Dear Reader,

True Colors was one of

wrote. It is still one of r

of revenge and its ultimate price, as well as the terrible danger of jumping to conclusions. I love this book, and not only for its plot. I wrote it in 1991, when I first went back to college, in my forties. I was bristling with courses in American history and anthropology and I had a ball putting some little-known facts into print.

I have studied the Little Big Horn battle for many years, and I mentioned some key qualities of Native American culture in this book. The heroine had Crow ancestry, but my fascination for all the protagonists in the fight has always carried me mostly toward the mysterious and intelligent Crazy Horse, who was Sioux. In fact, this great war chief was Oglala, which is one of the tribes of the Lakota (as the Sioux people I mention in the book more properly call themselves).

If you've read my books, you know that I frequently deal with the issues of native peoples. My extended family is heavily Native American. I also have a small connection to the Lakota people, since this year I established a nursing scholarship at the Oglala Lakota College in Kyle, South Dakota, in memory of my mother.

To my friend Marilyn Pourier at the Oglala Lakota College, and also to Nursing Department Chair Sarah Coulter Danner and President Thomas H. Shortbull of the same institution, I send my most heartfelt respect for your hard work and your dedication to the field of higher education.

Sincerely,

Diana Palmer

Also by Diana Palmer

RENEGADE
AFTER MIDNIGHT
LAWLESS
DIAMOND SPUR
DESPERADO
THE TEXAS RANGER
LORD OF THE DESERT
THE COWBOY AND THE LADY
MOST WANTED
FIT FOR A KING
PAPER ROSE
RAGE OF PASSION
ONCE IN PARIS
AFTER THE MUSIC
ROOMFUL OF ROSES
CHAMPAGNE GIRL
PASSION FLOWER
DIAMOND GIRL
FRIENDS AND LOVERS
CATTLEMAN'S CHOICE
LADY LOVE
THE RAWHIDE MAN

DIANA PALMER

True Colors

ISBN 0-373-77015-4

TRUE COLORS

This edition published by arrangement with Harlequin Books S.A.

www.HQNBooks.com

Printed in U.S.A.

IN MEMORIAM

Patsy Lovell Christopher
1955–1990

CHAPTER ONE

MEREDITH STOOD by the window watching the rain beat down on Chicago, while her companion watched her with worried eyes. She knew her face was showing the strain of business, and she'd lost weight, again. At twenty-four, she should have had a carefree outlook on life. What she had was a burden of pressure twice the size most women could carry.

Meredith Ashe Tennison was vice president of Tennison International's huge domestic enterprises, much more than a shadowy figurehead who avoided publicity like the plague. She had a shrewd mind and a natural aptitude for high finance which her late husband had carefully nurtured during their marriage. When he died, she had stepped into his shoes with such capability that the board of directors reversed their decision to ask her to step down. Now, two and a half years into her term of office, company profits were up and her plans for expansion into new mineral and gas reserves and strategic metals were well under way.

That explained the set of Meredith's thin shoulders. A company in southeastern Montana was fighting them tooth and nail over mineral rights they currently owned. But Harden Properties was not merely a formidable rival. It was headed by the one man Meredith had reason to hate, a shadow out of her past whose specter had haunted her through all the empty years since she'd left Montana.

Only Don Tennison knew the whole story. He and his late brother, Henry, had been very close. Meredith had come to Henry a shy, frightened teenager. At first Don, to whom business was a primary concern, had fought against the marriage. He relented, but he'd been faintly cool since Henry's death. Don was now president of Tennison International, but also something of a rival. Meredith had often wondered if he resented her position in the company. He knew his own limitations, and her brilliance and competence had impressed harder heads than his. But he watched her very carefully, especially when she drew on her nervous energy to take on too many projects. And this fight with Harden Properties was already taking its toll on her. She was still getting over the aftereffects of a rough bout with pneumonia that had come on the heels of a kidnapping attempt on her five-year-old son, Blake. If it hadn't been for the inscrutable Mr. Smith, her bodyguard, God only knew what might have happened.

Meredith was brooding over her forthcoming trip to Montana. She felt she had to make a brief visit to Billings, home of Harden Properties and Meredith's own hometown. The sudden death of her eighty-year-old great-aunt who had lived there had left Meredith with the house and a few belongings of Aunt Mary's to dispose of. Meredith was really her only surviving relative, except for a few distant cousins who still lived on the Crow Indian reservation several miles from Billings.

"You arranged the funeral over the phone—couldn't you do that with the property, too?" Don asked quietly.

She hesitated, then shook her head. "No, I can't. I've got to go back and face it. Face them," she amended. "Besides, it would be a God-given opportunity to scout out the opposition, wouldn't it? They don't know I'm Henry Tennison's widow. I was Henry's best-kept secret. I've avoided cameras and worn wigs and dark glasses ever since I took over."

"That was to protect Blake," he reminded her. "You're worth millions, and this last kidnapping attempt almost succeeded. A low public profile is invaluable. If you aren't recognized, you and Blake are safer."

"Yes, but Henry didn't do it for that reason. He did it to keep Cy Harden from finding out who I was, and where I was, in case he ever came looking for me." She closed her eyes, trying to blot out the memory of the fear she'd felt after her flight from Montana. Pregnant, accused of both sleeping with another man and being his accomplice in a theft, she'd been driven from the house by Cy's mother's harsh voice while Cy looked on in cold agreement. Meredith didn't know if the charges had ever been dropped, but Cy had believed she was guilty. That was the hardest to face.

She'd been carrying Cy's son, and she'd loved him so desperately. But Cy had used her. He'd proposed to her, but she'd learned later that it had only been to keep her happy in their relationship. *Love you?* he'd drawled in his deep voice. Sex was pleasant, but what would he want with a gangly, shy teenager in any other respect? He'd said that in front of his vicious mother, and something in Meredith had died of shame. She remembered running, blinded by tears, her only thought to get away. Great-Aunt Mary had bought her a bus ticket, and she'd left town. Left under a shadow, in disgrace, with the memory of Myrna Harden's mocking smile following her….

"You could give up the takeover bid," Don suggested hesitantly. "There are other companies with mineral holdings."

"Not in southeastern Montana," she replied, her soft gray eyes fixing on him calmly. "And Harden Properties has leases we can't break. They've made it impossible for us to get any mineral leases in the area." She turned and smiled, her oval face and creamy complexion framed by an elegant sweep of blond hair. She had the look of royalty, and the graceful carriage. That confidence was a legacy from Henry Tennison, who'd given her far more than control of his business empire by the time he died. He'd hired tutors for her, to teach her etiquette and the art of hostessing, to educate her in business and finance. She'd been an eager, willing pupil, and she had a mind like a sponge.

"He'll fight," the thin, balding man said stubbornly.

She smiled, because Don looked so much like Henry when he set his lips that way. He was ten years Henry's junior and ten years Meredith's senior. He was a good businessman, even if he wasn't her best friend in the world. But Don was conservative, and Meredith was aggressive. More than once they'd locked horns over company policy. The domestic operation was her baby, and Don wasn't going to tell her how to run it. Her steady, level gaze told him that.

"Let him fight, Don," she replied. "It will give him something to do while I'm taking over his company."

"You need rest," he said with a sigh. "Blake's a handful by himself, and you've been ill."

"Flu is inevitable with a child in kindergarten," she reminded him. "I didn't expect it to go into pneumonia. Besides, the takeover bid is crucial to my expansion plans. Regardless of how much time or energy it takes, I have to give it priority. I can ferret out a lot of information while I'm deciding what to do with Great-Aunt Mary's house."

"There shouldn't be a problem. She left a will. Even if she hadn't, Henry paid for the house."

"Nobody in Billings knows that," she said. She turned from the window, arms folded over her high, firm breasts as she nibbled her lower lip thoughtfully. "I wrote to her, and she came out here to see me several times. But I haven't been to Billings since—" She caught herself. "Not since I was eighteen," she amended.

But he knew. "It's been six years. Almost seven," he added gently. "Time is a great healer."

Her eyes darkened. "Is it? Do you think six years or sixty would be enough to forget what the Hardens did to me?" She turned toward him. "Revenge is unworthy of an intelligent person. Henry drilled that into me, but I can't help what I feel. They accused me of a crime I never committed, sent me out of Billings in disgrace and pregnant." Her eyes closed and she shivered. "I almost lost the baby. If it hadn't been for Henry..."

"He was crazy about Blake, and about you." Don grinned. "I've never seen a man so happy. It was a shame about the accident. Three years out of a lifetime isn't long for a man to find and lose everything he values."

"He was good to me," she said, smiling with the bittersweet memory. "Everybody thought I married him because he was wealthy. He was so much older than I was—almost twenty years. But what nobody knew was that he didn't tell me just how rich he was until he talked me into marrying him." She shook her head. "I almost ran away when I knew what he was worth. This—" she gestured around the elegant room with its priceless antiques "—terrified me."

"That's why he didn't tell you until it was too late," Don mused. "He'd spent his whole life making money and living for the corporation. Until you came along, he didn't even know he wanted a family."

"He got a ready-made one." She sighed. "I wanted so much to give him a child...." She turned away. Thinking about that would do no good at all. "I have to go to Billings. I want you to check on Blake and Mr. Smith every day or two, if you don't mind. I'm so nervous, about both of them, after that kidnapping attempt."

"Wouldn't you like to take Mr. Smith with you?" he asked

hopefully. "After all, there are Indians up there. Grizzly bears. Mountain lions. Crazed Winnebago drivers…."

She laughed. "Mr. Smith is worth his weight in gold, and he'll take very good care of Blake. There's no need to have much contact with him, since he disturbs you so much." He didn't look convinced. "Blake loves him," she reminded him.

"Blake isn't old enough to realize how dangerous he is. Meredith, I know he's worth his weight in gold, but you *do* realize that he's a wanted man…?"

"Only by the state police in that South African country," she said. "And that was a long time ago. Mr. Smith is forty-five if he's a day, and we did commandeer him from the CIA."

"Are you sure it wasn't the KGB?" He threw up his hands. "All right, I'll try to keep watch. But if I were you, I wouldn't have that animal of his near me."

"Tiny lives in an aquarium," she said defensively. "And she's very tame."

"She's a giant iguana," he muttered.

"Iguanas are vegetarians, and she's not quite that big. Yet. Besides, he's still grieving for Dano."

"Dano was a five-foot iguana," he said. "He actually petted the horrible thing. I think it ate my dog, that day you and Blake visited me and he brought the vile thing with him."

"Your dog ran away. Iguanas don't eat dogs."

"And he's raising a replacement for it," he moaned. "Can't he put it up if I have to come over here?"

"I'll ask him. It's just for a few weeks, until I see to Great-Aunt Mary's property and organize a way to get those mineral leases away from the Hardens. I'll have to do some scouting first," she added. "I want to see how the Hardens are placed these days." Her face darkened. "I want to see how *he's* placed."

"He probably knows who you are by now, so be careful."

"No, he doesn't," she replied. "I made a point of finding out. Henry was very protective of me at first, so he never told people anything about me. Since he always called me 'Kip,' there's very little likelihood that Cyrus Harden has any inkling about my connection with Tennison International. He only knows me as Meredith Ashe. If I leave the Rolls here and don't flash my diamonds, he won't know who I am. More important," she added coldly, "his mother won't know."

"I've never thought of Cy Harden as a mama's boy," he mused.

"He isn't. But Mama is a prime mover, a secretive manipulator. I was eighteen and no match for her shrewd mind. She got rid of me with ridiculous ease. Now it's my turn to manipulate. I want Harden Properties. And I'm going to get it."

He opened his mouth to warn her but after a second thought gave up. She'd known Cy Harden as a man, even as a lover. But she knew nothing about the business head on those broad shoulders, and if she pursued the takeover bid, she was going to find herself in over her own head. Others had tried to take on Harden, to their cost. He was a formidable foe, among the most ruthless of businessmen. He and Henry had butted heads several times. Probably Harden didn't know why Tennison hated him so, or deliberately tried to foil deals for him. It had been a shock to everyone when Henry was invited to sit on the Harden Properties board of directors. Harden had engineered that move so that he could keep an eye on Tennison's business deals, but it had worked to Henry's advantage as well, so he'd accepted. Naturally Don went to the meetings, and Meredith's name was never mentioned.

"You don't think I can do it, do you?" she asked, narrow-eyed.

"No," he said honestly. "His is a family-based company. He holds forty percent and his mother has five. That means you have to get his great-uncle's ten percent and the fifteen percent held by his directors and the remaining shares from his unrelated stockholders. I don't think any of them are brave enough to go against Cy, despite the financial rewards."

"By the time their next board of directors meetings rolls around, I expect to have those proxies," she told Don firmly. "And is Mr. Harden due for a surprise when I show up with them, and you, in his boardroom."

"Just be careful that your surprise doesn't backfire," he cautioned. "Don't underestimate him. Henry never did."

"Oh, I won't." She stretched lazily. "What's on the agenda for this afternoon? I have to do some shopping." She indicated her expensive suit. "Little Meredith Ashe could never have afforded anything like this. I don't want anyone to think I've prospered."

" 'O what a tangled web we weave, when first we practice to deceive,'" he quoted dryly.

"And hell has no fury like a woman scorned," she shot back. "Don't worry, Don. I know what I'm doing."

He shrugged. "I hope so."

DON'S MOROSE TONE haunted Meredith all day. As she packed her new clothes that evening in Mr. Smith's borrowed second-hand suitcase, Blake sprawled on her queen-sized bed in their Lincoln Park home, frowning.

"Why do you have to go away?" he muttered, his little face dark and sullen. "You're always going away. You're never here."

She felt a twinge of guilt. Her son was right. But she couldn't afford to give in to that stubborn determination of his. Blake was as formidable in his young way as she was.

"Business, my darling," she replied, smiling. She stared at him lovingly. He looked nothing like her. He was his father, from his dark hair to his deep-set brown eyes and olive complexion. He was going to be tall like Cy, too, she guessed.

Cy. Meredith sighed heavily and turned away. She'd loved him so much, with all the passion of her young life. He'd taken her chastity and her heart, and in return he'd given her grief and shame. His mother had done her part to break up what might have been an honest love affair. God knew, he'd always felt guilty about her. Probably he'd have felt even more guilt if he'd known that she was only eighteen to his twenty-eight. She'd lied and told him she was twenty. He'd said even then that it was like robbing the cradle. But his passion for her had been a helpless, deeply resented one that had cost him his stoic self-control time and time again. She often thought that he'd hated her for that, for making him vulnerable.

His mother had hated her, certainly. The fact that Meredith had been living with her great-aunt and uncle on the Crow reservation—and the fact that her great-uncle was a respected elder at that—had been a scandalous shock to Mrs. Myrna Granger Harden. Myrna belonged to the social set and made no secret of her snobbery. That her son had dared to embarrass her by dating the niece of one of his employees had haunted her, especially when she'd already hand-picked a wife for him—one Lois Newly, a local debutante whose people had property in Alberta, Canada, and could trace their ancestry back to royal England. Myrna had never even bothered to ask Meredith if she was Indian. She'd taken it for granted, when actually Meredith was only related to Uncle Raven-Walking by marriage.

There were dark-skinned people in Cy's background. Myrna swore they were French, but Meredith had once heard someone mention that Cy's ancestors contained a full-blooded Sioux on his father's side. Many Plains people had mixed ancestry, but most of them weren't as prejudiced and snobbish as Myrna Harden.

Blake Garrett Tennison would someday have to be told the truth about his parentage, Meredith thought worriedly. She didn't relish that at all. For now, he accepted that the tall, fair man who used to laugh and bring him things was his real father. In most senses, he was. Henry had spoiled Meredith shamefully, attended LaMaze classes with her, treated her pregnancy as if he'd been responsible for it, and showered her with luxuries when little Blake was born. He stayed with her through the delivery, and he cried when the child was placed in his arms. Oh, yes, Henry really was Blake's father in so many ways. He'd earned the right.

She often wondered why Cy had apparently never considered the possibility of Meredith becoming pregnant during their brief affair. Presumably his women were usually on the Pill, because he'd never even asked if she was. Not that he'd been in any condition to ask, the first time or the others. She dreamed about him sometimes, about the fierce pleasure he'd taught her to share with him. But she never told Henry about the dreams or compared him with Cy. It wouldn't have been fair. Henry was a gentle, skillful lover, but she'd never attained the heights with him that Cy had taken her to so effortlessly.

Blake cuddled his plush toy alligator. "Isn't Barry the Alligator nice?" he asked. "Mr. Smith let me pet Tiny. He says you should let me have an iguana, too, Mommy. They make very nice pets."

She laughed gently at Blake's adult-sounding speech. He was almost six, and he already had a tremendous grasp of language. He would be ready to start first grade next year. This year he attended private kindergarten until one each afternoon, and he was learning fast. Meredith knew that Cy had never married. She allowed herself to wonder for one long instant what Myrna Harden would think of her grandson. It was unlikely that the elderly woman would covet him, of course, since he was Meredith's. And a grandchild would tarnish the youthful image she tried so hard to project.

"Can't I have an iguana?" Blake persisted.

"You can pet Tiny, when Mr. Smith lets you."

"Doesn't Mr. Smith have a first name?" he asked, frowning.

She laughed. "Nobody has the nerve to ask," she whispered.

He laughed, too, his young voice delightfully carefree. Had she ever been that happy, she wondered, even as a child? The premature death of her parents had left scars. Thank God there had been Aunt Mary and Uncle Raven-Walking to look after her. They'd loved her, even if nobody else ever had.

Blake sighed. "I wish I could go with you."

"One day soon," she promised. "Then I'll take you to the Crow reservation and you can meet some of your Indian cousins."

"Real Indians?" he asked.

"Real Indians. I want you to be proud of your ancestry, Blake," she said seriously, smiling at him. "One of your distant relatives actually scouted for General Custer before the battle of the Little Bighorn."

"Wow!" he said, all eyes. He frowned. "Who was General Custer, Mommy?"

"Never mind." She shook her head. "Time enough for that when you're older. Now, I have to pack."

"Blake!"

The thunderous voice echoed along the upstairs landing.

"In here, Mr. Smith!" Blake called.

Heavy footsteps echoed down the hall, and a tall, balding hulk of a man walked into the room. Mr. Smith had a Marine

Corps tattoo on one brawny arm, and he wore khaki slacks with an olive drab T-shirt. He was the ugliest, and the kindest, man Meredith had ever known. He had to be in his middle or late forties, but nobody knew just how old he was. He had a spotless service record and had come from a successful career in the CIA to work for Henry Tennison. After Henry's death, Meredith had inherited him, so to speak. From his big nose to his green eyes and square face, he was a treasure. He'd aborted the kidnapping attempt on Blake. And nobody bothered Meredith when he was with her. She raised his salary every year without his having to ask. Next to Blake, he was the most treasured person in her private life.

"Bedtime for you, mister," Mr. Smith told Blake without cracking a smile. "Front and center."

"Yes, sir!" Blake saluted, laughing, and ran to the big man, to be swung up on his shoulders.

"I'll settle him for the night, Kip," he told Meredith. His eyes narrowed. "You shouldn't go. You need another week in bed."

"Don't fuss," she said gently, and smiled at him. "I'm all right. I have to do something with Aunt Mary's things you know. And it's a dandy opportunity to reconnoiter the opposition."

"Recon what?" Blake asked.

"Never mind," she told him. She leaned forward and kissed his rosy cheek. "Sleep tight, my lad. I'll be along to tuck you in."

"Mr. Smith is going to tell me about Vietnam!" Blake told her excitedly.

Meredith grimaced. Vietnam War stories hardly seemed the proper bedtime tales for a young boy, but she didn't have the heart to argue.

"I want to hear about the snake again."

She frowned at Blake. "The what?"

"The snake. Mr. Smith is teaching me about all the animals and stuff in Vietnam," he continued.

She flushed. She'd thought the stories were about something else entirely.

Mr. Smith saw the flush and almost smiled. "Fooled you, huh?" he asked smugly. "That's what you get for misjudging innocent people."

"You're not innocent people," she pointed out.

"I'm innocent of a few things," he argued. "I never shot anybody twice."

She looked toward the ceiling. "My bodyguard, the saint."

"Keep that up and I'll go back to the government," he promised. "They treat a guy right."

"I'll bet they never bought you kidskin moccasins and your very own Jacuzzi," she said haughtily.

"Well, no."

"And they don't give you three weeks' paid vacation and offer you free hotel rooms and carte blanche at restaurants," she continued.

"Well…"

"And they don't hug you like I do," Blake exclaimed, throwing his arms around Mr. Smith's thick neck as hard as he could.

Mr. Smith chuckled, returning the hug. "Got me there," he admitted. "Nobody in the CIA ever hugged me."

"See?" Meredith asked smugly. "You're well off and don't know it."

"Oh, I know it," he said. "I just like to watch you squirm."

"One of these days," she began, pointing a finger at him.

"That's our cue to leave, Blake," Mr. Smith said, turning with the boy in his arms to head for the door. "She's good for an hour on that subject."

Meredith hid a smile and went back to her packing.

TWO DAYS LATER she arrived in Billings on the bus. She could have flown, but that was an admission that she had money. A bus ticket was considerably cheaper, and besides, the bus station was located next door to the office of Harden Properties, Inc.

She waited for her suitcase, her hair loose around her shoulders, wearing a pair of jeans and a faded denim jacket over a sweatshirt. She wore a pair of scuffed boots she'd used for riding back home, and she'd left off her makeup. By and large, she looked very much as she had the day she'd taken the bus out of Billings six years before. Except that she had a different secret now, one she was going to enjoy keeping until the proper time.

In an office building just catercorner to the bus station, a man sitting at a desk happened to notice the movement of passengers disembarking. He got out of his swivel chair and moved to the one-way window, staring down with dark eyes that seemed to burst with mingled emotions.

"Mr. Harden?"

"What is it, Millie?" he asked without turning.

"Your letter...."

He had to force himself to turn away from the window. Surely not, he thought. That couldn't be her, not after all these years. He'd seen her in crowds before, only to get closer and find another face, the wrong face. But he felt as if it were Meredith. His heart began to beat with the fierce rhythm she'd taught it. He felt alive for the first time in six years.

He sat down, his tall, fit body in a dark blue suit so striking that even his secretary of many years stared at him. He was thirty-four now, but sometimes his lean, deeply tanned face seemed older than its years. There were lines around his eyes, too, and threads of gray in his thick, black hair. He had an elegant look for a man whose primary interest was agricultural properties and acquisitions and who had a ranch and spent time with cattle and horses.

"Forget the letter," he said abruptly. "Find the address of Mary Raven. Her husband was Crow—John Raven-Walking, but they're listed in the phone directory as Raven. They moved into town two or three years ago."

"Yes, sir." Millie left to find the address for him.

Cy continued to sit, turning to read some new contracts and an inquiry from one of his directors about a few mining leases he'd refused to cede to Tennison International. He looked at the papers without seeing them as memories flooded back, memories six years old of a woman who'd betrayed him and left town under a cloud of suspicion.

"Sir, there's an obituary here," Millie said as she returned thumbing through the local paper. "I saw it last week and meant to mention it. Well, I remembered, you know, about that Ashe girl who was involved in the theft six years ago."

Cy bristled. "Her part in it was never proved," he corrected.

Her eyebrows arched, but she was concentrating on the column and hardly heard him. "Yes, here it is. Mrs. Mary Raven, and here's the address—they print it, you know. She was buried two days ago. No family is listed at all. I suppose they didn't know about Miss Ashe at the newspaper…."

"Give me that." He took the paper and pored over it. Mary was dead. He remembered her from the Crow reservation, where she and Raven-Walking had lived until the old gentleman's death two years ago. Mary had moved into town. God only knew how she'd managed to afford a house on her Social Security. Cy hadn't seen the house but knew about it because he'd seen her one day in Billings. He'd questioned her harshly about Meredith, but she wouldn't tell him anything.

She was frankly evasive and even a little frightened. He grimaced, remembering his desperation to find Meredith. The old lady had practically run to get away from him. He hadn't followed her, but he'd been tempted to go and see her. Then he'd realized that it would accomplish nothing. He'd only upset her more. Besides, the past was dead. Meredith was probably married by now, with a house full of kids.

The thought hurt him. He sighed angrily. Well, she'd be coming back, surely. In fact, that could have been Meredith he'd just seen. Someone would have to tie up all the loose ends that Mary's death created. He knew that Meredith was Mary's closest living relative.

He sat back in his chair, scowling. Meredith was here. He knew she was. He didn't know whether he was sorry or glad about it. He only knew that his life was about to be disrupted all over again.

CHAPTER TWO

IT WAS TOO MUCH to hope for that Cy would walk out of his office building and run headlong into her, Meredith decided as she watched the city bus head toward the Billings station. He might not even be in town. Like Henry, and now herself, business demanded frequent trips to business meetings and conferences. And for her to run into the object of her youthful desire today would require a ferocious kind of coincidence or a helping hand from fate.

She boarded the bus and got off several minutes later near the Rimrocks. Her aunt's little house sat on a dead-end street sheltered by towering cottonwood trees. This house, thank God, held no memories for her. When Meredith lived here, Great-Aunt Mary's home was a small matchbox on the reservation. When she dated Cy, they always wound up in the penthouse he kept at the Sheraton, the tallest building in the city. She ground her teeth, remembering. Perhaps it had been a mistake to come back here after all. With the city of her youth around her, memories hurt more.

She unlocked the door with the key Mr. Hammer, the Realtor, had sent her. September was chilly here in southeastern Montana, and the snows weren't far away. She hoped to be long gone before they trapped her.

The house was cold, but fortunately Hammer had remembered to have the utilities put on for her. There was a gas stove with the pilot light already burning, and the electricity worked. He'd even been kind enough to leave her a few groceries. Typical Montana hospitality, she thought, smiling. People here looked out for each other. Everybody was friendly and kind, even to tourists.

Her eyes lingered on the old but functional furniture. Everything was done in Early American, because that was what Great-Aunt Mary liked. But she had kept many of her late husband's treasures. The medicine shield and bag that he always displayed so proudly were on the one wall. His pipe, with its exquisite decoration, rested on another peg, as did the bow and arrows his own grandfather had made for him in his youth. There were several parfleche bags filled with secret things in a coffee table drawer. There was a huge mandala on another wall, and assorted dried skins and woven hangings on the others. Dead potted plants covered almost every available surface. Great-Aunt Mary's plants had been her greatest treasures, but they'd gone without water since her death and now were beyond saving…except for one philodendron, which Meredith took to the kitchen and watered, then placed gently on the Formica counter.

When she noticed the telephone on the wall, Meredith felt a stab of relief. She was going to need it. She was also going to need her fax machine and her computer with its internal modem. Smith could bring all that equipment out, and she could make use of Aunt Mary's library as an office. It had a door that locked, to protect her secret from prying eyes in case any of the Hardens ever made it this far.

Meredith was a little concerned over the amount of time this project was going to take, but the mineral leases were her top priority right now. The domestic operation simply couldn't move ahead with its expansion program without them. She was committed, however long it took. She'd have to keep up with business through Don and the telephone and hope for the best.

Worst of all was the time away from Blake. He was becoming hyperactive in school. Her lifestyle was apparently affecting him more than she'd realized. And business had edged its way between them until she couldn't even sit down to a meal with her son without being interrupted by the telephone. He was on edge, and so was she. Maybe she could use this time to her advantage, to catch up on work so that she could have more time with him when she got home again.

She made herself a pot of coffee, smiling at the neatness of the little kitchen with its yellow walls and white curtains and oak furniture. Aunt Mary hadn't wanted to let Meredith and Henry buy her this house and furnish it, but they'd convinced her finally that it was something they wanted to do. Despite the fact that she had friends and cousins on the reservation, they wanted her close to her best friend, Miss Mable, who'd offered to look after her. Miss Mable had died only a few weeks before Mary. Perhaps they were together now, exchanging crochet patterns and gossiping on some ghostly front porch. Meredith liked to think of them that way.

Her fingers were cold, and she almost spilled the coffee as she poured it. Aunt Mary's doilies were everywhere in the living room, intricate patterns of colored thread that she'd crocheted so beautifully. It was a shame to use them, and Meredith knew that she wasn't going to let them be sold with the house when the time came. She'd have to choose some personal items to keep, especially the doilies and quilts, and of course Uncle Raven-Walking's legacy for little Blake.

As Meredith's gaze lingered on the beautifully decorated parfleche bags she had removed from the drawer, she remembered sitting on Uncle Raven-Walking's knee while he told her stories about the long-ago times of the People and how they'd enjoyed their horse-taking forays into Cheyenne and Sioux camps, and vice versa. So much she'd read and seen about the Plains Indians was inaccurate. The thing she remembered most from her uncle was his teachings about giving and sharing, traits that were inherent in Crow society. The giving of gifts and the sharing of acquired wealth were commonplace among these Indians. Selfishness was virtually unknown. Even the religion of the Crow focused on brotherly love and giving to the less fortunate. Nobody went hungry or cold in the camps of long ago. Even enemies were fed and gifted and allowed to go their own way, if they promised never again to make war on the Crow. No enemy was attacked if he walked into camp unarmed and with peaceful intent, because courage was admired.

Courage…Meredith sipped her coffee. She was going to need plenty of that. Myrna Harden's face flashed before her eyes, and she shivered. She had to remember that she was no longer eighteen and poor. She was twenty-four, almost twenty-five, and rich. Much richer than the Hardens. It was important to keep in mind that she was equal to them socially and financially.

Her eyes settled on Uncle Raven-Walking's medicine pouch. It contained, among other things, kinnikinnick—willow shavings used as tobacco—and sage, some gray dust from the Custer battlefield, a tiny red rock, a red-tailed hawk feather and an elk tooth. She'd opened it once secretively and looked in. Later she'd asked her uncle about the contents, but all he was willing to say was that it was his own personal "medicine," to keep away evil and protect him from enemies and ill health. How ironic, she mused. Her people seemed to think money and power were the answers to the riddle of what made life bearable. But Uncle Raven-Walking had never cared about having things or making money. And, content to work as a security guard for Harden Properties, he was one of the happiest people Meredith had ever known.

"*Wasicun,*" she murmured, using a Plains Sioux word for whites. It meant, literally, "You can't get rid of them." She laughed, because it seemed to be true. The Crow word for whites was *mahistasheeda*—literally, "yellow-eyes." Nobody knew why. Maybe the first white man they saw was jaundiced, but that was the expression. Crow called themselves *Absaroka*—"People of the fork-tailed bird." Meredith had loved the huge Montana ravens as a girl. Perhaps the forerunners of the Crow had loved them, too.

She finished her coffee and carried her suitcase into the neatly furnished second bedroom, the one Aunt Mary had used as a guest room. Meredith had never used it—she'd been too afraid of seeing the Hardens to ever come back to Billings.

Her few things put away, Meredith took the bus to a small convenience store several blocks away and bought a sack of groceries. It had been years since she'd done anything so menial. She had maids and a housekeeper at her Lincoln Park house, and they took care of such things. She knew how to cook, but it wasn't a skill she practiced often. She smiled at her own shortcomings. Aunt Mary liked to chide her for her lack of homemaking abilities.

She decided to walk back. Passing the enormous Billings city park she sighed at its beauty. The towering cottonwoods formed a green canopy over the lawn. Here, in summer, there were symphony orchestra concerts and ice-cream suppers. There was always something going on. Billings was a huge city with well-designed wide streets and plenty of elbow room, spreading between the Rimrocks and the Yellowstone River, with railroad tracks through the city and all around, because plenty of trains came through here. Agriculture and mining kept things going. Refineries were everywhere. So were vast ranches and fields of wheat and sugar beets. To the west stood the towering Rocky Mountains, to the southeast the Big Horn and Pryor mountains. Buttes surrounded Billings, leveling off to flat plains and rolling hills farther east. Meredith loved the country out of town, loved the vastness of it, loved the absence of concrete and steel. Distances were terrifying to easterners, but a hundred miles was nothing to a Montanan.

Her arms tightened around the grocery sack as she reached the street on which Great-Aunt Mary's house stood. Odd, she thought, that sleek gray Jaguar hadn't been sitting on the curb when she left. Perhaps the Realtor had come looking for her.

Digging in her jeans for her house key, she didn't see the shadowy figure on the front porch until she reached the steps. Then she stopped dead. She felt her heart skip.

Cyrus Granger Harden was every bit as tall as Mr. Smith, but the comparison ended there. Cy was dark and dangerous-looking even in an expensive blue vested suit like the one he was wearing now. He stepped into the sunlight. Despite the anguish of the past six years, Meredith felt a surge of warmth shoot through her body as she looked at him.

He was older. There were new lines in that long, lean face with its high cheekbones, thick black eyebrows and deepset dark brown eyes. His nose was straight, his mouth a sensual delight, its firmly etched contours so familiar that Meredith had to drag her eyes back up. There was a Stetson tilted arrogantly over his broad forehead, covering hair that had the sheen of a raven's back. His lean, dark fingers held a smoking cigarette; so he hadn't quite given up that habit, she thought with faint humor.

"I thought it was you," he said without preamble, his deep, cutting voice as harsh as the unrelenting sunlight on her bare head. "I can see the bus stop out my window."

As she'd hoped. So he had seen her after all. She gave herself a quick, mental pep talk. *I'm older, I'm richer, I have secrets, and he has no power over me.* She repeated it.

Her full lips tugged into a careless smile. "Hello, Cy," she said. "Fancy seeing you over here in the slums."

His jaw tautened. "Billings doesn't have slums. Why are you here?"

"I came back for your family silver," she returned with a pointed stare. "I must have missed it on my last trip through."

He shifted uncomfortably, ramming one hand into his pocket. It drew the thin fabric of his slacks against the powerful muscles of his long legs, and Meredith had to fight not to look. Unclothed, that body was a miracle of perfection, all dark skin and dark curling hair that wedged sexily down his chest and his flat stomach and feathered his legs....

"After you left," he said hesitantly, "Tanksley admitted to my mother that you had nothing to do with the theft."

Tony Tanksley, she recalled, was the "accomplice" she'd allegedly been in love and sleeping with. Only a jealous fool could have imagined Meredith going from Cy to Tony, but since Myrna had paid Tony to invent the story, the details she'd given him had been perfect. A classic frame. But regardless of that, Cy had believed her capable of infidelity and criminal acts. Love without trust wasn't love. He'd even admitted that his only interest in her had been sexual. What a pity that her mother hadn't lived, couldn't have warned her about giving a man everything without counting the cost. The lesson she'd learned the hard way had been expensive.

"I wondered why the police hadn't come after me," she said easily.

His powerful shoulders moved under the fabric. "You couldn't be found," he said tersely.

Not surprising, considering the fact that Henry had stashed

her on a Caribbean island during her pregnancy, with Mr. Smith to protect her. Nobody, but nobody, had been told her real name. She was known as Kip Tennison after their marriage, period. Now she was grateful for that safeguard. She'd been afraid that the Hardens might try to track her, if for no other reason than to embarrass her.

"How nice to finally know that," she said with faint sarcasm, watching his eyes glitter as she shifted the bag of groceries. "A jail sentence wouldn't have appealed to me."

His face became more severe, his dark eyes narrowed under those thick brows as he studied her face. "You're thinner than I remember," he said. "Older."

"Twenty-five next birthday," she said breezily, but her smile didn't reach her eyes. "You're thirty-four now, aren't you?"

He nodded. He moved his gaze down her body and back up. He felt as if he were dying inside all over again. Six long years. He remembered tears on that young face, and the sound of her voice hating him. He remembered, too, long, exquisite lovings in his bed with her arms clinging, her soft body like quicksilver under the heated thrust of his, her voice breaking as she moaned her pleasure into his damp throat....

"How long are you going to be here?" he asked tightly.

"Long enough to dispose of the house," she replied.

He lifted the cigarette to his mouth. "You won't keep it?" he asked, hating himself for being vulnerable enough to ask the question.

She shook her head. "No. I don't think I'll stay. Billings has too many enemies in it to suit me."

"I'm not your enemy," he replied.

She lifted her chin and stared at him with pure bravado. "Aren't you, Cy? That isn't how I remember it."

He turned away, his eyes glancing down the wide street. "You were eighteen. Too young. Years too young. I never asked, but I'd bet I had your chastity."

Meredith flushed. Cy watched the stain in her cheeks with faint amusement, the first he'd felt since he'd seen her get off the bus.

"So I did," he murmured, tingling all over at having his suspicions confirmed.

"You were the first," she said coldly. She smiled. "But not the last. Or did you think you were going to be an impossible act to follow?"

His pride bristled, but he didn't react. He finished the cigarette and flipped it off the porch. "Where have you been for the past six years?"

"Around," she said simply. "Look, this bag is getting heavy. Do you have anything to say, or is this just a friendly visit to see how fast you can shoot me out of town?"

"I came to ask if you needed a job," he said stiffly. "I know your aunt left nothing except bills. I own a restaurant here. There's an opening for a waitress."

This was really too much, Meredith thought. Cy offering her a job waitressing, when she could easily afford to buy the place. Guilty conscience? she wondered. Or renewed interest? Either way, it wouldn't hurt to accept it. She had a feeling she'd see a good bit of the Hardens that way, and it fitted in nicely with her plans.

"Okay," she said. "Do I need to apply?"

"No. Just report for work at six sharp tomorrow morning," he said. "I seem to remember that you had a job in a café when we first met."

"Yes." Her eyes met his, and for an instant they both shared the memory of that first meeting. She'd spilled coffee on him, and when she'd gone to mop up his jacket, electricity had danced between them. The attraction was instant and mutual…and devastating.

"So long ago," he said absently, his eyes dark with bitterness. "My God, why did you run? I came to my senses two days later, and I couldn't find you, damn you!"

Came to his senses? She didn't dare dwell on that. She glared at him. "Damn you, too, for listening to your mother instead of me. I hope the two of you have been very happy together."

His eyebrows arched. "What did my mother have to do with you and Tanksley?"

He didn't know! She could hardly believe it, but that blank stare of his was genuine. He didn't know what his mother had done!

"How did you get him to confess?" she asked.

"I didn't. He told Mother that you were innocent. She told me."

Her heart trembled in her chest. "Did she tell you anything else?" she asked with affected carelessness.

He scowled. "No. What else was there to tell?"

That I was pregnant with your child, she thought darkly, that I was eighteen and had nowhere to go. I couldn't risk staying with Great-Aunt Mary with a theft charge hanging over my head.

She lowered her eyes so that he wouldn't see the fury in them. Those first few weeks had been the purest hell of her life, despite the fact that they'd strengthened and matured her to a frightening degree. She'd had to take complete charge of her own life and fate, and from that time she'd never been afraid again.

"Was there anything else?" he persisted.

She lifted her face. "No. Nothing else."

But there was. He sensed it. Her eyes held a peculiar

gleam, almost of hatred. He'd accused her unjustly and hurt her with his rejection, but her anger went deeper than that.

"The restaurant is the Bar H Steak House," he said. "It's off North Twenty-seventh past the Sheraton."

Meredith felt her body go hot at the mention of the hotel, and she averted her eyes quickly. "I'll find it. Thanks for the recommendation."

"Does that mean you might stay for a few weeks, at least?" he asked, frowning.

Her eyes fenced with his. "Why? I do hope you don't entertain any thoughts of taking over where we left off. Because frankly, Cy, I'm not in the habit of trying to superglue broken relationships back together."

He went very still. "Is there someone?"

"In my life, you mean?" she asked. "Yes."

His face showed nothing, but a shadow seemed to pass over his eyes. "I might have known."

She didn't reply. She simply stared at him. She saw him glance at her left hand, and she thanked God that she'd remembered to take off her wedding band. But the engagement ring Henry had given her—a diamond-cut emerald with small diamonds—was still there. She remembered how Henry had laughed at her choice, because the ring was so inexpensive. He'd wanted to give her a three-carat diamond, and she'd insisted on this ring. How long ago it seemed.

"You're engaged?" he asked heavily.

"I was," she corrected. True enough, she was, before Henry married her a week after the engagement.

"Not now?"

She shook her head. "I have a friend, and I care about him very much. But I don't want commitment anymore." She wished she could cross her fingers behind her. She'd told more lies and half-truths in two minutes than she had in two years.

His features were more rigid than usual. "Why isn't your friend here with you, then?"

"I needed a breathing space. I came alone to dispose of Aunt Mary's things."

"Where were you living?"

She smiled. "Back east. Excuse me, I have to get these things in the refrigerator."

He stood aside, hesitating. "I'll see you tomorrow."

Presumably he ate at the restaurant where she was going to work. "I suppose so." She glanced at him. "Are you sure they won't mind giving me work without references?"

"I own the damned restaurant," he said shortly. "They can't afford to mind. The job's yours, if you want it."

"I want it," she said. She unlocked the door and hesitated. Since he didn't know her circumstances, he was probably doing it out of pity and guilt, but she felt obliged to say something. "You're very generous. Thank you."

"Generous." He laughed bitterly. "My God, I've never given anything in my life unless it suited me or made me richer. I've got the world. And I've got nothing." He turned and walked to his car, leaving her staring after him with wide, sad eyes.

Meredith let herself into the house. It had shaken her to see him again after so many barren years. She dropped the groceries on the kitchen counter and sat down, her mind going back to their first meeting.

She'd been seventeen then, a week shy of her eighteenth birthday. But she'd always looked older than she was, and the uniform she wore as a waitress molded itself lovingly to every soft curve of her slender body.

Cy had stared at her from the first, his narrow eyes following her as she waited on one table and then another. She'd been nervous of him instantly, because he radiated self-confidence and a kind of bridled arrogance. He had a way of narrowing one eye and lifting his chin that was like a declaration of war every time he studied someone. Actually, she found out later, it was because he had a slight problem focusing on distant objects and was too stubborn to go to an ophthalmologist. She wondered if any of the people he'd intimidated with that level glare ever knew what caused it.

His table drew its regular waitress, and she'd seen him frown and ask the girl something. Seconds later, he'd moved to a table that was in Meredith's territory.

The very idea that a man who looked like that should seem interested in her made her toes tingle. She'd approached him with a gentle smile, her face flushing with excitement when he looked up at her and smiled back.

"You're new here," he'd said. His voice was deep and slow, with delicious sensuality in it.

"Yes." She'd sounded as breathless as she felt. She could still remember how cold her hands had suddenly become. "I just started this morning."

"I'm Cyrus Harden," he said. "I have breakfast here most mornings."

She'd recognized the name instantly. Most people in Billings did. "I'm Meredith," she said huskily.

He lifted an eyebrow, and the smile deepened. "Are you past the age of consent?"

"I'm…twenty," she said at once, lying through her teeth. If she'd told him her real age, she knew instinctively that he'd have dismissed her.

"That'll do. Bring me some coffee, please. Then we'll discuss where we're going tonight."

She rushed back behind the counter to pour the coffee, running headlong into Terri, the older waitress who worked with her.

"Careful, chick," Terri said under her breath when Cy wasn't looking. "You're flirting with disaster. Cy Harden has a reputation with women as well as in business. Don't get in over your head."

"It's all right. He…he's just talking to me," Meredith stammered.

"Not when you look that flustered, he isn't," Terri replied worriedly. "Your great-aunt must live in a world all her own. Honey, men don't automatically propose marriage to women they want—especially men like Cy Harden. He's out of our league. He's rich, and his mother would savage any woman who tried to get him to the altar unless she had money and connections. He's upper crust. They marry among themselves."

"But we're just talking," Meredith protested, forcing a smile while all her dreams crashed to earth.

"See that it stays just talk. He could hurt you badly."

The sound of authority made her bristle, but she couldn't really afford to antagonize a co-worker, so she just smiled and finished getting Cy's coffee.

"Was she warning you off?" he asked when she put the cup and saucer in front of him on the red-and-white-checked tablecloth.

She gasped. "How did you know?"

"I took Terri out once," he replied easily. "She got too possessive, so I broke it off. It was a long time ago. Don't let her get under your skin, okay?"

She smiled, because now it all made sense. He was interested, and Terri was just jealous. She beamed. "I won't," she promised.

Remembering her own naiveté that day, Meredith groaned. She rose from the chair she'd been sitting in and went to put the groceries away. How could anyone have been so stupid?

she asked herself. At eighteen, with a sheltered upbringing, she'd known nothing. To a man as worldly as Cy, she must have been a pushover. If she'd had any idea how things were going to turn out, she'd never have…

Who was she kidding? She laughed bitterly. She'd have done exactly the same thing, because Cy fascinated her. He still did, after all the grief and pain. He was the most beautiful man she'd ever seen in her life, and she remembered those long lovings in his arms as if they'd happened yesterday.

Now she'd landed herself back in his orbit again and taken a job that she had no business taking. She was living a lie. But as she remembered the reasons for her visit, her blood began to boil. Cy had discarded her like garbage, she and the child she'd been carrying. He'd turned his back on her and left her to fend for herself with a theft charge hanging over her head.

She hadn't come back to rekindle an old love affair. She'd come back for revenge. Henry had taught her that everyone had a weakness that could be exploited in business. And some people were better at hiding their Achilles' heels than others. Cy was a past master. She'd have to be very careful if she was going to locate his. But in the end she'd get the upper hand, and he'd be out in the cold. She meant to cost him everything, to put him in the same horrible position he'd put her in so long ago. Her eyes narrowed as she considered the possibilities, and a cold smile touched her disciplined mouth.

Meredith was no longer a naive eighteen-year-old deeply in love with a man she couldn't have. She held all the aces this time. And when she played her hand, it was going to be the sweetest pleasure since Cy's treacherous kisses.

CHAPTER THREE

MEREDITH HAD BROUGHT some old clothes with her, so that she wouldn't arouse Cy's suspicions by looking too prosperous. Now, as she dressed for her new job, she was glad.

She stepped into a neat denim skirt that matched her white cotton long-sleeved blouse. She put on soft-soled loafers and discarded her Gucci purse for a brown vinyl one. Then she put up her hair in a neat French braid at the back of her head and left the house to catch a bus to work.

Billings was gorgeous first thing in the morning, Meredith thought as she savored the cool morning air. This spacious city was a world away from the bustle of Chicago. She missed her son, and even Mr. Smith and Don, but the change had already revived her fighting spirit and made her feel less depressed. The incredible pressures she faced daily in her work had been getting to her lately.

Meredith stepped off the bus in front of the restaurant. It was a prosperous one, very large and attached to a hotel. She noticed through the window that all the waitresses wore spotless white uniforms. It had been a long time since she had felt nervous around people, but here, without the cocoon of her wealth to cushion her, she was ill at ease. She found the cashier and asked for the manager.

"Mrs. Dade is just through there," the woman said pleasantly. "Is she expecting you?"

"I think so."

Meredith knocked on the door and walked in, surprised to find the woman almost twenty years older than she was. Perhaps she'd been harboring the subconscious thought that Mrs. Dade might be one of Cy's old lovers, but she had to revise that opinion now.

"I'm Meredith…Ashe," she said hesitantly. The name sounded strange. She was so used to being called Kip Tennison.

"Oh, yes," Mrs. Dade said, smiling as she stood up behind her huge polished wood desk. She was a tall woman, her red hair mingling with silver above a broad, happy face. "I'm Trudy Dade. I'm glad to meet you. Cy said that you'd just lost your aunt and needed work. Luckily for both of us, we've got an opening. Have you had experience at waitressing?"

"Well, a little," Meredith replied. "I used to work at the Bear Claw years ago."

"I remember. I thought I recognized you." Her gray eyes narrowed thoughtfully. "I'm sorry about your aunt."

"I'll miss her," Meredith said softly. "She was the only real relative I had in the world."

Mrs. Dade's perceptive gaze swept over Meredith, leaving no detail untouched. She nodded. "It's hard work, but the tips are good, and I'm not a slavedriver. You can start now. You'll get off at six, but you'll have to work some evenings. That's unavoidable in this business."

"I don't mind that," Meredith said easily. "I don't need my evenings free."

Mrs. Dade's eyebrows arched. "At your age? For heaven's sake, you're not married?"

"No." Meredith didn't say it rudely, but there was something in her manner that made the other woman visibly uncomfortable.

"Off men, then?" Mrs. Dade smiled and didn't pursue it,

going on to detail Meredith's duties and her salary, along with information about uniforms and territory.

Meredith was busy giving herself a lecture on keeping to the part she was playing. It wouldn't do to assume Kip Tennison's persona every time someone pried too deeply. She forced a smile and listened with every indication of interest, while at the back of her mind she wondered how long it was going to be before Cy Harden made his next move.

LATE THAT AFTERNOON, Cy walked into the gardens at the huge Harden estate. His eyes lingered halfheartedly on the Greek revival columns on the house's wide front porch. He remembered playing on that porch as a child, with his mother nearby, watching him. She had always been far too possessive and protective of her only child, a condition that, in later years, had caused friction between them. In fact, their relationship had fallen apart with the departure of Meredith Ashe. Cy had changed, in visible and not-so-visible ways.

He hung his hat on the antique hat rack in the hall and wandered absently into the elegant living room, gathering the usual impressions of pastel brocades and thick neutral shag carpeting and the priceless antiques his mother loved.

She was sitting on her wing chair, crocheting. Her dark eyes lifted and she smiled at him a little too brightly. "You're home early, aren't you?" she asked.

"I finished early." He poured himself a stiff whiskey and sank onto his own armchair. "I'll be out for dinner. The Petersons are hosting a business discussion on some new mineral leases."

"Business, business," she muttered. "There's more to life than making money. Cy, you really should marry. I've introduced you to two very nice young women, debutantes…"

"I won't marry," he said with a cold smile. He lifted his whiskey glass in a mock toast. "I took the cure. Remember?"

His mother went pasty white and dropped her eyes to her thin, nervous hands. "That…was a long time ago."

"It was yesterday." He threw down the rest of the whiskey and got up to refill the glass. Remembering was painful. "She's back in town, did you know?"

There was a funereal stillness in the room. "She?"

The word came out sounding as if his mother had choked on it. He turned. "Meredith Ashe. I gave her a job at the restaurant."

Myrna Harden had lived with her terrible secret, and her guilt, for so long that she'd forgotten anyone else shared it. But Meredith did. Ironically, the very information she'd used to get Meredith out of town could now be turned against her with even more devastating results. The ensuing scandal could ruin her by destroying the failing relationship she had with her son. She panicked.

"You mustn't!" she said frantically. "Cy, you mustn't get yourself involved with that woman again! You can't have forgotten what she did to you!"

His face gave away nothing. "No, Mother, I haven't forgotten. And I'm not getting involved with her. Once was enough. Her great-aunt died."

She swallowed nervously. "I didn't know."

"I'm sure there are bills to pay, loose ends to tidy up. She came from somewhere. She'll probably go back there as soon as she's got it all together."

Myrna wasn't so sure. "She'll inherit the house."

He nodded, staring into his second whiskey. He swirled the liquid carelessly. "She'll have a roof over her head. I have no idea where she's been all these years, but I know she had nothing when she left town." His face hardened and he tossed down the whiskey as if it were water.

"That's not true," Myrna said quickly. "She had money!"

Myrna had given her a wad of bills which Meredith had promptly returned. Myrna had always refused to believe, however, that the girl hadn't kept enough of it to get out of town. It eased her conscience to think it.

Cy stared at his mother over the glass, curious about her expression and about the fear in her normally calm voice. "Tony gave back the money that was supposedly stolen. Had you forgotten?"

Her face went even paler. "I'm sure she had some money," she faltered, lowering her eyes with raging guilt. "She must have."

Cy's eyes were thoughtful and bitter. "I was never comfortable with her part in it," he said. "Tony gave us the story as if he'd learned it by heart, and Meredith swore to me that he'd never touched her, that they'd never been lovers."

"A girl like that would have many lovers," Myrna said, flushing.

Cy's eyes went dark as he remembered the way it had been with Meredith, the fever that burned between them. He could still see her trembling because she wanted him so badly. Could she have been that way with any other man? She'd been as obsessed as he had, every bit as involved. He'd been too insanely jealous and angry to listen at the time his mother had accused her. It took only a couple of days after she left town for him to begin doubting her part in the so-called theft. It really had been very convenient that Tony subsequently produced all the "stolen money," and that Myrna insisted the boy not be arrested. The whole matter blew over after Meredith left town. But she hadn't looked guilty. She'd looked...defeated.

He hadn't questioned that. Perhaps he should have asked questions, but he'd deeply resented his helpless attraction to Meredith at the time. It had been almost a relief to have her out of his life, to close once and for all the door to his sexual excesses, to the headlong, wanton passion she had kindled in him. There had been a brief affair or two since then, but no woman had been able to make him lose control the way Meredith had. He wasn't sure he was even capable of it now. He felt dead inside. That was how Meredith had looked the last time he'd seen her, standing with her head bent in the hall of his home. She'd looked as if something inside her had died, and her accusing eyes had burned indelibly into his mind. He could see them even now.

He turned. "It's all past history. There's nothing left to build on, even if I were tempted. She was a fling. Nothing more."

Myrna relaxed a little. "I'm glad to hear it. Really, Cy, a waitress with a full-blooded Crow Indian for a great-uncle. Not our kind of people."

Under his heavy brows, his eyes glittered. "Isn't that a little snobbish for descendants of a British deserter?"

Myrna actually gasped. "We don't speak of that!"

He shrugged. "Why not? Everybody has a black sheep in the family tree."

"Don't be absurd. Sheep don't climb trees." She put down her crocheting. "I'll tell Ellen that you won't be in for dinner."

She walked past him, her mind whirling with fear and new complications. She didn't know what she was going to do. She couldn't have Meredith Ashe in Billings, not now, when she was doing her best to get Cy married. Dragging up an old love affair was the last thing he needed. She'd have to get Meredith out of town, and fast, before she had time to play on Cy's sympathy or make any hints about what had happened.

The baby…had she kept the baby she was carrying? Myrna ground her teeth at the thought of Cy's child being put up for adoption. The baby would have been a Harden, her blood. She hadn't allowed herself to think of that at the time. She only considered what was best for Cy, and she knew Meredith wasn't. She'd cut that woman out of his life with surgical precision, and if Myrna could help it, she wasn't coming back into it now. But she did want to know about the child. If Meredith hadn't had an abortion, there might be a way to get the child. She'd think about that, and about how to explain it to Cy without involving Meredith in his life again. Having successfully coped with the menace once, she was confident of her ability to do it again.

THE DAY PASSED QUICKLY for Meredith. She gained confidence as she worked, and she liked the people she worked with. They all accepted her at face value, helping her learn the routine and covering for her when she was slow at getting orders to customers. She especially liked Theresa, who was twenty and a raven-haired brunette, a Crow, like Meredith's late great-uncle.

Mealtime, however, meant crowds. The food was of sufficient variety and price to attract local people as well as out-of-towners. Many conferences were held in Billings, and not only in the cattle industry. The visitors liked the simple but elegant fare provided—even the southerners. That morning she'd waited on a gentleman from Alabama who was disappointed that grits weren't served for breakfast this far north. She noticed that he was back for dinner, though, and giving her frankly interested looks. She fended them off politely. Men had no part in her life anymore.

He was persistent, however. Meredith was busy warding him off once again while he ordered his evening meal when a familiar face came into view at a nearby table. Cy. And not only Cy. Myrna Harden, too.

Meredith used all of her skills at diplomacy to release herself from the Alabama gentleman and quickly turned in his order. As she did, she remembered that once she'd have switched tables with another waitress to avoid Myrna Harden. Those days were over. She turned and walked over to the table—one of hers—with easy pleasantness, belied only by the cold cruelty of her eyes as they met Myrna Harden's for the first time in years.

"Good evening. Would you like something to drink before you order?" she asked politely.

Myrna's dark eyes flickered. "I don't drink," she said flatly. "As you might remember, Meredith."

Meredith looked straight at her, ignoring Cy altogether. "It might surprise you what I remember, Mrs. Harden," she said quietly. "And my name is Miss Ashe."

The older woman laughed, too high pitched and much too mocking for pleasant amusement. "My, aren't you arrogant for a waitress?" She toyed nervously with the utensils in the place setting. "I'd like to see a menu."

Meredith produced two. "I'll have a glass of white wine," Cy told Meredith, shifting back on his chair to gauge her reactions. His mother's hostility disturbed him. Surely he was the one with the grudges.

"Coming right up," Meredith said. As she stood at the bar waiting for the drink, she took the opportunity to study her two antagonists. Cy was wearing a dark suit with a conservative tie. His creamy Stetson was parked on a chair at the table, and his thick dark hair was swept back neatly. He didn't look as if anything would ruffle him, his lean face completely without expression, his deep-set brown eyes staring straight ahead. But his mother was fidgeting beside him. Meredith could see her eyes dart nervously from left to right.

That body language was revealing. Meredith found it as

explicit as a confession. She smiled, slowly and with cold malice, and at that moment Myrna looked at her.

Her well made up face went pasty. There was something in the expression on that girl's face, Myrna thought, something in that cold stare that made her backbone turn to jelly. This wasn't the same girl she'd sent packing. No. There was something very different about Meredith now, and it made her begin to feel nauseated.

Meredith took Cy's drink back to the table and placed it before him. She then produced her pad and pen with perfectly steady fingers, mentally thanking Henry for the poise and self-confidence he'd engendered in her.

"These aren't necessary," Cy said curtly, pushing the menu away. "I'll have a steak and salad."

"So will I," Myrna said stiffly. "Rare, please. I don't like well-done meat."

"Same here," Cy replied.

"Two rare steaks," Meredith murmured, letting her eyes slide sideways to meet Cy's.

"Rare, not raw," he said, uncannily reading the thought in her mind. "I don't want it to get up and moo at me."

Meredith had to fight down a smile. "Yes, sir. It won't be long."

She left them to give in the order, then served it minutes later with cool courtesy.

"She's very efficient, isn't she?" Myrna said icily as they ate. "I can remember one time when she spilled coffee all down my dress, when you took me to that horrid little café for lunch."

"You made her nervous," Cy said tersely. He disliked the memory. His mother had gone out of her way to make Meredith uncomfortable, sniping at her constantly.

"Apparently I don't anymore," Myrna said with faint apprehension. She cut a piece of steak very delicately and raised it to her thin lips, chewing it deliberately before she swallowed. "Maybe she's married. Did you ask?"

Cy glared at her. "I didn't have to. She obviously isn't."

Myrna smiled. "If you say so. Odd, though, isn't it? A pretty girl of her age, still single."

"Maybe I'm a hard act to follow," Cy said cuttingly, and smiled in that unpleasant way that made Myrna shift on her chair.

"Don't be crude, dear. Pass me the salt, please."

Cy obliged her. He finished his meal, but he hardly tasted it. Watching Meredith move around the restaurant disturbed him. She was as graceful as ever. More so. There was a new carriage about her, a new confidence combined with a total lack of inhibition. She was nothing like the shy, loving, uncertain girl he'd taken to bed so many years ago. But she still made him burn. His reaction to her was as potent as ever, and he was fighting it with everything in him. Regardless of his mother's inexplicable hostility toward Meredith, he knew that he couldn't let the younger woman conquer his senses again. He'd been free from her, and he wanted to stay that way. Being taken over wasn't in the cards. Never again was he going to give in to that sweet madness.

Meredith brought the check and thanked them with a friendly smile, even adding that she hoped they had a nice evening. It was the way she said it, looking straight into Myrna Harden's eyes, that made it a threat instead of a farewell.

Myrna was silent all the way home. No, this wouldn't do, it really wouldn't. Presumably Meredith wasn't a woman of means, even if she did now own her great-aunt's house. A little money, a few words of warning, might be enough to remove the threat once and for all. She'd work it out.

Cy drove down the wide streets, unaware of his mother's

plotting. He was trying not to think about how that neat uniform covered Meredith's assets as he fought down the memories once more.

MEREDITH WAS WORN OUT by the time she started home. It was late, and her feet hurt. It had been a long time since she'd been on them all day.

She liked this city. She'd grown up outside Billings, in a tiny community several miles north of the Yellowstone. Her parents were shadowy figures in her mind, because they'd been killed in a wreck when she was just a small girl. Her only real memories were of Great-Aunt Mary and Great-Uncle Raven-Walking, who'd taken her in without hesitation and raised her as their own daughter. Since they had lived on the Crow Indian reservation, some of Meredith's earliest memories revolved around great celebrations and ceremonial occasions, her great-uncle in full Crow regalia. Meredith used to own a buckskin dress and a beaded headband that a Crow cousin had made for her. It seemed forever ago, now. Once painful, these memories had became bearable. The past was a safe place. Unchanged. Nothing could alter it. The good memories lived inside her, like the love she still had for the dark-eyed man who looked like her son.

She got off the bus near the house she'd bought for Great-Aunt Mary. It was a beautiful September evening, just right for walking. She enjoyed the invigorating cool weather. But snow wasn't far off, just another month or so. In this part of the world, it could be more than an inconvenience. Out in the isolated rural areas, it could be deadly to animals and humans alike when huge drifts of snow blocked roads and made travel impossible for long periods of time.

Amazing, she thought, how far she'd come from the ragged little girl living in the matchbox house on the Crow reservation with her relatives. She was wealthy now. No more homemade dresses and secondhand shoes. All the same, her childhood had been full of love. That was surely worth more than all the money in the world. Remembering those good days with her kin had made her keenly aware of the plight of the people on the reservation. She regularly contributed to causes that would benefit the Plains Indians, and she still did her share of gift giving to her cousins and their families. With no return address, of course. It was still only a drop in the bucket to what was needed. But every little bit helped. Family was family.

She locked the door behind her and sat down on the sofa, her eyelids falling listlessly. But she couldn't go to sleep. She had to call home. She'd promised Blake that she would.

Drowsily, she dialed the number direct and waited for Mr. Smith to answer it.

"Tennison residence," his gravelly voice greeted.

She smiled. "Hi, Mr. Smith," she said lazily. "How's everything?"

He chuckled. "Blake flushed his rubber duck down the toilet. Not to worry, I rushed out and bought him another. The plumber unstopped the overflow. Everything's fine." There was a pause. "How are you?"

"I'm working," she replied. "I got this great job waitressing at a local restaurant. I make minimum wage plus tips, isn't that great?"

There was a longer pause. "You have a job?"

"Just temporary. It's Cy Harden's restaurant, you see. Proximity to the enemy may give me a small advantage while I search out his weak spots."

"Be careful that he doesn't find yours," he cautioned. "Don's here. He had to get some papers from your desk. Want to talk to him?"

She frowned. Odd that Don would be at her home this time of night. "Yes."

Don picked up the line, sounding a little uncertain. "Nice to hear from you," he said. "I, uh, had to have the Jordan file. You brought it home."

Her brows knitted. "I was working on the Jordan merger. You know that. Why do you want it?"

"Jordan and Cane insisted that we get the deal through this week. Unless you want to fly up here to ramrod it…?"

"No," she said abruptly. "Of course not. Go ahead. I should have phoned you earlier about that, but it slipped my mind."

"That's a first," he said.

"I suppose so. You'll still need my signature, won't you?"

"Yes. You can fax it…."

"I don't have a fax machine," she said. She grimaced. "Send the papers express. I'll have them back within a day."

"Will do. You need a fax machine."

"I know. Mr. Smith can bring it out next week and fetch my office equipment with him. I may be here for a few weeks, but I'll make sure the business doesn't suffer because of it. I can handle my end at night. I'll call in every day and check on everything at the office."

"Are you sure such a long absence is wise?" Don asked cautiously.

"Yes, I'm sure," she said darkly. "Listen, Don, I'm not some flighty female with no business sense, and you know it. Henry taught me everything he knew."

"Yes, he did, didn't he?"

Don sounded bitter. Meredith wondered sometimes if he didn't resent having part of his brother's corporation headed by an outsider. He was pleasant enough, but there had always been a little distance between them, as if he didn't quite trust her.

"I won't let you down," she said. "This mineral deal is the most important thing I have on my agenda, regardless of how much time it takes. If I can find a weakness in Harden's stranglehold on the property, I can take advantage of it."

"Are you sure that it's the corporation you're concerned with, and not taking vengeance on Harden himself?"

She didn't answer that. "I'm glad to have the Jordan matter dealt with. Will you put Mr. Smith back on, please?"

He cleared his throat. "Of course. I'm sorry if I sounded antagonistic. I'm tired. It's been a long day."

"Yes. I know how it is."

"Meredith, are you sure Smith should have that iguana running loose in the house? The thing weighs almost ten pounds, and it's got claws like a cat and teeth like a snake…."

"Tiny is part of the family," she said simply. "She doesn't bother anything. She just sits on the back of Mr. Smith's chair until she's hungry, then she goes to the kitchen and eats her vegetables. She has a litter box in the bathroom, which she uses, and she never attacks anybody. Blake loves her, too."

"It's unnatural, having a big reptile slithering around everywhere. The plumber screamed when he came to unstop the commode. Tiny was sitting under the shower, having a bath."

"Poor plumber," she murmured, smothering a giggle.

"Yes, well, he said not to call him again. See what I mean? That reptile is a menace."

"Tell that to Mr. Smith. I'd do it from behind a door, though."

"I see what you mean. All right. Your house, your problem."

"It should have been your house, Don," she said unexpectedly. "I'm sorry it worked out this way. You're Henry's brother, his only blood relative. The bulk of the estate should have been yours."

Don sighed sharply. "Henry had the right to do what he pleased with it," he said, and the hostility abruptly left his voice, to be replaced by a tone that was almost regretful. "You were his wife, after all. He loved you."

"I loved him, too," she said. She meant it. Henry had been her refuge in that terrible storm of anguish Cy had caused. It wasn't the kind of love she'd felt for Cy, but it was love all the same. Given enough time, with Cy's presence removed permanently, she might have come to love Henry with the same fervor he'd offered her.

"This mineral monopoly the Hardens have," Don said, his voice strange. "Are you sure you want to go through with this? Harden is a formidable businessman. You could be risking more than you realize."

"Expansion without risk is like bread without butter. No flavor. Take care, Don. Let me speak to Mr. Smith again, please."

"Okay. I'll call him. Take care of yourself."

"Sure."

Minutes later, Mr. Smith was back on the line. "He's gone," he said curtly. "I don't trust him, Kip. Neither should you. I think he's up to something."

"I'll bet you're the most suspicious man on earth. It must be that old CIA experience affecting your brain. Don's all right."

"He said Tiny should be kept outside," he said after a minute.

She laughed. "Tiny would be miserable outside. It's my house. As long as it *is* my house, Tiny lives inside. Okay?"

He relaxed. "Okay." He made a rough sound. "Thanks."

"I want you to come out here next week." She gave him a list of the things she needed and set a time. "Call Blake, will you?" she added. "I hate being away from him so much. At least we can talk on the phone. I know it's late, but I do want to say hello."

"He'll be glad to do that. He's already missing you again."

She sighed. "I do travel a lot, don't I? Too much, sometimes."

"Uh, about Tiny…"

"I'll get a new plumber," she promised. "Don't worry."

She could almost see him grin. "Okay."

Seconds later her son picked up the phone. "Mama, when are you coming home?" he asked sleepily. "My rubber duck fell in the cubbymode and Mr. Smith throwed him away. He got me a new one. Did you buy me a present? I can count to twenty, and I can write my name…."

"That's very nice. I'm proud of you, son. You're coming to see me soon, and I'll have a present for you." She crossed her fingers. She would have, by then.

There was a brief pause. "Can't you stay home then and play with me sometimes? Jerry's mama takes him to the park to see the ducks. You never take me places, Mama."

She had to grit her teeth not to make some sharp reply about the necessity for her work. "When I get home, we'll talk about that," she said.

"That's what you always say, but you go away again," he muttered angrily.

"Blake, this isn't the time for an argument," she said firmly. "Now, listen. Mr. Smith is going to bring you out here very soon. There's a lot to see, even some real cowboys, and we'll have time to spend together."

"We will?" he asked with such delight that she felt guilty all over again.

"Yes," she promised.

"All right, Mama. Can we bring Tiny? Uncle Don says we ought to eat her. I think Uncle Don's mean."

"Now, now. We aren't going to eat Tiny. Mr. Smith can bring her with you when you come out here to see me. But not just yet, okay?"

"Okay." He sighed sadly. "Can Tiny sit with me when we come?"

"Tiny's carrier can sit with you," she corrected, remembering vividly the last time Mr. Smith had taken Tiny in the limousine with them on a trip. A small-town garage attendant had refused to pump gas after Tiny had pressed her nose against the window to look at him. People shouldn't carry monsters around in their cars, he'd added scornfully. Mr. Smith had gotten out of the car to answer that insult, but the attendant was already out of range. Ever since then, Tiny rode in a carrier because Meredith insisted.

"I love you, Mommy," Blake said.

"I love you, too, darling. I'll call you tomorrow. You mind Mr. Smith and be a good boy."

"I will. Night-night."

"Good night."

She hung up, fingering the receiver tenderly. Blake was the most important thing in her world. Sometimes she regretted bitterly the time she had to spend away from him on business. He was growing up, and she was missing some of the most precious days of his life. Would he resent that when he was older? Was she being fair to him not to let Don assume more of the responsibility for the domestic operations or to designate another corporate officer to help her? Perhaps her own pride was adding to the problem, because she felt obligated to carry on the role Henry had originally carved out for her. But would Henry have given her so much responsibility if he'd realized how it would affect her relationship with Blake?

No, she thought. He'd have delegated to give her more time with her son. He would have been with her himself, too, playing with Blake, taking him places, encouraging his curiosity about the world around him. Henry had loved Blake so much.

She turned away from the phone. Sometimes life without Henry was very hard. She wondered what it would have been like if Cy Harden had ignored his mother's accusations and believed in Meredith, if he'd married her. They'd have been together when Blake was born, and perhaps the delight of having a son would have bound Cy to her.

She laughed coldly. Oh, certainly. Blake would have warmed his cold heart, and he'd have fallen madly in love with Meredith and kicked his manipulative mother out on her ear.

All of it whirled around in her head, blinding her. The pressure of business, Blake's indignation and resentment of her absences, Cy Harden's renewed presence in her life. She tugged at her thick blond hair and remembered something she'd read about "primal scream therapy." She wondered what the neighbors would say if she went out into the street and screamed at the top of her lungs. She'd be locked up, that's what, and then who'd take care of Blake, acquire new contracts, and deal with Cy Harden and his vicious mother?

She went upstairs and took a tranquilizer. She didn't take them often, but sometimes the pressure was so terrible that she couldn't cope. Alcohol, thank God, had never appealed to her. Neither did pills. She only took them when she had no other option. This was one of those nights.

With a long sigh, she showered and dressed for bed. It did no good at all to agonize and theorize over problems. Henry had taught her that. The only way to deal with a situation was with action, not mental gymnastics.

She lay down and closed her eyes. The tranquilizer began to work and she left it all behind, drifting off into a twilight of semiawareness. Sometimes, they said, a good night's sleep was all that stood between an anguished person and suicide. She wasn't suicidal, but oblivion was sweet, just the same.

CHAPTER FOUR

AS DAWN STREAMED THROUGH the curtains in Great-Aunt Mary's immaculate bedroom, Meredith lay drowsily between the clean white sheets of the four-poster bed. She was remembering back. Cy's cold aloofness, Myrna's hot accusations, Tony's confession… She could still feel the sickness as she ran from the Harden house to her Great-Aunt Mary's. She couldn't even tell the worried old lady or her great-uncle the truth about what had happened. It was too shameful to share.

She'd packed her bags and gone straight to the bank to withdraw her pitiful savings from her restaurant job. With no clear idea of what she'd do when she got there, she'd bought a one-way bus ticket to Chicago and kissed her worried relatives good-bye before she boarded the Greyhound and said a silent farewell to Cy.

Even then, she'd hoped that he might come after her. Hope died hard, and she was carrying his child. She'd even hoped that Myrna might relent and tell him the truth, because Myrna knew about her pregnancy. The older woman had made that apparent just before Cy came into the room that long-ago morning. But no one came. No one rushed to the bus station to stop her.

The Chicago bus terminal had been unwelcoming, crowded and busy. Clutching her worn suitcase in her hand, Meredith had fought down the instinctive fear of being alone and without visible means of support. There was always the YWCA if everything else failed. She'd find some place. But she felt sick and afraid, and always there was the threat of Myrna pursuing her over that supposedly stolen money.

The first three nights she'd spent at the YMCA in tears, mourning Cy and the life that could have been. But then she'd been told about another place, a Christian home with only a few tenants. She'd decided to try her luck there, hoping for a little more privacy in which to spend her grief without the prying, compassionate eyes of the other downtrodden women at the Y.

She remembered leaving the YWCA, wandering aimlessly down the cracked sidewalk while the cold winter wind whipped her long hair around her thin, pale face. As a few snow flurries touched coldly against her cheeks and eyelids and lips, she wondered what to do next.

Fate took a hand when she stepped off the curb without looking and found herself flat on the pavement, beside a very expensive limousine.

A minute later, a quiet, intelligent face came into focus, a face with deep blue eyes and thin lips, high cheekbones and brownish blond hair.

"Are you all right?" asked a velvety voice. "You're very pale."

The voice had what sounded to Meredith like a definite New York accent. She'd heard it often enough in the café when tourists passed through. She smiled. "I'm fine," she murmured. "I guess I fell."

The man's eyes lit up. "I guess you did. But we helped a little, didn't we, Mr. Smith?"

A second man came into view. This one was a giant with thinning dark hair and big, deep-set green eyes, with an imposing nose in a chiseled face. He was wearing a chauffeur's uniform. "I couldn't brake quickly enough," he said. "But I'm sorry. It was my fault."

"No," Meredith said weakly. "I felt faint. I'm pregnant…."

The two men exchanged a speaking glance. "Your husband?" the first man asked. "Is he with you?"

"I don't have…a husband," she whispered, and tears sprang to her eyes. "He doesn't know."

"Oh, boy." Henry smoothed back her long, disheveled hair with a gentle hand. "Well, you'd better come with us."

In her naive way, Meredith equated big black limousines with organized crime. This man was dressed fit to kill, and his driver looked every inch a mobster. She hadn't run away from one dangerous situation to land herself in another.

"I can't do that," she blurted out, her big eyes saying more than she realized as she looked from one of them to the other.

"Will it help if we introduce ourselves?" The thin man smiled. "I'm Henry Tennison. This is Mr. Smith. I'm a legitimate businessman." He leaned closer, his lazy eyes smiling at her. "We're not even Italian."

One look at the humor in his face, and all her apprehension disappeared.

"That's better. Help me get her in the car, Smith. I think we're becoming the center of attention."

Belatedly, Meredith realized they were blocking traffic. Other drivers were making their irritation known with their horns. She allowed herself to be put in the back of the limousine with Henry Tennison while the formidable Mr. Smith stashed her luggage in the trunk.

She looked around her at the luxurious interior of the car. Real leather. Not to mention a bar, a television, a cellular phone, and some odd kind of computer and printer. "You must be worth a fortune," she said without thinking.

"I am," Henry mused. "But it's not all it's cracked up to be. I'm a slave to my job."

"Everything has a price, hasn't it?" Meredith asked sadly.

"Apparently." He leaned back and folded his arms as Mr. Smith started the car and pulled into traffic, leaving the loud horns behind. "Tell me about the baby."

Without knowing why she trusted him implicitly, a man she didn't even know, she began to talk. She told him about Cy and the beginning of their love affair, her voice quiet and slow as she skipped over the passion to his mother's interference and her speedy departure in disgrace.

"I guess I must sound like a tramp to you," she concluded.

"Don't be absurd," he said gently. "I'm not an impressionable youth. Is the father going to come after you?"

She shook her head. "He believed his mother."

"Too bad. Well, you can come home with me for the time being. Don't worry. I'm not a lecher, even if I am a certified bachelor. I'll look after you until you find your feet."

"But, I can't—"

"We'll have to get you some clothes," he said, thinking aloud. "And your hair needs work, too."

"I haven't said—"

"Delia, my secretary, can look after you while I'm away. I'll have her move in, just to keep everything aboveboard. And you'll need a good obstetrician. I'll have Delia take care of that, too."

Meredith caught her breath at the way he was arranging her life. "But—"

"How old are you?"

She swallowed. "Eighteen."

His eyes narrowed on her thin face. "Eighteen," he murmured. "A little young, but it will work out."

"What will work out?"

"Never mind." He leaned forward, his hands dangling between his knees as he stared straight into her eyes. "You're still in love with him, aren't you?"

"Yes."

He nodded. "Well, I'll cross that bridge when I come to it." He sat back again. "Do you like quiche?"

"What?"

"Quiche. It's a kind of French egg pie— Oh, never mind. I'll show you when we get home."

Home was a penthouse apartment in one of the most expensive hotels in Chicago. Meredith, who'd never known anything grander than Great-Aunt Mary's small house, was shocked and delighted at the luxury. She stood in the entrance to the living room and just stared.

"Don't let it intimidate you," Henry said, smiling. "You'll get used to it in no time at all."

Incredibly, she had. Without quite knowing how, she became Henry Tennison's possession. She was maneuvered into marriage scant weeks later and shipped out of the country to one of Henry's houses in the Bahamas, near Nassau. Her name became Kip Tennison. Henry undertook her advanced education in business tactics and strategy, in between natural childbirth classes with a registered nurse he hired to live in and look after Kip. During this time, he anticipated the baby with all the delight of its real father, spoiled his young wife, and seemed to lose twenty years of age as he involved himself with her pregnancy.

She sighed, remembering how it had been. Slowly, she had begun to replace Cy's face with Henry's, to trust her husband, to confide in him. She warmed to him. When the baby was born, he was with her at the delivery in Nassau, and as the tiny infant was placed in his arms, tears fell from his eyes.

It was only later that she discovered Henry was sterile, that he could never have a child of his own. It was why he was single at the age of thirty-eight—why he'd never asked anyone to marry him until Meredith came along. But fatherhood seemed to come naturally to him, and he treated Blake as if the infant were his own blood child.

In all the months they'd waited for Blake, he'd never touched Meredith. She wouldn't have refused him. He was kinder to her than anyone had ever been. He worshiped her, and slowly she began to return his warm affection, to look forward to their time together.

Then, almost inevitably, he came to her one night. It was as if there had never been a woman, he told her softly while he loved her. And while it wasn't the intense passion she'd shared with Cy, it wasn't at all unpleasant. Because Henry loved her, she was able to indulge him. He was a tender, expert lover, and she felt no revulsion at being touched by him. And if he ever suspected that, with her eyes closed, she sometimes thought of Cy as she gave herself to him, he never said so. They were compatible. They got along well together, with mutual respect and affection, and Blake was their world.

It had all fallen apart the day Henry left on a business trip and his plane crashed into the Atlantic. Meredith had felt something with him the night before that she hadn't experienced in their marriage. A merging, a oneness, that left her sobbing in his arms afterward. For the first time, she'd curled into his body and refused to let go. She was glad about that, when the news came. She'd finally told him that she loved him. If he'd lived…

She sat at the funeral with anguish in her eyes, and even her brother-in-law, Don, who'd been so distant with her, softened as he realized how genuine her grief was.

Henry was gone. But he'd been a good tutor, and Meredith had been an excellent student. She didn't stop learning after he died and left her with control of the domestic operation. Possessed already of a keen, intuitive mind, she found the give and take of negotiating right up her alley. In her first month, she astounded the corporate directors with her ability to size up a potential acquisition and land it with a minimum of fuss. Despite their initial desire to kick her out, the directors became her greatest fans—to the chagrin of Henry's brother, who was secretly nurturing a jealous resentment of Meredith's power that grew by the day.

Unaware of that resentment, Meredith barreled through business like a velvet bulldozer. She was enjoying power for the first time in her life and loving her job as mother to Blake. All the while, as Meredith grew in strength, she never stopped thinking about Cy Harden and his venomous mother. Don had been right about one thing. Her interest in Harden Properties went far beyond mineral rights acquisitions. She wanted to back Cy into a corner and cut him to ribbons, while his arrogant mother stood by helplessly and watched. She wanted Myrna Harden to suffer along with her son. Meredith was so far gone with regard to the Hardens that revenge was the only thing that registered. Whether Don liked it or not—and of course, he didn't—she wasn't leaving Billings until she had the Hardens on their knees, no matter what it took to get them there.

She got up and dressed, taking time to pour herself a cup of coffee before she left the house. Mrs. Dade didn't like her employees having breakfast on her time. She was a good boss, and a fair one, for all that.

The phone rang and Meredith yawned lazily as she answered it.

"Good, you're home," Mr. Smith said. "Don had me fly out with those Jordan papers for your signature. He said express mail was too slow. I'll be with you in five minutes."

"All right." She hung up, surprised. It wasn't like Don to send the corporate jet just for some routine papers. Perhaps the merger was more complicated than she'd realized.

She met Mr. Smith at the door with a cup of strong black coffee. He grinned as he took it.

"Here." He handed her the papers, then produced in short order her computer and printer, the fax machine, and boxes of paper. Meredith had him put them in the library, which she then locked.

"Now, I've no excuse not to work." She laughed, having only just realized how free she'd been until that dreaded equipment arrived. "How's Blake?" she asked.

"Fine. I left him with Perlie just for the morning. I'll be back before he misses me. I brought you this, too." He handed her a case of fresh orange juice. "You'll need plenty of vitamin C to help you build back up."

She laughed. "Well, I guess this qualifies as necessary equipment."

"Essential, if you're going to live in Billings for a while." He sipped coffee while she signed documents. "Heard from Harden?"

"Not today. He and his mother had dinner at the restaurant last night."

"How's it going?" he asked.

She glanced at him ruefully. "It's painful. But I expect the end result will be worth it."

His green eyes narrowed as they scanned her face. "Don't get caught again. Mr. Tennison wouldn't like having you hurt twice."

She smiled at him, remembering how Henry had cosseted her. Mr. Smith did, too. It was almost like having Henry back again when Mr. Smith was around. "You're good to me, Mr. Smith," she said.

He looked uncomfortable and averted his eyes. "No trouble to be good to someone like you. Sign those papers, please, so I can get out of here. Your brother-in-law was impatient to get the merger finished."

"So I see." She took her time reading the documents, suspicious at Don's eagerness. But the papers were just routine, no surprises. She didn't understand why it was so urgent. Then it occurred to her that Don was literally taking the merger out of her hands, and it all made sense. He was showing her up.

"You look worried," Mr. Smith remarked.

She shrugged as she handed the papers back. "I never credited Don with one-upmanship."

"Competition runs in the Tennison clan."

"Yes. Funny that I didn't realize it before, isn't it?"

"You've had a lot on your mind," he replied noncommittally. "Don't sweat it. Maybe the boss is just trying to give you a hand. God knows you could use one sometimes. You push yourself too hard."

"Do I?" she mused.

"Too many long hours, too much time on the run. You're several pounds light."

She grinned. "Send me down to the gym and build me up, then."

"Wish I could. Can't keep you still long enough." He went to the door, pausing with his hand on the knob. "Watch your back. It gets dangerous up in the high altitudes."

"I have noticed that," she agreed.

Mr. Smith opened the door and walked out onto the porch, idly noting a car that hesitated as it passed the house. Nosy neighbors, he thought mockingly, motioning to the cabdriver.

"I'll phone you tonight," she said. "Tell Blake I love him."

"He knows that."

"It never hurts to tell him, all the same."

He grinned and got into the cab. "Okay."

Meredith watched the cab drive away. Mr. Smith was like family. When he was gone, she was alone again. Just like old times, she thought as she turned back into the house.

The knock on the door ten minutes later startled her. Perhaps Mr. Smith had forgotten something, she thought as she went to answer it.

Meredith opened the door to an unexpected visitor. Myrna Harden stood rigidly on her doorstep, dressed in black, her thin, pinched face hard with contempt and repugnance.

"I've been expecting you," Meredith said with icy calm. "Come in."

Myrna walked into the house, looking around with disdain. She took the best of the living room chairs and crossed her elegant legs, her purse clutched tightly on her lap.

"I'll come straight to the point," she said primly, producing a check. She held it out to Meredith. "That should make it worth your while to leave Billings for good."

Meredith didn't take it. She smiled vacantly. "Would you like coffee?"

"Thank you, no," Myrna said stiffly. She waved the check. "It's for ten thousand dollars," she announced. "Take it and go away."

Meredith eased down onto the sofa and crossed her jean-clad legs comfortably. "I went away, once."

"Why didn't you stay?" Myrna's face stiffened even more. "What do you want? My son doesn't care about you! He never did, or he'd have gone after you, surely you must realize that?" she demanded in an almost frantic high-pitched tone.

Yes, of course Meredith realized it, and almost winced at the old pain. "My great-aunt died," she said with dignity.

Myrna's inherent good manners flinched at the reminder. "I did know that. I'm sorry. But you must have been offered something for the house...."

"I don't want to sell the house. It has pleasant memories for me. I don't want to leave Billings just yet, either," she added quietly, and some of the steely makeup Henry had taught her was coming into play. She looked straight into Myrna's eyes, her posture open and threatening, her face giving away no weaknesses. "It will take more than ten thousand to get me out of Billings. It will take more than you've got."

Myrna gasped. "You arrogant backwoods brat!"

"No name calling, if you please," Meredith said easily. She studied the lined face without haste. "You haven't worn well, have you? I'm not surprised. The guilt must have been terrible at times."

Myrna actually paled. She clenched her purse tightly. "I don't feel guilt."

"You lied to your son, falsely accused me, cost me my home at a time when I desperately needed it...you don't feel guilt for any of that?"

"You were a child, playing games," Myrna rasped.

"I was a woman, deeply in love and pregnant with your grandchild," Meredith said, the words delivered with the precision of a merciless scalpel. "You lied," she accused, her eyes contemptuous.

"I had to," Myrna cried. "I couldn't let my son marry someone like you!"

"You never told Cy the truth, did you?" Meredith persisted.

Myrna swallowed. "I'll give you twenty thousand dollars."

"Tell him the truth."

"Never!"

"That's my price," Meredith said, rising. "Tell Cy what you did to me, and I'll go without a penny."

The older woman looked frail. Damaged. She stood up, her lips trembling. "I can't do that," she said, shaken.

"You'll wish you had, before I'm through," Meredith said, her eyes as cold as Henry Tennison's had ever been. "Did you really think you were going to get away with it forever?"

Myrna dug out a handkerchief with trembling fingers and dabbed at the corners of her mouth. She looked pasty. "Abortions are easy these days," she said. "I gave you enough for one. I gave you enough to go away."

"And I had it sent back to you, along with all Cy's gifts, didn't I?" Meredith challenged.

Myrna squirmed, but she didn't answer.

"You told Cy I'd robbed the company of thousands, Tony and I. You had Tony tell him that we'd been lovers, that I'd betrayed him."

"It was the only way I could get rid of you. He wouldn't have let you go if I hadn't. He was obsessed with you!"

Meredith laughed bitterly. "Obsessed, yes. But that was all. He didn't love me. If he had, you and all your plotting wouldn't have made the slightest difference."

Satisfaction smoldered in Myrna's eyes. "So you know that, do you?"

Meredith nodded, the heat building in her body from a temper suppressed too long. "I was naive, all right. I didn't realize just how naive until you shot me out of here."

"You haven't fared badly, have you?" Myrna asked stiffly. "You look well. You're still young."

"There was a baby, Myrna."

"Yes." Myrna moved closer, her eyes calculating. "Did you have it? Did you put it up for adoption? I'll give you anything. Cy never has to know. The baby will want for nothing!"

Meredith looked at the older woman incredulously. "Suppose someone had made you that offer when you were carrying Cy?"

Something happened in Myrna's eyes. An expression came into them that Meredith had never seen there. An uncertainty. An anguish.

"All these years… You never knew where I was, or what I had to do to take care of myself, and you didn't care," Meredith said. "Now you waltz into my home and try to blackmail me out of town. You even have the audacity to try to buy a grandchild you didn't give a damn about six years ago."

"That isn't true," Myrna said, lowering her eyes. "I…tried to trace you."

"Because you felt guilty about letting a Harden be put up for adoption?" Meredith said with a mocking smile when the older woman flushed guiltily. "Just as I thought."

"You put him up for adoption, didn't you?" Myrna persisted. "We could still find him. Or her. Which is it?"

"That's something you can wonder about to your heart's content," Meredith said. "Whether I had an abortion, whether I had the baby and put it up for adoption, all of it. And you can take your offer of money with you. I'm afraid I still can't be bought." Meredith stood up.

Myrna rose from her chair looking nervous and shaken. "Everyone has a price," she said. "Even you."

"Oh, that's true enough," Meredith agreed. "But then, you know what my price is, don't you?"

The older woman started to speak, but Meredith opened the door in a way that was more than a suggestion that she leave.

Myrna stopped in the doorway. "Your male visitor was very formidable, wasn't he?" she asked. "Are you living with him?"

Meredith couldn't find an answer fast enough. Myrna smiled venomously. "I'm sure Cy will be interested to hear that he's been replaced in your affections. Good day."

There was nothing she could say, nothing she could do, that would stop Myrna from taking news of Mr. Smith's visit home to Cy. Not that she cared, really, she told herself. It would only fortify his opinion of her. Probably he couldn't have a worse one. He'd accused her of being unfaithful many times, not just with Tony. Myrna Harden had said she was sleeping with Tony, and Tony had been paid not to deny it. Cy had thought of her as a tramp. She had no reason to suppose his attitude had changed over the years.

She went to work, and fortunately it was a busy day. She didn't have to think. But dinner brought Cy back for the second night in a row, and his whole posture spelled trouble.

"May I get you something to drink?" she asked politely with carefully schooled features and a blank smile.

Cy's dark eyes stared back at her from a face like a wall. "Who was the man your neighbor saw leaving your house early this morning?"

"It wasn't a neighbor," she replied carelessly. "It was your mother."

He scowled. Apparently Myrna hadn't shared her visit with him. Meredith smiled.

"Didn't she tell you she came to see me? Pity. She offered me ten thousand dollars to leave town."

"That's a lie," he said coldly.

She shrugged. "Okay. What would you like to eat?"

His face hardened. "My mother doesn't need to pay you to leave town. I can get rid of you whenever I like."

"Can you really?" she asked with genuine interest. "It would be fascinating to watch you try."

"You don't believe it?" His smile was calculating. "For instance, I could buy the mortgage on your aunt's house and foreclose."

"The house doesn't have a mortgage," she said easily. And

it didn't. Henry had paid it off, anonymously, through a Realty company in Illinois.

Cy was surprised. Something niggled at the back of his mind for just an instant before he dismissed it. "I could fire you."

"I can get another job," she said. "Even you can't control quite every business in Billings. I seem to remember that you used to have enemies. I could go to one of them for work."

His eyes flashed. "Try it."

"Why don't you ask your mother why she wants me to leave?" she asked quietly.

"I know why. She thinks you'll worm your way into my life again and leave me bleeding, like you did years ago."

She laughed softly. "You don't bleed," she said huskily. "If you did, it would be pure gold, or silver."

"You cheated on me and helped another man steal from me. You're the one who might bleed money, not me."

"Think so?" The pain and anguish of the past contorted her features, made her eyes darker. "What you and your mother did to me didn't count?"

"We did nothing to you," he said tersely. "Although we could have. I could have sent you to prison for that theft."

She shook her head. "Because a good attorney would have cut Tony to pieces on the witness stand. Where is the dear boy now?"

"I don't know," he said coldly.

"Don't know, and don't care." She nodded. "Well, that's too bad. I liked Tony, despite what he and your mother did to my life."

"My mother did nothing to you!"

Her gaze was level and unflinching. "Nothing?" She leaned forward. "Ask her. I dare you. Ask her why I'm here, why I won't leave. Ask her for the truth."

His eyes glittered. "I know the truth. Don't push me. You're only here on sufferance." He threw down his napkin and got up, towering over her. "You won't find me as vulnerable this time."

"The reverse is also true," she said quietly. "And you can tell your mother that my price is now beyond her pocket."

"Careful, honey," he said softly. "You're on my home ground now, and I fight to win."

"Then you'd better start polishing your sword, big man," she replied. "Because this time you're going to have to make the first cut count. Have a nice evening."

She turned and walked over to the next table without batting an eyelash.

CHAPTER FIVE

MYRNA HARDEN ATE NOTHING that evening. Her interview with Meredith hadn't gone at all the way she'd planned it. She hadn't wanted to make threats, but the younger woman had frightened her. This wasn't the shy young girl who'd once cringed at her cold tone, who'd been beaten and sent packing. No. This new Meredith was an unknown quantity, and when Myrna hadn't been able to ruffle her composure, she'd said things she never meant to say.

She'd wanted to tell Meredith how desperately she'd searched for her, how upset she'd been at her own irrational actions. She hadn't wanted to leave a young, pregnant girl at the mercy of a heartless world, and when Meredith had sent back the small wad of bills she'd given her, along with all the expensive things Cy had tried to give her, she was even more afraid. Meredith's people wouldn't have had much to give her. The young girl, alone and pregnant in a large city, would have been at the mercy of any stranger who wanted to hurt her.

Shocked and horrified at what she'd done, Myrna had hired private detectives, unbeknownst to Cy, in a furious attempt to track Meredith down and provide for her. The thought of her own grandchild being aborted or put up for adoptions by strangers had haunted her for years. Her best efforts hadn't produced one scrap of evidence that would point to Meredith's whereabouts. The girl might have disappeared from the face of the earth.

Myrna gave up trying to eat and pushed the plate away. She was alone tonight, as she frequently was. Cy had business, he'd said. Even his attitude had changed over the years. He was no longer the loving, considerate son he'd once been. Meredith's departure had twisted something inside him, made him hard and uncaring and cruel at times. He blamed the girl, when it was Myrna's manipulating that had caused his pain. She closed her eyes. Meredith had accused her of feeling guilt, and of course, she had. Guilt, shame, anguish, all those things. She felt the weight of her villainy tonight, along with her memories. Meredith's pleading face, Cy's unyielding one, Tony's innocent complicity, came back to torment her. Cy had stayed drunk for days afterward, refusing to leave his room, even to speak to his mother. When he regained his composure, he became a playboy of the worst kind, and for months the business suffered.

He'd weathered his storm, but he wasn't the same. Myrna laughed bitterly. She wasn't the same, either. Her plotting had caused so much tragedy that even the terrible fear that had triggered her actions couldn't justify them. She thought of the child and wished she knew if Meredith had really had it. Was it safe? Was it happy? Was it in the hands of loving people and not sadists who might abuse it? The same thoughts had grieved her all the long years, had given her no peace. She got up from the table, leaving the maid to clear away, and she strolled aimlessly into the living room. A mausoleum, she thought, looking around at the exquisite decor. She was entombed in this luxury, with no real friends and no living relatives except her son. She was alone, as perhaps she deserved to be.

Her long fingers touched a Ming vase on a side table, caressing its beauty, its faded colors. She was like that, she mused. Old and faded and delicate, for all her bluster. Meredith hated her, and it was no more than she deserved. She hadn't really expected to get away with her sins. Nobody did. Payment might take twenty years, but inevitably your trespasses ricocheted right back to you.

Myrna shivered as she felt the approaching storm. Meredith couldn't be bought, she couldn't be intimidated. There was no way to make her leave, and if she stayed, there was every chance that Cy would learn the truth. All of it.

Her eyes closed on a shudder. Her son would hate her when he learned what she'd done.

Restlessly, she walked over to the darkened window and looked out at the cold, bare silhouette of the trees on the horizon. Farther, in the distance, were the lights of the refinery near the Yellowstone, like beacons against the dark sky. She couldn't confess her crime, not yet. She'd just have to bide her time. There was so much Cy didn't know about her past, about the reasons she'd fought so hard for respectability. She'd even married Frank Harden for that, when she didn't love him. The man she'd really loved had gone off to Vietnam shattered by her cold mercenary plotting, and he'd been killed there. That, too, was on Myrna's conscience. She'd sacrificed love all her life in the pursuit of wealth and power, to arm herself with the things that would protect her son from the devastating childhood she'd had to suffer.

Nobody knew, not even the one great-uncle she had left, what she'd had to endure as a little girl because of her mother. No one would know, ever, she swore. She'd made her bed, now she had to lie in it. But what she'd done to Meredith, to Cy, to the man she'd loved—her soul ached with the bruises her actions had dealt it.

But there might still be time to spare herself the humiliation of having Cy know what she'd done. If she begged, she might gain Meredith's compassion and get her out of Billings in time. The damage was done, the child was lost. She was almost certain now that Meredith had placed him or her up for adoption. The only possible course of action was to convince her that revenge was an empty pleasure, to ask her to spare them.

It would scorch her pride, but perhaps it was no less than she deserved. She'd hurt so many lives with her determination to have Cy marry into the proper bloodlines. She laughed mirthlessly. Myrna's fierce need for social acceptance had probably cost her any hope of grandchildren, because Cy refused even to consider marriage anymore. The only grandchild she'd ever had was lost to her, through her own arrogance. She closed her eyes and shivered. Paradise lost, she thought. How cold were the dead dreams of the past. She turned slowly and wandered back into the living room to sit down.

IT WASN'T LATE WHEN Meredith left the restaurant. Cy had walked out just after their brief quarrel. How silly of her to expect that he might ask Myrna for the truth, when he'd believed his mother's lies from the beginning.

If she felt any consolation at all, it came from Myrna's uncertainty about the fate of her only grandchild. It was a bitter pleasure at that, because Meredith didn't like hurting people—not even people like Myrna. All that pain, all that anguish, and for what? Myrna had wanted Cy to marry a local socialite he'd been dating infrequently, but that had obviously come to nothing. Cy was still single and showed no interest whatsoever in becoming anyone's husband. There was a cold cynicism in him now that Meredith didn't recognize, a hardness that completely overshadowed the sensitivity she remembered. He'd changed, as she had. Only Myrna remained the same: icy and arrogant and certain of getting her own way. But not this time, Meredith told herself. Oh, no, not this time. She wasn't leaving town until Cy had the truth of it, no matter what it took. And she had a few surprises for him before that day came.

Meredith called the office as soon as she reached Mary's house. Working eased her aching heart, made her whole again. She wanted to check with her contacts on the inquiries she was making into Harden Properties. Cy had to have an Achilles' heel. She'd noticed that most of his executives ate at the restaurant where she worked. She smiled at that irony. He'd given her a job at the very best place to eavesdrop on his business. How would he feel, she wondered smugly, when he found out?

During the next few days, she made it her business to be especially courteous to his executives and become friendly with them. That being the case, they were much less guarded in their conversation, assuming that she wouldn't know what they were talking about. But she did. From the information she gleaned, she gathered that one of Cy's directors was quietly working against him, trying to obtain a majority of the stockholders' votes to oust Cy from his own company. She mentioned that over the phone to Don the night she heard this. He agreed to find the director and cultivate him.

Little bits and pieces of conversation, small tidbits of gossip, fueled her secretive inquiries, provided her with insight into the best avenues to pursue as she sought a foothold in Cy's company.

Cy hadn't been back to the restaurant since they argued, which was something of a relief. Neither had Myrna, and Meredith began to wonder if something was afoot.

Meanwhile, Mrs. Dade had noticed Meredith's special attention to the Harden executives, and she asked her employee into the office late one evening to discuss it.

"You're a good waitress," Mrs. Dade said with a steely look, "but I don't like the attention you're giving Cy Harden's employees. Not only does it not look good, but you're making a spectacle of yourself in front of the other help."

Meredith's eyebrows rose. "I wasn't aware that I was paying them any special attention, Mrs. Dade," she said innocently. "They're very nice tippers…." She added that last bit with a calculating look and saw with pleasure that she'd given exactly the impression she meant to.

Mrs. Dade's face relaxed into a smile. "I see."

I thought you would, Meredith thought with silent satisfaction.

"Well, if that's all it is," Mrs. Dade continued. "But you mustn't pay them such obvious attention. It does look bad. And I'd hate to have to let you go."

That would be interesting, she thought. She wondered what Mrs. Dade would do if she fired Meredith and Cy found out. It might be the restaurant manager who was out on the streets looking for work, because Cy didn't like anyone undermining his orders.

"I'll be very careful not to let it happen again, Mrs. Dade," Meredith promised.

The older woman smiled. "Okay. No harm done. I know how much you young girls depend on tips to keep you going. And you are very good at your job, Meredith."

Meredith suppressed the desire to curtsy. "Thank you, Mrs. Dade."

"I'll see you tomorrow morning, then."

Dismissed, Meredith got her light jacket and walked to the bus stop, laughing softly to herself. She wondered what the businesslike Mrs. Dade would say if she knew how her erstwhile employee really was. It was like having a secret identity, and she loved the subterfuge. Of course, it wouldn't do for her to lose sight of the reason she was here, she reminded herself, and the smile faded. The acquisition of those mineral rights was the bottom line, and she had to remember it. If Cy Harden and his mother got their noses bloodied in the fight, that wouldn't bother her in the least. But she was holding the reins of Henry's domestic operation. It wouldn't do to let things get too personal. She had to keep her mind on the objective, without allowing herself to be too much diverted by the past. There were hundreds of Tennison International employees whose jobs hinged on the decisions she made. It was an awesome responsibility, and it allowed little leeway for personal revenge.

The wind was picking up, and it felt cool. Meredith closed her eyes, drinking in the feel of the breeze on her face. Until she'd come home to Billings, she hadn't even realized that she'd missed it. Despite the long hours and hard work, this job was like a vacation, a safety valve from the pressure that had jeopardized her health. The aftereffects of pneumonia—the weakness and cough—had already disappeared. She felt stronger by the day, perhaps because she was finding her roots all over again. It felt good to be home, except that she missed Blake so terribly.

The bus was late, and Meredith was the only person waiting for it. When a sleek, light gray car pulled up beside her with the window down, she almost jumped out of her skin. Then she recognized the driver and her teeth clenched.

"You don't need to be out here alone at this hour of night," Cy said curtly. "It's dangerous."

"This is Billings, not Chicago," she said without thinking.

He scowled, and she felt her heart stop, because she'd given away a tidbit of information she'd never meant to divulge.

"Know Chicago, do you?" he asked softly.

She smiled. "I know a lot of cities. Chicago is one, yes." She put her hand on her hip and moved it suggestively. "One city is pretty much like another, if you know which streets are the best pickings."

His eyes flashed as the insinuation penetrated. "And you did?"

She tossed back her long hair and gave him a blank look. "What do you think?"

His face hardened even more. The thought of Meredith having to go on the streets to stay alive at the age of eighteen made him sick, even sicker than the certainty that he'd condemned her to it. He had to block out the images of other hands touching her…

"Oh, for God's sake," she said harshly, borrowing one of Henry's favorite euphemisms, "I didn't become a streetwalker!"

He relaxed visibly, and she hated herself for reacting to that horrible expression in his eyes. She should have let him think what he liked.

"Get in," he said, weary with relief. "I'll drive you to the house."

She didn't argue. It was a dark and lonely night, and she'd never liked being on her own after dusk. Usually she wasn't; Mr. Smith was always somewhere nearby.

"Who is he?" he asked as the powerful car purred away from the curb and down the long, wide street.

"He?"

"Don't play games. The man leaving your house that morning."

"His name is Mr. Smith," she said simply.

"Is he your lover?"

She leaned her head back against the seat with a long sigh. "Isn't it a nice evening?" she mused. "I always did love Billings at night."

"You haven't answered me," he said impatiently.

"I won't, either," she replied. She turned toward him, her eyes steady and accusing. "You have no right at all to ask anything about my personal life. Not after what you did to me."

He didn't look at her. His hands tightened on the steering wheel. "Why didn't you go with him?"

"He works in Chicago," she said. "I work here. For the time being."

His dark eyes narrowed angrily. "Is it serious?"

Her thin shoulders rose and fell. "Not really. He's a friend."

He let out a held breath.

"Why would it matter to you?" she asked, conversationally. "What we…did was over long ago."

He looked at her while he stopped for a traffic light, his gaze slow and possessive. "I burn every time I look at you," he said gruffly. "I ache for you. There hasn't been one woman who could block you out of my mind for five minutes."

Her face burned. "That's lust," she said, enunciating the word clearly. "That's all it ever was to you. You wanted me. You couldn't get enough. You'd have come to me from your deathbed if I'd asked you, and we both know it. But it wasn't enough then, and it isn't now."

"I don't remember you having so many moral scruples at the time," he said mockingly.

Her head lowered. "I had none at all. I was in love with you."

He made a sound. The flat statement had shocked him. He'd never really questioned Meredith's motives for the affair. He'd always assumed that she felt the same helpless, raging desire that he did.

"Sure," he said after a minute, his voice harsh. "That's why you fell into bed with Tony."

She tilted her head toward him and smiled coldly. "I went

to you a virgin. I was so besotted with you that I couldn't have given myself to another man if I'd been stinking drunk."

"Maybe that was how you got him to help you steal the money," he persisted, his eyes calculating.

She laughed. "Tony gave all the money back, though, didn't he?" she asked icily. "And if you'd pushed him hard enough, he'd have told you that we never had either a conspiracy or a relationship."

Cy looked straight at the road. "Tell me, Meredith," he said unexpectedly.

"Tell you what?"

"The truth." He looked at her. "Tell me all of it."

She smiled, unblinking. "I offered it to you six years ago and you didn't want it."

"Now I do."

"Then ask your mother," she said. "Ask Myrna Harden for it."

"You won't get anywhere by trying to drag my mother into this," he said. "We both know she disapproved of you."

"She hated me," she corrected. "I have Indian relatives, remember? I come from poor people, from ordinary stock. My parents had a very small farm until they died, and I can remember needing shoes and having to wear secondhand ones before my great-aunt and great-uncle took me in. But even afterward, I didn't have social status or money, and that's what your mother wanted for you. I wasn't good enough. It had to be a blue blood."

He turned into the street that led past her great-aunt's house. His face was rigid with pent-up emotions. "Most mothers want what's best for their children."

She thought of Blake and nodded. "Yes. But all mothers don't interfere to the point of making decisions for them. I never would," she added.

He pulled into her driveway and turned off the engine and the lights, turning to look at her in the porch light.

"Why are you still here?" he asked quietly. "If there's a man waiting in Chicago, why haven't you gone back to him?"

She looked into his face, and all the anguish came flooding back, all the rejection, all the love. "I have my reasons," she said.

He slid his arm over the back of the seat, tugging the fabric of his gray jacket closer to his muscular body. He smelled of spice and soap. Meredith remembered how it had felt to lie in his arms with nothing between them except the beads of sweat they generated as they melded together in passion.

He seemed to sense those memories. His voice was husky when he spoke. "The first time was under a tree by the lake on my ranch," he recalled quietly, as if he'd read her mind. "We'd gone riding, but by then, we were both burning with need of each other. I pulled off your top and you let me. I put you down on the grass and you let me. I undressed you, and myself, and I couldn't even wait long enough to arouse you. I had you—" his voice deepened as he moved closer "—in one long, hard thrust."

She flushed. "Don't!"

"Does it embarrass you?" he asked. He jerked her against him, imprisoning her against his chest. "You were tight and afraid, and when I started convulsing, you asked if I was hurt." He bent and whispered into her ear, then her mouth. "But the second time, I kissed you from head to toe and bit the inside of your thighs and your nipples, and when I took you, you were ready for me. We were all over the ground that second time, thrashing, shaking. We came apart because I was too explosive, and you came after me, sitting over me to finish it. I watched you," he breathed into her, his tongue following the words into the soft darkness.

Meredith's eyes stung with tears as she reached up to him, her arms clinging. Vivid memories flashed through her mind.

"Yes," he groaned. His mouth opened, insistent, while his hands fought under her blouse and bra to find the soft warmth of her body.

She didn't think about the changes he was sure to find. He knew her body as well as she did in the old days. It was inevitable that her maturity would be noticeable.

His fingers pushed softly at one breast before his palm slid under it, lifting it. He raised his head, and his eyes burned into hers. "You're bigger."

"I'm older," she said huskily.

He moved, and before she realized what he meant to do, he had the blouse and bra up past her collarbone, and he was looking at her. His breath caught at her soft firmness, at her delicate color.

"Oh, baby," he breathed.

Her lips parted at the reverence in his tone. "I'm not...a girl anymore," she whispered, trying to divert his curiosity.

"My God, I know that." His eyes lifted back to hers. "You became a woman in my arms. Did you really think I could ever forget?" His thumbs rubbed down against her nipples as he spoke, and she shivered.

"Meredith," he whispered hoarsely. He bent his head, his mouth poised over one taut nipple, his breath warming it.

The glare of headlights and the roar of an engine caused his head to jerk up. Meredith took advantage of his diversion to tug her clothing down and pull out of his arms. By the time the passing vehicle was out of sight, she was out of the car.

Cy managed to catch her as she reached the porch, his lean hands insistent as they turned her to him. "I want you," he said, his voice ragged.

"I know that," she replied tersely. "I'm just as vulnerable as I was at eighteen, and apparently every bit as stupid when I get close to you. But that won't work twice. I'm not going to be your mistress a second time. I learned my lesson the hard way."

He was breathing hard, his eyes still faintly glazed with desire. Her gaze fell and she could see the blatant evidence of his frustration.

"You still want me," he said. "I could take away every choice you have. I could make you get on your knees and beg me for it." He smiled contemptuously. "In fact, I did. Do you remember?"

She did. It had been just before his mother had filled his head with lies about Tony, that last wild loving—before the confrontation with his mother. He'd humbled and exalted her, and she'd been too much in love and too weak to resist him. She hadn't known that Tony and Myrna had sold her out. She'd given in because she loved him, because she thought he was in love with her, too. But he hadn't been. Ever. It had all been a means to an end. He'd only wanted her.

"I remember," she said, stiffening as he drew her against his body. "Let go of me."

His voice deepened. "That isn't what you want."

"It's what your mother wants," she replied, playing the only card she had left. She hoped that it would divert him, because her body was betraying her. It had been so many years since she'd been with Cy. She wanted him until it hurt, but she didn't dare give in.

He hesitated, and she pulled back.

"Remember your mother, Cy?" she asked coldly. "Nothing's changed. She still hates me."

"She doesn't have to love a woman I sleep with," he said, resorting to cruelty as frustration and pain gnawed at him.

"But I'm not sleeping with you, Cy," she said, holding her purse protectively over her sensitive breasts.

He stood there, towering over her, struggling to breathe normally. It was just like before, just like old times. He was falling headlong into her web, and he wanted her so much that he couldn't even save himself. He looked at her and ached like a boy.

"Tell me you don't want me, Meredith," he said mockingly.

She moved toward her door, fumbling in her purse for the key. "What I want doesn't enter into it," she said. Wearily, she unlocked the door and turned, her eyes big and sad in her tired face. He looked only a little less worn himself. "I don't want that madness again, any more than you do. Go home, Cy. I'm sure your mother will be glad of the company."

"She didn't come to see you, did she?" he probed. "That was a lie."

"It amazes me," she said, searching his face. "Even now, you automatically think that if someone's in the wrong, it must be me. Myrna should be proud. She's taught you that the only truth is hers."

"At least she's capable of it," he replied.

She smiled. "Once I thought you might love me," she said. "But I knew the minute you sided with your mother that it was only desire. Love and trust are both sides of the same coin. One is nothing without the other."

He clenched his teeth. "You can't accept the fact that my mother has any virtues, can you?"

"You don't know what she's cost me," she replied coldly, "because you don't want to know the truth." She smiled again. "Someday, you'll have it. I swear you will. And when you know what she's cost *you,* you'll wish to God you'd listened to me. Good night, Cy."

She was inside with the door locked before he had time

to reply. She wasn't at all surprised to find that she was shaking.

Outside, Cy strode back to his car, bristling with temper and frustration. As usual, she had him weak in the knees. She was just as much woman as she'd ever been, and his response to her was powerful, immediate.

He fought himself out of the sensual fog by the time he got home, but something Meredith had said was disturbing him. You don't know what your mother has cost *you,* she'd said. He frowned as he went into the house. Did she mean money? Or was it something intangible? Perhaps she meant her love. But he knew how treacherous she was. She'd betrayed him. Or had she?

That was a thought he didn't want to entertain. He passed the living room, still deep in thought.

"Oh, you're home," Myrna said, rising from the sofa. "I waited up. You've been very preoccupied the past several days. I thought…you might want to talk."

"About what?" he shot at her.

She swallowed. "About whatever's bothering you."

He moved into the room, his dark eyes threatening. "Did you go to see Meredith?"

That was a question she hadn't wanted to answer. She could have lied, but what if one of the neighbors had seen her? It would be a risk to lie.

"I…did," she said finally.

He scowled. "Why?"

"You know I don't approve of Meredith," she said quickly. "I was only trying to convince her that bringing back old memories won't help either of you. I asked her to go away."

"I gave her a job," he reminded her.

She twisted her hands together, her face tormented. "Oh, Cy, she's not for you! Don't make it worse."

"Make what worse?" he demanded. "What do you know that I don't?"

She actually paled. "Cy..."

He moved forward, determined to get it out of her. Just as she panicked, the telephone rang, diverting him. Fortunately it was someone on business, and she excused herself quickly with a rushed "Good night."

By the time she got upstairs, her heart was beating her to death. It was like a nightmare. Why hadn't she realized the implications of what she'd done all those years ago? Her chickens had come home to roost, now. She didn't know how she was going to survive if she didn't get Meredith out of town fast.

CHAPTER SIX

BLAKE WAS ANGRY when Meredith phoned Chicago.

"Why won't you come home?" he demanded. "You said a few days, didn't you?"

"It's taking longer than I anticipated," she defended herself, sick over Cy's rekindling of her physical needs and the slowness of her progress. "Blake, don't push. You know I'd be home if I could. I have to support us, little man. I have to work."

He sighed. "I know. But I miss you, Mommy."

Her eyes closed. "I miss you, too," she said, and it was true. She missed him more every day. Seeing Cy was like looking at a mature image of Blake. The pressure of trying to conduct business from a long distance, missing Blake, and dealing with the Hardens kept her nerves on end.

"Tell you what," she said after a minute. "My secretary reminded me earlier when I phoned in that I have to go to a banquet Saturday night in Chicago. Suppose I fly up Friday night and spend the weekend? How about that?"

"Oh, Mommy, that's radical!" he exclaimed.

Already, she thought, he sounded like a typical boy of the nineties. She laughed. "I hope that means you're glad I'm coming. Now, put Mr. Smith on, please."

"Yes, ma'am."

"I gather that you're coming home?" Mr. Smith asked with droll humor.

"For the weekend," she emphasized. "I need to pick up some more diskettes for the computer and conduct a few personal visits to clients I seem to have been neglecting." She added that last bit because her secretary had mentioned that those clients had reacted to some comments of Don's that Meredith was taking a working holiday. How like him to forget to mention that it was on company business. He'd made it sound as if she were off enjoying herself to the company's detriment. "Have one of the jets pick me up at the Rimrocks at six sharp Friday night. I'll get off from work early."

"Can't get much work done on the weekend," he murmured.

"Stand back and watch me. Or don't you remember that Henry did most of his plotting at cocktail parties?" She grinned to herself. "The Harrisons are having that banquet for Senator Lane Saturday night, and Don promised to tag along. We can discuss the new computer operation and the personnel shift at the same time. Remind Don."

"Will do. How do you plan to manage this project, the acquisition, and hold down a full-time waitressing job at the same time?"

"Don't fuss," she replied, although it touched her that he was concerned for her health. "I'll see you Friday."

She hung up before he could argue. It would be a lot of pressure. But, then, she'd had nothing except pressure since Henry died—and even before. She was young and strong and willful. Besides, it wouldn't be forever. The pressure would end for a while once she had her hands on those mineral rights. Except that it was looking more and more as if the only way to do that was to get enough proxies from Cy's stockholders to assume control of his company and force him into relinquishing the mineral rights. In fact, she'd determined that nothing less was going to work, so she'd already set the wheels in motion. And the thought of ousting him and his mother so delighted her that it had helped to stem the frustration she felt at being away from her son.

Cy hadn't been to her house since the night he'd picked her up when she was working late. But Wednesday evening he came to the restaurant for dinner. He didn't come alone. His companion was a beautiful redhead with long legs, wearing an outfit that had probably cost more than a week's take at the restaurant. He was getting even with Meredith for his loss of control. She knew it instantly. Not that it did much for her ego or lessened the pain of seeing him with another woman. She'd heard plenty about Cy's reputation with women since she'd started work. It was depressing, because he hadn't been a rounder when he was with her.

She put on her best smile and let nothing she was feeling show as she greeted them and produced menus. "Would you like something to drink while you wait for your order?" she asked politely.

"I'll have a German lager," the redhead said carelessly, and named the brand she wanted. "And do make sure that they don't substitute foam for beer, will you? I detest being shorted."

"Yes, ma'am," Meredith said pleasantly. "And what will you have, sir?"

"White wine," he said curtly. He didn't look at her. That sunny bright greeting had taken the starch out of his sails. He'd brought Lara here to make Meredith jealous. And he'd kept his distance, hoping that she might miss him. He wasn't sure of his own motives, except that he ached for her. He wanted her more than ever, but she'd dug in her heels and wasn't giving an inch. It was going to be an uphill battle all the way to get her back into his arms. Lara's presence didn't even seem to faze her. The old Meredith would have been in tears.

Meredith served them with the impeccable control that Henry had taught her. Cy looked darker and angrier by the minute as she did her best impression of a star-struck waitress serving her betters. Lara swallowed it, insisting that he leave a huge tip. Cy only glared at Meredith, his eyes promising retribution. She had to resist the urge to rage at him. She knew what he was doing, but it didn't help her bruised feelings.

He was showing her that he attracted other women, beautiful women. Inadvertently, it helped her get a bridle on her own need for him. Nothing had changed. He was a playboy now, and he had no use for commitment. She'd do well to remember the way he'd thrown her to the wolves before, so that she wouldn't have to repeat it.

FRIDAY NIGHT, she changed hours with one of the other waitresses—with Mrs. Dade's permission—and called a cab to take her to the airport. She changed into a black wig and expensive coat, so nobody at the airport would mistake her for Meredith Ashe. It was just a precaution, in case anyone who knew her saw her getting into a Tennison International jet. Cy probably wouldn't even know that she was away for the weekend, nor would he care. He was avoiding her lately with a vengeance. But just in case, she'd make sure she was seen leaving the Billings bus terminal Sunday afternoon.

She boarded the small corporate jet quickly, and in minutes she was bound for Chicago.

Blake was waiting at O'Hare with Mr. Smith. He ran to her, recognizing her through her disguise, outdistancing even his companion in his excitement.

"Mommy!" he shouted.

Meredith bent and picked him up, swinging him around with laughter brimming over inside her. It had been such a dismal week and a half, and she'd missed Blake so badly.

"Welcome home, ragamuffin," Mr. Smith mused, his eyes pointedly assessing the dark wig and the worn jeans and sweatshirt under Meredith's open coat.

"Well, I couldn't very well go to work in a Liz Claiborne original, could I?" she asked with a mischievous grin.

"Point taken. Your brother-in-law is still out of town, but he promised to be back in time for the banquet tomorrow night."

"Very good. And the Jordan merger?"

"Went through with flying colors."

"Oh, Mommy, don't talk business," Blake wailed as they got into the car.

She pulled him close and kissed him. "Okay. I'll try. Until tomorrow night, we'll just do what you want to."

"Honestly?! Great!"

It wasn't until she was failing miserably at the Nintendo controls with Blake that she realized how much she missed being with him. Even a simple game like this—at which she was terrible—was so much fun. Blake laughed and flaunted his superiority at eye and hand coordination while Meredith rolled on the floor with glee at her own failure.

They watched a nature special together after supper, and then Meredith read bedtime stories for half an hour. When Blake fell asleep in her arms, she looked down at him with aching tenderness. She'd never be alone, not while she had Blake. It even eased the pain of losing Cy. There was so much similarity between Blake's small features and those of his father, she thought wistfully. The resemblance really was striking, especially when he opened his dark eyes. Her child...hers and Cy's. Not that Cy would ever believe it, she told herself.

Meredith tucked in her son and walked back downstairs into Henry's old study, which was now hers. Passing the fax machine and computer, she walked over to her desk and sat down. She started to pore over contracts and memos and correspondence that seemed endless. Although work had piled up in her absence, Meredith still looked upon the past week and a half as a vacation. Even the physical work of waitressing wasn't a patch on the mentally exhausting routine she was used to. The exercise was rather relaxing, in fact.

She worked far into the night on current projects without really getting caught up. The most she accomplished was to answer the more immediate correspondence on tape for her secretary to type and Don to verify. She'd have to pack up and take the rest back to Billings with her. She could fax and use the phone to catch up on the rest. She hoped. Most deals were best conducted in person. Well, if all else failed, she could sneak out on the corporate jet for meetings. But that was risky. Seeing the Tennison International conveyance too often at the Rimrocks, upon which Billings' airport was located, could tip Cy Harden to a move on his company. And that she didn't want.

Blake wanted to go to the park the next morning, so Meredith dressed him warmly and walked him the four blocks east to the playground. Mr. Smith brought up the rear. The rugged ex-mercenary never left them alone. She knew it was driving him crazy that he couldn't be around in Billings to look after her. He was as loyal as he was trustworthy.

Meredith and Smith sat on a wooden bench watching the sun play off the vast expanse of Lake Michigan. "How's it going?" he asked while Blake was swinging on the playground equipment.

Meredith leaned back on the park bench and pulled her cashmere coat closer around her body. "I'm surviving. It isn't easy. I tried to get to some of the executives and almost got fired for fraternizing."

He smiled, something he did rarely. That hard face was

scarred and laced with mementos of the violent lifestyle Mr. Smith had led. One of the executives once told Meredith that his scars were the result of his being shot to within an inch of his life in a commando raid, after which they'd practically had to put his face back together with superglue. She could believe it. He was rugged and indomitable. She always felt safe with him, as she had with Cy.

"Giving up?" he taunted.

She glanced at him and grinned. "What do you think?"

His green eyes searched over her face quietly, lingering just a second too long before he averted them. "I think Don's right. You've found yourself one formidable adversary. There's no shame in cutting your losses."

"I haven't started yet," she reminded him. "I've got McGee working on proxy acquisition behind the scenes. All I'm doing is keeping the head honcho diverted while they work."

"No, I don't think so," he replied.

She folded her arms and watched Blake, waving back when he waved and called for her to see how high he could go. "All right," she said finally. "I got a little too close to the fire and singed my wings. But I won't make the same mistake again."

"I hope not. I haven't forgotten how broken up you were that night we found you."

She looked up at him warmly. "You saved my life."

"I almost cost it," he replied. "I didn't even see you."

"Did I ever tell you that you and Henry made me want to live?" she asked wistfully. "You even went to Lamaze classes with us, to learn natural childbirth in case Henry was out of town when Blake was born and you had to coach me. We did so many things together." Her eyes grew sad. "I miss him."

"So do I," he replied. "He gave me a job when nobody else would. I was under indictment for murder. No prospective employer wanted me around. But Henry believed I was innocent. He hired me, got me the best criminal lawyer in town, and I was acquitted."

"I know. Henry told me."

He glanced at her wryly before he stuck a toothpick in his mouth and began to gnaw on it. "You used to hide from me at first."

"I thought you might be ex-Mafia." She chuckled. "But after a while, especially after Blake was born, you were just family. I couldn't have imagined you changing diapers or washing an infant."

"Neither could I, six years ago." His eyes softened as he looked at Blake. "But now I can't imagine not doing it. I don't have anyone," he added slowly. He didn't look at her.

"Yes, you do," she said, her voice warm and caring. She touched his big hand briefly. "You have Blake and me."

He took a steadying breath, and Meredith saw a tiny crack in that armor. It pleased her that Mr. Smith was touched, and it amused her that he worked so hard not to show it. But her face gave away none of her thoughts. Neither did his, really. She'd been around him long enough to see through his mask. Probably, the reverse was also true.

"The boy is having some problems with bullies," he said, quickly changing the subject. "I took the liberty of starting martial arts training."

Her eyebrows arched. "You're going to teach my son how to kill people?" she asked.

"I'm going to teach your son how not to kill people," he corrected. "It will also teach him a body posture and assertiveness that will dissuade bullies from trying him. He'll learn to focus his mind, to concentrate. Most of all, he'll learn discipline. That's important for a boy."

She relaxed. "Yes, I know it is." She studied him for a minute before she looked back toward Blake. "Okay. I don't mind."

It was a major victory, because she hated violence. He grinned, pleased with himself.

That night, Don arrived early to pick her up. He greeted Meredith with his most polite smile. Wearing a dinner jacket with dark slacks and a ruffled white shirt, Don looked very elegant. Not as elegant as Henry had looked, but not bad. Don had always been a shadow of his formidable older brother, and Meredith always felt a little sorry for him. Since Henry's death, he'd been a tower of strength, though, and his business sense had pulled them out of more than one tight corner.

"You look lovely," he told her.

She smiled. She was wearing a Paris original, emerald-green velvet and satin in a contemporary design that emphasized her slender figure and highlighted her blond hair and silky skin and gray eyes.

"Thank you, Don. You're not bad yourself."

"Have you read my memo on the Camfield Computer acquisition?"

"Yes, with the other notes," she replied as he escorted her down to the car, where Abe, one of Mr. Smith's operatives, was waiting to drive them in the limousine. "You're very good at what you do, Don," she said seriously. "You're meticulous and cool under pressure. Henry would be proud of the way you've pulled this deal out of the fire."

Don looked surprised. He glanced down at her. "I wasn't aware that you noticed what I do."

"Well, technically I shouldn't, should I?" she mused. "After all, the foreign operation is none of my business. But I can admire business skill. I get a lot through the grapevine, you know. Your people would follow you over a snakepit."

He smiled faintly. "High praise."

"But earned," she said. She got into the back seat and so did Don before Abe closed the door and climbed behind the wheel. "Don, do you ever get tired of the pressure?"

His eyebrows jerked. "Not really," he said. "Business is my life these days. I enjoy the challenge, I guess." He studied her shrewdly. "How about you?"

"I sometimes wish I had more time to spend with Blake," she confessed, toying with her purse. "Not that I don't enjoy my work. It's just that it's very demanding sometimes."

Don averted his eyes. "You might consider delegating more."

"Henry wouldn't approve."

"Henry is dead," he said coldly.

She started at his tone, her eyes searching. "Yes, I know. But I owe him everything, don't you see?"

He started to speak and caught himself. "I know you're grateful for what he did for you," he said. "But you have to consider what you did for him. He was alone, totally alone, before you came along. He was literally working himself to death. You changed him, you and Blake. He died a happy man."

She was touched by the comment. "I did love him, you know," she said honestly. "Not at first, although I was terribly grateful for what he did for me, and very fond of him. But by the time he...by then, he was becoming my whole world."

Don glanced at her. "It was a pity that he died when he did. I should have been on that plane. He was covering for me."

"Oh, Don, don't," she said. She touched his sleeve, smiling sadly. "I'm a fatalist. I think the very seconds of our lives are numbered, that death is preordained. If it hadn't been in a plane crash, it could have been some other way. He didn't suffer. It was quick. Given a choice, that's what he would have wanted."

"I suppose so." He took a slow breath. "I suppose it is."

"You don't resent me, do you?" she asked suddenly, puzzled by a look on his face.

"Resent you, how?" he asked, and his voice sounded strained.

"That I got such a chunk of the corporation when, by all rights, it should have all gone to you."

"No...of course, I don't resent you."

She didn't believe him. His eyes wouldn't meet hers. "I'm sorry, all the same," she said. "It was Henry's doing, not mine."

"I know that," he said stiffly. He crossed his long legs. "How are you proceeding on the Harden project?"

The change of subject caught her off guard, but she recovered quickly and filled him in. "The only way is to outvote him at the board meeting, and in order to do that, I have to get enough proxies to force him either to relinquish the mineral leases or risk being thrown out as president of his own company. I'm still working on the proxies. Cy Harden doesn't seem to be noticing that his outstanding stock is being wolfed up, or that his out-of-town stockholders are being courted for proxies." She smiled in a faintly predatory way. "Hopefully, I'll be able to move in before they know what hit them."

"It's always a mistake to involve personalities with business," he said quietly. "Even with noble motives."

She blinked. "It isn't...really personal," she said, trying to defend herself. "I have to have those mineral rights for my expansion program."

He gave her a knowing smile. "Yes, but we could get them in Arizona or Wyoming or even Colorado. It doesn't have to be Montana."

"We?" she asked with faint hauteur, staring at him until his cheekbones flushed. "The domestic operation is my domain,

Don," she said gently but with authority. "Whatever decisions are necessary, I make. Henry left it that way." She lifted her chin, her fingers clenching her purse as she remembered what he'd already said to some of her clients about her "holiday." Her eyes narrowed. "There's one other little thing," she added. "Some of our mutual clients seem to have the idea that I'm having a holiday at company expense."

"I wonder where they got that idea?" he asked after a minute with a bland look.

"I wouldn't know," she replied. She shifted, angry that she couldn't flush him into the open. "Well, anyway, unless you have in mind bringing me up before the directors on charges of mismanagement, you have no real authority to challenge my business decisions."

He was silent. "Don't be absurd," he said after a minute.

She glanced at him. "Expansion always involves a modicum of risk. Henry was like me, he was progressive. You're conservative. We'd never agree on how to manage projects, which is exactly why Henry split the corporation and put us each in charge of our respective interests. I'll make money when I get those mineral leases. You don't have to approve, but I'm going to get them, Don, even if it means the threat of forcing Cy out of his company to make him give them up."

"You may find yourself baiting a trap that you'll be caught in," he said slowly, his eyes steady on hers. "I've told you already that Harden is one tough customer. Don't think you'll blind him to what you're doing behind his back. He was playing this kind of game while you were still in school, and in business you can't trust anyone. Haven't you learned that yet?"

"Surely I can trust you, Don," she said with a calculating smile.

He averted his face. "Of course you can," he said harshly. "After all, I'm family."

"I know."

He shifted, his eyes narrowing as they gave her a quick appraisal. "You're right. I have no business trying to tell you how to run your part of the corporation. So if you'd like some help on those proxies," he said, "I could contact the people on the East Coast for you."

She smiled. It was an olive branch, and one she was grateful to grasp. He had contacts that she didn't. For a moment she hesitated, but after all, he wouldn't do anything that would hurt Henry's corporation. The business was his whole life. "Would you have time?"

He nodded. "I'll make time. Have you got a list of the stockholders?"

"Indeed I have," she replied. "I'll run you off a copy tonight."

Don looked visibly relaxed after that. He didn't mention the proxies again or the fact that he was crossing over his boundary to focus his efforts on what was basically Meredith's territory. Meredith felt as if she had a real ally for the first time.

"I'm grateful for your help, Don," she said when they pulled up at the Harrisons' driveway, where guests were being taken up by limousine to alleviate the parking situation.

"I'm on your side, Kip," he said easily. "You know that."

But he didn't sound very convincing, and the conversation played on her mind for the rest of the evening.

She moved from guest to guest, lingering with Senator Lane, who was very pro-conservation. He and Meredith had a lot in common, and he was sponsoring a bill that would benefit one of her companies. The Harrisons had to drag him away from her to give other guests a shot at his company.

When she went to find Don, she came upon him unexpectedly, overhearing the piece of a conversation that puzzled her.

"Ah, Kip," he said a little too loudly once he noticed her.

"This is Frank Dockins," he introduced his companion. "He's comptroller for Camfield Computers."

She held out her hand with a smile. "I'm very pleased to meet you," she said. "This is the first time I've had the opportunity to tell you how pleased we are that you've merged with us. Don has told you, no doubt, that I'm shifting some of the high-level executives in Tennison's domestic computer operations to work with you. We want the transition to be as smooth as possible."

"Uh, yes," Mr. Dockins replied, clearing his throat. "Don was just telling me about that. You run the domestic operation, don't you?"

She nodded, smiling at his accent. Camfield Computers was a very British industry, and Mr. Dockins, for all his time in the States, still retained the crisp enunciation of his countrymen. "Henry groomed me for it," she explained. "He found that I had a natural aptitude for picking companies that fit into our corporate structure, and a fairly workable financial talent. He developed me," she said with dry humor. "He used to say that I was one of his better acquisitions."

Charmed, Mr. Dockins laughed, too. "Don says you have a young son. Doesn't the stress make home life difficult?"

"More than you know," she replied, aware of Don's searching look. "I cope, I suppose, but Blake's childhood is passing me by. I'm not terribly good at delegating. I don't really trust people. Except Don, of course," she added with a smile at her brother-in-law. He frowned slightly and looked away.

Mr. Camfield shifted his feet. "Nice party. Do you know Senator Lane?" he asked.

"Not well. But I voted for him." She chuckled. "He was born and bred on the east side. A real gentleman, and he came up hard."

"A good worker, too. He's been helpful to the conservation movement. Can't be bribed, either," Don added. He chuckled at Camfield's expression. "And no, I don't know that from experience."

The Englishman chuckled himself, and the odd tension vanished as if it had never been.

Meredith moved away to finish her small cocktail, and her mind drifted back to her first banquet. She hadn't even known which utensils to use. Henry had tutored her, pressing her hand warmly under the table, his blue eyes sparkling.

"Don't worry," he'd whispered. "I'll guide you through it."

She'd laughed, and his expression had warmed.

"It's true what they say about pregnant women glowing," he'd said quietly. "You're beautiful, Kip. You've changed my life, you and the baby."

His hand had gone gently to the soft mound of her belly, and his eyes had searched hers intently. "This is mine," he'd whispered. "Despite the fact that I didn't put him there. I'll love him, Kip. I'll love you, too, if you'll let me."

The tears had been involuntary. Lack of manners or not, she'd put her arms around Henry's neck and hugged him right there. Incredibly, the other guests had smiled approvingly at her spontaneity and her obvious affection for her husband. After that night, no one ever accused Kip Tennison of marrying for money. Least of all Henry himself.

Her hand touched her belly involuntarily as she remembered. Expensive perfume drifted to her nostrils, the rustle of satin and the soft whisper of silk and crepe de chine assaulted her ears along with soft conversation and background music. But Meredith was far away. The day Cy had sent her packing had been the very day she planned to tell him about the baby.

For one long instant, she allowed herself to think about how he would have reacted. They'd been engaged. He'd never said he loved her, but children hadn't been something they'd ever discussed. He seemed not to want any. But he was wonderful with them. He'd had cousins with children of their own, and he was Uncle Cy to every one of them. Somehow Meredith knew that he'd have wanted Blake as Henry had, but she'd never know. His reaction had been denied her.

Cy never knew the price he'd paid for her loss. Only Myrna Harden knew that, and Meredith doubted if any coercion was going to drag the secret out of her. She'd told Myrna she'd leave town if the older woman would tell Cy the truth, but she knew Myrna never would. Meredith would leave town when she had her mineral leases or Cy's company in the palm of her hand. At the same time, she might let Myrna see the grandchild she'd banished. The thought gave her a little pleasure, the first she'd felt all evening.

That night, as she looked in on Blake before going to bed, she saw the resemblance in his face. He was the very image of Cy. Myrna would see that. But she wouldn't be able to acknowledge it without letting Cy know what she'd done. That would be her punishment, to see the grandchild she craved and know that he was lost to her forever.

A cold shiver of fear moved along Meredith's backbone as a line of Scripture stabbed into her mind. "Vengeance is mine." She swallowed. Well, even if vengeance was God's domain, didn't He sometimes use people to carry it out? She closed her mind to any other interpretation. She'd waited too long, suffered too much, to back down now.

She hugged Blake good-bye Sunday afternoon and promised to let Mr. Smith bring him out to Montana shortly for a visit. Then she put on her wig and expensive coat and boarded the jet for Billings.

TAKING A CAB to the bus station, she ducked into the ladies' restroom and exchanged her fancy gear and wig for Meredith

Ashe's working clothes. She walked out of the bus station with every appearance of having gotten off a bus and whistled as she walked on down the street to catch the bus home.

Her eyes wandered lovingly over the city of her childhood. Billings was special to her. She'd damped down her hunger for it during the long years of exile. But now that she was back, it was as if she'd never left. Wide-open prairie, rolling on the infinity of the horizon, stretched far beyond the city, beyond the banks of the Yellowstone River and the railroad tracks. She hadn't realized how much she loved it until she'd been exiled to Chicago. Now that she was back, she wondered how it would be if she could raise Blake here, let him grow up where his pioneer forebears had lived. She could tell him all the stories that her mom, dad, and Great-Aunt Mary had told her about his Irish and Scottish heritage, as well as the stories that Uncle Raven-Walking passed down about the Crow people.

All the same, Montana was her home. She wished that it could be Blake's, too, but only time would tell if that was possible.

CHAPTER SEVEN

MEREDITH WAS TIRED from her weekend trip. She went to bed early but still felt as if she were dragging when she got up the next morning to fix herself some breakfast.

The knock at the back door caught her off guard and brought back painful memories. When Cy had come to get her years before, he'd always come to Great-Aunt Mary's back door on the Crow reservation. It was less formal, he'd said dryly when Meredith had questioned him about his motives. Now, she wondered who could be calling at such an early hour.

She pulled her pink chenille bathrobe closer around her body, because it was chilly even with the small gas heater, and brushed back her disheveled blond hair as she lifted the curtain to see outside.

Just like old times. The phrase leapt into her mind as she saw Cy Harden standing there, his dark head bare, a black Stetson in one big, lean hand. He was dressed for work, in a dark suit and a conservative patterned tie. He looked successful. Enjoy it while you can, Meredith thought to herself.

She opened the door, her face giving nothing away. "Got lost, did we?" she asked without expression. "The restaurant is that way." She pointed down the street.

"I know where it is," he said curtly. "What I want to know is where you were the whole damned weekend."

Her heart jumped. She might have guessed that he'd discover her absence. "You mean you actually had time to wonder about me? I would have thought your current flame would have kept you too busy for that."

The muscles in his jaw pulled taut. "She did."

Meredith forced a smile. "Good. To answer your question, I went to see Mr. Smith."

His dark eyes flashed fire. "I thought you were just friends."

"We are. We do visit occasionally. The bus is very nice on long trips, don't you think?" she added.

"I wouldn't know," he said, his eyes narrowing. "I fly."

"Without wings? Amazing!"

"Don't be cute. Have you made coffee?"

He eased in past her and got a cup, pausing to pour coffee in it before he pulled out one of the chairs at the kitchen table and sat down, tossing his Stetson carelessly onto a nearby chair.

"Make yourself at home," she invited sarcastically.

"I already have." His dark eyes studied her. "You're hiding things."

She thanked God for her poker face. "Am I really? What kind of things?"

"I don't know. But I'll find out." He sipped coffee while she poured her own. "Going to fix breakfast?"

"This is breakfast," she said, putting a saucer of cinnamon toast on the table.

"No wonder you're so thin."

She shrugged. "I run it all off anyway."

"Just like you used to," he mused, and for an instant his face softened. "You were bristling with nervous energy back then. I could hardly keep you still five minutes."

"I'm too restless to sit around," she said. She nibbled on the toast, tasting none of it.

"One of your neighbors saw a brunette leave here. A very ritzy one," he added, "wearing a fancy coat. She took a cab."

Her smile widened, and not one thing showed in her face. "Yes. That was Mr. Smith's sister. She was on her way to Chicago and stopped by for the night."

He glared at her, falling for the lie. "Thick with his family, are you?"

"Thicker than I ever was with yours," she said with faint hauteur.

"My mother saw through you, didn't she?" he asked, his voice deep and mocking. "You were a two-timing little thief, after my money all along."

"I got more than your money," she said, her eyes reminiscent as she thought of Blake.

But Cy was thinking of something entirely different. "Yes. My body, my self-respect, and plenty of expensive presents."

She'd sent those back to Myrna Harden after she left Billings. Myrna, of course, had never told him.

"You've really given up on the stolen money?" she drawled.

"I told you Tony returned the money," he said stiffly, and couldn't help feeling uncomfortable at the look on her face. Well, damn it, he'd tried to find her, hadn't he? "He never would tell me who his other accomplice was."

She laughed oddly. "He wouldn't have dared."

"You never wrote, not even to try and make me see the truth one last time," he said, his voice accusing.

"I thought I might be prosecuted for theft if I let you know where I was," she replied. "I had no way of knowing that Tony had confessed and given the money back."

His face went hard, his eyes bitter. "Of course. I never thought about that."

"As it happened, leaving here was the best thing that ever happened to me," she said. "I found plenty of friends in Chicago."

"I looked in Chicago," he said surprisingly. "Along with most other major cities. I never found you."

"You didn't look in Nassau, though, did you?" she returned, her eyes full of secrets. His puzzled expression gave him away. "Why should you have? I was young and poor and stupid. Hardly the kind of woman to end up living in luxury."

"As what? Some rich man's companion? That's all you were fit for, with your background," he said, stung by her attitude and wanting to hit back.

She gave him an icy smile. "However did you guess?"

"Mr. Smith's companion?" he fished.

"Mr. Smith is not a wealthy man," she said without thinking.

He studied her narrowly, leaning on his elbows with his coffee cup in both hands. "You've learned that money can't buy happiness, I gather."

"I've known that for a long time." Her eyes searched his handsome face and she grimaced. "Oh, go away, will you?" she said wearily. "I've had a long weekend and I have to be at the restaurant in thirty minutes."

He finished his coffee. "You've got a half day Thursday," he said. "I'll take you out to the Custer battlefield and buy you a pair of earrings."

She could have flinched. He'd done that once, when they were engaged. The earrings were northern Cheyenne, yellow-and-orange-and-black-beaded circles with long trails of beads. She had them still, tucked away in her jewelry box along with her diamonds and emeralds. She never wore them.

"I don't want any earrings."

"Come anyway," he replied. His eyes searched hers and they were suddenly as weary as her own, as bitter and sad. "You can't go back, they say. But just for one day, Meredith."

She hesitated. She didn't trust him. "Won't your girlfriend mind?" she asked, and without sarcasm.

His eyes darkened. "She was, like all the others, a passing attraction. None of them was you," he said.

"Don't," she said with quiet dignity. "I didn't come back to Billings to fan old embers. I'm just taking a rest. I have a life in Chicago that will be waiting for me when I'm through here."

"Taking a rest? Working in a restaurant for minimum wage?" he taunted softly.

She didn't speak for a minute. She'd almost given the game away. "Compared to working in a garment factory, it's a vacation," she said, without actually telling a lie. Probably it was easier than working in a garment factory, after all.

His eyes were assessing, but after a minute they lost their suspicious gleam. He got to his feet with easy grace and reached for his hat. He twirled it in his hands, hesitating.

"I won't back you into a corner again, if that's what's stopping you," he said after a minute. "Dragging up the past won't help. I should never have let things get physical again." He stared at her levelly, uncomfortable at the look that flared in her eyes. "I know you can't help how you react to me, Meredith," he said with resigned humor. "You might not believe it, but neither can I. I still want you. I imagine I always will."

"Wanting was all it ever was between us," she said proudly. "I don't have room in my life for that particular physical addiction again."

"I had less room for it when we were together," he replied. "I could never control what I felt. At times, I couldn't even hold back long enough to satisfy you. My God, it went beyond obsession. I thought of nothing except being with you!"

"It was the same for me," she confessed. "Whole books have been written on that kind of thing. I was much too young to be able to handle it, and you resented me more and more."

"You bewitched me," he said quietly. "I couldn't have denied you anything."

"I didn't ask for anything," she reminded him.

He hated remembering that. He'd accused her of theft, made her run away, destroyed her youth. He couldn't even blame her for keeping the presents he'd given her. She'd had nothing. These days she had every reason to mistrust and resent him. But it was his own obsession that had motivated him even then. He'd grasped at any excuse to get her out of his life, to break the engagement. He'd been terrified of finding himself nothing more than a helpless slave to his passion for her.

"I gave you nothing, Meredith," he said, his voice deep and haunted. "Except grief."

She wanted to tell him, then. She wanted to dig out her wallet and show him the little boy who was his image. He'd given her Blake. But that way lay disaster. She had to remember the pain.

"Don't tell me you feel guilty at this late date." She laughed.

He didn't smile. "I've felt guilt every day of my life since you left Billings. I expect to feel it on my deathbed. You were innocent. I even robbed you of that."

Her heart wasn't hard enough to ignore his look of pain. She moved close to him, reaching out hesitantly to touch his cheek. He caught it, holding it there, his eyes steady and dark as they met hers.

"You robbed me of nothing," she said gently. "I couldn't help what happened any more than you could. I wanted you so badly, Cy."

His broad chest rose and fell heavily. "Do you now?"

Her fingers moved down to his hard mouth and pressed there. "I can't afford to want you," she said, remembering her responsibilities and what she had to do to carry them out. Her eyes fell to his square jaw. "Oh, Cy, it's too late…."

His hands slid to her shoulders and he drew her, unresisting, against him. He didn't try to kiss her or even to hold her intimately. His arms enfolded her and he laid his cheek against her soft hair, closing his eyes.

"Don't pull away, sweetheart," he whispered into her ear when he felt her stir. "Just give me this."

She stiffened when she felt his slow, hot arousal pressing against her belly.

"All right," he said quietly, moving back. "You don't like feeling that, but there's nothing I can do about it. The poor damned thing can't think."

She laughed in spite of herself and pulled away. "Go to work," she murmured.

"I might as well," he said with a rueful smile. He slanted his Stetson over one eye, so rakishly handsome that she had to bite her tongue to keep from throwing herself at him.

"Cy."

He turned at the door, with his hand on the knob.

"I'll go out to the battlefield with you Thursday," she said reluctantly.

His eyes brightened for an instant. But he only nodded, without speaking, and let himself out.

She didn't move for a few seconds, drinking in the lingering scent of him. Finally she finished her coffee and went to dress.

IT WAS A LONG WEEK. Mrs. Dade was openly curious about her "lost weekend," but she was kind enough not to ask leading questions. Meredith worked longer hours than she had the week before, but what tired her most was what she did after she left the restaurant. She stayed up until one and two o'clock in the morning faxing mail out, replying to proposals and memos, studying statistics. Twice, she had to sneak out of the restaurant long enough to phone Don when questions came up about the foreign operation and she didn't have the answers. The pressure was telling on her. By Thursday she was dragged out and almost asleep on her feet.

Cy picked her up at the restaurant, frowning at her listlessness. "You're tired to death," he muttered as he pulled away from the curb. "Do you want to go home and change?"

She glanced down at her jeans and sneakers and red-striped blouse which she wore with a white sweatshirt. At work, she wore a white uniform, which she left in her locker. "This will do," she said. "Can we stop in Hardin and get something hot to drink? I didn't get my coffee before I left."

"Have you eaten?" he asked.

She shook her head. "No time."

"I didn't mean to starve you," he murmured. "We can stop at a restaurant…."

"No, please, I'm really not that hungry. A bag of chips or some beef jerky will do me fine."

"Okay, then."

The road to Hardin was long, and there wasn't a lot to see on the way except rolling grassland and wheat fields and buttes, with the monotony occasionally broken by a herd of cattle or oil pumper wells. The horizon reached to the sky, and with hardly any trees there, it was truly big sky country. Meredith loved the vastness of it, the lack of crowding, the sparseness.

"Elbow room," she remarked absently.

He glanced at her. "That's why I stay here. I hate crowds."

She nodded, but she didn't speak.

"What does Mr. Smith do for a living?" he asked with quiet malice.

"He's a professional bodyguard." That much was gospel, and she smiled a little.

"Since he obviously wouldn't need to work for you, who employs him?"

Meredith had to fight laughter. The secrecy was all the more delicious because, inevitably, Cy was going to find out whom Mr. Smith worked for. "He has various employers," she replied. "He travels a great deal."

"If he works for the jet set, I don't doubt it." He didn't like the thought of Mr. Smith. He fumbled a cigarette out of his shirt pocket and lit it. He was wearing jeans today with a blue-striped western shirt and his heavy shepherd's coat. It was pretty cold, and the heater in the car felt good.

"You still smoke," Meredith mused.

"I did quit, for a while," he replied, not mentioning that he'd only started back when Meredith reappeared in his life. He cracked a window and blew out a gray cloud of smoke.

"How's business these days?" she asked carelessly, though her eyes were wary.

"Successful," he murmured.

"It's nice to have no shadows on your horizon, I guess."

He gave a curt laugh. "I didn't say that. There are always problems, in any large company. Lately we seem to spend most of our time fighting takeover bids."

Her heart jumped. "What?" she asked, pretending ignorance.

"Rival companies see potential in us and try to absorb us," he explained patiently.

"They can't just take you over, surely," she said.

"No. But they buy up stock and then try to sway our stockholders to side with them."

He frowned as he thought about the rumors he'd heard just lately about a new threat from Tennison International. Old Henry Tennison was dead, but his brother, Don, was very much alive, and there was a widow who was said to have extensive business acumen and nerves of steel. Odd, he thought, that there was never a photo of her in the Annual Report. Rumor said she refused to let her picture ever be used. He had one of his directors, Bill Marson, checking on that rumor. Bill had assured him there was no truth to it, but lately Bill had been fighting every decision he brought before the board. He sighed roughly. He was probably overreacting, he thought, glancing sideways at Meredith. Lately his business had taken a back seat to her, again. He spent far too much time brooding over her presence in his life.

"You haven't been back, have you?" he asked suddenly. "Not since you left here."

She shook her head, staring blankly out the window. The pain was still there, just under the surface. "I wanted to," she replied. "I missed Great-Aunt Mary. Phone calls and letters aren't the same."

"You never told her why you stayed away."

"No," she said. "It would have served no purpose, except to upset her."

"That wouldn't have stopped most women from crying all over her."

She looked at him, her eyes steady. "I'm not most women. I don't need to punish other people for my own problems."

His face hardened. "Is that a dig?"

"You tell me, Cy," she replied. "You were never happy about the way you were with me. You hated the hold I had on you, and you wanted no part of commitment. I think you were looking for an excuse to push me out the door. Tony gave it to you on a platter. With a little help."

"From whom?" he asked.

"That's not for me to say," she replied. She leaned back against the seat, wondering if Myrna Harden had done any more thinking about the proposition Meredith had made her.

Probably not, she decided. Myrna would hide her head in the sand as long as possible, hoping that Meredith would have to leave eventually. Certainly she hadn't heard from the woman again.

"My mother doesn't like having you in Billings," Cy said after a minute.

"I'm not surprised," she told him. "But she can't get me out. Not this time."

"What do you mean, this time?"

She smiled at him and didn't answer. "Have you been out to the battlefield since the archaeological team was here?"

"Yes. The fire that swept the area served a useful purpose. The excavation that followed it cast a lot of new light on the actual battle. As you know already, Custer sent a message back to Benteen to bring the pack mules with the extra ammunition. That was the last anyone heard from him until a couple of days after the fight, when the bodies were found."

"Which is why nobody knows exactly how Custer deployed his men or what his original position was when he mounted the attack on the combined Sioux and Cheyenne forces," she added. Great-Uncle Raven-Walking had been a storehouse of information on the battle. One of his ancestors had been a scout for the Seventh Cavalry at the time of the Little Bighorn battle. He'd often walked Meredith over the battlefield when she was small, holding her spellbound with his stories of the old days. But it was the time she'd been here with Cy that she remembered so vividly.

"That's right," Cy told her. "The surviving accounts from Crow scouts indicate that at one point Custer was warned that there was a big encampment of Sioux and Cheyenne on the Little Bighorn, but apparently he didn't heed them. Even when he saw the camp, he might have only noticed women and children. He might have thought the warriors were far away hunting and that he had the element of surprise."

"The Indians certainly had it, from all accounts," she returned.

"Yes. His Crow and Arikara scouts later said that Custer's men were overwhelmed by sheer numbers."

"Didn't a lot of officers employ two translators when they spoke to Indians, to make sure there were no mistakes when they were trying to decipher the sign language the Indians used?" she asked.

"Yes, they did. But Custer was known to be fairly proficient with sign language."

"Fascinating."

"I find the whole history fascinating. I never tire of going through the museum or wandering over the battlefield."

They turned off the main highway outside Hardin and onto the small paved road that led past the guard station, where they paid the fee that allowed them a day pass into the historical site. They parked in the museum lot and walked up the long paved path to the last stand. A number of graves were marked by white crosses in a large square area bounded by a black wrought-iron fence.

Atop the hill was a monument listing the names of the men who died in the battle. At one time it had been a mass grave for all the Seventh Cavalry dead, but the body of Custer had long since been taken back to West Point for burial. On the other side of the museum, under transplanted fir trees, were graves of many other men, including Vietnam veterans. Major Marcus Reno was buried there.

"What about Captain Benteen?" Meredith asked.

"He died and was buried in Atlanta, Georgia," Cy replied. He leaned over the fence and stared down the ridge to the banks of Medicine Tail Coulee far below.

"It's a long walk to the coulee," she remarked. "I remember we did it one Sunday afternoon in summer, and it was so hot."

He glanced down at her. That had been in the early days of their relationship, when they'd barely been able to exist apart.

"Do you remember what we did when we got back to my apartment?" he asked huskily.

She remembered all right. He'd stripped them both and carried her into the bathroom, placing her in the cool water of the Jacuzzi before he climbed in beside her. He'd turned her so that the jets gave her a shattering climax, and while the tremors were still shaking her, he'd joined his body to hers in one of the most satisfying bouts of lovemaking they'd ever shared. Before it was over, he'd had her on the floor of the bathroom, the carpet of the bedroom, and, finally, in bed.

It had taken days for her to recover from the experience, which had left her sore in ways she'd never been since. That had been only days before his mother had accused her of theft.

She lowered her eyes to the ground.

"It was the last time we made love," he said quietly, staring out over the battlefield while his body gnarled with memories of almost painful pleasure. "I couldn't have you for days after that, because I'd been so insatiable with you." His eyes closed. "Before we could be together again, Tony came to me with that money...."

Her gaze wouldn't lift. She didn't want to look back, to remember that last feverish coupling. He remembered nothing but the pleasure, and then the so-called betrayal. It was all physical with him, right down to the memories.

"I'll die without ever experiencing anything like that afternoon again, Meredith," he said, his voice giving nothing away. "What I had with you I can't find with other women."

"Can't you?" she asked with a cynicism far beyond her years. "I thought sex was satisfying with any partner, for a man."

He looked down at her, scowling. "Did you find that kind of pleasure with anyone else?"

She lifted her eyes to his and thought of Henry and how much he'd loved her. She remembered the night before Henry's plane crashed and the first stirring of love she'd felt for her husband.

"I came very close," she said quietly, her eyes clouding with pain.

Jealousy raged through his body. He hadn't expected her answer or the look in her eyes, the faint haunting. "Did he?"

"He loved me," she said with pride, with reverence, for Henry's memory. She looked at Cy without flinching. "I was his world. If he hadn't died, I'd be with him still, and I'd never have given you a thought for the rest of my life!"

He paled. His hand clenched and he cursed, his dark eyes dangerous with feeling.

"Go ahead, lose your temper," she said calmly, knowing that he wouldn't. "I don't belong to you anymore. I'm not your slave. That was why you brought me out here, wasn't it, to see if I still loved you, to see if I was vulnerable." She put her hands on her hips, aware of the solitude on the hill. Only a few tourists had come today because of the cold and threatening snow, and most of them were in the museum. "Well, I like kissing you, Cy. I might even enjoy an afternoon in bed with you. But I could still walk away afterward and never look back." She smiled with pure malice, lying through her teeth and enjoying the fact that he actually believed what she was saying. "So lose control, if you like. It won't change anything, though. It won't make me love you again."

"Did you ever?" he asked roughly.

"What does it matter now?" She stuck her hands in her pockets and turned her face back to the battlefield. "Like what happened down there—" she gestured toward the slope of the hill "—it's ancient history. The details have been swallowed up in the aftermath. Dead is dead, Cy. Who cares in the final analysis how it happened?"

He didn't reply. He lit a cigarette, shocked by the intense emotion he still felt with her. His own behavior made him uneasy.

"Would you have taken out your anger on me?" she asked after a minute and without looking at him. She wanted him to admit that he couldn't.

His eyes searched hers. "Not ever, little one," he said quietly. He turned. "Let's go down."

They wandered through the museum, where a copy of Custer's last command to Benteen survived, in the handwriting of his adjutant, Cooke. There was also a duplicate of the white buckskin suit Custer had worn that hot June day in 1876 when he left for the Little Bighorn with his column. Indian artifacts were presented along with bits and pieces of equipment from the battle. The colorful Indian regalia looked odd beside the sedate blue of the soldier's uniforms—almost celebratory.

She mentioned that to Cy as he towered over her at the glass cases containing the memorabilia. "Remember, when a Sioux went to war, he dressed in his best clothing—or at least carried it with him with the intention of being buried in it. He decorated his face and body with his medicine symbols, sometimes even decorated his horse the same way, and carried his medicine shield before him. As he charged, he sang his death song. It was an occasion when a warrior went into battle."

"They fought individually, though," she recalled. "Not under orders from company commanders, like in the army."

"The warriors, Sioux and Cheyenne, belonged to a warrior society. Each society had its own chiefs and subchiefs. During the battle, the societies attacked together, one at a time, but it was the individual efforts which were noted and later recited around the campfires. It was why soldiers had such a time fighting the Indians, because they waged war on an individual basis, not as a group."

"Not at all like some southwestern tribes," she murmured, "which frowned on individual achievement and rewarded group achievement."

He glanced down at her with a smile. "You know your subject. I forget sometimes that you grew up on the Crow reservation. I suppose you learned a lot about Indians."

"Yes, and from reading," she agreed. She didn't add that Henry had bought her volumes on American Indians while she was expecting Blake, to give her something to pass the time. "Crow society is fascinating. Its structure is an ideal one for mutual cooperation and harmony."

He led her to another exhibit in a glass case. "The arrows always fascinated me," he said, indicating a quiver of them. "Each tribe had unique ways of making arrows, and each warrior as well. You can tell by the makeup of the arrow who it belonged to. The funny thing is that an Indian could shoot eight arrows before the first hit the ground, and never miss his mark. But Indians were notoriously the worst rifle shots around."

She laughed. "Great-Uncle Raven-Walking certainly was. I wonder why?"

"Because the way you sight a rifle and the way you sight a bow are different, I expect," he said, smiling at her.

"Did you ever read *Memoirs of a White Crow Indian* by Thomas H. Leforge? The one Dr. Marquis helped him put down on paper?" she asked. "I had an old, old copy that my great-uncle gave me. It's like a textbook on how the Crow once lived and what they believed."

"Honey, everybody who knows anything about Custer or the Little Bighorn has read Leforge's story. It's one of the foremost sources on the Crow way of life and, indirectly, on the Little Bighorn campaign. But nobody, and I mean nobody, in my opinion comes close to *Son of the Morning Star,* Evan S. Connell's compilation of all known information about the battle. The bibliography goes on for pages. It's a monumental work, and interesting to read as well as factual."

"I know." She grinned up at him. "I've read it."

He chuckled. "I should have known. Look at the Sioux knife stick."

It was an odd implement, made of iron spikes along a lance. There were also Sioux war clubs, huge foot-size rounded rocks from the Yellowstone River tied to wooden handles with rawhide. The Cheyenne seemed to prefer iron, because their tomahawks were made of it.

"That's a coup stick," she told him, pointing to another artifact. "My great-uncle had one that his grandfather carried. I think I've still got it at the house somewhere."

"I remember seeing it," he said. "The Plains Indians considered touching a live enemy much more courageous than just killing one. Counting coup was a great feat."

"There's a soldier's watch," she murmured as they turned to another case.

"Several Indians walked off with those, and threw them away when they stopped making their magical noise," he said, smiling.

"So long ago." She sighed, thinking about how it must have felt to the soldiers when they saw the great numbers of Indians surrounding them and knew they were going to die. And afterward, the Indians running for their lives, forever threatened because of what had happened to Custer, regardless of whether or not their particular branch of the tribe had any part in it.

"Lots of the soldiers were green recruits from back east who'd never even seen an Indian before," Cy remarked, resting his lean hands on her shoulders to look past her at the case. "The Indians were painted, like their horses, screaming their death chants, firing captured guns and their own bows and arrows, and blowing eagle-bone whistles. There was dust and noise and the screams of the wounded. Worse, the Indians were all seasoned warriors, comfortable in battle. The recruits were outmatched from the start."

"But Custer was experienced," she said.

"Oh, yes. There were any number of seasoned soldiers in his command, like Reno and Benteen and many of the noncommissioned officers. Custer himself was a veteran of the Civil War, where he fought old classmates from West Point like Robert E. Lee and J.E.B. Stuart. That's where he got his battlefield commission as brevet general. He led charge after charge right into the enemy ranks. But his luck gave out here. So many things went wrong for him that it was fate more than coincidence that he fell. He left his artillery pieces behind because he didn't want to be slowed down, he refused to take along companies of Montana militia, he either disbelieved or disregarded intelligence from Crow and Arikara scouts about the strength of the Indian camp, he split his forces between himself, Major Reno, and Captain Benteen..."

Cy shook his head. "Historians will argue the outcome as long as there are historians alive. But only Custer and his men know what really happened here, and whether or not it was inevitable. Some say Reno and Benteen should have rushed to his assistance, but they were pinned down and very nearly destroyed. Eyewitnesses said there was no way they could have gotten through the mass of milling Indian warriors even if they'd had sufficient strength to lend aid to Custer."

"Reno was court-martialed, wasn't he?"

"He asked for the inquiry," Cy corrected, "because he was tired of the gossip about his actions at the Little Bighorn. He was cleared of all charges. Benteen, too, was exonerated of any blame for Custer's death. The whispers followed them all their lives, though. Reno died of cancer. After the Little Bighorn battle, he was court-martialed for behavior unbecoming an officer, after having allegedly been peering late at night through the window of a woman with whom he was infatuated. Benteen was happily married and died of old age."

Meredith didn't say any more. The exhibits made her sad and full of regret for the soldiers and the Indians. It had always amazed her that Cy knew so much about the battle. They had that interest in common, along with plenty of others. But in the old days, there had been too much passion between them for long talks and lazy afternoons out of bed. She followed Cy out into the cold sunlight and back to the car.

Outside the gates of the battlefield park, Meredith noticed several small tables and any number of Indians selling their wares.

"Northern Cheyenne." Cy grinned as he nodded toward one group. "Ironic, isn't it? The battlefield is on Crow land. Back in the old days, Crow and Cheyenne were mortal enemies, like Crow and Sioux."

"There are so few of both tribes left that fighting hardly accomplishes anything today," she said. "It takes a lot of work just to keep the few rights they still have, and to fight off speculators who want their land. They can't even sell it, you know, without government approval. There are lobbies working for them in Washington, but it's an expensive business." She stopped short, almost having blurted out that she financed one. That wouldn't have done at all.

THEY DROVE BACK TO TOWN without speaking. "You still haven't eaten," Cy remarked when he pulled up at Meredith's house.

"I'm not hungry."

"I could go out and get supper," he said as he cut off the engine. His dark eyes caressed her face. "We could talk some more."

Her heart was beating so fast. She remembered oh, so well, the last time they'd seen the battlefield together and what had come afterward. She had to think about her new life, about her son.

"Meredith."

His voice was velvet. It almost purred. She looked up into his eyes. It was fatal. The old electricity was still there, even stronger with maturity, and the years fell away. The same hunger she felt was mirrored there, a need so desperate that it overcame all her protective instincts. He was the only man she'd ever loved. *Once more,* her mind whispered. *Just once more, while there's still time....*

"I'll...cook something," she whispered, but she was saying much more than that, and he knew it.

With deft, somber movements Cy got them both out of the car and into the house. As he closed the door behind him and turned to Meredith, all the years in between dropped away. His chest rose and fell heavily, his heart shaking him. She was here, no longer a dream. The reasons he shouldn't touch her vanished like smoke. He could hardly bear the throbbing need that consumed him.

"I want you," he said roughly. "Oh, God, I want you so!"

Meredith shivered with a need of her own. Precautions

never entered her mind; neither did consequences. For these few minutes, nothing mattered except Cy and her relentless love for him.

"I want you, too," she whispered, her eyes adoring his face.

"There's no tomorrow, Meredith," he said, his voice as deep with feeling as his eyes, caressing, coaxing. "There's no yesterday. There's only now."

"Yes," she said softly. And he reached for her.

CHAPTER EIGHT

MEREDITH KEPT REPEATING to herself, silently, all the reasons why she should stop Cy. But as his warm, hard mouth closed on hers and fitted itself hungrily to her lips, the years rolled back and she was a young girl with her first love, her only love, in her arms.

"Don't fight me," he breathed into her mouth as he lifted her. "Don't fight me, little one, I need you so badly!"

He carried her effortlessly into the bedroom and settled onto the narrow mattress with her.

It was like the first time. He was slow and careful and infinitely tender. She yielded completely after a faint protest and watched him slide the fabric away from her body.

He looked at her, finding all the subtle differences between the girl's body he'd possessed and the woman's body before him now. Frowning slightly, he touched her belly, where the faint bikini-cut scar made a thin white line. She'd had to have a cesarean section with Blake, despite all the weeks of Lamaze training. She held her breath, wondering if Cy would recognize it for what it was.

"An accident?" he asked softly, his eyes seeking hers.

"An operation," she said quietly. "I…there was a female problem," she fibbed.

"Are you all right? Did you recover fully?" he persisted.

"Yes."

His big hand traced her belly up to the swell of her pretty pink breasts with their hard, mauve crests, noting their increased size. "You were always beautiful," he said softly. "But you're much fuller than you were, more voluptuous."

Her skin tingled as his fingertips traced over it. She felt the old sensations winding through her again. It had been so long!

She must have whispered it, because she heard him echo the words against her mouth. He shifted and one long leg inserted itself between both of hers in a lazy, arousing rhythm.

He'd been expert even when she was a girl. Now he was much more knowledgeable. He did things to her, whispered things to her, that she'd never experienced with him.

As the lazy minutes dragged by, with his mouth sucking hungrily at her breasts, her belly, even the inside of her thighs, she became a wild thing, bent only on satisfaction, lost to reason entirely.

She pulled at his shirt and he smiled even through his fierce arousal as he helped her divest his body of clothing. He was more muscular than he had been six years ago, more powerfully athletic. The muscles her hands touched were bigger now, and his body had filled out with maturity. He was still more man than most women could handle, and she felt a sting of pride that she could accommodate him so easily.

He laughed gently as his body began to penetrate hers. "You're tight," he whispered huskily. "Wasn't your last lover as well endowed as I am?"

"No," she replied, flushing a little at the intimacy of the question.

"You always fit me like a glove," he breathed, nipping at her lower lip arousingly. "Even the first time, when I had to hurt you. You never said a word, you never told me I was the only man you'd had. But I knew, just the same." He shifted, nudging one of her long legs gently. "Like that, sweetheart," he murmured at her mouth. "And try to relax a little, if you can. I don't want to make you any more uncomfortable than I have to."

"It's been…a long time," she whispered, jerking as he furthered his possession of her, his glittering eyes looking straight down into hers.

"I can tell." He stopped to catch his breath and bent, drawing his mouth tenderly over her damp forehead, her closed eyelids. "Do you want me to stop and arouse you again? Will that make it any easier?"

He would have done that. Despite his raging need, she knew all she had to do was ask. He was the most considerate lover she could ever have imagined. If he'd loved her, every time would have been exquisite.

"No," she said softly. "It's all right now." She lifted her hips experimentally and grimaced as she felt him begin to fill her completely. But she didn't draw back. She arched, pushing, and heard his involuntary gasp of pleasure when she took him completely. Before Blake was born, she'd never been able to do that.

"Never," he ground out. "Never like this. Never…!"

Her unexpected movement startled him into a quick, mindless drive for satisfaction, his body corded, in agony. He began to move convulsively, his hoarse apology like a litany in her ears as the springs creaked noisily beneath his formidable weight and the helpless rhythm of his hungry body. He grabbed the iron headrail and held on for dear life as he drove for fulfillment, blind, deaf, and dumb to anything except the agony of his need.

Meredith lay quietly, watching him, glorying in his tormented expression, in the sudden still arch of his body before it convulsed in a throbbing rhythm that was echoed in the hoarse groans that tore out of his throat.

Even at that blind moment, he suddenly jerked back and upward, so that he spared her the risk of pregnancy. Amazing, she thought, watching him, that he could manage that.

He dropped onto her damp body seconds later, shuddering in the aftermath, wet all over with the sweat of his passionate exertion. "You didn't have time," he whispered at her ear. "I'm sorry."

She didn't answer him. It had always been like that. His need of her reached through all barriers, until he was out of his mind. But he always made it up to her, and that was why she smiled. He had remarkable stamina and he was generous.

Sure enough, seconds later, she felt the slow, delicate touch of his mouth moving down to her breasts. He brushed them with kisses, teasing them lazily until her nipples went rigid. He nibbled and touched and kissed them until he built her hunger back to fever pitch. All the time, his hand was easing its way between her soft thighs, wickedly expert as it found the very core of her femininity and kindled it to a flame so high that she cried out.

The first tremors were already working up her spine when she felt him shift his weight over her. She gripped his arms hard and her eyes opened just as he went into her with one hard, fierce thrust.

The predatory smile on his hard lips blurred into fire as he moved and then moved again. She clung to him, her breath stuck in the back of her throat as she echoed the piston movement of his hips, reaching blindly for fulfillment. It came like a lightning bolt, lifting her, killing her with its hot pleasure.

She arched into him with a sound that she hadn't made since her last time with him, crying out as the painful ecstasy corded her muscles into unbearable tension and suddenly snapped them like a rubber band.

She wept all the way back down, piteous tears that recognized the brevity of nirvana, the black anguish of losing him again, the pain of all the years without this…

He was smoking a cigarette when she opened her eyes. He had one knee drawn up, the sheet lightly over his hips, and he was staring blankly into space. She tugged the sheet over her swollen, red-marked breasts and sat up. She felt cheap and easy, having given in to him without even a struggle.

"You aren't on the Pill, are you?" he asked.

"No," she replied. "I haven't needed to be, for a long time."

"So I noticed." He glanced down at her, suddenly ripping the sheet from her hands so that he could see the faint marks of passion that he'd left on her silky body. His face hardened and his eye went dark with memory. "I kept from making you pregnant, this time," he said. "I can't promise to hold back again. I'll make sure I have something with me from now on."

"Are all your other women protected?" she asked with cold pride.

He laughed shortly and threw the sheet over her again before he got to his feet and started dressing. "These days, women are more liberated than men," he said. "I don't have to worry about precautions, as a rule." He looked down at her. "Not that I probably needed to resort to them with you. You never got pregnant by me, and we never used a damned thing in the old days."

No, they hadn't. But she didn't reply. She fiddled with the sheet and pushed back her disheveled hair to keep from answering him.

"You could be barren," he remarked, and hated the statement the second it was out. Why it should bother him, he didn't understand.

"Yes, I suppose so," Meredith replied, enjoying an ironic joke she couldn't share with him.

"All the same, I don't want to take chances. I don't want children."

She looked up as he buttoned his shirt. "Never?" she asked hesitantly.

Dressed now, he picked up his cigarette and drew hard on it. "Children mean commitment. I told you a long time ago that commitment wasn't something I wanted."

"I remember," she said, averting her eyes. Well, what had she expected, that he'd changed in six years? It was certainly a forlorn hope, judging from today's performance.

"And apparently you don't want it, either," he persisted. "You've never married."

She had, but now wasn't the time to admit it. "I like my own company."

"Do you?" He chuckled harshly. Part of him was ecstatic that she still wanted him, that her body betrayed the length of time it had been without sex. But another part hated the ease of her submission, hated the way his own body had reacted to hers. He couldn't control himself with her. He lost his edge. He was like a young boy, and it made him doubt his own manhood.

"Now that you've gotten what you came for, why don't you go home?" she asked quietly.

He finished the cigarette. "I might as well. I thought you were going to feed me."

"I don't feel like eating."

"You always used to, after we made love," he recalled, watching her through narrowed eyes. "It gave you an appetite."

"That was long ago," she said.

He put out the cigarette in an ashtray. "Well, if you've had men in all that time, they haven't left much impression on you," he said, remembering angrily what she'd said about the man who'd loved her. His eyes looked straight into hers. "You were starving to death for me."

"That works both ways, doesn't it?" she asked with icy poise. "You couldn't even hold back the first time!"

His face went rigid. He didn't say another word. He jerked up his hat and slammed out the front door, leaving Meredith sprawled on the bed.

"So much for you, big man," she told the empty room. "If you can't stand the heat, get out of the kitchen."

She got up and took a long shower, trying to wash off the scent of him, the feel of his hands on her. But it was hopeless, because the memories couldn't be washed away. He still hated the thought of marriage, and he wanted no part of children. She hadn't expected anything else, but it hurt all the same. He had a beautiful son. Now she wondered how he was going to react when he found out about Blake, because inevitably he was going to.

What bothered her most was the way she'd given in to him. Now, without a doubt, he was going to expect that easy submission. He was going to try to use her all over again, trade on her need of him. Well, she'd soon put that false notion to rest, she told herself. Even if it cut her to the quick to give up the ecstasy only he could give her, all over again.

HE WAS AT THE RESTAURANT the next morning as she went to work. His eyes watched her with smug possession, and memories of the day before lay open in his face. Apparently he'd forgiven her parting shot, because it wasn't dislike that flamed in his eyes when he looked at her. It was desire, hot and urgent.

She presented him with a menu and her customary smile. "Good morning, Cy. May I take your order, or would you like a few minutes to study the menu?"

"I'd rather have you again than anything that's on the menu," he murmured.

"I can recommend the country ham," she said politely, ignoring the innuendo. "And the coffee is fresh. Shall I get you a cup?"

He sighed angrily. So that was how she was going to play it. He handed her back the menu. "Yes, bring me a cup of coffee. And I'll have bacon, eggs and toast."

"Yes, sir, coming up."

She served it minutes later, having made him wait for the coffee. He was irritated, and it showed. He complained about everything, even the strength of the coffee. But Meredith was polite and courteous, and not much more.

He left without a backward glance. And, she noticed, without a tip. She smiled with wicked glee and went back to work.

That night she called home and talked to Mr. Smith and Blake, leaving a message for Don about a letter she'd received. She missed home, especially after what had happened with Cy. She wanted to run, but she couldn't. She was committed.

The knock on the door wasn't really surprising. She'd expected that Cy might try to wear her down after hours. She let him in, frowning as he produced a huge designer box from under one arm and tossed it on the couch.

"What's that?" she asked.

"Something for you. I'm taking you to a charity ball tomorrow night."

He was not, because Mr. Smith was going to fly down with some urgent contracts tomorrow afternoon. But she couldn't very well explain that.

She opened the box and her face went white as she saw the kind of dress he'd bought her. It was a flaming cherry red, sequined, with hardly a bodice, no back, and a long side slit. Just the dress a man might buy for his mistress, but not at all the sort he'd give any woman he really cared about.

"Is that a message?" she asked, turning to face him.

His eyes ranged down her ragged sweatshirt and jeans and back up to her eyes. She looked worn, as if her job were killing her. Not that it could be, he assured himself. After all, she was only waiting tables.

He didn't know what she was doing after hours. She was glad she had the fax machine and her computer, printer, files, and mail in the library she used as an office and that she'd locked it when she heard the car drive up.

"The dress, you mean?" he asked. "It's just a dress."

"It's a very expensive dress," she replied. "The kind a man takes his mistress dancing in."

"Isn't that what you were, six years back?" he asked insolently, because what she'd said made him uncomfortable.

"I loved you six years ago," she said. "That's why I slept with you."

"Bull," he replied easily. "You loved my money and the luxury of my apartment, and the pretty things I bought you."

"Convinced yourself of that, have you?" she asked.

"You weren't even an adult, honey," he said, shrugging his powerful shoulders. "I didn't expect love from a kid like you. Your body was all I wanted."

"I found that out the hard way," she replied. "Couldn't you have left me alone?" she asked suddenly, her eyes tormented as they met his. "You had nothing to offer, but you deliberately took everything of value I had to give. My love, my virginity…"

"You gave that last item," he said shortly. "Gave it with a passion that knocked the breath out of me, and without my having to ask for it. You did everything short of stripping in public to catch my eye."

That was true. She didn't have a comeback, because she'd certainly given that impression. Her eyes lowered again to the dress in its pristine, elegant box.

"Life teaches hard lessons," she murmured.

"Why won't you take the dress?" he asked.

She glanced at him. "Because I'm not your mistress."

He smiled, but his eyes were cold and angry. "Aren't you?" He moved toward her.

She backed away, extending a hand. "No," she said firmly, and her face echoed the word. The very calmness of her voice stopped him in his tracks.

"You want me," he said.

"Of course I want you, Cy," she replied. "But I'm old enough now to make sensible choices. And the last complication I need is to drag up an old affair."

"Because of your precious Mr. Smith?" he asked mockingly.

She didn't react to the dig. "Because I have too much pride," she said. "You used me once. I won't let you do it again. Yesterday was an accident. A mistake. I let the past blind me to the present. But it won't happen again."

He stood very still, his big hands clenched by his sides. "You wanted me."

"I suppose I always will," she confessed. "You and I are addicted to each other in bed. That's a sad quirk of nature, nothing we can do anything about. But I want more than a few feverish hours in bed. Once, it was magic and I didn't have to think ahead. Now I do."

She sounded mature and very businesslike. That registered even through the words that were kindling his temper.

"You have no real ties," he said, trying a softer approach. "Neither do I."

"You're a Harden," she returned. "Your mother considers me a different species. She'd separate us again, if you didn't toss me aside or find some reason to push me out of your life. There's no future in what I feel for you, Cy. I'd have better luck with Mr. Smith."

He let out a harsh word. "My mother never separated us in the first place. Your own greed did that!"

"Think what you like," she said tiredly. "Just go home." She picked up the box and handed it to him. "Take that with you. I don't have anyplace to wear something that fancy."

"So blasé," he chided. "God knows you've probably never seen a dress that expensive before, and you're refusing it."

In fact, she had seen dresses that expensive. Her closet was full of originals even more expensive than the one she was giving back to him.

"I like the gift. I just don't like the strings it's attached to," she said.

"Imagine that," he drawled. "Pride, from a woman like you."

She stiffened. She didn't like the insinuation, and it showed.

"Insulted?" he taunted, his hand gripping the box roughly. "Why should you be? Women with no morals can't afford the luxury of taking themselves too seriously."

"You think you know me so well," she said in a harsh whisper, almost shaking with anger.

"I know you inside out," he returned in a tone equally gruff. "My God, all I have to do is touch you and you're mine!"

"Get out," she said.

He gave her one last bold appraisal, ignoring her white face and wounded eyes. "Just as well you wouldn't go to the ball with me," he murmured. "You probably haven't gained any social graces in the past six years. I'll bet you don't even know which damned fork to use at a properly set table or where to put a napkin."

She was quivering with rage by now. "I know where I'd like to put one right now. Get out!"

He hesitated, but only for an instant. He laughed coldly. "Good night, Meredith. Sweet dreams," he said before he went out and closed the door behind him.

But once he was in his car and on the way home, he cursed himself for the things he'd said. Meredith was as helpless as he was when they touched, but he'd made it sound as if she were a slut. That wasn't what he'd meant to do at all. Her refusal to give in to him was painful. He'd thought they were starting over, but she'd closed the door in his face.

Just as well, probably, he mused, trying to soothe his pride. His father had shown him that faithfulness to one woman just wasn't possible for a Harden. He'd seen how his mother's life had been destroyed by her husband's blatant unfaithfulness. It had warped his opinion of marriage, of love. Nothing lasted, least of all infatuation. That's all it had been on his part and on Meredith's. Just infatuation.

Remembering her passion and his, he didn't feel that way. Their need for each other had lasted all the long years, and the way she'd welcomed him still made his head spin. He'd never felt with any woman what he felt when he loved Meredith in bed. It was like dying all over, in the most exquisite way.

He groaned out loud as the pleasure washed over him, fiery hot and sweet. He was going to lose her all over again, and he didn't know how he'd bear it a second time. If only she was modern enough to take what they had together in her stride, without promises of forever. Didn't she know by now that nobody had forever?

He turned his car toward home, turning over what she'd said in his mind. She kept insinuating that his mother had caused their breakup. He knew that wasn't true. His mother, for all her faults, loved him. She'd never do anything to hurt him.

The dress on the seat beside him made him angry. Impulsively he stopped the car on the bridge, got out, ripped the dress from its box, and hurled it down into the river far below. As he watched it float away in the dim light from the street lamps, he felt as if he were watching an instant replay of the past. He shouldn't have said those things to Meredith. It was going to make everything that much more complicated.

MEREDITH WAS CONSIDERING her own options as she sat alone on her sofa. Part of her wanted to get on the next plane for Chicago and throw up the whole deal. But she couldn't do that.

Don reported making some progress with the East Coast proxies, Meredith recalled as she pulled out the list of names of people across the country who held large blocks of Harden stock. Her anger at Cy lent impetus to her determination.

The fourth name on the list was a great-uncle of Cy's, one of his more deadly business enemies. The old man was a brother to Cy's grandfather, and a formidable adversary. He'd never pretended to like Cy. Of course nothing made friends like a common enemy, but she couldn't afford to trust the old man until she saw him.

She picked up the phone and dialed, giving an assumed name as she spoke, asking about his voting shares and mentioning a surprise she'd like to spring on Cy. The old man said little, but in the end Meredith arranged a meeting with him for very early the next morning.

As she hung up the telephone, she was thinking ahead to the board meeting that Cy's company directors had planned for two weeks from now. If everything worked out, she was going to have one hell of a surprise for Cy Harden and his mother.

She didn't regret the surprise, either. Over the years the Hardens had given her plenty of grief. This was poetic justice, to have a hand in watching them lose everything.

It was sad that she and Cy couldn't form a permanent relationship. It would have been nice for Blake. But now the die was cast, and she couldn't afford to backslide. No more romantic interludes or revisiting the past with Cy. Now she was in deadly earnest, and she had only a little time left to spread her net.

CHAPTER NINE

LAWRENCE HARDEN was seventy-two years old. He lived in a small clapboard house on ten thousand acres of prime pastureland on the way to the Big Horn Mountains in southern Montana.

He welcomed Meredith with grace and old-world courtesy, pausing to make coffee and offer store-bought sweet rolls.

"Now," he said when he was comfortably situated on his rocking chair and she was perched on his sofa. "What's this about my proxy?"

Meredith smiled. It was just past daylight and she was dressed in nice clothes today, a soft gray suit with a blue plaid blouse, her hair in a plait down her back. She looked the successful businesswoman, and she could see that her appearance gave her extra points with Cy's great-uncle. She'd counted on that.

"Can I trust you not to go to Cy if I tell you?" she asked point-blank.

He nodded. "I like your honesty," he replied, his blue eyes twinkling. "Yes, you can trust me. I'll give you my word."

"In that case, I'm after your great-nephew's company," she said simply. "I want it all—lock, stock, and barrel—and I'm prepared to pay top dollar for any outstanding stock. What I can't buy, I want to control through signed proxies."

"Once you have the company, what do you plan to do with it?" he asked warily.

"Incorporate it into mine," she said.

"You have your own company?" he asked, impressed.

She smiled. "Yes."

"Times change."

"Indeed they do." She outlined what she wanted to do with Cy's mineral leases and why she needed them.

"So he wouldn't sell them," he murmured. "Not like him to forgo a deal like that. No company can afford to turn down that kind of money."

"His reasons are his own, of course. I understand that his board of directors wasn't too thrilled at his line of reasoning either. But I need those mineral rights, and I'll go to any lengths to get them."

He leaned forward, scowling. "Why? This isn't just business, is it?"

"You see too much." She crossed her arms. "No, it's personal. He and his mother did me a bad turn some years ago. They chased me out of town and left me alone in the world."

"You're Meredith," he said at once.

She caught her breath. "How did you know?"

"Whole family knew, despite Myrna's efforts to cover up." His old eyes narrowed angrily. "She set you up, didn't she? A cold, hard woman, Myrna. Forever pretending to be something she never was. Married to that bounder of a playboy, never anything she loved except her son. A woman shouldn't be that possessive of a child, it comes to no good."

"So they say," Meredith murmured, thinking about how protective she was of her own son, how involved with his welfare, even though she had to spend time away from him. She hated understanding Myrna Harden. It was somehow easier now that she had a son of her own.

"I always figured you'd come back someday. Myrna knows you're here, I reckon?"

She nodded. "But she can't buy me off. And yes, she tried."

"A hard woman," he repeated. "She'll pay for what she did one day. Not up to you to see to that, however," he added levelly. "God's business, revenge. Dangerous to take it into your own hands. It could backfire."

"Not if I get your proxy." She laughed, refusing to be frightened off. "What do you say?"

He thought about it for a minute, his wrinkled eyes narrowed. "Okay. You can have it."

"And you won't tell Cy, or Myrna?"

"Never had any use for her," he scoffed. "Cy might have turned out better if Myrna hadn't kept him away from me so much. Thought I wasn't good enough to associate with him," he said gruffly. "I live out here in the wilds, run cattle and such. My people could have bought and sold hers in the old days, back before the turn of the century. But now, I'm an embarrassment to her."

"My great-uncle was a full-blooded Crow," Meredith said with pride in her voice. "I have cousins on the reservation, and they're no embarrassment to me."

He grinned. "Good for you. No shame in honest kinfolk, rich or poor. Too bad Myrna's got her nose so far in the air. I know things about her she wouldn't want told. She wasn't always a rich society matron."

"They say your sins catch up with you," Meredith said quietly. "We'll see."

He got up to get his cashbox. "I'll sign the papers for you. Mind you don't try to play judge," he cautioned as he opened it. "What goes around comes around."

"How well I know," she said.

With the proxy in her hand, she drove back to Billings in the car she'd rented. It had been careless to do that, because Cy was probably keeping an eye on her. But she didn't really care anymore. Soon enough he was going to find out her secrets anyway.

She changed and went to work, to discover from one of Cy's executives that the boss had gone out of town the day before and wasn't expected back for a week. All her worrying had been for nothing. He didn't care enough to stay around and watch her, she decided. But she didn't know if she was relieved or disappointed by the news.

Meredith watched Myrna Harden walk into the restaurant for lunch and seat herself in Meredith's station. Apparently since Cy was gone, she felt safe enough bracing Meredith on her home ground.

Meredith placed a glass of water on the table and offered her a menu with her usual courtesy. She only had another hour to go on her shift, then she had to rush home, because Mr. Smith would be there soon with the contracts.

Myrna's hands trembled as she took the menu. She was wearing a terribly expensive designer dress in muted pastel colors. She gave Meredith's uniform a look that spoke volumes, and Meredith only thought, Enjoy it while you can.

"I only want coffee and apple pie," Myrna said, putting the menu aside. "And I want to know how much longer you're going to stay here. I know you went with Cy to the battlefield Thursday. He came home upset and he left yesterday morning without a word to me."

"He's thirty-four," Meredith pointed out. "I think that's old enough not to need your permission to leave home."

Myrna looked up at her with mingled contempt and pleading. "Don't," she said through her teeth. "I'll give you anything if you'll go away. Anything! My son is all I have left."

Meredith just stared at her.

"You must need money," the older woman persisted, almost frantic now. "You're still young, you can find someone to love. You can marry and have a family. I'll help you make a new start somewhere else."

Meredith looked down at her blankly. "It's too late for that. You know my conditions."

"I can't tell Cy," came the piteous reply. "I can't! He'll hate me…."

"You're his mother. He can't hate you."

"Meredith, for the love of God, don't do this to me," Myrna begged, and the tears in her eyes were real. She clutched at Meredith's apron with talonlike hands. "He's my son. I only wanted what was best for him."

"And I wouldn't do," she said coldly.

"You were eighteen. You came from poverty. I wanted a woman to match him, someone who could bring him stability, security, a happy future. He wanted you, but his lust blinded him to what you were," Myrna explained feverishly. "It could never have lasted. He resented you. He never wanted to get engaged to you, but he said he'd had to do it to keep you sweet, so you wouldn't walk out on him, that he was only playing along with you…."

Wincing, Meredith closed her eyes. She'd always assumed that Cy had loved her. Now she knew it all. It had only been desire. He'd never had permanence in mind, despite what he'd said to her when he proposed that they get married.

The pain in Meredith's face made Myrna even more uncomfortable than she already was. She was making a bad situation worse, but she'd been desperate. She dropped her hand with a heavy sigh. "I had no idea what I'd done until it was too late. Private detectives searched for over a year, but they couldn't find you. I would have made it up to you somehow."

"There are some things nothing can make up for," she said quietly.

"The baby." Myrna's haunted eyes lifted. "Did you have him? Did you put him up for adoption?"

Meredith didn't reply. She stared down at Myrna with contempt. "You can spend the rest of your life wondering," she said instead. "And even then you won't know the hell I went through because of you."

"No. I don't suppose I will," the other woman said, and for an instant there was something like understanding in her eyes as she looked at Meredith. Myrna took a deep breath. "I shouldn't have come at all. But Cy is hurting. Really hurting. If you can't feel pity for me, can't you feel it for him?"

"The only reason he's hurting is because I've denied him my bed," Meredith said bluntly, watching the older woman flush. "He never loved me. It was only ever a raging desire, you just said so yourself. Once I'm gone, he'll find someone else again and again," she added on a cold laugh. "Just like he did when I left here."

Myrna twisted the napkin in her hands, staring at it. "He's been different since you left. So many women. He looks for you everywhere and he can't find you." She lifted her eyes. "If I'd let you stay, it might have burned itself out eventually. He might have tired of you."

"He'd already tired of me," Meredith said wearily. "He was looking for a reason to throw me out. You gave it to him, that's all." She pushed a stray wisp of blond hair back from her cheek with a slender hand. "Do you really want anything? I'm off in twenty minutes, and I've got a backlog of work to get through."

"Housework, I suppose," Myrna said with a faint smile. "I don't have to do that anymore, but I remember…" Her face closed up. "If you should change your mind, about leaving, I mean," she added solemnly, "I could manage twenty thousand."

"I've told you. You can't buy me."

Myrna got up from her chair, so small and frail that she seemed almost childlike. "I never could. It was the one thing about you that I admired." She smiled hesitantly. "I was like you…once." She picked up her purse, clutching it like a talisman, her silver hair neat and clean. She met Meredith's eyes with a quiet, searching gaze and actually winced. "You still love him, don't you?" she blurted out, and then quickly looked away from the pain that washed over Meredith's composed features. "That makes it so much worse…."

She was gone before Meredith had time to consider the enigmatic statement. She'd never considered Myrna to be perceptive, but she'd certainly missed the mark this time. Meredith didn't love Cy. She hated him. She kept telling herself that all the way home, right until Mr. Smith showed up on her doorstep with his arms full of documents.

"That's it, that's it, kill me with paperwork, bury me in statistics," she moaned as he deposited the stack of files in his attaché case onto her neat coffee table.

"You're the one who wanted to be Ms. Executive," he reminded her.

"So I did. How's my baby?"

"Missing you, of course." He handed her a sealed envelope. "Don said to give you that. It's the progress report on the proxies he's been obtaining. And he said to tell you that Harden had been tipped off royally about the takeover bid. He knows it's coming, and from where."

Meredith knew her face had gone white. "Does he know about me?"

"How could he?" Mr. Smith replied. "Kip Tennison is just a name to him, as it is to most other people. Nobody knows what you look like except family."

"I hope you're right," she murmured. She unsealed the envelope and read over the list of names and proxies that Don had managed to obtain. "I'll write a note for you to take back to Don. I got the outstanding family stock vote from Cy's great-uncle. I think that's going to put us over the top. What I need now is for Don to approach one of Cy's board members directly—the one named Bill. He's working against Cy. Don knows the directors. I don't dare stick my nose in just yet."

Mr. Smith was fingering the attaché case, his green eyes pensive. "When's that annual meeting?"

"Two weeks away," Meredith replied. She pulled a pen and paper from her purse and jotted down a quick note to Don. "Mrs. Harden has been doing her best to buy me off," she mused, glancing up at him. "Her latest offer was twenty thousand."

"Chicken feed, but she doesn't know it, does she?"

She shook her head, signing the note absently. "I almost feel sorry for her. When Cy finds out what she's done, he'll never forgive her."

Mr. Smith took the note she handed him in its envelope. He stared at the handwriting on it without speaking.

"You don't approve, Mr. Smith," she said, her gray eyes narrowing as she almost read his mind.

"No." He lifted his eyes to hers. "Revenge is stupid and expensive. Wasted emotion. So you force his mother to tell all and destroy her relationship with her son. You take his company away from him and send him packing. Then what?"

She frowned. "What do you mean, then what?"

"After you bring him to his knees, what do you do?"

"I have the satisfaction of seeing him and his mother paid back for what they did to my life!" she raged.

"You didn't help?" he countered, watching the shock in her eyes. "You ran. You didn't try to defend yourself, you didn't try to fight the old lady. You didn't give Harden the chance to learn about Blake, or to regret what he'd done. I'm not saying Henry didn't help you put up the smokescreen, but he had ulterior motives for not wanting Harden to find you."

"I tried to tell Cy," she said, turning away. "He wouldn't listen."

"His mother wouldn't let him. I can understand why you want her brought down, but it seems to me that Harden is pretty much a victim himself."

"Cy?!" she asked coldly.

"He's got a five-year-old son that he doesn't know about," he told her flatly. "When he finds out, if he finds out, you and old lady Harden had both better look for a deep hole to hide in."

Meredith hadn't considered that part of it. She tried to imagine how Cy was going to feel and realized Mr. Smith was right. The company takeover was going to be the least of her worries if he learned about the pregnancy that had sent her into Henry Tennison's arms. The fact that Blake had been legally adopted by Henry was going to be another fly in the soup.

"You'd better do some hard and fast thinking before you get your pretty head in too deep to pull out," Mr. Smith told her gently. "If you want the company so much, take it. But the past is better left alone, unless you really want to sacrifice Blake on the altar of revenge. Or don't you think Harden would fight you with everything he's got once he discovers he has a son?"

Of course he would. She paled. Cy would be a force to reckon with, and he had influence and contacts. In court, if he could prove his paternity, there was the faintest chance that he might take Blake away from her. Myrna would do her best to help. She'd thought she had the edge, but Mr. Smith was convincing her that she might have opened up a very deadly can of worms with her little scheme.

"What am I going to do?" she asked, foundering for the first time in memory.

He moved closer, his green eyes oddly sympathetic as he looked down at her. "Get out, while you can."

She shook her head. "I've set the wheels in motion. I can't stop now. It's too late."

"Then pull back to a safe distance, at least. Let the past die."

The thought made her sick. The past was Cy, and she was going to have to leave Billings and go back to a life that was nothing more than the acquisition of more wealth and power. It had been enough when revenge had driven her. Now, it seemed to loom ahead like a vast emptiness, with only Blake to keep her sane.

She put a hand to her forehead.

"I've upset you. I'm sorry." He touched her blond hair gently, something he rarely did. He wasn't demonstrative. "Kip, I don't want to see you destroyed. You've underestimated Harden all down the line. He's nobody's fool. Hedge your bets. Get out."

She smiled sadly. "Okay. I can use the proxies to force him into giving me those mineral rights—threaten him with the takeover and ram it through if I have to. But I'll leave Myrna alone."

"Good girl." He packed the attaché case. "People pay for their mistakes," he said gently. "It's built into the system. Hurt somebody and you get hurt."

"Does the hurting ever stop?" she wondered, remembering her hopeless love for Cy. Even now, all he wanted from her was sex, not love. He'd never loved her.

"I don't know," Mr. Smith replied. He looked at her in a way she didn't see before he turned to the door. "I don't guess so. Eat more. You're losing weight."

"I'm tired," she said, crossing her arms over her chest. "Two jobs at once would reduce most people to spare bones."

"You could quit the restaurant job."

"And give up minimum wage? Bite your tongue!"

He chuckled at her impish look. Sometimes she looked much younger than her twenty-four years. "Okay. No more advice. I'll be in touch."

"Thanks, Mr. Smith."

He shrugged. "You're the only family I've got. I have to look out for you."

He left, and she had to fight tears. He cared about her. That was the only reason she hadn't cut him dead when he started pointing out the folly in what she was attempting.

She closed the door and turned back inside, her stomach clenching as she began to contemplate all the consequences she could face because of what she was doing. She couldn't lose Blake, surely not! The thought ate at her insides. She knew how ruthless Cy could be. He didn't mind hitting below the belt. Myrna had taught him how to do that.

Ironically, her threat to ruin Myrna could ricochet and destroy her own life. If Myrna realized it, there would be no stopping her. The older woman might feel guilt and regret, but it wouldn't even slow her down if Meredith threatened her relationship with her son. Of course, she reminded herself, Myrna didn't know about Blake. She wasn't sure there was a child.

She began to calm down. And there was always another country. She could take Blake anywhere in the world to live, someplace where Cy couldn't find them. Yes. She didn't have to worry about custody suits as long as she had the financial means to fight back, and she did. Henry had made sure of it.

Meredith smiled in relief. She'd just panicked. She could pull it off. Everything would be all right.

She worked through the night, grateful for the paperwork

that kept her mind off her worries. She phoned home the next day to speak to Blake and went to bed late, only to toss and turn and hardly sleep.

It was almost noon before she woke up Sunday. Frequently when she was at home in Chicago, she took Blake to church. But she hadn't attended services since she came to Billings. There was something vaguely disturbing about going into a church when she was taking vengeance into her own hands.

She had made a pot of coffee and was just tying a ribbon to hold back her disheveled blond hair when she heard a knock at the back door. Smoothing down her pink track suit with nervous hands, she stood still, wondering if she could refuse to answer it. But someone knocked again, and again, and she knew who it was before she opened it.

"It's Sunday," Cy said with a cruel twist of his lips. "You don't go to church, I gather?" He'd obviously just been, because he was wearing a very handsome dark charcoal vested suit with his dress Stetson and boots.

"Isn't your mother with you?" she asked.

"I sent her home with one of her church friends for lunch," he said. His dark eyes slid over her with pure malice. "Aren't you going to offer me some coffee?"

"Coffee's all that's available," she said, making her voice firm even though her knees felt like rubber. She stood aside. "Come on in."

His eyes went around the neat kitchen quietly while she poured his coffee and placed it on the table with hers.

"Looking for something?" she asked politely.

He took off his Stetson and sprawled on the chair, elegant even at ease as he studied her across the table. "Not really. You're a good housekeeper. You always were. Mary taught you well, didn't she?"

"She taught me how to cook, too."

He lifted his coffee cup with a long sigh. There were new lines in his face, new silver threads in his dark hair.

"You look worn," she said without thinking.

He laughed bitterly. "I don't sleep." His dark eyes pinned hers. "All I think about is you in my bed."

Her jaw set. "Lust," she said through her teeth. "That's all it is, and you know it."

A rough sigh passed his lips as he fumbled a cigarette out of a pack and lit it, waiting for her to fetch him an ashtray. He pocketed his lighter without looking at it, but Meredith recognized it with a start. It was one she'd given him while they were together six years ago—a cheap one, because she hadn't much money then. Amazing that he still used it, even if he seemed totally unaware of its significance.

"You still blush," he said quietly, studying the faint ruddy color on her cheekbones. "You were so shy, in the old days. All wide-eyed innocence and generosity."

"Ignorant and overstimulated," she corrected with a cool smile. "Habits you were kind enough to cure."

"Sarcasm doesn't suit you," he said.

"You'd be amazed how lethal a weapon it can be in the right quarters," she returned, and something in the set of her head, in the flash of her eyes, caught his attention and stilled him.

"Sometimes you become an anachronism," he said absently with narrowed eyes. "I get the impression that I'm not seeing you at all."

She laughed. "Do you really? Perhaps I've just changed."

"Changed, surely. In ways I can't quite comprehend." He blew out a cloud of smoke and stared at her. "I never told you about my father," he said out of the blue. "He was only two years older than my mother, a shrewd businessman with an eye to the main chance, as they say. There was nothing he wouldn't do to make money. He'd come up without it, and he was determined to die a rich man." Cy crossed his long, powerful legs, watching Meredith's face. "You don't understand why I'm telling you this. You will. My father thought nothing of sleeping with an executive's wife to have some leverage with her husband. He'd use any methods, regardless of how unscrupulous, to get ahead. What his grasping philandering did to my mother didn't bother him."

"She stayed with him," she pointed out.

"In her day, women of wealth didn't work. Divorce was a stigma. I don't think she loved him. Her family was poor, and his prospects caused them to push her at him when they saw he was interested. Apparently she was as susceptible to his line as other women, because I was born a month premature."

That was shocking. Somehow Meredith couldn't imagine the very straitlaced Myrna Harden doing anything as unsuitable as getting pregnant out of wedlock.

"My father had one affair after another all his life, and he died in one of his lovers' arms," he said bitterly. "Everyone knew it. The scandal very nearly destroyed my mother's life. What there was left of it, after the damage he did to her pride during almost twenty years."

Meredith stared at him without seeing him. She wondered how it would feel to have a husband who was totally without morals, and she knew suddenly how it would affect her. She'd have become like Myrna, all ice on the outside, totally removed from emotion.

"That's why you've never married," Meredith said suddenly, looking straight at Cy.

He shrugged. "Not really. I've never found anyone I wanted to spend my life with," he said with deadly intent, watching her. "But I have learned the hard way that fidelity doesn't exist," he said with a mocking smile. "I don't think I could settle down, even if I didn't find the very thought of commitment repulsive."

She lowered her eyes to his broad chest. "I see."

"I never talked to you about this, in the old days," he said. "You were such a child, little one. Too young to comprehend how cruel life can be. You wanted happily ever after."

"While you only wanted sex without any strings," she replied with weary cynicism. "How uncooperative of me. That was why you proposed, of course," she said, startling him. "Because you knew I'd stop seeing you if I thought all you wanted was a quick affair."

He started to speak and couldn't. He turned his attention to his cigarette. "You were special. More special than you knew."

"But you had nothing to give me." She finished her coffee and fingered the cup absently. "I've blamed you all these years for the way you treated me, for making me nothing but a sex object. I don't suppose in all that time I ever really tried seeing things from your point of view." That was true. Myrna had opened her eyes to the truth. She lifted her eyes to his. "I was just a backwoods country girl with no breeding, no manners, and, it must have seemed to you, no morals. I wouldn't have fit into your world in a million years."

"Any more than you would now," he said bluntly. "I'm sorry, I didn't mean to sound superior. But you have no idea of my lifestyle, of how I live on a daily basis. You were warm and sweet and I wanted you. I still want you. That won't ever stop. But I'm no more oriented toward marriage than I was six years ago. I don't want ties or permanence. I want my freedom more than I want anything else. Even," he added quietly, "more than I want you."

"I understand."

"No arguments?"

She shrugged. "I have nothing to give you, either, Cy," she

said in a soft, sad tone. "Nothing except what we had the other day, and that's self-defeating and futile. I'm too old for that kind of live-for-today relationship."

"Yes." His mind tightened, like his body, at the exquisite memory of it.

They didn't speak for several minutes. Meredith felt drained of all emotion. He'd stolen her thunder. She didn't know what to say. He'd just told her that he felt nothing for her but a lust that he was putting in the past, where it belonged, and that he could never settle down. She'd known, but hope died hard. Her secret dreams of a family that included Cy and Blake, were dying in her eyes.

Cy saw the light go out of her and felt guilty. He was fighting a rearguard action against her, just as he had six years ago. She could take him over, own him, with less effort than she realized. But he had to ward it off, to prevent it, because Meredith could become his life. He'd lost her once and barely survived. He knew he could never let her go again. It was so much better not to start things he couldn't finish. She could never fit into his world.

"I wanted you to understand," he said suddenly, lifting his eyes. "I shouldn't have forced you back into my bed that afternoon we went out to the battlefield. I had no right."

That was new, to have him feel guilt at seducing her. He'd never seemed to be aware before that it was seduction.

"It wasn't all your fault," she said honestly, her eyes avoiding his. "I wanted you very much."

"An aberration we both share," he said. "But one with no future. I should never have touched you."

"It takes two." She leaned back and looked at him, feeling vaguely guilty herself about what she was planning for him. Her vengeance, so sweet only a month ago, was turning more sour by the minute. "Give your mother a message for me," she said.

He scowled. "What?"

"Tell her she doesn't have anything to worry about," she replied. "Don't ask," she added when he started to speak. "It's something personal. Just tell her. She'll understand." She got to her feet, looking elegant and somehow fragile. "Good-bye, Cy."

He stood up, too, towering over her. He was hurting in ways he remembered so well from the past. His mouth twisted. "Paradise lost," he said huskily, letting his eyes slide over her body with aching need. "I'll regret you all my life. But to invite that madness a second time is insanity."

"Yes." She went with him to the door and held it open. She didn't look up. "I…won't be in town much longer."

"Where will you go?" he asked dully.

"I haven't decided."

"To the man waiting in Chicago?" he taunted, his temper kindling at the thought of some other man giving her what he couldn't—marriage, children.

The sarcasm touched her on the raw. "Why not?" she asked. "There are men in the world who want permanence."

"Fools," he said.

"No. Just ordinary men, who are tired of living alone."

"I don't have to be alone, honey," he said with a cool smile. "All I have to do is snap my fingers."

"I know." She searched his hard face. "As long as the money lasts, that's right. But who would sit with you when you were sick, if there was no money? Who would read to you if you went blind, hold your hand if you were dying?"

His eyes closed briefly, and he could hardly stand the pain. Meredith would have done all those things, because she'd loved him. But he couldn't, he wasn't capable of returning that kind of feeling. He didn't dare….

"I have to go," he said harshly. He didn't look back. He

walked straight to his car and got in, starting it viciously. Meredith watched him drive away before she closed the door. She should be grateful to him, she supposed, for making the break for her. Now she could get on with her plans, with her life, without dreaming any more impossible dreams. Now she saw exactly how impossible they'd been.

She needed desperately to get away for a day or two, and there were business meetings with clients that she couldn't put off. She phoned Mrs. Dade at home and begged for Monday off to see about the sale of Great-Aunt Mary's house. It wasn't the truth, but it was enough to get her out of work.

Minutes later she phoned for the Tennison jet to be sent out to collect her. She put on the wig and the expensive coat two hours later, called a taxi, and was waiting at the airport when the chartered jet came in for a landing. That afternoon she was safely home, with Blake wrapped tight in her arms. She had time, at least a little time, to come to grips with Cy's final rejection. She was going to use it to her best advantage.

CHAPTER TEN

BLAKE SAT in Meredith's lap that night while she watched the money segment on the twenty-four-hour news channel, her eyes keen on the stock market report and the company stock quotes. Her son. She felt warm and feminine just looking down at him. Cy had said that he didn't want children. That was a pity. He'd never know the joy of seeing generations of his family in Blake's face or of being loved by the child. Meredith adored him, now more than ever. He was all she'd ever have of Cy.

"Mommy, why do you watch that boring stuff?" he asked.

She started at the interruption to her thoughts and laughed. "My darling, that boring stuff helps me keep the edge on the competition, like my *Wall Street Journal* and the *Forbes* magazine and *Fortune* magazine I subscribe to."

"Are you a businessman, Mommy?" he persisted.

"I'm a businesswoman," she corrected. "You know that."

"I guess so. I got a hundred in spelling," he volunteered. "But I throwed a block at Betty, and I had to go to the office and see Mr. Dodd."

She whistled. "Did he call here?"

"He called Mr. Smith," Blake replied. His eyes twinkled. "Mr. Smith said two bad words and told him that if Betty hit me again, I should throw another block at her. He told Mr. Dodd that if he fussed at me again for fighting back, he'd go and feed Mr. Dodd a knuckle sandwich. Mr. Dodd was *very* nervous the next day."

Meredith had to smother a laugh. Mr. Smith had that effect on most normal people. "You shouldn't hit girls, all the same."

"Why not, if they hit me first?"

The phone rang, sparing her an answer, and Smith stuck his head in the door. "It's McGee. He wants to know if you'll be in the office tomorrow."

"Tell him yes, and ask him... Never mind, I'll ask him myself," she murmured, putting Blake gently aside. She ruffled his hair. "Back in a minute, sport."

"Sure," he said on a long sigh, knowing she wouldn't.

She had McGee, her first vice president, set up appointments with her officers and several clients, determined to make the most of her time in town.

The next morning she was at the office before it officially opened, using her master key. She looked every inch the lady executive, from her dark suit and white silk blouse to her no-frills black pumps and leather bag. Her hair was in a neat chignon, very little makeup and small earrings completing her executive look. Dressing frivolously or in a flashy manner had a way of undermining a woman's authority. She'd taken a course on how to dress and how to behave in predominantly male company. It had worked. Nobody thought Kip Tennison was a marshmallow. Except, perhaps, one gentleman back in Montana, who was shortly to be disabused of that impression.

Meredith sat down behind her huge oak desk and read through the latest mining reports on molybdenum and its enhanced military uses thanks to a new discovery in superconductivity. She smiled. This was a good time to get back into production; the corporation had given up its mines during a glut of moly. It had been a good business move at the time, but now was a good time to buy more. Those mineral leases of Cy's would stand the corporation in good stead with its military hardware contracts. And with the situation in the Middle East, it wouldn't hurt to step up domestic oil production and fund more research in the corporate labs on alternative fuel sources.

As she worked, fielding telephone calls that came in two a minute, or so it seemed, her mind wandered to Cy's little speech. He was giving her up because she couldn't hold her own in his world. She permitted herself a tiny smile. What would Cy say when he learned that he might not fit into her world?

The possibility that his refusal to budge on those mineral leases might require a complete takeover of his company began to bother her. Was she only doing it out of revenge? Was she doing the right thing for the corporation or for herself? And if she had to force Cy to give up the company he'd worked all his life for, could she live with it? Don had said that she could get those leases elsewhere, and she probably could. But what he wasn't considering was the cost of production. In Montana, where the corporation owned land and had processing facilities, mineral leases would involve very little cost for transportation. The railroad ran through their holdings and to the leased properties she wanted, and back to the processing plant. If she mined moly in any other state, it would require either cutting another company in on the profits to get the mineral processed or shipping it to one of their processing plants in Montana. That cost would put them in the red. Perhaps Don didn't know it, but Meredith did. She'd left nothing to chance in her preliminary examination of the project.

No, Don was wrong, she decided. She had no choice but to proceed. She'd spent too much money already to back out now.

McGee, a tall, balding man with a brain like a steel trap, knocked briefly and walked in, closing the door gently behind him.

"How long can we keep you?" he asked bluntly.

"Today," she said. "Perhaps tomorrow, if I call in sick. Never mind," she added when he frowned and started to ask why she had to call in sick. "I've got clients coming in at eleven, one, two, three, and four. What do you want?"

"To know if you've realized how much time your brother-in-law spends at this office and what he's pulling out of your files."

"Do you realize exactly what you're saying?"

"Certainly. I'm saying that Don Tennison is working against you at every opportunity. You've put a weapon into his hands with this Harden Properties fight, and he's going to blow you up with it if you're not careful."

Meredith's gray eyes narrowed. So her suspicions weren't totally unfounded. "Tell me more."

"He's belittled you for your absence, told clients you're on holiday, diverted queries to his own office, bribed your old secretary to come to work for him, and in his free time he's been cultivating your executives at cocktail parties. And he's been going down the line on those Harden Properties stockholders, talking to each one, not just the ones you asked him to approach."

She let out a whispering breath. "Toward what end, I wonder?"

"I think you know," McGee replied grimly. "We think he's going to ask for a no-confidence vote at your next directors meeting. And he may very well use this fight with Harden Properties to do it."

"Will he get a no-confidence vote?" she persisted.

"Not from me. Your profit record is hard to ignore, even if

these mineral leases are iffy. I'm with you. So are five others. But Don's got a lot of weight with some of the rest, and he's throwing it around. Watch out."

"I'll do that." She stood up, gazing out the window at the misty city. "The mineral leases are necessary, you know," she said. "I've been working on a memo to explain my position. I'll leave it with you. Make sure all the directors get a copy. I don't want anyone thinking I'm on a revenge kick." She turned to face him. "I had reasons to want Cy Harden ousted. But I've dealt with them. Now it's business. Strictly business. He's refused me mineral leases I have to have in order to fill upcoming military contract obligations. The cost of transporting ore from other states to our processing plants would be exorbitant if I have to go outside Montana for it. Besides that, Harden has no legitimate reason for refusing me the leases, and his directors are aware of it. I can push hard enough to make him let go of them. And I'm going to, Don or no Don."

McGee grinned. "Good for you. I never believed you were into vengeance. You're too level-headed."

Thank God he didn't know it all. It was true, though, that she'd lost her taste for vengeance. She'd realized how much she had to lose, and she felt no real desire to see Cy or Myrna humbled anymore. She just wanted it over. She was tired of the deception, of hiding her true colors under a blanket of assumed poverty and deprivation. It was time to start fighting in the open. Besides all that, she was tired. So tired. Tired to the bone.

"You've lost a little weight, haven't you?" he asked, frowning.

"Probably. I always fall off in cold weather. Bring me those figures on the Camfield Computers merger, will you?"

McGee grimaced. "I can't. Don has them."

Her eyebrows lifted. "But we're supplying him with support people. Surely we have every right to access the particulars of the contract."

"I'll see what I can do," McGee said heavily. "You don't realize how much he's involved in everything we do here. Your absence, even if it was that necessary, has given him just the opportunity he needed to come in here and stick his nose into our business."

She caught her breath. It was a web she and the people who worked for her were being snared in, and Don had woven it very skillfully. "In that case," she said stiffly, "suppose we find out just exactly what he knows and bait a trap for him."

McGee brightened. "Tell me more."

"I hope you're still single."

His eyebrows arched. "I beg your pardon?"

"Are you?"

"Well, yes…."

"And is Don's executive secretary still sweet on you?"

He paled. "Oh, my God, you can't ask me to do that!"

"Yes, I can," she said easily. "Make reservations at the ritziest club you can find and get her talking. She'll tell you everything she knows."

"That's not ethical," he muttered.

"No, it isn't," she agreed. "Neither is Don sneaking in here and trying to kick me out of my own company. Fire with fire. Do it."

He threw up his hands. "All right. What else?"

She smiled slowly and folded her arms across her breasts. "Make an alternate list of those stockholders in Harden Properties and see every one of them who lives in Chicago personally. Wine and dine them, show them what profits we can produce for them. But don't tell Don if you get their proxies. I'll do the same thing in Billings. Find one other director you can trust and assign him the other accessible shareholders. It's going to take some fast work, but I think we can swing it, despite Don's attempts to interfere. Are you with me?"

"What a stupid question," he said. "Here I am, willing to sacrifice myself to that Sanderson woman on the altar of corporate intrigue, and you can question my loyalty! Have you *seen* her?"

Meredith had. "I admire your courage," she said, laying it on with a trowel. "We'll have a medal struck, for bravery above and beyond the call of duty."

"No thanks. I have some awful ideas about where you'd pin it," he muttered. He thought about what he'd said and flushed. "Anything else?" he asked when she grinned.

"Not a thing. Thanks, McGee."

"Any time."

Meredith spent the rest of the day talking on the phone to clients and colleagues, closing deals, agreeing to clauses the legal department insisted on, signing endless letters, answering inquiries and worrying about Don.

Blake was already in bed by the time she arrived home. She'd forgotten to phone Mrs. Dade, too, worse luck. Well, she could do that tomorrow. She fell into bed and was asleep before her head hit the pillow.

The next day was a repeat of the first. She convinced Mrs. Dade that she was dying of a virus and pleaded with the woman not to send anyone around to see about her, because it was contagious. She had her day, plus another, now that she had an excuse. Cy was still out of town, from what she'd been able to extract from the woman. So far, so good.

But she was worn to the nub by the end of the third day. It didn't help that Don stopped by the house that evening to get her signature on yet another contract that should have been processed by her department.

"You're doing a lot of this, aren't you?" she asked when she'd scrawled her signature on the contract.

"A lot of what?" he asked innocently.

"Negotiating contracts on domestic enterprises."

He shrugged. "You haven't been here," he said uncomfortably. "I was just trying to expedite matters."

"The Harden board meets next week. I'll expect you out the day it convenes," she said firmly. "Don't disappoint me. And in the meantime," she added, "anything that comes up on the domestic front is to be brought to my attention, by my people. I will expect to be consulted, even if it's only on new toilet paper for the janitorial staff of some second-rate computer supply firm. Is that clear?"

Don had had few opportunities to see Meredith in fighting form. He felt himself shiver at the ice in her voice and in her eyes. She looked surprisingly like Henry in a temper, and he had a brief qualm about what he was plotting. At least, thank God, she had no idea what he was trying to do. He had guarantees for several of Harden's company proxies, and he was going to get more. In fact, he'd already talked to Cy Harden, tipping him off about the takeover and offering his help. Cy didn't know about Meredith. Don hadn't dared divulge her connection, but Harden had readily agreed to cooperate. That would be his downfall. Don had every intention of grabbing those proxies and ousting Harden. He'd have control of the company, with his own people in position, of the mineral leases, and when he could show that Meredith had done it all for revenge, he'd have Meredith's scalp as well. He'd end up with the whole corporation, as he would have before Meredith came on the scene. All he had to do was keep Meredith, and Harden, in the dark for a little bit longer.

"Oh, it's clear," Don agreed. He smiled. "I'll try not to overstep again."

"I rather doubt that," she said. And she didn't smile. Don left shortly thereafter, with a strained atmosphere between them for the first time in memory.

Blake wailed when she announced that she had to go back to Billings.

She wiped away the tears. "I'm almost through," she said. "You and Mr. Smith are coming back with me," she added. "We're leaving first thing in the morning."

His face brightened. "I can come, too?!" he exclaimed.

She hadn't meant to take him out there. She was afraid that Myrna Harden or some neighbor might see him. She was afraid that Cy might see him. But Blake was upset. She couldn't leave him crying for her. It was just as well. The board meeting was Monday. She'd go to work for two more days, and then she'd spring her little surprise on Cy and his board. And, subsequently, on Don. She'd done her homework. Now she was going to stand the test.

Hours later, she and Mr. Smith, with Tiny in a carrying case, and Blake boarded the Tennison jet with their bags. The bait was set. Now she had to wait for the quarry to take it.

CHAPTER ELEVEN

THE END OF THE WEEK dragged. Meredith spent two days at the restaurant and then returned to Great-Aunt Mary's house in the evenings, where Mr. Smith was organizing the meals and housekeeping and watching over Blake. She'd taken him out of kindergarten for the week, so that they could be together.

Hiding Blake and Smith at the house was the hard thing. The rental car had to be parked nearby in a neighbor's driveway, with permission. Blake could only play outside in the backyard, which had a high privacy fence. He couldn't even be seen in the window. That put a strain on things, but Meredith was so delighted to have him with her that she managed it with a minimum of stress.

Meanwhile, she worked in the restaurant and at the desk in the library at night, coordinating what McGee found out from Ms. Sanderson with the information she gleaned from other sources. Cy was being sold down the river by Don and a director named Bill, but that was going to have to wait. Right now those mineral leases were too important for diversions of any kind. She had to work fast, to get all the proxies in before the board of directors met Monday night.

She called her office from Mary's house during her lunch breaks, and by sitting down at her desk in the evenings, she got through at least half her workload. She phoned clients at home at night to advise them of progress on various projects, then talked and read stories to Blake. Meredith and her son were enjoying a closeness they'd never really had, in between her work. The pace in Billings was slower, and she enjoyed the feeling of time it gave her. She wondered vaguely what it would be like to live here, to raise Blake in this wonderful place, to let him grow up where she had. Her childhood had been a happy one, in most ways. The death of her parents before she started school had been painful, but Great-Aunt Mary and Great-Uncle Raven-Walking had been very special substitutes. They'd loved and protected her, and she missed them even now.

Cy had been out of town, thank God, as long as she had. He still hadn't come around by the time she reported back to work. But Myrna showed up Saturday, and Meredith had to force herself to go to the woman's table and pretend nothing was wrong.

Myrna didn't look as if she were gloating. She couldn't quite meet Meredith's eyes, either. "Why did you change your mind?" she asked.

"Because Cy doesn't want me anymore," Meredith said bluntly. She couldn't very well admit her own fears about what might happen if Cy found out about Blake.

Myrna looked up at her. "He's brooding," she said. "It's been much worse this past week. He looks at me, but he doesn't see me. He doesn't hear what I say to him." She gnawed her lower lip. "He said…that he told you about his…father."

So that was it. Myrna was afraid that Meredith might talk about it, and damage the oh, so unblemished Harden name.

"You needn't worry," Meredith said coldly. "Your family skeletons aren't of enough interest to me to gossip about them."

Myrna frowned slightly and looked up.

"Wasn't that why you came?" she asked the older woman. "To make sure I didn't say anything?"

Myrna started to speak, but before she could, Cy entered the restaurant with his redhead on his arm, forcing himself to look infatuated as he led Lara to the table where his mother sat. Myrna looked as surprised as Meredith did, but Meredith wasn't watching the older woman's face and didn't see it.

"So this is where you are," Cy said curtly, glaring down at his mother with barely a reluctant glance at Meredith. "You were to have lunch at the house with Lara and me. It's waiting."

"Oh!" Myrna was flustered. It was the first time she'd ever forgotten a dinner engagement. Of course, this Lara person Cy was squiring around was hardly an improvement on Meredith. The woman was nobody's idea of high society. She had money, true enough, but she had no breeding and a tongue like a rapier. Myrna heartily disliked her. She couldn't prevent that from showing, either, as she deferred to Cy and allowed him to half drag her from the restaurant.

Meredith watched them go with a sinking heart. Well, she'd known he was seeing Lara, why should she let it hurt? She had much more important things on her mind.

She pleaded a headache and left the restaurant. It didn't matter now if Mrs. Dade fired her. Today was her last day anyway. She'd only kept the job to allay suspicions at this critical time anyway.

BACK AT THE ELEGANT Harden home, Cy seated Lara next to his mother and then slid onto a chair himself. The maids served, and Cy glared as Lara complained about the weak coffee.

"Why were you at the restaurant?" he asked his mother suspiciously. "Still trying to protect me?"

Myrna faltered. "No. I...I..."

"I thought we were going to the penthouse for lunch," Lara muttered at Cy, ignoring the innuendo around her. "And you didn't mention coming here until you saw your mother's car in town."

Myrna was taken aback. So she hadn't forgotten. She wondered what Cy's motives were and wondered if confronting Meredith with Lara had played a part.

"Never mind, baby," Cy told the redhead. He glared across at his mother. "Answer me. Why were you there? What are you and Meredith hiding?"

"I just want a salad," Lara told one of the maids haughtily, glaring at the beef and potatoes and beans in bowls on the spotless linen tablecloth. "With blue cheese dressing, on the side. I don't want it on the salad. And bring me a Perrier to drink."

"You'll starve on that," Cy remarked quietly.

"You'll get fat," Lara countered. "And beef is bad for you. You shouldn't eat it."

He was gritting his teeth. "You've forgotten that I still own a ranch?"

Lara bristled. "How cruel. I'll bet you brand the poor cattle. I belong to several animal rights organizations—"

"Not now," he said firmly, and the threat in his dark eyes stopped Lara in midsentence. "Besides, I won't get fat eating lean cuts of beef. I'm not a growing boy anymore."

"Oh, you are at times," Lara purred outrageously.

Myrna looked aghast.

Cy looked at Lara with banked-down fury. He hadn't meant to bring her here. He hadn't really meant to take her by the restaurant. He'd wanted Meredith to think that she was having an affair with him, but it wasn't true. He hadn't touched a woman since Meredith came back to Billings. He couldn't. But there was no way he could admit that now, even if he was bitterly regretting what he'd said to Meredith last Sunday. All he'd thought about since was how he was going to feel when she walked out of his life again. Bringing Lara to the restaurant was a last-ditch attempt to smoke out Meredith's feelings, to see if she still cared despite the way he'd hurt her. One sign, one indication of her interest, and he was ready to put aside his misgivings and give their relationship a real chance. But Meredith hadn't seemed to notice, or care, that Lara was with him.

His thoughts were interrupted by his mother's icy glare. "I have to see about the invitations to that charity tea I'm giving," Myrna said stiffly, rising. "Enjoy your lunch, Cy. I'll…see you again sometime, I hope, Lara," she lied, her eyes troubled as she left them there.

Cy watched his mother leave with mixed emotions. "I wish to God I knew what was going on."

"I guess I embarrassed her," Lara said on a laugh. "Doesn't she know you sleep with women?" she asked Cy bluntly.

"I don't sleep with you, and you damned well know it," he said, his tone cold and threatening. He got up. "I'll take you home."

"For heaven's sake, I just said…!" Lara protested as he grasped her arm.

"Let's go," he muttered.

FOR THE REST OF THE DAY, Meredith worried about Myrna Harden's visit. She wondered what the older woman had been about to say to her. But it no longer mattered. All she wanted to do was spring her trap on Cy and get out of Billings. She'd already wasted too much energy and time on a plan that hardly added to her credibility with the firm. Henry would have been ashamed of her for letting personal feelings interfere with the running of his business, despite the fact that she'd come to her senses. But her lapse could still provide Don with enough ammunition to take her on at her own board meeting and win control of the domestic branch.

She phoned him that Sunday night. "You are coming out for the meeting tomorrow?" she asked.

"That's the plan. I've got those proxies, and I've been the rounds of the directors. I'm cautiously optimistic that we can carry a vote."

She hoped that he didn't plan to sell her out, and Cy with her, at the meeting. She had to trust to luck on that matter. "I'll settle for the threat," she said. "If we can use the vote as leverage to get those mineral leases, force Cy into agreeing, I'll be satisfied."

There was a long pause. "I thought the whole point of the thing was to absorb Harden Properties?"

"I don't really care that much about taking over the operation, not if it's going to mean sacrificing half our domestic profits to accomplish it. The mineral rights are all we really need, and from what I can find out, Cy has the confidence of his directors. Even if I gain control, I won't be able to oust him and install my own managerial people." She paused to let that sink in. It might give him pause, hold him off until she could decide how to proceed. "Besides that, his company is in a good financial position to resist a takeover. It's operating in the black. The shares are commanding a good market price, and his reputation is keeping the company solvent."

"You've done your homework," Don remarked. "Yes, all that is true. And we'd have to go anywhere from twenty to thirty dollars a share over the market price in an offering to buy out the company. Hardly a sound financial move in our own present slump."

"I agree. But by expanding our mineral holdings, we could close the deficit and manage a tidy profit. There's a new use for molybdenum that our research people are sitting on right now. If we can get our hands on one mine, we stand to mop up when the demand hits. Moly production is at an all-time low right now, but the Concord Mining Company is still producing moly, and with the lease on that old Wellington property for which Harden Properties holds the mineral rights, we'd be sitting pretty."

"You're sure you want to go through with this, Kip?" Don asked quietly.

"No," she said. "But I've wasted too much time and energy to back off now. It's not a vendetta anymore, if that helps. I don't really have to have Cy Harden's head on a stick. I just want his molybdenum rights."

There was a pregnant pause. "In that case, things may work out very well. I'll be out there tomorrow. Can I bring you anything?"

"No thanks. I'll see you then."

The next day went by so slowly that she was actually seeing the seconds pass.

She wandered out into the backyard, where Mr. Smith and Blake were tossing a ball in the cold wind.

"Isn't it great here, Mommy?" Blake asked, laughing. "A real backyard! And Mr. Smith says there's a park. Can we go there?"

"Not today," Meredith said without smiling. "In a day or two."

"Aw, gee," he muttered. "Okay."

She smiled at his annoyance. He didn't understand that she couldn't risk having him seen just yet. Cy didn't know about him. She had to find a way to get him out of Billings before Myrna spilled the beans. But right now, she had priorities.

She glanced at her watch, grimacing. Don would be here in less than an hour. She had things to do.

She went upstairs and laid out her clothes meticulously. She couldn't afford to be anything less than elegant tonight, self-possessed and businesslike. But her mouth was dry and her legs felt like rubber.

The atmosphere became a little strained when Don arrived, especially when Tiny, Mr. Smith's big green iguana, came padding into the living room to see who the newcomer was.

"Why don't you make a hatband out of that thing?" Don muttered.

Mr. Smith picked up Tiny and let her sit on his shoulder, glaring at Don as he went upstairs with Blake to help him dress.

"Not a wise diplomatic move," Meredith mused, watching Don.

"I hate that thing," he replied tautly, glancing at his Rolex watch. "Shouldn't you be dressing?"

"I suppose so," she said reluctantly. "Funny, you get something you've always wanted, always waited for. And when the moment comes, it tastes like ashes."

Don glanced at her curiously. "It isn't as if you had a choice. Harden made it for you when he refused you the leases. I read your report," he added a little uncomfortably. "And I have to agree that it would be unproductive financially to pursue molybdenum anywhere but in Montana, where we have easy access to mineral processing."

She was taken aback. "I'm surprised."

He shrugged. "I know good business when I see it. You may have had less than laudable motives to start out, but you've got good business sense about acquisitions. Harden Properties would make a nice addition to our portfolio of companies."

"Yes, it would," she said, but she didn't mean it. She didn't really want Cy's company. Did Don? Her eyes narrowed. She'd have to keep an eye on him, a really close one. Maybe she owed Cy that, out of old memories if nothing else.

She showered and changed into a brand-new Guy Laroche tailored silk suit in a light blue, with a delicately embroidered silk blouse to match it. She wore leather pumps and put her hair in an elegant high coiffure, sweeping the blond mass back to her nape and securing it with combs. She looked in the mirror, approving the image.

Blake was wearing a suit, too, and he glared at her when she joined him downstairs, along with Mr. Smith in his chauffeur's uniform and a sedately suited Don Tennison.

"Why do I have to wear a suit, Mommy?" he muttered. "And I don't want to go out, I want to watch television."

"Sorry, my darling, but I need Mr. Smith and you can't stay here alone." She bent and kissed him warmly. "I'll make sure we have plenty of time together later. Okay?"

He grimaced. "Okay, I guess."

Don nodded as he studied her. "You'll do," he said. "Very much the Tennison executive."

She smiled. "I'm glad you approve." She glanced at her diamond-studded gold Rolex. "Well, it's almost seven," she said with butterflies flapping in her stomach. "Shall we go?"

"We might as well. You didn't want to be in on the beginning of the meeting, I gather?"

"No need," she replied. "As you said, they'll buzz our cellular phone when it's time for the vote. We'll present our proxies and make our bid and see what happens."

"Fair enough."

The Harden Properties building was ablaze with lights. Cy Harden and Myrna were already seated in the boardroom, recovering from a delicious buffet arranged by the caterer. It was good business, Cy's father had said, to feed men before you asked them to die for you on the corporate battlefield. So the policy had continued.

Cy was thinking about Meredith. Staying away from her had only made his hunger for her worse. He knew now that there was no question of substitutes. He wasn't going to let go of her. He was gearing up for action, and when he had this absurd takeover off his mind, he was going to do nothing but think up ways to get Meredith back.

He wanted to try again, to start over. But before he could go to Meredith's house and tell her that, urgent business had intervened, necessitating an out-of-town trip. When he got back, it was to learn that he was under the threat of a hostile takeover from Tennison International and that proxies had been obtained steadily, along with outstanding stock. The company was in a fragile position, and trying to block the takeover was absorbing all his spare time.

"Have you been able to reach Don Tennison?" he asked one of his directors.

"He'll be here," came the quiet reply. "Is he behind this takeover, do you think?"

"I don't know," Cy said instantly. He glanced at the man. "Do you have any idea who's after us?" he asked.

"Indeed I do. I think it's Henry Tennison's widow," the director said wryly. "She's one sharp lady. Runs the entire domestic branch of the corporation, and makes money hand over fist. They say Henry groomed her himself, had her tutored for years. She's as sharp as they come, and she's adamant about obtaining those mineral leases. We're standing in the way of her expansion plans, which could work to her disadvantage with her board of directors. They want results."

"I'm adamant about not giving them to her," he replied. "I'll be damned if I'm going to let some flighty rich widow come out here and tell me what to do with my own company."

"She's not flighty," the man murmured. "If she was, Don Tennison would be running the whole show. They say he stands in her shadow."

"Not a comfortable place to be," Cy mused.

The man nodded, turning to greet the rest of the board members as they filed in and took their places.

The big black limousine parked in front of the Harden Properties building waited until the cellular phone buzzed. Then Meredith kissed Blake's cheek and climbed out of the car.

She was wearing a cashmere coat, a heather-and-gray shade that enhanced her exquisite complexion. She walked just ahead of Don into the building toward the boardroom with his hand at her elbow.

"Nervous?" he asked as they paused at the closed door.

She looked up at him. "Not now," she replied. "Ironic, isn't it? I should be shaking, but it's suddenly very flat. I almost feel sorry for him."

He nodded. He opened the door and they walked in.

She could see Cy and his mother sitting at the head and right of the long board table, through a room filled with people and smoke. Cy noticed Meredith and his brows drew together, like his mother's.

The director who was speaking nodded toward Don. "There's a new order of business tonight," he said, directing his comments to Cy. "We've been approached by Tennison International with a takeover bid. I'll turn the floor over to Don Tennison, if there are no objections, and we'll hear his offer."

"No objections at all," Cy said with faint humor, his eyes going to Don with a conspiratorial gleam and then to Meredith with clear puzzlement. "But I'd like to know why we need a waitress tonight," he added, unreasonably irritated to find her in the company of Don Tennison. She was his!

Meredith was the only one, besides Myrna and Don, who got the joke. She didn't reply. She simply smiled at Cy, her mind whirling with his insults, his easy seduction, his treachery. The evening suddenly bubbled with evil possibilities, and she found herself looking forward to her role in it. Her anger at Myrna took second place to dishing out a little unpleasantness for Cy. God knew he deserved it. He'd hurt her enough in the past.

Cy clasped his big hands on the table in front of him when Meredith didn't reply, his gaze going to his directors. "It'll take more than a bid to unseat me, as you're damned well about to find out."

"Now, Cy, it isn't your leadership we're questioning," the director named Bill stammered, red-faced. "It's just that many of us feel you're being deliberately obstructive about these mineral leases."

"I'm entitled to be obstructive," Cy raged. "Or has it slipped your notice that Henry Tennison did everything in his power to put us out of business up until his death?"

Meredith hadn't known that. She glanced at Don, but he wouldn't meet her eyes.

"That has nothing to do with today's business," Bill continued, refusing to back down. "At least let the rest of us hear what Don has to say."

Cy leaned back in his chair, aware of his mother's curiosity as she stared at Meredith. He stared at her, too.

"I think I mentioned that this meeting is for stockholders only," he said, bitterly angry to find Meredith in the company of a Tennison, and dressed like that, in luxurious garments that she certainly couldn't afford on what he paid her to waitress at his restaurant. Was she involved with Don? Was he her friend in Chicago instead of Smith? It was puzzling, and he knew damned well Meredith didn't own any stock in Harden

Properties. So why was she here? "You're a little out of your element, aren't you, Meredith?" he asked coolly.

"Am I?" she murmured sweetly and with a smile.

"Is she with you?" Cy asked Don.

"It's rather the other way around, I'm afraid," Don said quietly. And he sat down, leaving Meredith to put her attaché case on the table and address the board.

"Sorry to spring this on you, gentlemen," she said in a clear, cold, businesslike tone, "but your president and CEO—" she glanced at a puzzled Cy "—has my back to the wall. We have to diversify. I need those mineral leases, and you've left me no alternative but to deal under the table to get them."

Cy sat up straighter, aware of his mother's shock and wide-eyed tension beside him. "What do you mean, we?" Cy asked, his very tone a threat.

"Haven't I introduced myself?" she asked pleasantly. "I'm sorry." She smiled, her cool gaze encompassing not only Cy, but his mother as well. "I'm Kip Tennison," she said, waiting for the impact to register, "Henry Tennison's widow. I'm vice president and chief executive officer of Tennison International's domestic operation."

The look on Cy's face was worth it all, she thought briefly. Worth six years of grief and anguish, worth all the pain. Myrna looked white in the face and near to fainting. But Meredith couldn't afford to take pleasure in the shock she'd handed out. She had business to conduct.

So she conducted it, her calm voice detailing the bid, outlining exactly what changes would be made, naming a price and sticking to it despite the outcry from the directors.

"You won't take over my company," Cy said coldly.

She lifted an eyebrow. "Yes, I will," she returned, her voice equally cold. "I have the necessary proxies. I can outvote you."

"You don't have my great-uncle's...."

She shot it across the table to him with chilling efficiency, watching his face stiffen.

"But, he wouldn't!" Myrna gasped.

"Your father's brother doesn't have a very high opinion of either of you, Mrs. Harden," Meredith said easily. "I'm afraid he would, and has. That ten percent of your stock puts me over the edge. It gives me the votes I need to gain control of the company, unless your attorneys can pull a rabbit out of the hat for you." She picked up her materials and closed them up in her attaché case with apparent unconcern. "I want those mineral leases," she said, her hard gray eyes staring straight into Cy's with determination and pure power. "I'll have them, even if I have to take over your company to get them. You can let me know your decision. I'd appreciate it by the first of next week. I have a government contract to fill, and if necessary, I'll have the appropriate agency intercede as well. I imagine you already know that the government doesn't like to be kept waiting for military hardware, especially right now."

She stood up and motioned to Don. "Thank you for your time, gentlemen," she said smoothly. "I'll be in touch. Good evening."

She left the room with Don close behind, smiling a little secretively as she heard the outburst that exploded behind them when the doors closed.

Cy didn't move. He barely breathed. Lightning flashed in his mind as he put all the things that had puzzled him into sequence and realised that Meredith had played him for a fool. Henry Tennison's widow, working for wages in a restaurant. Someday he might even be able to laugh about that irony.

Myrna touched his hand and he jumped, tension rippling through him.

"She's why Henry Tennison tried to destroy us," Myrna said through numb lips. "It was because of Meredith!"

Gossip filtered through his consciousness. Henry Tennison's devotion to his young wife, his obsession to protect her. Meredith had been Tennison's wife, married to him. He was the man she'd said had loved her….

"God," he breathed, choking on the pain. He'd chased her away, and she'd somehow met and married one of the wealthiest men in the world. Now she was the worst enemy he had on earth, and if he wasn't careful, she was going to destroy him.

"I'm sorry," Myrna said tearfully. She gnawed her lower lip. "It's my fault. All my fault…."

He barely heard his mother and didn't understand what she was saying anyway. He was hurting as he'd never dreamed he could. He'd told Meredith that she could never fit into his lifestyle, that she didn't have the sophistication. And she could buy and sell him. How she must have laughed.

She was as far out of his reach now as he'd been out of hers six years before. She was Henry Tennison's widow. She had an empire of her own and an incredible fortune to go with it. The means for a vicious revenge was in her hands, and she'd used it tonight. He closed his eyes. He'd thought she might still love him, despite everything. But she'd just shown him what she felt. She'd played him like a big fish, and now she was reeling him in. None of it had been real. Her only thought had been revenge, probably even when she was giving herself to him. She'd known that it would make the pain so much worse, to remember that and know that the only reason she'd done it was to keep him so interested in her that he hadn't realized the game she was playing. He'd been falling in love all over again, while Meredith had merely been hedging her bets for a hostile takeover. He got up and went to the window, looking out blindly. Somehow the threat of losing his company was nothing compared to the pain of Meredith's betrayal. It came to him without warning that this was how she must have felt six years ago....

It was thirty minutes later when Mr. Smith finally arrived for an impatient Meredith and Don, having had, of all things, a flat. That meant they were still waiting when Cy and Myrna Harden came out of the boardroom themselves and out into the lobby. It took all of Meredith's nerve not to back away from Cy when he came toward her with eyes as cold as death. She'd played her hand, now she had to back it up. She couldn't afford to show weakness.

"My God, was it all part of the plan?" he demanded of her, his dark eyes blazing.

She knew what he meant. She smiled, lifting an eyebrow. "Weren't you the one who used to say that in business, nothing is sacred?"

"Answer me, you female barracuda!" he said under his breath.

She looked past him to a shattered Myrna Harden with hardly any interest except a quiet, dull pity. She felt vaguely ashamed of herself.

"Yes," she said without emotion, lying to save her pride. "It was all part of the plan."

The contempt in his face was almost too much to bear, but she couldn't let him see how much she still cared. It was too late, and she had responsibilities she couldn't shirk. Worse, she had a child to protect. Letting Cy too close now could cost her Blake. Her eyes widened as she realized with horror that Mr. Smith, unaware of the undercurrents, was bringing Blake to the door!

She froze as the door opened and Blake came running in ahead of Mr. Smith.

"Mommy, we had a flat tire!" Blake told the world, holding out his arms to be picked up.

Meredith stooped to lift him into her arms, holding him far too tight, her eyes frightened as she held him. "My little man, were you worried about being late?" she asked, trying not to let the fear show. She knew without looking that Cy and Myrna were gaping at the child.

"Yes, and Mr. Smith said some *very* bad words. You must speak with him," he said in his adult tones.

Meredith would have laughed at that ordinarily, but this really wasn't any time for humor.

Cy was staring at her with venomous anger, as he realized that not only had she gone from him to another man, she'd had a child by that man. She was holding Henry Tennison's son, and he hated her for it.

Even more did he hate the burly man standing close beside her, looking overtly protective and threatening. "You're Smith, of course," Cy said coldly, eyeing the older man with fury as he realized who he had to be—Meredith's bodyguard.

"You're Harden, of course," came the gravelly reply.

Sensing trouble, Meredith got between them, but in her disturbed condition she hadn't counted on the effect Blake's presence was going to have on Myrna Harden. Cy might not have noticed the resemblance, but his mother certainly did, and she knew that Meredith had been pregnant when she left Billings—Cy did not. Myrna stared at the child with eyes gone huge in a face like rice paper. And without warning, she slumped to the floor in a dead faint.

Cy ran to her, his concern obvious. Meredith felt guilty, because it was her fault. She'd sprung more than enough surprises on Myrna tonight, even if she hadn't really meant to produce Blake. That had been an accident. But for the flat tire, Myrna would never have seen the boy at all. She didn't dare think about the consequences now, or she'd go mad!

She gave Blake to Mr. Smith and knelt beside Cy, her cool

fingers going to the pulse in the older woman's neck. The pulse was steady and regular, if a little weak.

"Shock," Cy said curtly, glaring at Meredith. "God knows she's had enough for one night. Cold as ice, aren't you, honey?"

She didn't react. Her eyes met his levelly. "Business isn't for the fainthearted," she replied. "Henry taught me how to play the game. I was a good student."

"You'll need to be," was all he said, but the way he looked at her made her nervous.

He got up to call an ambulance, leaving Meredith to look after Myrna. The older woman opened her eyes briefly, while the directors, all male, stood around trying not to look stupid. They had no idea what to do, leaving Meredith to it.

"The...child," she gasped, her fingernails biting into Meredith's hand, her eyes tormented. "The...child, Meredith!"

"Try not to move around," Meredith said quietly. "You'll be all right."

Tears blurred the older woman's eyes, making Meredith feel even worse than she already did. "I'm...sorry," she got out before her eyes closed again.

"So am I," Meredith said dully, her face going hard as she confronted the result of her attempt to play God. Justifying her actions was going to be harder than she'd ever dreamed. If anything happened to Myrna, there would be no stopping Cy. What had seemed simple before was now a complicated, horrible mess.

The ambulance seemed to take forever, and Cy paced and smoked when he wasn't accusing Meredith silently and verbally for his mother's incapacity. When it arrived he ushered the attendants in and stood guard over them while they loaded his mother into the ambulance. Then he climbed in beside her, leaving the directors and Meredith and all the threats behind.

He held his mother's cold hand as they roared toward the hospital, his mind whirling with new knowledge. Meredith had certainly found her feet, he thought bitterly. Kip Tennison. Henry's wife. Henry Tennison's hidden treasure. And as his mother had said, probably the reason Tennison had tried so hard to bury him. He'd been carrying out Kip's revenge, Meredith's revenge, for the pain and anguish he'd caused her.

He'd pushed her out of his life and sent her running apparently right into Henry Tennison's arms. So much for her profession of love, he thought bitterly. She'd loved him so much that she'd married another man almost immediately and given him a child. He hadn't known who Kip Tennison was, but he'd certainly heard about her. It was common knowledge in business circles that Henry Tennison's devotion to his business came a poor second after devotion to his pretty young wife. They said Henry had kept her hidden from all eyes but his own, he was so besotted with her. There were also rumors that his devotion was returned, that no one believed Kip had married him for any reason other than love.

The gossip hadn't been of much interest to him at the time. Now it assumed paramount importance. Meredith had remarried, had been desperately in love, her husband had died. And there was, obviously, fruit of that love. He'd watched the little dark-haired boy running to her, heard him call her "Mommy." Something in him turned to ashes at the memory. He'd rarely ever thought of children, but when he had, they were always his and Meredith's. The pain almost doubled him over as he realized how complete her revenge was.

A moan caught his attention. He lifted his mother's blue-veined hand in his and held tight. "Hello," he said gently, smiling down at her.

She moaned again. Tears were staining her cheeks. "Cy, the child," she whispered. "Did you see...the child?"

He scowled in concern. She must be rambling. "Mother, how do you feel?"

"What?" She opened her eyes wider and looked at him. "I fainted."

"Yes, you did," he said. "We're on the way to the hospital."

"But it was just a faint."

"We'll let the doctor tell us that," he told her firmly. "You just lie back and be still. You'll be all right now."

She clenched her fingers around his. "Meredith," she began.

"Quite a surprise, wasn't it?" he asked, his voice bitter. "I actually gave her a job waitressing. She could buy the restaurant out of her petty cash fund, if their last annual statement was any indication of the corporation's assets."

Myrna was just beginning to realize that. Her bribe of twenty thousand dollars must have amused Meredith no end. She hadn't known, hadn't dreamed, who Meredith was. Now the surprise continued to echo through her frail body like a gunshot. The past had caught up with her. Not only had Meredith borne Cy's child, she still had him. Cy didn't know. He assumed that the little boy was Henry Tennison's, and if Myrna told him the truth, her own guilt would have to be revealed. It would mean destroying their tenuous relationship. Worse, it would lock the child into a custody battle the likes of which the Hardens and Tennisons had never seen.

Could she do that, even to obtain her grandchild? Could she allow the little boy to become nothing more than a pawn, to satisfy her hunger for a grandchild, for Cy's son to carry on the Harden name?

She put a hand over her face. So much deceit. So many lies. Meredith had said that it was finished, that her thirst for revenge was over. She obviously planned to take the child back home with her and forget about Cy and Myrna. But now Myrna couldn't forget. She had a grandson whom she would never know. Cy had a son whose very existence was unknown to him. That was Myrna's fault. He wouldn't forget, how could he? But by withholding the information, she would be damaging him even more than she already had.

"Don't worry so," he chided, bending to kiss her forehead. Her consciousness gave him hope, relieving some of the strain of worry on his hard face. "I'm not going to sit back and let Meredith take our company away."

"I never thought you would," Myrna whispered. Her eyes closed. "Even if it would be no less than I deserved…."

He frowned, but she was drifting in and out again, and he let it go. Her behavior worried him. It wasn't like his mother to let things get her down, but Meredith's revelation had affected her more than anything else in recent years. In fact, Meredith's very presence in Billings had upset her. He wondered what secret the two women shared that had driven Meredith to secrecy and plotting, that had reduced his mother to a frightened shell. But before he could worry the subject too much, they were pulling into the emergency room parking lot.

In the car back to Mary's house, Meredith sat on the seat next to Blake.

"That lady fainted, Mommy," he said. "Why did she faint? Did I scare her?"

"No, darling, she'd just had a shock," Meredith said stiffly. "Now sit here like a good boy and listen to your new tape." She plugged the headphones in for him.

"Didn't she know about Blake?" Don asked Meredith.

"Not until tonight, not for sure, anyway," she said wearily. "I never meant for her to know at all. If it hadn't been for the flat tire, I was just going to pack up and leave town."

"Tough break," he said.

"Yes." She lifted her eyes to his. "Will the board go for our offer?"

"I doubt it," he said, but with an odd uneasiness. He stretched. "They'll bulldoze Cy into those mineral leases, but I don't think they'll go along with new management or yield to a hostile takeover. Not even at the price we're offering." Not yet, anyway, he was thinking. He still had plans, and neither Meredith nor Cy could be allowed to know what they were until he was ready to spring his own surprise on both of them.

"As long as something good comes out of this, I don't mind," she said.

"You look drawn," he murmured, his expression faintly guilty. "This has been rough on you, hasn't it?"

She didn't look at him. "Yes. I...didn't mean to upset Mrs. Harden that much. I didn't think—"

"She'll be all right."

"Oh, Don, I do hope so," she said, remembering Cy's pained face. Even though things between them were strained and hostile, she didn't really want to cause him any more anguish.

Later that night she phoned the hospital, to be told that Mrs. Harden was simply suffering from exhaustion and was doing very well. It was the only bright spot in a horrible day.

At least she hadn't caused Cy's mother to have a heart attack. But now she had another problem. Myrna had seen Blake. Would she tell Cy the truth? And if she did, what then?

CHAPTER TWELVE

MEREDITH HAD TRIED TO GET Don to stay the night, but he was adamant about getting back to Chicago for an important meeting the next morning. Just as well, Meredith thought. McGee could watch him once he was back in Chicago. She wanted his companionship no more than he wanted hers. The gloves were finally off. He took the corporate jet out barely an hour after they left the Harden Properties building, leaving a subdued Meredith to deal with Blake.

Mr. Smith left the limousine in the driveway. There was no longer any need to pretend, and if eyebrows were raised at the rented limousine, it no longer mattered.

Blake was still asleep when Meredith dragged herself out of bed late the next morning to cook breakfast.

"You should get a maid," Mr. Smith remarked as he nibbled bacon while Meredith took biscuits out of the oven. "You look out of place in the kitchen."

She glanced at him with a wan smile. He looked out of place in a kitchen himself, in his jeans and olive drab T-shirt. But he could cook better than she could.

"We do what we must," she reminded him. She pushed back the untidy plat of her long blond hair and sat down at the table, like him in jeans and T-shirt. Except that now the jeans had a designer label, and the T-shirt was silk. "Have a biscuit."

He reached for one just as an impatient hand pounded on the back door.

"I'll get it," Mr. Smith said, ignoring her impulsive movement.

He opened the door and Cy gave him a hard glare as he walked into the kitchen, tossed his Stetson onto the clean counter and sat down.

Meredith was totally stunned. She couldn't even speak. She hadn't expected to see Cy again, and certainly not here, not after last night.

"Make yourself at home," she said finally.

"Haven't I always?" he asked carelessly. He scowled at Mr. Smith, who sat back down with his usual imperturbability and began to eat his breakfast. "Am I interrupting anything?" he added.

"Just breakfast," she said. "Get a plate if you want some."

He did, to Smith's irritation, and filled it.

"How is your mother?" she asked.

He lifted his dark eyes to hers. "She'll be all right. It wasn't a stroke, thank God."

She pushed the eggs around on her plate. "I'm glad."

"What the hell is going on between you two?" he asked flatly, watching her jerk in surprise. "I've never seen my mother faint, but she went white as a ghost last night after your…revelation. What have you got on her that makes her so afraid of you?"

"Nothing that should worry her," she told him. "I've given up vendettas. They're too wearing."

"I'm sorry to hear that," he mused, watching her. "I've been looking forward to the fireworks when you try to pry my company out of my hands."

"You don't think I can?" she asked with faint cynicism.

"No. But you're welcome to try," he added.

"Thank you so much for your permission." She put down her fork. "You withheld those mineral leases against the advice of your attorney and your directors. And you did it for less than business reasons."

"Of course I did," he agreed. He lit a cigarette, ignoring the glares he got. "I didn't understand why Henry Tennison went out of his way to antagonize me—not until last night—but handing over those leases went against the grain. I don't do favors for the enemy."

"The enemy had you outflanked this time," Meredith said, smiling at him. "Caught you off guard, I daresay."

He nodded, his eyes narrowing. "I was diverted."

The way he said it brought color to her cheeks.

"Mommy!"

The laughing voice brought her head around as a pajama-clad Blake wandered in, dragging his stuffed rabbit by the ear and rubbing his eyes. "Mommy, I got woked up," he murmured, leaning against her.

Her eyes grew tender as she lifted him onto her lap and cuddled him, smiling at the sleepy face.

Cy had to bite down hard to keep his temper. Henry Tennison's child, and the love in her face was impossible to hide. She'd looked at him like that once, with that same soft wonder. He'd withdrawn from it, not trusting her, and pushed her out of his life. Now he was just beginning to realize what he'd thrown away. He didn't like feeling second best.

Smith saw the expression on the younger man's face. Jealousy. He knew the look.

Cy glanced in his direction, dark eyes glittering. He hated the idea of Smith more than he envied the child. It disturbed him to see the man sitting so comfortably with Meredith, living with her.

"Tiny's in the washing machine, Mr. Smith," Blake murmured. "Does she want a bath?"

"Let's go see. Up and at 'em, boy." He took Blake from Meredith, his face softening as the boy grinned at him. "I'll get him dressed."

"Thank you," she said.

Cy watched them go, gazing at the child with cold hunger. He and Meredith might have eventually had a child together if things had been different. He might have looked like that. He almost winced. He doubted if he'd ever have a child, because marriage wasn't in his vocabulary. God knew, none of the women he'd dated over the years had even wanted them. Only Meredith. Why hadn't she told him that she and Tennison had a child together? He felt betrayed, wounded to the bone.

"Who's Tiny?" he asked stiffly.

"Mr. Smith's iguana," she replied. "Why are you here?"

He fingered his coffee cup and sighed. "I didn't have anywhere else to go," he said.

She couldn't let him get to her. She didn't dare. Her eyes fell to his hands, long-fingered and dark-skinned. She remembered the feel of them so well.

"I'm sorry about your mother."

"She'll be all right." He finished his coffee and his cigarette and stared at her. "Did you love your husband?"

"Yes," she said. "It's easy to love people who care about you. Henry treated me like fine china. He spoiled me, protected me, loved me with all his heart." She glanced down, feeling the grief all over again. "He was so alone."

He drew in a sharp breath. "He hid you out, didn't he? That's why I couldn't find you."

She nodded. "Looking back, I suppose he could quite easily have found out about any criminal charges and fixed them.

He could have solved all my problems in an hour or so. But as my brother-in-law once said, Henry had ulterior motives for not wanting you to find me." She looked up at him. "He would have done anything to keep me."

Cy didn't find that surprising. He could barely drag his eyes away from her face. "By then you were pregnant, weren't you?"

This was shaky ground. She had to feel her way. "Yes," she replied. "Blake was Henry's whole world." If only he'd say something, anything, about Blake! But he couldn't know that Blake was his child. He seemed to be trying to pretend that the child wasn't even here.

"And yours?"

She smiled softly. "Oh, yes. And mine. He's the reason I get up in the morning."

"Does your lifestyle leave you much time for him?" he asked. "Oh, yes—" he nodded when he saw her surprise "—I know what the demands are. Meetings, trips, conferences, snags in business deals, wining and dining clients, coaxing directors to vote your way…I do that every day of my life. But I don't have a child to neglect."

"I don't neglect my son," she said hotly.

"You've been here for over a month," he returned.

"And I've talked to Blake every night on the telephone."

"How nice for him."

Her fingers clenched on the table. "This is just what I need," she flared. "A bachelor telling me how to raise my child!"

"If I had one, I'd make damned sure he didn't grow up by himself."

"You're insinuating—"

"What's the rabbit's name?"

She blinked. "I beg your pardon?"

"His stuffed rabbit. What does he call it?"

She knew, but he had her rattled and she couldn't immediately remember.

He cocked an eyebrow at her flush. "Well, that says it all, doesn't it?" he asked.

"My son is none of your business," she muttered.

"I agree. Henry Tennison's son is the least of my worries right now," he added coldly. "My mother wants to see you."

So that was why he'd come. She wouldn't admit to herself that she'd hoped it was for any other reason. "Why?" she asked.

"I have no idea. But she's in for observation and tests for at least two more days, and she wants to talk to you. I told her I'd ask."

She slid the coffee cup around on the table. "We don't have anything to say to each other," she said.

"She says you do." He leaned forward to trace patterns on the back of her hand. "Meredith, tell me what's going on."

Her hand withdrew gently from the arousing touch. "It's nothing to do with you," she lied.

He caught her fingers in his and held on, his eyes flashing. "You don't want me to touch you anymore, is that it?" he asked angrily. "Now that you think you've beaten me out of my mineral leases, you don't need to pretend you want me anymore?"

She looked at him helplessly, her heart throbbing in her chest at the contact. "It wasn't...that," she whispered, because she couldn't bear what he was thinking—that she'd slept with him just to keep him in the dark about her takeover plans.

His face seemed to lose some of its tautness, and the fingers gripping hers became caressing. He looked at them, his eyes on the engagement ring that still graced her third finger, the one Henry had given her. "You were mine long before you were his," he said. "I hurt you, and I'm sorry. I suppose you were entitled to any revenge you wanted." She might not know it, and he didn't say it, but giving Tennison a child had been her best revenge. Nothing hurt him more than that child.

He let go of her hand all at once and stood up, and the fire in his eyes went out. "Go and see Mother, if you will, so she'll stop dwelling on whatever's between you. She's nobody's idea of congeniality, but there are reasons for her lack of it. She's all I've got left."

Her eyes closed. It hurt to hear him say it, even though she realized it was true. She didn't want to have to confront Myrna Harden again. But she wasn't going to be able to get out of it without arousing his suspicions and, perhaps, pushing Myrna into doing something desperate.

"All right," she said. "I'll go."

His face was as bitter as hers was sad. He scooped up his Stetson and looked down at her with quiet intensity. "You'll be leaving Billings now, I gather."

She nodded. "I have to get back to work." She smiled ruefully. "As you say, my life is one business meeting after another. It's been difficult running things from here, despite the fax machine and the phone."

"And the airport?" he asked. "Yes, I heard about the corporate jet traffic we've been getting from Tennison International. Now it makes sense. You went to a lot of trouble to keep me in the dark."

"You don't know exactly how much," she murmured.

"I think I might even tell Mrs. Dade why you don't need the job anymore," he said with dry humor. "You must have laughed your head off about it."

"I enjoyed it," she said. "After what I do in a day's time, waiting tables was a vacation."

He only nodded. His eyes fell to her mouth, lingering there. "I thought I was playing a pat hand, but you had all the aces, didn't you, honey?"

"I had to have the mineral leases," she said simply. "My expansion plans depend on them."

"There are mineral leases available all over the western states, including Arizona, if you're after moly. You are, aren't you?" he added with keen perception, watching her face give the show away. "Why didn't you just go to Arizona in the first place?"

"Because you weren't there," she said flatly, her eyes flashing.

"That's right," he replied. "You weren't after leases, you wanted my neck in a noose. You think you've managed to maneuver it there. But you don't know how strong a hold I have on my board of directors, or how hard I'm willing to fight to keep control of them." He smiled slowly. "I like a good fight. Come on, honey. You want my company, come and get it. But I play hardball."

"So do I," she returned with a calm smile. "Henry taught me how."

The mention of her late husband hardened his face. "He had the killer instinct," he said softly. "So do I. But I don't think you do, little Meredith. It takes more than your married name to spook me."

"I've got the proxies," she reminded him.

"And they've already changed hands once," he replied cheerfully. She didn't know it, but her own brother-in-law was his best ally. That made him just a little arrogant. His eyes twinkled. He was actually enjoying himself. From the bitter revelations of the night, and the worry, was emerging something else. "You never competed with me in the old days. You gave. You never took."

"Times change," she said, lifting her coffee cup.

"Count on it." He slid his hat over his dark hair, slanting it toward one eyebrow. "I won't give up and I won't give in. You've got the upper hand right now. Let's see how long you can keep it."

"I'll send you a postcard from Chicago," she drawled.

"Are you leaving right away?" he asked, letting his eyes run over her. He moved closer, looming over her deliberately, with one lean hand resting on the chair beside her shoulder. His breath stirred the hair at her forehead as he spoke. "Stick around," he whispered, tilting his head so that his mouth was poised just above hers. "I'll take you to the penthouse and we'll make love on the carpet."

"I don't want to—oh!"

Her protest died as his hand found her soft breast and his thumb traced the suddenly hard nipple.

"Oh, what?" he whispered, and his mouth closed on hers while his hand claimed her with blatant possession.

She pushed backward, only to find that she was overbalanced. He held her in that vulnerable position, so that she had to cling to his neck to keep from falling. And while she clung, he kissed her, hotly, intimately, his tongue thrusting so deep into her mouth that shards of pure electricity ran into her loins and all but convulsed her.

He tore his mouth away and righted her chair, standing over her with no visible sign of emotion except for a faint, mocking smile on the lips that had bitten hers into submission.

"You're mine," he said quietly. "You always have been. You always will be. Run while you can, but you're not getting away. Not this time. I won't let go."

He turned and went out the back door, closing it firmly behind him. He meant it. Even the child wouldn't deter him. He had Meredith in his grasp, and he was going to keep her, no matter what it took. The past six years had been the purest kind of hell. He wasn't going through that again, not if it meant pulling Meredith out of her office and tying her in his house. Don would help him get her off the Tennison board and out of her office permanently. Then she was going to be his forever. In what capacity, he'd worry about later.

Blake's laughter finally got through to her as he and Mr. Smith came bouncing down the stairs and back into the kitchen. Smith lifted an eyebrow at her swollen mouth and scarlet flush.

"Ran him off, did you?" he murmured, smiling wickedly.

"He left voluntarily," she said. She got up. "His mother is asking for me. I've got to go to the hospital and see her. I promised."

"What does his mother want, do you think?" he asked.

She looked, and felt, worried. "I don't know," she said. "I'm almost certain it's something to do with you-know-who," she added so that Blake wouldn't get too curious. "I don't think she'll tell him, but I can't be sure."

"What if she does?"

Her eyes mirrored her concern. "You said yourself, we'd both better find a hole."

"I'd bet on it."

She grimaced. "Well, maybe it needn't come to that. First I've got to see what's on her mind." She looked at her watch. "Hamilton is supposed to phone me this morning. Can you call Don for me and ask him to intercede?"

"Sure thing."

"Thanks."

She kissed Blake and left Mr. Smith to feed him while she disappeared into her bedroom. She had one dress here she hadn't worn—a soft paisley print in silk. She put that on, fixed her hair neatly, and stepped into her hose and high heels. To beard the lioness, she might as well dress to the teeth, she told herself. It might give her more confidence than she really had.

She wouldn't allow herself to think about Cy and what he'd said, or what he'd done. Her mouth still bore the imprint of his, and she could taste him on her lips. He wanted her. That hadn't changed. But she couldn't give in to him again. She had to get Blake out of Billings, along with herself, before Cy found out the truth.

Myrna Harden was sitting up in bed, looking wan and dull-eyed. She straightened when Meredith came in the door, her whole demeanor nervous and preoccupied.

"Thank you for coming," Myrna said when Meredith stopped by the bedside. "Please, sit down."

The younger woman dropped elegantly onto the one padded chair by the bed, her chin lifted, her eyes calm and level. "What do you want?"

"Are you going to tell Cy?" Myrna asked solemnly.

"I told him to tell you that you had nothing to worry about," Meredith said stiffly. "I meant it. No, I'm not going to tell him. You're perfectly safe."

Myrna flushed. Her eyes fell to her cold, trembling hands on the sheet. "What will you do?"

"Nothing. I'll go home to Chicago, and you can get on with your life."

"And the takeover?"

Meredith's expression didn't waver. "I need those leases. I'll have them, no matter what I have to do."

Myrna studied the other woman intently. "You're very strong, aren't you?"

"Yes, thanks to you," came the terse reply. "I grew up fast when I left Billings. Being on the streets and pregnant at the age of eighteen would make most people strong, if it didn't kill them."

Myrna's eyes closed. "I've lived with it all these years," she said in a faint monotone. "I've watched my son go wild, when he wasn't brooding or working himself half to death. I've thought about you, and wondered and worried about the unborn child. Finally, I managed to forget, at times. I was…I was learning to live with it. And then you came back."

"Our sins catch up with us, isn't that the maxim?" Meredith asked quietly.

Myrna sighed, her dark eyes seeking Meredith's gray ones. "Oh, yes. And mine have. But you're making Cy pay for them. It's me you should be punishing, not him."

"Isn't that what I've done?" Meredith asked softly.

Myrna flushed, averting her gaze. "I see."

"The sins of the father, visited on the child. Or in this case, the mother," Meredith said. "I hated you. I lived for the day I could pay you back for what you'd done to me, for what you'd cost me. I thought of nothing else. When Henry died, vendetta became the very breath in my lungs, the most important thing in my life. You owe me!"

The older woman clenched her hands together and winced.

Meredith had to restrain herself forcibly. She swallowed, twisting her purse in nerveless hands as she struggled for composure. "I lost my home, my security. I lost the only man I ever loved. I lost my honor, my reputation…everything! If it hadn't been for Henry Tennison, I might have lost my life."

Myrna's face looked pinched with nerves. "He adopted the child?"

"Yes," Meredith said. She looked at the purse. "Blake was the light of his life. He made it legal. On the birth certificate, he is listed as Blake's father." Remembering that eased her fear. It occurred to her that the birth certificate was her ace in the hole. No matter what claims the Hardens might make, that document would stand in any court of law. She looked up, her eyes gleaming with triumph. "To all intents and purposes, Blake is a Tennison. So you don't have to worry that Cy might find out the truth. I won't tell him. And you won't have to."

"I thought that was what I wanted," the other woman said quietly. "Not to have my sins laid out for his inspection. But have you thought what it means? What you're denying Blake?"

Meredith nodded. "That can't be helped. It's too late."

"Cy...would love him," she whispered.

Meredith caught her lower lip in her teeth. Her eyes closed. "Yes."

"Oh, Meredith," Myrna said, tears in her voice, in her eyes. "I thought Cy would get over you. I was sure he'd find someone else, get married, have children. I didn't realize how...how involved he was with you, emotionally."

"It wasn't emotional on his part," Meredith said coldly. "It was just physical attraction. Physical obsession."

"No." Myrna shifted against her pillows, looking old and frail and somehow vulnerable. "No, it's lasted far too long for that. It's in his eyes when he looks at you, even when he talks about you."

"You don't understand," she returned, leaning forward. "He came to see me, before the board meeting. He told me about your husband so that he could make me understand why he doesn't want commitment. He said that he never wanted marriage, or children. He doesn't believe that fidelity exists."

Myrna was taken aback. "He never said any such thing to me."

"You're his mother," Meredith replied. "He's very protective of you. He always was. But he was telling the truth. I was just a novelty. He knew I couldn't fit into his lifestyle, he never planned to marry me at all. You were right about that. The engagement was just a sham, to keep me with him."

"He feels something for you," Myrna said doggedly.

"Certainly. But I don't want him," she replied. "I won't spend the rest of my life being used like a company car. I have my own responsibilities and a son to raise. I'm not cut out to be Cy Harden's mistress!"

Myrna flushed, but she didn't look away. "Would you marry him, if he asked you?"

"No." She got to her feet. "He's thrown me out of his life twice now. I have no intention of inviting a third rejection."

"But he doesn't know," Myrna said fervently. "Meredith, he doesn't know about the child, about what I've done…"

"And he won't." She was tired, and she felt it. Looked it. "Mrs. Harden, revenge is a stupid thing. Someone tried to tell me that, but I wouldn't listen. I wanted to get even with all of you, but now I just want to go back to my own life and get on with it as best I can. I'm sorry that I've made things hard for you, and for Cy."

"I can't believe that you're asking me for forgiveness," Myrna said quietly, "after what I've done to you."

"I have a son," Meredith said. "I'd do anything for him, anything to protect him, to spare him pain." She hesitated. "I…understand."

The older woman sighed. "Yes. A mother will make any sacrifice for a much loved child. Cy was all I had. He still is. I loved him and protected him perhaps too much. My good intentions seem very selfish now, considering what I've cost him. He has to know about the child, Meredith," she said firmly. "Even if he hates me when he knows what I did. He has every right to know about his son."

"I won't tell him," Meredith said. "I told you, it's too late. It would serve no purpose except to upset Blake's life."

"I can take you to court," Myrna said recklessly. "There are chromosome tests that can prove paternity."

"Yes, but for that you'd have to have my permission, and I won't give it," Meredith told her. "I won't let Cy have my child. The two of you wanted nothing to do with me six years ago. Fine. Now I want nothing to do with either of you."

"Is it fair, to punish the child for mistakes I made?" Myrna demanded.

"Look who's talking about fairness," Meredith said in a dangerously quiet voice.

The old woman actually flinched. She lay back against her pillows, her dark eyes accusing, her strength drained. "Very well. Do what you will. But I'm going to tell Cy."

Meredith felt the fear all the way to her feet. She couldn't admit how frightened she was or show her reluctance. There was still a slim chance that Myrna was bluffing, that she might change her mind.

"Do what you want to," she said proudly.

Myrna let out a long sigh. "You can't imagine that I really want to tell my only son what a mess I've made out of his life, or what I've cost him out of misguided love?" she asked. "I'm the villain of the piece, and I'll get what's coming to me. But I won't let Cy go through life not knowing he has a son."

Meredith glared at her. "And what about Blake? What about the mess you'll be making of his life? He thinks of Henry Tennison as his father."

"Blake has the right to know his real father, doesn't he?" Myrna asked. "He might come to hate you one day, when he found out the truth."

That was a fact Meredith had already faced, but it didn't make things any easier. She clutched her purse tightly. "I won't give up my child."

"Nobody is asking that," Myrna said, her voice almost gentle. "Can't you accept that this is every bit as difficult for me as it is for you? Cy is going to hate me."

"You're his mother. He won't hate you. He'll hate me." She gave a bitter laugh. "It will give him one more reason, as if he needs it."

"He doesn't hate you, either," Myrna replied surprisingly. She smiled. "He said that he was looking forward to taking his company away from you. It was the first spark of life I've seen in him for years, as if he finally had a reason to smile."

Meredith averted her eyes. "He won't get custody."

"You sound as if you think he'll go to court the minute he finds out about Blake." Myrna sat up slowly. "Meredith, he'll know what you went through. He's not going to blame you. I think he has some idea already of how badly he hurt you. Don't paint him completely black. Even if he is my son, he isn't totally without feelings."

Meredith stared at her purse, feeling insecure, young. "Blake is all I have," she whispered.

Myrna's eyes stung with tears. The evidence of her hard-heartedness was painted on that young, tragic face, and the sight of it reduced her to sick humility.

"Meredith…"

"I have to go. I…" She turned and almost ran out of the room, giving Myrna the victory for this battle. She had no heart for any more fighting.

Myrna watched her go with anguish. She hadn't meant to upset the other woman so badly. Now she might bolt and take Blake, run away as she had once before. She didn't know what to do. Cy had to know, but telling him was only going to cause Meredith more pain. She was genuinely sorry for that. Her attitude toward the younger woman had changed completely over the past few weeks. She didn't like the idea of hurting Meredith any more. But the choice was well and truly out of her hands now. She had to grit her teeth and tell the truth. If Cy hated her for it…well, it would be no more than she deserved. At last she'd have it off her conscience, and one step toward putting things right would have been taken.

She picked up the telephone and dialed Cy's office number.

CHAPTER THIRTEEN

IT HAD BEEN A LONG TIME since Cy Harden had worried about his mother's health. But the strained face in the hospital bed made him uneasy. Myrna looked weaker than ever, despite the fact that her doctor had just presented them with the test results and pronounced her in the peak of health and quite ready to go home.

"This wasn't why I asked you to come," Myrna murmured as he loaded her into the car, along with her overnight case. It was almost dark by the time he'd been free to pick her up.

"It was good timing, all the same," he replied. He smiled at her as he started the car. "I'm glad it was nothing serious. You had me scared."

She averted her gaze to the window. "It was a night for surprises," she said. Her nervous fingers picked at the skirt of her silk dress. "Imagine little Meredith Ashe turning out to be the notorious Mrs. Henry Tennison."

"And I gave her a job working as a waitress for minimum wage," Cy mused, lighting a cigarette as he drove. "I don't imagine she's stopped laughing yet. Did she go to see you?"

"Yes. That…that's why I phoned your office."

His dark eyes narrowed. "Well?"

"It's a long story. Can it wait until we get home?"

He shrugged. "Suit yourself."

They drove the rest of the way to the elegant house in silence, while Myrna brooded and tried to work up enough courage to tell him what she'd done. Her hands were trembling as he helped her out of the car, but she knew there was no help for her now.

She had Mrs. Dougherty, the housekeeper, bring a tray of coffee to the living room. Then she sat down and waited for it to be served before she spoke to Cy about anything except routine matters.

"If it's about those proxies, you needn't worry," Cy told her when they were sipping hot black coffee from Myrna's elegant old china cups. "Meredith doesn't know it, but her own brother-in-law is undermining her. He wants her out of the corporation. He's offered me his cooperation in getting control of the outstanding stock and proxies before the board makes a final decision on the takeover bid."

Myrna frowned. "But that's not fair," she said involuntarily. "It's underhanded."

His eyebrows arched. "I thought you were Meredith's worst enemy?"

She looked down into her cup. "In many ways I have been," she said. She drew a steadying breath and glanced at her tall son, her eyes full of sadness and regret. "Cy, I've done something terribly bad."

"Join the club."

"I'm serious." She put down her cup and saucer and clasped her hands on her lap. She felt her age for once, and finding the right words was difficult. "Cy, I paid Tony Tanksley to rob the safe and implicate Meredith," she said tightly. "I gave him the combination."

He didn't seem to react at all. He stared at her with slow comprehension, his dark eyes steady and unblinking. "You did what?" he asked.

She swallowed. "I set her up, is that the right terminology? Cy, she was eighteen and hopelessly naive and unsophisticated…"

"I didn't know she was eighteen," he said roughly. "Not until you and Tony confronted her that day. She told me she was twenty."

That was news. She hesitated. "I didn't realize."

"I felt like ten kinds of a fool when I knew the truth," he said with quiet regret. "I had no right to hurt her the way I did." He looked at his mother with bitter comprehension. "Did you know she'd run?"

"I had a pretty good idea that she would," Myrna said, her face paling. "You see, she was proud and she wouldn't have asked you for help after…after you believed the lies Tony and I told you about her."

"She didn't need help, did she?" Cy asked. "You gave her enough money to get out of town, I gather?"

"Yes." She brushed back the hair from her cheeks, feeling old and worn. It was harder than she'd dreamed. "But she sent it back to me, along with all the things you gave her, and I never told you. The jewelry, all of it, is in one of my dresser drawers."

He stared straight ahead, his mind whirling with the anguish of it. "How could you have done that to her?" he asked. "Didn't you know how badly I'd already hurt her?"

"I was afraid you meant to marry her, Cy," she said. "God forgive me, I wanted a debutante for you, someone of good family, good breeding, with money and…and respectability. I'd sacrificed so much to get us in society, to keep us there…" Her eyes closed. "I thought you'd get over her."

"So did I," he said dully. "But I never did."

She saw the pain in his eyes and flinched. "In the end, I almost couldn't go through with it. I wouldn't let you prosecute Tony for fear that he might tell you the truth, and I gave him a plane ticket and had him taken to the airport before you could question him. Even then I was afraid you might go after her."

"I did," he said. "I hired private detectives. But she vanished."

"Yes. I…hired some of my own," she confessed, smiling at his surprise. "I felt so guilty about what I'd done. I couldn't live with not knowing if she was all right. Especially under the circumstances."

The insinuation went right over his head. "That's what she was holding over your head, wasn't it?" he asked.

"That was part of it," Myrna replied. She paused, hoping for a reprieve, but his steady gaze was formidable. "Cy, when she left Billings, she was pregnant."

He didn't think he could keep breathing. His lungs seemed to be paralyzed, like his mind, his heart. He felt the horror of those words in every cell of his body as he stared helplessly at his mother. Pregnant. Meredith was pregnant. Pregnant with his child!

Myrna moaned, burying her face in her hands. "Forgive me," she whispered. "Cy, forgive me! I must have been mad. I'll never forgive myself for what I've done."

"You sent her away, knowing she was carrying my child?" he asked hoarsely. He stood up, his face white, his eyes almost black with feeling. "You let her go, like that?!"

She cringed from the contempt in his face. "You said you didn't want marriage, or children!" she cried.

"You thought I wouldn't want my own child?" he demanded. A little boy's face flashed in front of him, a child dressed in pajamas and dragging a stuffed rabbit. He gasped as it sank in. "Oh, my God, that little boy in her house isn't Henry Tennison's son. He's mine!" The reality was more than he could bear. No wonder Meredith hated him! The child's face burned into his brain, and he didn't understand how he could have looked at hair and eyes like his own and not have realized it.

Myrna's shoulders slumped in defeat. "Yes," she said heavily. "He's yours."

His fists clenched at his sides. He started to speak, and the words choked him. He whirled on his heel and went out the door without looking back, his brain on fire with what he'd just learned.

Myrna ran to the door to stop him. She didn't know what he might do. He'd looked murderous. Surely he wouldn't go and attack Meredith?

Cy got into his low-slung Jaguar and spun gravel getting out of the driveway. He wasn't thinking or feeling, he was numb from the neck down. Meredith had been carrying his child, and his venomous parent had known it. She'd framed Meredith, run her out of town, and his own fear of commitment had helped her destroy the younger woman's life. If he'd been less wary of permanence, Meredith might have felt confident enough to tell him she was pregnant. If she had, he'd have married her at once, despite his misgivings. But he hadn't even been given the chance. Myrna had made sure that Meredith got out of his life, out of reach. And fate had placed her within Henry Tennison's grasp.

He had a son who didn't know him, a son who bore the Tennison name and would be raised a Tennison. Meredith knew and hadn't told him. But how could he blame her? She was the real victim in all this, the innocent sacrifice. She'd been used and cast aside, hurt and hounded, all because his mother didn't think she was good enough to become a Harden.

He wheeled out onto the main highway without any real idea of what he was going to do. He had to come to grips with it, he had to deal with what he'd been told. Years of anguish, of loneliness, missing Meredith and wanting her. Now she'd come back, and he'd been banking everything on a second chance at making things right. But she was playing games with him. No longer a child, she was an executive in her own right, with enough power to take his company right out from under him if he wasn't careful.

Did she hate him? God knew she had every right. She must have planned this takeover bid carefully, worked it so that she could spring her trap without the Hardens being any the wiser. It had almost worked, too, except that Meredith's brother-in-law wanted power more than he wanted mining leases. He was the key to Cy's own victory.

He remembered the way the child had looked that morning in Meredith's arms, a little dark-haired boy with eyes like brown velvet. Something inside him twisted at the memory. He'd never really thought much about children. Now he realized how empty his life had been. He'd listened to his executives talk about their kids, about the routine of family life, and he'd felt superior because he was free to do what he liked. But despite the glamour and wealth of his lifestyle, he was totally alone except for Myrna. His heart had grown cold since Meredith's defection, and now he had to face the fact that he'd run her off for all the wrong reasons. He'd hated the hold she had on his emotions. That had been the real reason he'd let himself believe she was guilty. In his own way, he'd been running, too.

He'd accused her of being mercenary, of selling him out. He'd really believed she could stab him in the back like that. And all the while she'd been pregnant with his baby and couldn't even tell him.

He groaned out loud, gunning the engine furiously. How could Myrna have done that to Meredith? It was the shock of learning Meredith's real age that had blinded him to the rest of the lies—something that shamed him so much that he'd never even admitted the shock to himself, much less to anyone else. He'd cold-bloodedly seduced a teenaged girl, not the woman he'd thought, and his conscience had put him on the rack for it. His head had been spinning wildly with guilt, and he hadn't been quite lucid. But after Meredith was gone, and he realized what he'd lost, her age had no longer mattered. He'd missed her beyond bearing. He hadn't really believed that she'd stolen from him. Despite Tony's so-called confession and the evidence, he'd never bought it, because Meredith had loved him.

Love. He'd never said the word and meant it. But when Meredith lay moaning in his arms, he felt it. What she gave to his starved senses was beyond price. She made everything all right. She made him feel safe and wanted. He hadn't wanted to call it love. He'd branded it an obsession and hated himself for giving in to it so fiercely. He'd hated being prisoner to that blind ecstasy. But its hold on him was unbreakable. For six years it had held him in thrall. It still did. He had only to look at Meredith and he knew that he'd die to have her. Lust? Not likely.

He had to make Meredith understand that. He had to show her that he genuinely cared for her. Not because she was Kip Tennison and held enough proxies to jerk his company out of his hands. Not because she had wealth and power. But because she was the only woman he'd ever really cared about, and because she'd borne him a child.

There had to be a way to convince her that he'd changed. He wanted commitment now. He wanted to get to know his child, to learn how to be a father to their son. He knew Meredith had lied when she'd said it was all just part of her plan for the takeover, when she'd slept with him. She loved him. He could make her forgive him, if he worked at it. Love didn't die. Oh, God, he thought, it couldn't! Hadn't Meredith been his whole world all these long, empty years?

His heart brightened as he considered the possibilities. It could all work out, if he kept his head. He wouldn't think about his mother, not just yet. It was going to be a long time before he could forgive her for the years she'd cost him, for the time he could have been with his son and Meredith. Right now the only thought in his mind was how quickly he could get to Meredith and tell her how he felt, ask her to give him one last chance.

The Jaguar purred as he threw it around a last deep curve and down a long hill. Just a few more minutes....

Even as he was thinking it, the glare of another car's headlights startled him. He jerked the wheel, but too late. The lights splintered into terrible darkness, and he saw nothing else.

MYRNA HARDEN WAS PACING the living room minutes after Cy had left the house, her nerves tangled as she wondered where he'd gone. Probably he was on his way to see Meredith, to talk to her. Myrna didn't know how she was going to live with his contempt and hatred now that he knew the truth. But she'd had no choice about telling him. As she'd told Meredith, she did owe him that.

Her fingers worried a handkerchief. She was still crying. The look on her son's tormented face hurt. She'd have given all her good intentions to turn the clock back and let Cy live his own life, but it was too late. She'd done so much damage. And he still didn't know everything....

The doorbell rang. Usually she let Mrs. Dougherty answer it, but she was strung out on nervous energy. She went to answer it.

Two Billings policemen stood on the porch, with quiet, solemn faces.

"Mrs. Myrna Harden?" one of them asked.

She clutched her bodice with shaking fingers. "Yes. Is it Cy? Has something happened to my son?" she asked with cold foreboding.

"I'm afraid so, ma'am," the second officer replied. "You'd better come with us. We'll drive you to the hospital."

"Is he alive? Please, is he alive?" she asked frantically, tears streaming down her cheeks as she grabbed her purse and followed them out the door.

"He was when the ambulance got there, ma'am," the younger officer replied. "I'm sure they'll do all they can."

She let them put her in the patrol car, her hands clutching her purse in a death grip. Cy was going to die, and that, too, was her fault. She'd let him go, after having destroyed his peace of mind. Had Meredith been right after all? Would silence have served a better purpose? Had she killed him?

The questions tormented her during that wild ride to the hospital. She ran into the emergency room and stood by, shaking, while the admissions clerk asked question after question about Cy. She answered them blindly, waiting for someone, anyone, to tell her something about her son.

Dr. Bryner, the attending physician, came out to talk to her five minutes later. He sat down beside her in the waiting room.

"Cy is alive," he said, alleviating her worst fears. "But he's in critical condition. His spine is badly bruised and there are internal injuries, along with some torn ligaments and nerve damage. I can't even tell the extent just yet. If you'd like to leave your number, we can telephone you as soon as we know something."

"I won't go home," she whispered. "I can't."

"Do you have any family that we could call for you?" he continued, his face sympathetic.

She shook her head. Then she realized that she did have family. Sort of. Cy had a family, even if he'd only just learned about it. "Yes. Yes, I have," she said.

MR. SMITH HAD JUST PUT Blake to bed. Meredith was sitting in the kitchen when the telephone rang.

"Ignore it," he said. "Go to bed."

She smiled wearily. "It's probably Don. I can't afford to ignore it." She lifted the receiver. "Hello."

"Meredith?"

It sounded like Myrna Harden. "Yes," she said, her tone curious.

"Meredith, there's been an accident," the older woman said tearfully. "I'm at the city hospital. Can you come down here, please?"

Meredith felt sick to her stomach. She sat down, all but gasping for breath. "Cy?" she asked. "Is he dead?"

"No," Myrna said. "But he's…he's very bad. Please, can you come?"

"I'll be there in five minutes," Meredith said. She hung up. "It's Cy. He's been hurt."

"I'll get Blake dressed and we'll drive you. No arguments," he added when he saw her face. "Get a coat."

She did it automatically, letting Mr. Smith take charge, as he always did in emergencies. It was wonderful not to have to worry about how to get things done. Before she knew it, he had them in the hospital waiting room, where a frightened, tearful Myrna Harden was waiting for news.

Meredith left Mr. Smith to take care of Blake while she sat down next to Myrna. "Tell me what's happened," she said, and listened, white-faced, to the particulars.

"You were right. I should never have told him," Myrna whispered miserably. "I wouldn't listen…. He'll die, and that's my fault, too!"

"Stop that," Meredith said firmly. "He won't die."

"He's so badly hurt…."

Meredith got up and asked to speak to the attending physician.

"I'm Dr. Bryner," he introduced himself, shaking hands with her. "Are you a friend of Mr. Harden, Mrs. Tennison?"

"A very old one," she replied. "What can be done?"

He gave her an abbreviated version of Cy's injuries, including the preliminary findings, more serious than he'd thought at first. "Immediate orthopedic surgery is indicated, before his condition deteriorates. We have an orthopedic surgeon, but he feels that a neurosurgeon should do the procedure. It's very involved."

"Who's the best person in the field?" she asked without hesitation.

He smiled. "Dr. Miles Danbury, of the Mayo Clinic."

"Can you get him?"

"If you can afford the fees and get me a chartered jet, yes."

"Get on the phone," she replied.

It was amazing, she thought, what money and influence could accomplish. In minutes Danbury had agreed to take the case and Meredith had a Tennison corporate jet waiting at the airport to bring him to Billings.

"You've just improved his chances of walking again by seventy percent," Dr. Bryner told Meredith.

"Anything you need," she told him. "Anything at all. Money is no object."

"We'll keep you informed. You'll be with Mrs. Harden, I gather?"

"Yes," she said. "Thank you."

He smiled. "Thank you. I'm fond of Cy myself."

Myrna had watched the scene with rapt, quiet eyes. "You're very efficient," she said hesitantly. "I...wouldn't have known what to do."

"I'm used to organizing," Meredith said. "It's just a matter of doing what needs to be done."

"I could have managed the fees, but the corporate jet…" Myrna shrugged. "We'll pay you back, of course," she added with cold pride.

"Cy is my son's father," Meredith said, equally stiff. "I'm as much to blame for the wreck as you are."

"He was furious at me." Myrna's voice was quiet, her eyes sad and red-rimmed. "I don't blame him. But he may never speak to me again."

"I'm sure he'll get over it, in time," Meredith replied. "I'm in the same boat you are. Not only have I withheld his son, I've tried to rip off his company. I guess on points, I'm a few ahead of you."

The older woman smiled faintly. "If he gets well, I won't care if he hates me."

Meredith returned the smile. "Neither will I."

"Mommy, I want to go home," Blake grumbled, moving close to lay his cheek on her lap.

"Mr. Smith can take you, darling," she said softly, kissing his dark head.

"No, Mr. Smith can't," muttered the older man. "How do you expect to get home?"

"I'm not going home until this is over," Meredith said, her eyes sparking at him. "I'll be here for the duration. Put Blake to bed and you get some sleep, too. You'll have to look after him while I'm away."

"You can't sit in a waiting room all night!" Mr. Smith exploded.

"Yes, I can," Meredith said shortly. "I'm not leaving until I know how he is, until I'm sure he's all right."

"Women!" Mr. Smith snorted.

"Men!" she snorted right back. "Go on."

"All right," he muttered then he sighed roughly. "I hope it goes well," he added.

"So do I." She hugged Blake and kissed his cheek, aware of Myrna's steady, hungry gaze on the child. "Sleep tight, chicken," she whispered. "Mommy will be home in the morning, okay?"

"Okay." He let Mr. Smith pick him up and carry him out.

"He's a beautiful child," Myrna said gently.

"Yes. Inside and out. He's not spoiled, either," she added. "No designer toys and outlandishly expensive clothes and other luxuries. I want him to grow up understanding that money won't buy everything."

"A wise precaution," the other woman replied. "I wish somebody had told me that when I was younger. I've only just learned what a curse money can be."

"Or a blessing, in this case," Meredith said quietly, thinking of the chance Cy would have because of her own wealth.

"He'll be all right, won't he, Meredith?" Myrna asked with almost pathetic vulnerability. "He'll live?"

"Of course he will," came the firm reply.

They sat quietly, drinking black coffee and talking listlessly, while the hospital routine carried on around them.

It was hours later, almost daylight, when the neurosurgeon arrived. He'd slept on the plane, thank God, and was wide awake and alert. He shook hands with Meredith and Mrs. Harden and then went directly to Dr. Bryner to discuss the case. Barely two hours later, Cy was wheeled, heavily sedated, into the operating room. He'd come around only briefly and was in too much pain to speak or even be aware of his surroundings. Myrna had cried at the sight of him, lacerated and bruised, his dark face drawn in lines of terrible pain. Meredith had to bite back tears of her own. She had to be strong.

Memories of the day Henry died came careening back, haunting her. She stared out the window, remembering.

It had been raining. She'd been sitting with Blake, because he'd had a slight cold and she'd been worried about him. Her mind had been lingering on the sweetness of the night before. For once, Cy Harden was out of her thoughts as she considered how lucky she was to have someone like Henry to take care of her, to love her. She was weaving daydreams, because his ardor had been thorough and so potent that she still trembled just remembering how completely he'd satisfied her. By then it had been three years since she'd left Billings, almost three years since she and Henry had been married. She'd reconciled herself to the fact that she'd never see Cy again, that her only loyalty now was to Henry. She was making the best of her situation, but it wasn't as difficult as she'd imagined. For all of that one long night, she hadn't thought of Cy. It had been like an omen, giving her hope that she could find happiness with Henry.

The phone rang, and she'd smiled to herself. No doubt that was Henry, phoning from the airport to say good-bye again. She left Blake playing with his toys in bed and ran into the bedroom she and Henry shared to answer it, breathless and happier than she'd been in the whole three years of her marriage.

The voice on the other end of the telephone was Don's. He wouldn't talk to her. He asked her to put Mr. Smith on.

Puzzled, she called her bodyguard and waited while Mr. Smith's stoic face registered first shock and then grief. He put down the receiver.

As if it were yesterday, she could see the sequence unfolding in her mind.

"Sit down," Mr. Smith had said, very gently. He'd knelt just in front of her and gripped both her hands. "Hold on, real hard," he'd told her. "Henry's plane just crashed. He's gone."

It hadn't registered. She'd stared at Mr. Smith with gray eyes that didn't really see him. She was aware of her nails biting into his big hands, but she didn't quite feel any contact.

"He's gone?" she'd repeated blankly, her eyes wide and trusting.

"He's dead, Kip," he'd said quietly. "I'm sorry."

Sorry. Sorry. Sorry. The word echoed until she found herself saying it. The numbness was crushed in a solid wave of anguish. She remembered screaming as she finally realized what had happened.

Mr. Smith had gathered her up close, cradling her, while the terror and grief rippled through her slender body in throbbing waves. She'd cried until she was totally exhausted. Mr. Smith had carried her to bed, tucking her under the coverlet like a child, leaving her only long enough to phone the family physician and see to Blake.

The long, terrible days went on, like a nightmare, with Meredith walking through them like a zombie. Don and Mr. Smith had kept her going, through it all, until the memorial service was over and the will was read. Even that didn't really make much of an impression on her. She'd lost Henry, just when she was beginning to love him. It didn't seem fair. It seemed that her life was destined to be nothing but one long tragedy. And now she might lose Cy as well.

Mrs. Harden touched her shoulder, and when Meredith turned, the look in the younger woman's eyes made her flinch.

"Are you all right?" she asked gently.

"I was remembering when Henry's plane went down," Meredith said numbly. "I felt...like this." She wrapped her arms around her body and shivered. "I can't go on living if Cy dies," she whispered, her wide, frightened eyes seeking the older woman's.

Myrna read the depth of feeling in those tortured eyes, and

she didn't know what to say. She loved her son, but it had been a lifetime since she'd loved a man. Her husband had hurt her pride, although he'd never mattered to her. Not like the other man. Her eyes softened as she remembered the beloved dark face that still haunted her dreams. She'd loved once, too, with all the passion Meredith felt for her son, and she understood. She'd betrayed him, just as she'd betrayed Cy and Meredith....

"He'll be all right," Myrna said. "I know he will."

Meredith took a steadying breath and averted her eyes, embarrassed by her outburst. She didn't trust the older woman, and she was afraid of giving away too much of herself. She went back to her seat and picked up her cup of coffee. It was cold, but the bitter taste of it stung her senses back to life. She couldn't give in to weakness now. She had to be strong, for Blake's sake.

She wouldn't allow herself to think about what life would be like if Cy died in that operating room. Her pride, her vendetta, her need to even the score, all took a back seat to her prayers for his life. The past didn't seem very important when the present might take away the only man she'd ever really loved. She didn't dare think about the future. If Cy died, she wouldn't even have one.

CHAPTER FOURTEEN

THE SURGERY TOOK several hours. Lack of sleep finally drugged Meredith into semiconsciousness. Her dreams were wild and disturbed, and she jerked when a gentle hand shook her.

"Meredith, he's out of the operating room," Myrna said, her eyes bright and her face smiling. "And it went well!"

"Oh, thank God." Meredith put her face in her hands and sighed heavily, fighting tears. "Thank God, thank God."

Myrna sat down beside her, her own eyes bloodshot and her face wan and drawn. "We won't be able to see him until he comes out of the recovery room, but Dr. Danbury says he's almost certain he's repaired most of the damage. At least Cy won't be totally paralyzed."

Meredith sat up slowly, her eyes widening as that last remark registered. "What do you mean, totally?"

Myrna hesitated. She took Meredith's hands in hers. "He may not be able to walk," she replied.

Tears slipped unnoticed down Meredith's cheeks, and her fingers clenched around Myrna's. "But the surgery…!"

"It depends on how well he mends," Myrna said wearily. "They won't know for several days."

That was frightening. Cy was so vital and alive, so much an outdoorsman. Being confined to a wheelchair would cripple his mind more than his body.

"He can't be told that," Meredith said quickly. "He mustn't be told that there's any chance of paralysis."

"I've already made that clear to the doctors," Myrna agreed. "I know him as well as you do, you see. Even if I've been less of a mother than I should be, he's my son and I love him very much."

"I never doubted that," Meredith said.

Myrna hesitated, looking for sarcasm, but she didn't find it. Like herself, Meredith was far too drained for arguments.

When they were finally allowed into the intensive care unit to see Cy, Meredith was all but asleep on her feet. She stood by his bedside, watching Myrna smooth back the dark hair from his broad, pale forehead. His eyes were closed, long dark lashes lying thick on his cheek, his high cheekbones emphasized by the drawn appearance of his face. He was so pale, she thought. Like death. He was hooked up to wires and tubes so profuse that he seemed almost part of the machinery around him.

"Cy, can you hear me?" Myrna asked in a whisper. "Dear, can you hear me? It's Mother."

There was no reply. Not even the flutter of an eyelash. His chest rose and fell very slowly, shallowly. Meredith watched him with quiet despair. He was a strong man, but would he want to live, knowing the condition he might have to spend the rest of his life in? Even if they hadn't been able to tell him, might he not sense it? She remembered reading somewhere that even comatose patients could hear what was going on around them.

She moved closer to the bed, her fingers lightly touching his chest. "You'll walk again," she said, her voice strong and carrying, surprising his mother. "You'll get back on your feet, because you're a fighter. You'll need to be, unless you want me to walk off with Harden Properties."

"Meredith!" Myrna gasped.

But the younger woman put a finger to her lips. She was watching Cy's face. He didn't stir, but his heavy eyebrows drew together and he grimaced.

"Yes, you can hear me, can't you?" she asked, bending closer. "You have to fight your way out of this. You can, if you want to. And you want to, don't you? A Harden doesn't lie down and die when there's a war on."

"Fight," he mouthed the word. Then he drew in a slow breath, grimaced again and seemed to sink back into unconsciousness.

Myrna followed Meredith out the door, her face worried. "Should you have said that to him?"

"Oh, yes." Meredith nodded, facing her. "Didn't you notice that he responded to the challenge? He had to have a reason to live. I've given him one."

"Will you really take the company?" Myrna asked.

"I haven't decided if I want it," Meredith mused. "I do want those mineral leases. Cy and I are evenly matched. The domestic operation of Tennison International and the scope of Harden Properties are about equal. It all comes down to who controls the most votes."

"He'd never forgive you," the older woman reminded her.

Meredith shrugged. "He'll never forgive me for Blake. What's one more sin on my conscience?"

"I'm the one he'll hate." Myrna sighed wearily. "Not you."

"Don't bet on it," Meredith said. "He'll come out from under the anesthesia and remember everything, including the fact that I played him for a fool while I gathered those proxies from under his very nose. That won't sit well. Neither will my married name, and my business acumen. Cy remembers an eighteen-year-old girl who never discussed anything more important than food or the weather with him. I'm not that woman anymore."

Myrna picked up her purse and coat. "Cy didn't know you were eighteen, that day at the house when I…sprang my surprise on you."

Meredith stared at her frowning. "What?"

"You'd told him you were older, hadn't you?"

She hesitated. "Yes. I knew he wouldn't have anything to do with me if he knew I was just turning eighteen." She moved restlessly. "I didn't know he'd ever found out the truth. After we became involved, I was too afraid of losing him to say anything."

"He told me that he was stunned when he knew the truth. It was one reason he let you go. Barely two days later, he was certain that Tony had lied, but by then I had Tony safely out of the country and he couldn't find him." Myrna's face showed every year of its age. "I was so thorough. I knew you weren't eating breakfast, because I had spies at the café. I knew your uniform was too tight in the waist, and that you were fighting bouts of nausea. It didn't take much guesswork to assume you were pregnant, and your expression when I confronted you confirmed it. I tried to justify what I did, but it wasn't easy. It was one thing to shoot you out of the city. It was quite another to cold-bloodedly push my grandchild away." She brushed at a spot on her jacket with eyes that didn't see. "I must have been mad. I didn't even know you. I wouldn't make the attempt. I closed my mind to everything except arranging a suitable marriage for Cy, to insure that he never had to go without money."

"Money was something of an obsession with you, if I remember," Meredith said stiffly.

Myrna lifted her eyes. "I grew up in poverty," she said in a tight whisper, and managed a smile. "My mother was a…a prostitute." She closed her eyes, groaning. "I can't talk about it. Let's go. I'll drop you off at your house on my way home."

Meredith was staggered by what Cy's mother had said. She wondered if the other woman had ever told Cy that, or anyone else. Perhaps it was lack of sleep and worry that had lowered her formidable barriers. Meredith was certain that she'd regret it and that she'd have them firmly back in place the next time they met. She couldn't afford to give in to sympathy. This woman wanted her child. That made her dangerous.

"I can phone Mr. Smith to come for me…." Meredith hesitated.

Myrna stopped as they reached the lobby and stared at Meredith blankly. "Meredith," she said. "I've just realized, I don't have a car. I came here with the police."

Meredith smiled. "Well, in that case, it's definitely Mr. Smith."

He came driving up in the limousine minutes later, glaring as Meredith and Mrs. Harden got into the back seat with a bright, laughing Blake.

"All night and half the day," he grumbled. "You need your head read. You can't go without sleep and food."

"I had other priorities," Meredith informed him, hugging Blake to her. "I hope you were good for Mr. Smith?"

"Yes, Mommy."

"No more flushing rubber ducks down the commode?"

"Oh, no," he promised. "Just washcloths."

Meredith groaned.

"Cy used to do that," Mrs. Harden murmured. "And once, he put the car in gear and rolled down the hill in it. We were frantic when we got to him, and he laughed and said he wanted to do it again."

Meredith smiled, trying to picture Cy as a child. She knew less than nothing about his private life or his past. They'd never really talked. He'd been too hungry for her in those days. He took her to bed and out to eat and rarely anyplace else. Even when they talked, it was always about something impersonal. They never talked about themselves or the future. He seemed to think it didn't exist. Perhaps it hadn't.

"You said that Cy didn't know I was eighteen. That...mattered to him?" she asked Myrna.

"It mattered a great deal." She turned on the seat, facing Meredith. "Young women of eighteen are notorious for falling in and out of love. There was also the matter of your ignorance about men. He'd assumed you were experienced, I gathered."

Meredith averted her eyes. "Yes. I...wanted to go out with him. The other girls said that he wouldn't have anything to do with good girls."

"Oh, Meredith," Myrna said heavily.

"Hindsight is a marvelous thing, isn't it?" she asked, absently kissing Blake's dark hair. "I made so many mistakes. I did love him, so much."

"He didn't know that."

"He didn't want to know it. He told me time and time again that he wanted no part of commitment. Marriage meant fidelity, and he didn't believe in it." She leaned her head back against the seat and closed her eyes. "I'm so tired."

"So am I. You...will come back?"

"How could I stay away?" Meredith mused. "He'll need a scapegoat." She glanced at Myrna. "In fact, Mr. Smith said earlier that you and I had better find a nice, deep hole now that he knows the whole truth."

Myrna managed a smile in return. "Well, I suppose I could buy the shovel, if you'll help me dig."

Meredith laughed. "As long as he's fit enough to throw us into it, I guess I won't mind."

"Yes indeed."

They dropped Myrna off at her house, and Mr. Smith drove Meredith back to Great-Aunt Mary's.

"How is he?" he asked her when Blake was settled in front of the television watching a program on the educational channel.

"Critical, but they think he'll live. I went in and dared him to let me take over his company. I think that did it. He was fighting when I left."

"Good incentive," he mused.

She smiled ruefully. "Wait until he comes to. I don't want to be within earshot. And his mother is going to catch hell for certain."

"You haven't gotten over him at all, have you?" he asked.

She turned away, refusing to answer him. "I need a few hours' sleep. Will you call me about five?"

"Sure thing. I'll look after the little one. Don called."

"Did you tell him about Cy?"

"No. That's your business."

She grinned at him. "I like your sense of loyalty, Mr. Smith."

"I worked for Henry, not his brother." His green eyes narrowed. "Don's up to something."

"I'm not blind," she replied. "I've caught bits and pieces of conversation for weeks, and I found out plenty the last time I flew to Chicago. I know what he's up to." She pursed her lips. "I'll bet you ten cents to a dollar that he's dealing behind my back. When I'm less sleepy, I'm going to double-check on those proxies. If he's trying to cut me out with Cy, he'll have to have firm promises of support for his position."

"Do you think any of his contacts will talk?"

"Most of them wouldn't dare. But Cy's great-uncle is a man of his word, and he will. He likes me."

Mr. Smith smiled at the picture she made, even disheveled and half-asleep. "I don't blame him. I like you, too."

She frowned. "Cy never did. He wanted me. He was obsessed with me. But he never really knew me. I know more about your past than I know about his. I don't think we ever talked about a single personal thing."

"You were a different person six years ago," he suggested.

She nodded. "Yes. I'm not the woman he remembers. I wonder if he realizes that."

"Give him time and he might."

She lifted her eyes. "I hope he has time. I hope he can walk again."

"Time will tell."

"Yes."

She went up the staircase, her steps dragging a little. But when she lay down and tried to sleep, memories kept coming back to haunt her.

The first time they made love, Cy had taken her out riding on the family ranch that was located outside town. They lived in town because Myrna refused to "rough it" in the country. She had no taste for that kind of life, Cy had mentioned once. It wasn't, apparently, a socially acceptable kind of setting for her. Cy loved it. He kept Arabians, and it was two of them that he'd saddled for an outing.

Meredith had met Myrna Harden for the first time that morning, at the big Harden mansion in Billings where Cy had gone to change clothes. The older woman had been instantly cold and hostile, hardly acknowledging Meredith on her way to a bridge club meeting. She'd made it patently obvious that she had no interest in one of her son's women, and she'd made a pointed reference to a date Cy had that evening with a local debutante.

The incident had left a bad taste in Meredith's mouth. In the past few days she and Cy had gone on a picnic, and he'd taken her out to eat one night. They'd hardly had any time to be completely alone. Now she began to see that he might have other irons in the fire, and she knew she could never compete with a debutante. She didn't have the clothes or the money or the poise. She only had a body that he wanted. But if she gave in to him—and she knew all too well how badly he wanted her—it might be the last time she ever saw him. She wished she had a woman she could talk to about sex. Her great-aunt Mary wouldn't have been able to discuss the subject at all, and her great-uncle, well, that was out of the question. She was on her own, and she didn't know how to handle her blatant hunger for Cy or his for her.

Cy had tied the horses to nearby trees and led Meredith to a grove of huge cottonwood by the banks of the stream that cut through his property. He was wearing jeans, as she was, with a chambray shirt and a gray Stetson. Meredith had on a pink blouse. It was summer and hot, and the stream sounded cool. The area was deserted, miles from the house or anything else. There wasn't even a line cabin around.

"I thought you said this was a small ranch," Meredith murmured dryly, smiling at him as he leaned back against the tree trunk with his hat over his eyes.

"It is small, honey," he murmured. "Barely a thousand acres. That's a thimbleful of land by Montana standards."

"Well, it looks awfully big to me." She looped her arms over her updrawn knees and rested her chin on them as she watched the water flow. The wind blew her long blond hair all around her face. She didn't notice the tug on it at first, until Cy's hand buried itself in the tangled mass and dragged her backward, throwing her off balance so that she fell to the ground.

He flung a powerful leg across both of hers and looked down at her with glittering dark eyes.

It was like every dream she'd ever had of him. She could smell the expensive aftershave he wore, the scents of smoke and leather that clung to him. He was muscular, and she felt his warm strength and savored it. The press of his leg over hers was intimate, like the way his hard chest crushed her soft breasts. She loved the position. She loved him. For days she'd wanted so desperately for him to touch her, but he'd carefully kept his distance. This was the first time she'd been close to him, and it made her body throb in a new and frightening way.

Cy was feeling something similar. His hunger for her had kept him on the rack, but he couldn't wait any longer. He needed her. She was submissive and sweet and old enough to know her mind. There was no reason to hold back anymore.

"I've waited days for this," he said huskily. His eyes fell to her mouth. "Afraid of me, Meredith?"

"No. Not ever of you," she whispered, even though she was. A man's passion was something she'd never experienced, and in their present position she could feel the strength and heat of his arousal against her leg. It occurred to her that some men were much more generously endowed than others, and she had a moment's panic as she wondered if she could even accommodate him, with her lack of experience.

He didn't know that she was innocent, because she'd led him to believe otherwise. He thought she was twenty, when she was just eighteen. So many lies, and now the moment of truth was catching her unawares.

He bent to her mouth and brushed it open with his in lazy, smiling movements. "Soft," he whispered. "And sweet as sugar. Open it."

His tongue penetrated the dark recesses of her mouth with a slow, sensual rhythm that had a strange effect on her body. The rhythm seemed to call up something from her blood, because it made her nipples harden and kindled heat in her loins. She dug her fingers into his hard arms and heard him laugh softly under his breath.

His long leg insinuated itself between both of hers and began to move with the same rhythm as his tongue. And instantly the teasing stopped. Seconds later he stripped the blouse and bra from her, and his hard, hungry mouth fastened on her naked breast with a ferocity that almost convulsed her with pleasure. She never had time to be embarrassed about his eyes on her bare breasts, because he enmeshed her in a passion so sweeping that nothing mattered except the pleasure he was giving her.

After that, everything blurred into headlong ecstasy. He had their clothes off before she realized it, his hair-roughened body on hers, his thighs forcing hers apart.

He lifted his head and his dark eyes looked straight into hers as he went into her with one furious thrust.

The sharp pain was overshadowed by the incredible shock of penetration, so stark and raw that she felt him and only then realized that they were completely joined. Even so, she was vaguely aware that she couldn't quite absorb all of him.

"God, you're like a virgin," he said through his teeth. But his eyes closed as the heat of her burned around him, her involuntary movements triggering his desire to explosive force. He drove for satisfaction, barely lucid enough to catch her hips and ease her into the rhythm with him. He convulsed almost at once, groaning harshly at the most complete ecstasy he'd ever experienced in his life. He shuddered against her forever until his tense muscles gave, all at once, and left him shaken and sweating, dead weight on her soft body.

"I'm sorry," he whispered after a minute. His mouth found her eyes wet, but he smiled, thinking the tears were because he'd left her hanging. He nibbled gently at her mouth. "I'll wait for you this time, little one."

And he did. The second time, he kissed her and touched her in ways she'd only read about. Her body was on fire long before he drew her to him, lying on her side, and set about reducing her to tears and helpless ecstasy. She cried out, because the pleasure was so terrible she thought she might die of it, lost in the shivering oblivion of being so completely filled that she seemed to exist only as part of him.

Afterward he held her for a long time, her cheek pillowed on his damp, hairy chest while he smoked a cigarette and savored the silken brush of her bare skin against his chest, his hips, his legs, in the still afternoon. They didn't dress, because there was no need. His enjoyment in her nudity was obvious, even if he hadn't softly described her body with exquisite pleasure. He finished his cigarette and lay looking at her. Just looking, as if he found a beauty in her that he'd never thought to experience, from her long legs to the thrust of her soft pink breasts with their dark rose tips that grew slowly hard as he looked at her. She hadn't been embarrassed, she recalled. His delight in her had chased away all her inhibitions. Her first time had been sheer bliss. She wondered if he knew, but she didn't have the courage to ask.

At last he kissed her, with slow tenderness, and helped her dress. That had been the first of many long, sweet lovings. He never spoke of his feelings or made promises. Meredith in her naiveté assumed he took for granted that they would be married, since she'd given herself to him. She had no way of knowing that it was only her body he wanted, not forever.

Finally, she was reduced to tears after he took her to the penthouse and spent the day making love to her, that last time after they left the Custer battlefield. She accused him of making her his mistress, of being ashamed of her, of making her feel cheap.

Perhaps his conscience was hurting him even then, because he said that they'd get married, if that was what she wanted. But he didn't say it with pleasure, and there was no mention of a ring. He put off naming a date, even though he took her home to Myrna and mentioned to his mother in an offhand way that he and Meredith were thinking of marriage. His mother murmured something and left the room. She'd come around, Cy promised. Then he took her home and left her there.

It was three days later, early in the morning, that Myrna Harden phoned and asked her over to the house. She even sent a car for her. Meredith hoped it was an olive branch. She was so excited, waving to all Great-Aunt Mary's Crow neighbors on the reservation as the limousine wove around the small, pastel-painted houses and occasional backyard teepee on her way to the Harden estate. She was smiling.

The smile soon vanished when she got inside the house and found a cold-faced Myrna waiting for her.

"I know you're pregnant, you little tramp," Myrna whispered fiercely. "But it won't do any good to tell him, because your hold on him is about to be royally broken!"

She led a shocked Meredith into the waiting room. Cy was in there, quietly condemning her with his eyes. Tony Tanksley, who worked for Cy, was there as well, a nice young man whom Meredith liked. She smiled at him. She didn't know him well, but they'd talked often when he'd come to the café where she worked.

That smile helped tighten the noose around her neck.

In a cool, cultured voice, Mrs. Harden began to state the case against her. She'd helped Tony rob a safe in Cy's office. Meredith had been there frequently, and Cy knew that she'd seen him open it. She began to turn pale as she realized suddenly what was being done to her. She tried to protest, but Cy silenced her in a quiet, curt voice that had as much impact as a vicious shout.

Mrs. Harden went over the theft with a fine-tooth comb,

prompting Tony, who said that Meredith had helped him get into Cy's office with a skeleton key made of a wax impression from the keys in Cy's pocket. Not only that, he and Meredith had been intimate, he said, many times when Cy was out of town on business.

Myrna didn't give Meredith a chance to say anything. She dragged up Meredith's real age, hoping that Cy didn't know the truth, and added a rider to the effect that Meredith had been bragging at the café about her rich suitor and how she was going to take him to the cleaners.

Cy cut Meredith off immediately when she started speaking, his eyes black with fury, his fists clenched at his sides in almost demonic rage and sexual jealousy. She was nothing but a two-timing tramp, he accused. She could get out of his life and take her lover with her, but she wouldn't get money for it. He was going to have her arrested for the theft and watch her rot in prison!

At last, Myrna's whispered warning hit home. She could tell him she was innocent, but she was damned in his eyes. She didn't dare even tell him about the baby, because now he'd think it was Tony's. Oh, how could Myrna Harden have been so cruel, and to someone she didn't even know!

She ran. It was the hurt of having him believe such lies about her that made her run. Myrna Harden caught up with her at the back door and pressed a wad of bills into her hand. Get out quick, she told Meredith, and leave Billings. She'd try to hold Cy off long enough for her to get away, but she must never think of coming back again, as long as she lived. She'd be arrested if she even thought of it.

Meredith was hysterical, scared to death, completely at the mercy of her emotions. What if Cy called the police? Tony had already confessed and blamed her. If he testified against her, how would she manage in jail and pregnant? And what would it do to Great-Aunt Mary and Great-Uncle Raven-Walking—especially since her great-uncle worked for Harden Properties?

She ran and kept on running. She let the limousine take her back to Great-Aunt Mary's house, where she said nothing. She simply packed and kissed the worried old lady goodbye, telling her tearfully that she'd write and explain everything very soon. She gave Mary the things Cy had given her as presents, all neatly wrapped up, along with the wad of money Myrna had given her, and asked her aunt to make sure it got back to Cy Harden. Then she went to the bus station and caught the first outbound bus, which happened to be headed to Chicago. There, fate caught her up and changed her life.

Meredith opened her eyes and stared at the ceiling. Full circle, she thought numbly. Her life had started here. Now it was all but ending here. Cy might never stand again. Not that it would matter, because she could have accepted him even without legs. But bitterness and regret were poor foundations for a relationship, and pity was even worse. She still couldn't resist him physically. He was, as usual, bulldozing over her wishes. Now he'd have to ease off, while he healed. After he was back in good health again, she could begin sorting out her feelings.

Then, too, there was Blake. He was the one wild card in the deck. She didn't know how Cy was going to react to being a father. He might blame Myrna and Meredith, or he might blame himself for those six years of Blake's life he'd lost. There was also the possibility that he'd meant what he said years ago about not wanting children, and he might reject the boy entirely.

Meredith closed her eyes again and tried to force her working brain to relax. She'd just have to face those problems as they arose. Meanwhile she was Kip Tennison and she couldn't just give up the corporation because her nerves were shot. She had work to do.

Work. That brought Don to mind. She pursed her lips and smiled. So her brother-in-law was making a play for Henry's legacy and Cy's company all at once. Good enough. Perhaps Don was entitled to Tennison International, but he wasn't going to get it without a fight, not even if Meredith had to take on her brother-in-law and Cy at the same time.

If a challenge was what it took to get Cy in fighting shape, it might as well serve Meredith, too, by honing her own combat skills. She felt suddenly equal to anything fate threw at her, and she gave a silent nod of gratitude to Henry, who'd taught her a great deal about how to come out ahead.

CHAPTER FIFTEEN

IF MEREDITH'S SUSPICIONS about her brother-in-law hadn't been cemented, Don's phone call late that afternoon would have reinforced them.

"Listen," he said after she'd told him about Cy's accident, "why don't you take a few weeks off. Think of it as a vacation. There's nothing urgent, and I can handle anything that comes up. I'll send Foster overseas in my place and I'll ramrod this Harden Properties takeover for you."

"I'm in a better position to handle that than you are," she reminded him dryly.

"Well, of course, proximity and all that," he said after a minute. "I meant the paperwork."

She could almost read his mind, and she smiled to herself. "Okay. I'll need a little time while I cope with my past. But I still want to be advised of any decisions you make, and I'll handle my own correspondence. Nell can fax it down daily and I'll fax my replies back for her."

There was a pause and a sigh. "Very well."

"And, Don, thank you for your support," she said softly. "I know Henry would approve of the way you're helping me."

He cleared his throat. "I'll be speaking with you soon. Take care."

"You, too."

She put the receiver down on a harsh laugh. You can't trust anyone, she thought. Not even people who are supposed to be on your side. Henry would roll over in his grave if he knew how Don was trying to control the operation.

But as she went to the kitchen to get a cup of coffee, she had to rethink her position. After all, Don was Henry's own flesh and blood. He had every right to resent the fact that half the corporation had been given over to a very young woman with no real experience of business except what she'd been taught. Henry might have been besotted with Meredith, but Don certainly wasn't, and the corporation was his whole life.

She frowned as she sipped coffee, her mind vaguely registering her son's excited voice from the backyard, where Mr. Smith was teaching him how to play football.

They came in the back door, both flushed with exercise. "It's cold out there, Mommy!" Blake told her. "But me and Mr. Smith warmed up quick when we started passing the pigskin back and forth."

"He's a natural," Mr. Smith told her, ruffling the boy's dark hair. "Super Bowl stuff."

"Can I have coffee, Mama?" Blake asked.

"How about hot chocolate instead?" she teased, smiling at him. "Mr. Smith can have some, too."

"Mr. Smith would love some, but he can fix it," Mr. Smith informed her. "Sit down. You've had a long night."

"Who did you go see?" Blake asked her.

She hesitated. She didn't know how to put it. "A man," she said finally. "In the hospital."

"Is he going to die?"

Her heart skipped. "No," she said. "No, he isn't."

"Oh."

She absentmindedly watched Mr. Smith boil milk and chocolate. She couldn't help but wonder how Cy was going to react when he regained full consciousness. She looked at Blake and saw him in the darkness of his hair and eyes, the shape of his face. Cy would see the resemblance, too, but would it please him? Or would Blake just be another complication he didn't want?

"Stop worrying and drink your coffee," Mr. Smith said firmly. "Are you going back tonight?"

She shrugged. "I don't know."

She glanced at the clock. It was suppertime already, but she had no appetite. Mr. Smith insisted on making sandwiches, and she ate one, but without really tasting it.

The phone rang almost as soon as Meredith was finished, and she jumped to answer it.

"Meredith?" It was Myrna Harden. "I just wondered if you wanted to go back to the hospital with me."

"Yes," she said without hesitation. "I'll have Mr. Smith bring me."

"No need," Myrna replied. "I'll pick you up on my way. It'll be about fifteen minutes."

"I'll be ready."

She put the receiver down, amazed that the older woman actually wanted her company. Probably, she mused as she put on slacks and a pink silk blouse, Myrna was so upset that she just wanted someone with her, and there wasn't anybody else. Only Meredith had any real interest in Cy's future.

Myrna came to the door when she arrived. She stared down at Blake as he hugged his mother good-night.

"So handsome." The elderly woman sighed, smiling. "He's big for his age, too, isn't he?"

"Yes. I think he's going to be tall," Meredith agreed.

Blake looked up at the newcomer, his dark eyes steady and not at all shy. "I'm Blake Tennison," he told Myrna. "I'm five years old."

Myrna's eyelids flinched. Her dark eyes faintly accused Meredith before they dropped to the child. "Are you?" she asked. "Do you go to school?"

"Yes, ma'am."

"I have him in kindergarten in Chicago," Meredith said quietly.

"Our Presbyterian church has a good program," Myrna suggested.

"If we're here long enough, I might look into it. Shouldn't we go?" Another complication, Meredith thought miserably. She couldn't very well keep Blake out of kindergarten for very long.

"Yes, certainly. It was nice to meet you, Blake," Myrna said, shaking hands with him.

Meredith exchanged a speaking glance with Mr. Smith and followed her out to the car.

"Blake Tennison," Myrna said heavily as she started the car. The thought of Cy's son being raised as someone else's had a particularly keen effect on Myrna. She didn't blame Meredith—how could she?—but the pain was terrible. "Oh, Meredith!" she breathed.

"Henry was with me every step of the way through my pregnancy," Meredith told her. "He was in the delivery room when they took Blake. He helped me change diapers and give bottles, and he loved Blake even more than he loved me." Her gray eyes softened with the memory. "If ever a man worked to deserve fatherhood, it was Henry Tennison. Yes, I gave Blake his name. At the time, I had no idea that I'd ever see Cy again. I was reconciled to spending the rest of my life with Henry."

"Yes, I know." Myrna didn't look at her as she drove. The past was haunting her, and not just the part that included Meredith. There were secrets she'd kept all her life, but she was beginning to rethink her justification for keeping them. "You did the only thing you could. It's just that Blake will grow up never knowing his real father."

"Cy may not want him," she replied quietly. "Has that thought not occurred to you?"

"No. Cy loves children."

"Other people's."

"You don't think he could love his own son?"

"I never really knew Cy, except in obvious ways. He wouldn't let me close enough."

Myrna sighed wearily. "He won't let anyone close enough. I suppose his father did that to him. My husband was a past master at finding weaknesses and attacking them. He never wanted a child in the first place, but I was pregnant with Cy and I begged him to marry me, to give him a name."

Meredith stared at her. "Did you love him?"

"No." She didn't look at Meredith. "The only man I ever loved...was killed in Vietnam. He was a career officer. Cy's father was a friend of his." Her face went hard. "Frank Harden had money and prospects, and I wanted respectability and security. I threw away everything for it. I even got pregnant with Cy so that he'd marry me," she said. "But the price I paid...!"

"Have you heard from the hospital?" Meredith asked after a long pause.

"They said that Cy was resting comfortably and out of danger," Myrna replied. "I only pray that he's going to recover fully. What you said to him must have done some good, because the nurse told me that he's conscious."

Meredith studied the purse in her lap. "I wonder if we ought to congratulate ourselves on that before we've seen him?" She smiled wanly. "I have visions of being pelted with bedpans and IV bags on the way into his room."

To her surprise, Myrna Harden laughed. "Well, at least that would prove he's in fighting shape, wouldn't it?"

When they got to Cy's room—and it was a private room, because he'd been moved out of intensive care—he was lying in bed, his dark eyes open and accusing. The pain he was feeling, despite the drugs they'd given him, was as obvious as his anger.

"How do you feel?" Myrna asked him hesitantly.

"How the hell do you think I feel?" he asked, his deep voice a little slurred from medication, but cold as ice. "My God, you're brave. In your place, I'd be packing."

Myrna bit her lower lip. "Cy, try to understand...."

"I've been trying, ever since I came out from under the anesthetic. Do you know what you've cost me?"

"Yes." She averted her eyes, almost trembling. "I know all too well. But I thought I was doing what was best for you."

"I had the right to decide that. You didn't."

"Cy..."

He stared at Meredith with steady, unblinking eyes. "And you," he said in a husky tone. "Didn't you consider that it might have been worth your while to make me listen?"

"I was too afraid of being arrested to stay and try it," she said quietly.

"You could have written to me!" he raged.

She stared at her feet, without speaking. His mother was in enough trouble. She could have told him that she'd written, but she hated to make things even worse for Myrna.

"She did," Myrna confessed miserably. "I tore up the letter."

Cy cursed furiously, and his mother bit back tears.

"Get out," he told Myrna.

"Don't you do it," Meredith said when she started to leave. She moved closer to the bed and stared down at Cy. "It's ancient history. Nobody got hurt except me. You don't have to pretend that you were dying of love for me. You wanted me, and you had me. It was over before I left Billings, and you know it. You were glad of the excuse to shoot me out of your life. Certainly you had plenty of consolation after I left."

His jaw clenched. "I didn't know there was a child!"

She shrugged. "And if you had? You didn't want me in any permanent capacity. I can't imagine that you'd have wanted Blake, either."

"But your husband did?" he demanded.

"Oh, yes," she said huskily. "Yes, Henry wanted him, very much."

He gave a heavy sigh, grimaced, and closed his eyes again. His big, lean hands gripped the pillow.

"Oh, Cy," Meredith whispered.

"I'll live," he muttered. His eyes opened, glaring at the two women. "Unfortunately for you two."

Meredith glanced at his mother and grimaced, finding fellow feeling in those dark, resigned eyes.

"Do you need anything?" Myrna asked hesitantly.

"No." He bit off the word.

Meredith nodded to herself and called the nurse. After she'd given him a shot and left the room, Myrna went downstairs to get coffee for both of them. Meredith took the chair by Cy's bed and gently touched his drawn cheek.

His eyes opened, narrow and hurting. "Six years," he whispered.

She drew in a steadying breath. "Yes."

"I didn't know," he ground out. "Oh, God, Meredith, I didn't...know!"

Moisture brightened his eyes for an instant. Meredith leaned close to him, her hand smoothing his dark, damp hair, her cheek laid against his.

"Don't," she pleaded. "Cy, I can't bear it...!"

His fingers clenched hard on the pillow and he groaned.

Her lips touched his cheek, his closed eye, his chin, the corner of his hard mouth.

"Darling," she whispered. "Darling, I'm sorry, I'm so sorry."

He moved his head just enough to let her reach his lips. She kissed them with aching tenderness, a brief touch that seemed to take some of the pain out of his face. She rested her forehead on his broad shoulder in its plain hospital gown, the scent of antiseptic and medicine that clung to him reminding her painfully of the accident.

"Will I walk?" he asked.

"Of course you will," she said, praying that she hadn't told him a lie. "Try to sleep. You need all the rest you can get."

"My mother…lied to me," he bit off.

"A mother will do anything for a child she loves," she said dully. "Please, don't dwell on it. You have to get well. Try not to blame her too much."

He tried to speak, but he was too weak and pain-racked to get the words out. His eyes closed on a rasping sigh, and the medicine began to do its work. Silently Meredith let the hot tears escape her eyes.

Myrna paused in the doorway, grimacing as she saw the anguish on Meredith's vulnerable face. She deliberately backed away, leaving the younger woman her privacy. How well she understood that look. It made her guilt so much worse….

ANOTHER DAY PASSED before Cy was able to sit up in bed and eat. He was pale and weak, and he lost weight, but none of that had affected his temper. He was outspoken, rude, and totally hostile to everyone around him as he began to understand the extent of his injuries and the very real possibility that he might not be able to walk when his fractures and the scar from his back surgery healed.

"You lied to me," he accused Meredith. "You said I'd walk. The surgeon isn't sure that I will."

"You know very well he said that it depends on how well you recuperate from the surgery, and how hard you're willing to work with the physiotherapist after you're released from the hospital," she replied calmly. "Dr. Danbury thought there was every chance."

"Danbury flew in from the Mayo Clinic," he said, staring at her narrowly. "On a Tennison International jet."

She shrugged. "I beat your mother to the punch, that's all. She'd have done the same thing."

"You and I are adversaries," he said softly. "I'm grateful for what you've done, but it's not going to make any difference in a business sense. I'll fight you tooth and nail for my company."

"Oh, I never expected anything less," she mused. "I do like a good fight."

He shifted in the bed, grimacing a little. "Damned stitches pull."

"They come out in five more days and you can go home," she informed him.

He closed his eyes and lay back on the pillows. He looked pale and drawn. "I'll have to have a room downstairs," he said, thinking aloud.

"Yes." She crossed her long legs, watching him quietly.

His eyes opened, catching her at it. He studied her face, seeking out the telltale signs of fatigue. "You haven't left the hospital since I came in, except to sleep."

"Myrna needed someone. You don't have any other family."

"Imagine you, caring about my mother."

"I have a son of my own," she said stiffly. "Perhaps I understand her now a little better than I once did."

His expression stilled. His eyes averted to the window. "Do you have a picture of him?"

"Him?"

His jaw tautened as he glared at her. "My son."

Waves of sensation rippled down her body at the deep tone, the faint possessive note in it. "Yes," she said, and fumbled in her purse for her photograph of Blake with hands that were suddenly clumsy.

She brought it to Cy. He caught her wrist with a steely dark hand and held it while he took the photograph in his free hand and stared at it for a long time without speaking.

"He has your eyes," he said after a minute, "even if they're the color of mine. But he has my nose and my chin."

"He's going to be tall, too," she said hesitantly.

His gaze lifted to her face, and he watched the slow flush spread across her cheekbones. "When did we make him?" he asked.

Her body felt hot all over. She didn't want to remember.

"When?" he whispered.

"The first time," she said.

"My God." He looked at the picture again, something in his expression so foreign, so mystifying, that Meredith stared down at him helplessly.

Everything had been so cut and dried before. She and Henry had done the natural childbirth classes together, he'd been with her when Blake was born, he was always there as the child grew and thrived. But now she realized just how much a substitute Henry had been for what she'd really wanted—for Cy, doing all those things with her. Cy, holding her at night when she worried about labor; taking her to the hospital when the time came; staring down at his first child in his arms. Tears stung her eyes.

He looked up and saw them. His chest rose and fell heavily,

and his eyes were dark with sadness and pain. He let go of her wrist and handed the photograph back.

"I wouldn't have known," he said, almost to himself. He stared out the window without seeing anything. "I'd never have seen him."

If Henry had lived, he meant. Meredith traced her son's dark hair on the photograph before she put it back in her purse and sat down again. "One day I'd have told him," she said eventually. "Henry and I both agreed that he had the right to know who his real father was."

Myrna Harden had come into the room while Meredith was speaking. She stood quietly in the doorway, grimacing as she listened to that last damning statement. So she'd have told Cy eventually. Perhaps it was just as well to have it out in the open now.

"Back so soon?" he asked sarcastically. "If that's for me, I'm tired of coffee."

Myrna handed a cup of black coffee to Meredith, taking the other to her own seat by the window. "It's not for you," she told Cy with magnificent unconcern. This was how she handled his furious temper, by ignoring it. He'd been hostile for days, and it hurt, but she wasn't going to let him see how much, even if she did realize that she deserved everything she was getting.

"I feel like hell," Cy muttered on a weary sigh. "The company's going to pot while I lie around doing nothing."

"Your vice president is coping quite nicely," Myrna informed him.

"Is he? Coping, and keeping predators away?" he added with a meaningful glance at Meredith.

"This predator is too tired to nip away at your company," Meredith replied. "For the moment, anyway. I'll wait until you're back on your feet."

"Sporting of you," he mused. His eyes darkened. "And if I'm never back on my feet?"

"Dr. Danbury said you will be," she replied. "He's the best in his field."

He looked at her for a long moment, reading truth in her expression. He seemed to relax a little. "All right."

"You'll be able to come home in a few days," Myrna said.

"I'll move into the penthouse apartment," Cy announced, watching his mother turn pale.

"No, you will not," Meredith said firmly. "You'll go home, where you belong."

His eyebrows lifted. "Are you going to make me?"

"No. But Mr. Smith will," she told him. "I'm going to lend him to your mother for a week or so, just until you're settled in. Mr. Smith is very good at physiotherapy."

"Like hell I'll have your lover in my house!" Cy raged.

"Mr. Smith is not, and has never been, my lover," Meredith said calmly. "He's my bodyguard. There was an attempt to kidnap Blake earlier this year. If it hadn't been for Mr. Smith, I don't know what might have happened."

He scowled, feeling protective stirrings deep inside himself. "Kidnapping?"

Her gray eyes searched his face. "Cy, do you have any idea of my net worth as Henry's heir? That kind of money makes anyone close to me a target. Especially Blake. Mr. Smith never leaves him for a minute, unless he's certain we're in a secure area."

"What a hell of a life for a child," he said quietly.

"And for his mother," she agreed. "It wears on my nerves from time to time. Mr. Smith is ex-CIA, and he was a mercenary for some years. Believe me, he knows his business."

Cy seemed to relax a little, but his eyes were still glittering with feeling.

Myrna was thinking while she listened. She had a solution that was going to make everything all right—even give her a buffer against her son's righteous anger.

"Meredith," she began slowly, "why don't you move in with us while Cy recuperates?"

The younger woman gaped at her. She should have expected the suggestion, but she hadn't.

"Yes, why don't you?" Cy asked without offering a single argument. "It's a big house. Plenty of room. You can even bring Mr. Smith," he added curtly, "as long as you keep him away from me."

"It's an ideal arrangement," Myrna coaxed. "We have an excellent cook and housekeeper. You can work from the house. We have a telephone and a fax machine...."

"Yes, Meredith, you can work on taking over my company from my own phone," Cy drawled, glaring at his mother.

"Talk about inside sabotage," Meredith murmured dryly.

"Think about it." Myrna's dark eyes pleaded.

Meredith was weighing alternatives in her mind. Cy had perked up considerably since Myrna made the suggestion. It would give her the opportunity to help spur him to recovery. But Myrna would get close to Blake, and that was definitely a risk. Of course, Cy would get close to him, too....

"All right," she said finally, and Cy and Myrna both seemed to relax. "But there's a condition. Blake isn't to know anything about the past," she added, looking directly at Cy's mother.

There was a definite hesitation. But Myrna knew she had no other choice, and she relented because it was the only way she was going to get to see her grandchild at all.

"Fair enough," she told Meredith.

The younger woman nodded. The conversation changed,

but for the rest of the day Meredith wondered if she'd done the right thing. And she still had to break the news to Mr. Smith, who was certainly not one of Cy's biggest fans.

CHAPTER SIXTEEN

THE HARDEN HOME was as elegant as Meredith remembered it. It was difficult not to dwell on the last time she'd been here or the anguish she'd felt as she left. Mr. Smith glared at her as he helped move suitcases and equipment into the rooms Myrna had prepared for their use. "Are you out of your mind?" he asked. "Don't you know what she's plotting?"

"She wants to get to know her grandson," Meredith replied. "And I'm handy to keep Cy from eating her alive. Yes, I know why we're here."

He sighed heavily, eyeing her. "Still crazy about him, aren't you?"

She smiled and nodded.

He shrugged. "Okay. We'll settle in. Mrs. Harden just appropriated Blake and herded him into the kitchen. I'll bet she's planning to stuff him full of sweets. Not good for him. He needs healthy food."

"I'll go tell her right now." She paused in the doorway. "Bear with me. It's a difficult situation all around. I have to decide what to do. I can't walk out on Cy while he's in this condition. He's convinced himself that he won't walk, even though he's got feeling in his legs. He's weak and can't stand, and he thinks it's permanent."

"What did that specialist really say?" he asked.

She moved back into the room, so that there was no danger of anyone overhearing. "A disk in Cy's back was ruptured. If the nerve roots had been damaged, he'd never have walked again. There's a lot of bruising, and muscle damage. Dr. Danbury repaired it, but he's going to have some numbness and tingling and weakness for a while longer."

Mr. Smith whistled through his teeth. "Poor guy."

"Cy doesn't believe that he's going to improve. So he needs all the support he can get right now. I can't leave him. Regardless of what happened in the past, he is Blake's father."

"No getting around that," he agreed. He smiled faintly. "Looks just like him."

She smiled back. "Yes, he does."

As she walked into the kitchen, Myrna was supervising the preparation of little cakes just for Blake.

"Look what the lady's making me!" Blake enthused, laughing up at his mother. "Tea cakes! Mrs. Harden says that she used to make them for her little boy."

"Her little boy is quite grown now," Meredith said, smiling at him. "You mustn't be any trouble."

"I won't be, I promise. I like cakes."

"Is it all right?" Myrna asked belatedly.

"I don't mind. Mr. Smith does." She grinned at Myrna Harden. "What he doesn't know won't hurt us."

Myrna grimaced. "It's like having Cy duplicated, isn't it?" she murmured. "He's very…formidable."

"Marshmallow underneath. Honest," Meredith added.

"I'll reserve judgment. Do you want some coffee?"

"Yes. Shall I take a cup to Cy?"

"Let's both do it," Myrna said. "We might take Blake with us."

"Safety in numbers?" Meredith asked under her breath.

"Don't you think it's wise?"

"Considering the language I heard when we first came in, yes," Meredith said without argument.

Blake was all questions as they went down the long hall to the room Cy was using on the ground floor. It was, like the rest of the house, filled with priceless antiques, including a huge four-poster bed. Cy was lying against pillows on the headboard, a sheet thrown haphazardly across his hips, his broad, hair-roughened chest bare. He glared at them, uncomfortable from the ride in the ambulance and the unfamiliar hardness of the mattress he was lying on.

"This was my grandfather's bed," he said without greeting them. "No wonder he died young."

Meredith had to smother a giggle.

"You came to see my mommy," Blake recalled, going right up to the bed to stare at the dark-haired man in it. He'd been warned about getting on the mattress and shaking the man, but nobody said he couldn't rest his arms on it, and he did.

Cy hadn't been quite prepared for the fact of the child so close to him. He stared at the young face that was almost a mirror image of his own and felt something sick in his throat. His son. Until now children had been a vague thought. But this was his flesh and blood, part of him. Part of Meredith. His face tautened and color shot along his cheekbones as he stared with pure possession and a shock of joy at the child who looked so much like him.

"You're Blake, aren't you?" Cy asked to fill the tense silence.

"I'm Blake Garrett Tennison," the boy agreed, without knowing how the name hurt the man sitting so still in the bed. "I'm five years old and I can spell my name. Do you like iguanas? Mr. Smith has one. She lives with us."

"She's living with us now," Myrna said. Amazingly, she'd been fascinated with the giant lizard and not at all afraid of it. Something that couldn't be said for the housekeeper and cook, who had threatened to quit on the spot.

"She likes Tiny," Blake said, his small face animated. "Do you like lizards?"

"I've never thought about it." Cy hadn't taken his eyes off Blake since the child had come into the room. "I suppose I can get used to one."

"Tiny has her own cage. She sleeps in it at night. But sometimes she sleeps on the curtain rod."

"Iguanas like high places, don't they?" Cy asked, his voice more tender than Meredith had ever heard it.

"Are you sick?" Blake asked.

"I was in an accident," Cy replied. "I have to stay in bed for a while."

"I'm sorry. Does it hurt?"

Cy's jaw went taut. "Yes," he said huskily. "It hurts."

Meredith knew instinctively that he wasn't talking about any physical injury. She didn't know what to say. While she was trying to formulate words, Cy's dark eyes shot up to catch and hold hers. The look in them was so intense that she blushed.

"Let's check on your cakes, Blake, shall we?" Myrna asked with a smile, and held out her hand.

Blake took it unhesitatingly. "I'll come back to see you, if you like. I'm sorry you feel bad," he told Cy.

"Thanks," the man replied heavily.

The door closed behind Myrna and Blake, and Meredith looked down at Cy with confused emotions.

"You let me give you a baby," he said unsteadily.

"I didn't know anything about birth control," she hedged, folding her arms over her breasts. "I was afraid to admit it. I always thought men took care of that."

"I assumed you were on the Pill. Or maybe I didn't," he

said after a minute. "Pregnancy never occurred to me. Certainly not that first time. I wanted you so badly, I don't even remember how I got you on the ground."

She flushed, because it had been just that way for her. She stared at her feet.

"You could have had an abortion," he persisted.

She smiled at him and shook her head. "That was never an option."

"Not even after what I believed about you?" he asked with pained eyes. "Thinking I hated you?"

"When I got to Chicago, one of the first things I did was to get caught in the rain and fall under the wheels of Henry's car." Her eyes softened with memory. "He and Mr. Smith sort of took me over, right there. Before I knew it, I was married."

"You wrote to me, you said," he asked.

"Henry insisted. He knew very well how I felt about you." Her face turned toward the curtained window. "He wanted to make sure I knew there was no chance you might still want me. When I got no reply to the letter…well, I assumed you were out for blood."

"I never saw it."

Her eyes met his. "What if you had?"

His face went even harder. "It hardly makes any difference now."

He didn't want to remember. She read that in his dark eyes. Well, he was right, it didn't make any difference. "Are you hungry?" she asked, changing the subject. "I could bring you a salad or a sandwich."

"Are you going to tell the boy about me?" he asked.

She hesitated. She didn't know what to say. Her own emotions were still in a state of flux. She'd lived on vengeance since Henry's death. "I don't know."

He shifted against the pillows. His back was giving him

hell. They'd taken out the stitches that held the incision together, and he was taking painkillers, but all the moving around had made him uncomfortable. And, worst of all, he still couldn't stand by himself.

"Why can't I stand up?" he asked, slapping at one hard muscled thigh impotently. "Why are they so damned weak?"

"You've been in a terrible accident," she said softly. "You can't expect to get well overnight. The muscles were badly damaged."

"My spine was badly damaged as well," he replied, his eyes catching hers. "That's what the surgery was all about, but you and my mother got to the doctor before I did. He won't tell me a damned thing."

"He's told you the truth," she said firmly.

"Will I walk again?" he demanded.

She couldn't have lied to him. Those dark eyes seemed to see right through her. "Yes."

"You don't know," he persisted. "You don't have the faintest idea if I will or not. You're guessing."

"I'm not guessing! Will you listen? They wouldn't have let you come home if they weren't sure you'd walk again."

"So you keep saying."

"It's the truth."

"Why are you here? Because you care about me or because I'm Blake's father?"

"Both."

His hard face didn't relax. "Did my mother tell you that I was on my way to your house when this happened? Is that why you feel guilty?"

"No," she faltered. "She didn't know where you were going. She only said that she'd just…just told you about what happened six years ago."

His chest rose and fell heavily. "I went wild. The truth was hard to swallow." His eyes were remorseful as they met hers. "I wouldn't listen to you when you tried to tell me you were innocent. That hurt most of all, didn't it, that we'd been intimate and I still took other people's words above your own?"

"Yes," she replied. She sat down on the chair by the bed, crossing her jean-clad legs. "I loved you." She smiled faintly. "I suppose I had some crazy idea that you felt the same way, that you really meant it when you said we'd get married." She dropped her eyes to her lap, missing the expression that crossed his face. "I should have known better, but I was eighteen and in love for the first time. I wasn't looking ahead."

"Neither was I. I thought you were twenty. I told myself you were experienced, even though I really knew the truth that first time, when you cried and tried to push me away...." He lay back and closed his eyes. "I couldn't quite handle innocence. Until you came along, I'm not sure I believed it existed in grown women."

"I knew you wouldn't have anything to do with me if you knew how green I really was," she said honestly. "I lied to you. I suppose you wondered if I even knew how to tell the truth when you found out."

His dark eyes slid over her face, to her mouth and lower, to her soft breasts outlined under the green silk T-shirt she was wearing. "I was addicted to you," he said. "I dreamed about you, ached for you. When we were apart, you were all I thought about. I was bitterly jealous of you as well. Tony's accusation only emphasized the fears that popped up when I found out your age. I thought you were too young and fickle for any lasting relationship. It was the main reason I let you go." He touched his chest idly. "Afterward, I regretted that assumption. I wondered if my own fear of commitment had pushed you into Tony's arms. I had no idea that my mother had orchestrated the whole damned mess, of course," he added bitterly. "When I began to suspect the truth, it was too late. I couldn't find Tony. I couldn't find you, either."

"Henry sent me down to the Bahamas after we were married, to his estate. I spent my whole pregnancy there."

"My detective wasn't looking for Kip Tennison," he agreed. He studied her. "Why Kip?" he asked with a faint smile.

"I had a passion for kippered herring while I was carrying Blake. Henry had to ship it in by the case for me." She smiled ruefully. "He started calling me Kip as a joke, and it stuck. After a while I forgot that I'd been called anything else."

"Mother said you had a hard time with Blake."

She nodded. "They had to do a C-section. I still don't know what went wrong. They let Henry into the delivery room—something they never made a practice of—because they thought they were going to lose me."

He scowled. There was something else, something she wasn't saying.

"Why?" he asked quietly.

"Does it matter?"

"Come here."

She hesitated. He held out his hand, waiting. Finally she gave in, sitting gingerly on the bed beside him while he pressed her fingers to his chest and looked at her.

"Why did they think they might lose you?" he repeated softly.

"I didn't want to live," she whispered, staring at his fingers covering her own. "Henry knew it. He...he stood beside me and talked to me the whole time. He described Blake and how perfect he was, and how I had to stay alive because Blake would need me." She met his eyes. "That's why I talked to you, in the intensive care unit. I remembered what Henry said to me, so I must have heard him. I realized that you could probably hear what the doctors had said, about your back. I had to give you a reason to live, just as Henry gave me one."

His fingers contracted around hers. "Did you think about me, when you saw Blake?"

"Yes. It…made things so much more difficult. Henry loved me desperately. I felt such guilt that I couldn't return his feelings for me." She curled her hand into his and studied it. "The night before he crashed was the first time in three years of marriage that I…really wanted him. I'm glad," she added, lifting her eyes to his bravely. "I'm glad I gave him that memory, and the hope that I might grow to love him, so that he didn't die with nothing."

He caught his breath at the feeling that showed in her tormented eyes. "God, what I've cost you…. Come here!"

He drew her down into his arms and closed them around her, holding her, letting the hot tears seep onto his bare chest as she gave way finally to all the grief and all the pain.

His fingers sifted through her soft blond hair and he kissed her forehead absently, aware of her floral scent, her vulnerability. His body began to stir involuntarily, until he could feel the raging desire that she kindled.

He caught his breath audibly. "My God!" he gasped.

She lifted her head and met his eyes curiously. "I'm sorry, did I hurt you?" she asked, sniffing as she wiped away the tears.

"It isn't that." He drew her hand under the sheet and smoothed it gently over the raging force of his desire, his fingers clenching in protest when she instinctively jerked against them.

"No," he whispered. "Feel it. At least I'm still a man, even if I can't stand up."

Her hand relaxed, although she blushed scarlet as he positioned her fingers and moved them gently, so that the movement made him grimace and groan softly.

"Cy," she protested weakly, and drew her hand away. He let her, his chest rising and falling heavily until he managed to get himself under control.

"It's been a long time," he said with a rough laugh.

"Surely not," she murmured, still a little embarrassed. "Your friend Lara looks capable of giving you anything you need."

"She isn't you," he said quietly. "Nobody ever was. What you give me, I can't have with anyone else." He didn't even blink. "I had nothing from Lara. I never slept with her. Once you came back, it would have been impossible with anyone else."

The memories lay soft and hungry in his eyes, and he laughed suddenly as they teased his body into another fierce arousal.

Meredith's eyes fell to the sheet. He threw it off, letting her look, his expression half-amused, half-rueful.

"See what you do to me?" he asked. "One man out of twenty can make love time after time without rest. That's what the book says. My body doesn't know that it's supposed to be incapable of multiple orgasms."

She looked at him helplessly, her eyes lingering on the evidence of his desire with an almost tangible hunger to satisfy it. But that wasn't possible. Not in his condition. Rosy-cheeked, she forced her hand to move, to pull the sheet back up to his waist, her fingers trembling. "It never did," she whispered. "You never seemed to tire, in the old days. I remember once, we made love three times in a row without even stopping."

"The last time," he replied quietly. "The night before my mother's surprise." The smile faded. "I don't know if I can ever forgive her for that."

"You have to," she said. "Life goes on. We can't change what happened."

"You were bitter when you came back to Billings," he reminded her. "Out for blood, any way you could get it."

"Yes." She tugged at the thick hair on his chest. "When you wrecked the car, I suppose I got my priorities straight again. I've lived for revenge since Henry died. I wanted your mother to have to confess her sins to you." She winced. "Oh, Cy, if I'd known what would happen to you…!"

He linked his fingers with hers. "You'd have gone away. I'd never have known about Blake. I'd never have seen you again."

"You've done very well without me for six years," she reminded him.

"No." He studied her face quietly. "I've had one or two women. But it was physical, not emotional. And when I lost control, it was your face I saw, your name I cried out." His eyes averted to the wall and his jaw tautened. "And I felt guilty. As if I'd committed adultery."

"That's…that's how I felt, with Henry," she whispered.

His eyes slid back up to hers and searched them for a long, long moment. "I still want you."

"Yes. I know. But you can't," she said huskily. "Not with your back in that condition."

"You'd let me, wouldn't you?" he asked, one eye narrowing as he studied her. "If I couldn't take you, you'd take me, if I asked you to."

She swallowed. Her eyes ran hungrily over his broad, hair-matted chest. "Haven't I already proved that?"

"Yes." He reached up and drew her down over him, so that her mouth was just above his. "You've given me back my manhood. I wasn't sure that I could still function, you see."

She smiled as his mouth poised just under hers. "I was."

He chuckled. "Kiss me."

Her lips brushed his, lifted and settled. His lean hands caught her head and held it where he wanted it while his mouth made slow, hungry love to hers.

"I want you so much," he whispered, nibbling her lower lip. His whole body trembled with the need. "I want to be enveloped by that hot, silky softness…."

She moaned into his mouth, the words making her blood run hot. She clung to him, living on his kiss while the world spun around her.

"Take off your clothes and lie with me," he whispered into her lips.

"I can't."

"Yes, you can. Lock the door."

She smiled against his hungry mouth. "You aren't fit."

"Yes, I am." He slid her hand down his belly and proved it.

"That way, but not the rest of you." She nuzzled her cheek against his. "You'll undo all Dr. Danbury's good work."

He bit her upper lip sensually. "What did he do?"

"Scooped out the damaged vertebra and did a laminectomy."

"To relieve the pressure on the nerves."

"Yes."

His mouth slid down her throat, hesitating in the soft hollow of it before his lips trespassed onto her silk T-shirt and suddenly fastened onto the throbbing hard tip of her breast.

"Cy!" she cried out, convulsing almost at once from the merciless stab of pleasure.

His free hand slid under the shirt and unfastened her bra while his mouth fed on her. Seconds later she felt the air as he pushed it up and nibbled softly at her breasts, lifting her so that he could look at them.

"Did you nurse my son?" he murmured.

"Yes," she moaned.

"Did you let him watch?"

She trembled. She couldn't think, couldn't breathe.

"Did you let him watch?" he asked again, his mouth suckling hungrily at her breast.

"Yes!"

"Damn you," he bit off, and his lips were fierce and thorough, so that by the time he'd finally had his fill, she was shaking all over and flushed with the force of pleasure he'd aroused.

He held her firmly, the pain in his back forgotten as he looked up at her. Disheveled blond hair, flushed face, wide gray eyes, trembling, swollen mouth, beautiful bare breasts with hard rosy crowns. He caught his breath at his handiwork.

"You're going to give me another child," he said roughly. "But this time you won't run away. I'm going to watch you grow big with it. I'm going to be there when it's born. This next one is going to be mine from the instant you conceive it, and I'll never let you go."

"Cy, you…can't," she whispered.

He smiled slowly, his eyes falling to her stomach. "Yes, I can. Maybe not just yet. But in another few weeks, when the fractures and the surgery heal." His face hardened. "Even if I can't dash around, I can make love. So if you stay here, it's going to happen."

"Why?" she asked huskily as she righted her blouse and bra.

"I want my son, Meredith," he said. "If you're pregnant, you're much more likely to stay with me."

Her eyes darkened with pain. "I see."

"No, you don't," he said, his eyes steady and unblinking. "But you will, eventually. In the meanwhile, you and I might get to know each other. Really know each other."

"We never talked," she said.

"I know that." He smiled at her. "We've both changed in six years. I think it might be an adventure, just catching up. If you get pregnant, that's a bonus." His face hardened. "You belong to me. That hasn't changed."

She didn't want to think about that or what he'd threatened. Another child would tie her to him. But his motives still escaped her. Did he only want her? Or did he want Blake, as he'd said, and meant to get him any way he could? She didn't quite trust him, so it was just as well that he wasn't capable of intimacy just yet.

"Would you like some fresh coffee?" she asked, noticing that what she'd brought for them had gone cold.

"Yes. And a steak."

"I'll see what I can do."

"Meredith."

She turned, her hand on the doorknob.

He hesitated, his fist clenching on the bed beside him as he looked at her and tried to picture her as she'd been when she carried Blake. "Nothing."

"I'll be right back," she told him, and quickly left the room.

SHE SAT WITH HIM that night. She and Myrna had been taking turns at the hospital, one sleeping while the other kept watch, in case he needed anything or took a turn for the worse. She still didn't feel comfortable in bed while he was in pain. The fractures still hurt, and the physical therapy he endured daily seemed to aggravate his suffering.

In the early hours before daylight, he awoke, moaning as the pain lanced through his back and legs.

Meredith was awake instantly, smoothing back his dark hair over his sweaty brow. "Need something for the pain?" she whispered.

"Yes." His jaw clenched. "Damned exercises."

"They're helping. Here." She handed him the pain capsule and a muscle relaxant that the doctor had prescribed, letting him swallow them down with water.

He grimaced as the agony overwhelmed him, his hands clenching the covers.

"I'm sorry," she whispered. "Cy, I'm so sorry!"

He opened his eyes and saw the torment in hers. His hand reached up and touched her cheek, almost in wonder, as he realized just how deep her feeling for him went. He'd never considered that before, nor how empty his life had been without her. She made anything bearable, even pain.

"Come here, little one," he said quietly. "Lie with me."

"But your back..."

"It can't hurt more than it already does. Let me hold you."

She hesitated, but it was beyond her to refuse him anything in his condition. She eased down beside him, letting him fold her against his powerful body under the sheet and blanket. He was nude, as he always slept, while she was still wearing the jeans and silk T-shirt she'd had on earlier. He molded her body against his with a long, shuddering sigh, his face in the soft hair at her throat.

"Silk against bare skin is very seductive, did you know?" he whispered as he smoothed her breasts against his hard chest. "And you smell of wildflowers."

"Perfume," she murmured. "It's mostly worn off." Her eyes closed and she sighed, drinking in the feel and warmth of him, smiling as she let drowsiness wash over her.

"I've never...slept with anyone," he said slowly. His hand stroked her hair. "Made love, yes. But I never stayed all night. I never wanted to."

"I remember."

"I suppose you slept with him?" he asked, his voice harsh.

"Not all night," she whispered. "We had separate rooms."

She felt him relax, felt some of the tension ease out of him. He kissed her forehead with breathless tenderness and eased her cheek against his hair-roughened chest. He caught her hand and tangled it in the thick hair, pressing the soft palm against his skin.

"Tell me about Blake. Does he play baseball, watch game shows? What is he like?"

"He's all boy," she said proudly, her voice hushed and soft in the darkness. "He likes to play football with Mr. Smith. He watches *Sesame Street* and *Mr. Rogers* on TV, he likes to be read to. He's stubborn and he has a violent temper when he can't do something the right way the first time he tries it. He loves cake and chocolate ice cream, and trips to the zoo and picnics."

"Do you take him on picnics?"

"Mr. Smith and I do," she said. "It's much too dangerous for us to go alone, in Chicago."

He didn't like that. His body tensed. "I don't like the idea of Mr. Smith, necessary or not."

"He doesn't like you, either," she pointed out. "But you'll have to get used to each other, if I stay around here very long, because he's part of my family."

He tugged on a lock of her hair. "What do you mean, *if* you stay?"

Her nails traced a path on his broad chest. "When you're back on your feet, you might not want me here."

He scowled. Did that mean she wanted to go? Was she only with him out of pity?

When he didn't reply, she assumed that he was agreeing with her, that he only needed her while he was helpless. If Cy Harden could ever be called helpless, she thought in silent amusement. It was like lying in the clutch of a bear, warm but precarious.

She nuzzled closer, refusing to think ahead. "Hold me," she whispered.

His arms contracted obligingly. "You can't be comfortable like that," he whispered. "Ease your leg between mine."

"I can't. I might hurt your back."

"It won't hurt. Do it."

She obeyed him, the soft stuff of her expensive jeans making a quiet noise as her long leg insinuated itself gently and forced his apart. She heard him catch his breath and seconds later felt why.

He laughed harshly. "Easy," he said in a strained tone. "Watch where you move."

"Are you shy?" she teased, deliberately moving her hand so that it brushed his lower body.

He groaned and shivered. His fingers caught her hand and dragged it back to his chest, holding it there. "You witch," he growled. "Stop that!"

Her smile was buried against the crisp hairs on his chest. "You might sound a little more grateful. Now we know you're not impotent."

"Keep in mind that I'm in no condition to prove it."

"Yes," she said sadly. "I'm trying to."

His hands moved to her back, lightly caressing. "Will you give yourself to me when I get on my feet again?"

"Of course I will," she said without hesitation.

"Promise."

"I promise."

His chest rose and fell on a heavy breath. "I'll hold you to that. Turn off the light, honey. Let's try and get some sleep."

She reached up and turned the switch on the bedside lamp, letting him settle her against him before he tucked the covers over her. She felt his mouth against hers for an instant before he lay back and closed his eyes.

"Heaven," he murmured as he sank into sleep.

Meredith barely heard him, but she smiled.

CHAPTER SEVENTEEN

MEREDITH WAS SPRAWLED OVER Cy's body when consciousness seeped into her tired brain at daylight. She felt his big hand at the base of her spine and something uncomfortably blatant against her belly. She moved gingerly, only then discovering that one of her legs had eased its way across both of his, so that she was lying almost completely on him.

"Cy?" she murmured.

"What?" he whispered, his own voice slurred.

"I have to get up," she said. "This isn't good for your back."

"It's great for the other parts of me," he murmured. "Take your jeans off and help me get rid of this," he coaxed, moving her blatantly against him.

She lifted her head and looked down into his dark, smoldering eyes. Her eyes smiled. "No," she said. "Not until you're well."

"What if I don't get well?" he asked curtly. "I can still barely stand without Smith to help me, despite the exercises...."

"You have to give it time, Mr. Impatience," she whispered, smiling as she bent down to kiss his mouth. "Now let me up, before you do any more damage to yourself."

Both his hands were behind her now, crushing her down on him. "I need you," he said. "God...!"

He shuddered from pain as much as desire, and she felt guilty all the way to her bare feet, but she didn't dare let him do what he wanted. It was too great a risk, and she said so.

"It's been…weeks," he groaned, his face tormented as he looked up at her. "Weeks since I had you. Don't you understand?"

He was a sensual man. He always had been. For him, sex was as much a necessity as breathing, but what he was asking was too dangerous. For his own good, she had to help him abstain.

"I understand very well," she whispered. "But we can't." She eased away, and he let her, with evident reluctance.

She bent, drawing her lips softly over his face, touching them to his closed eyes, his nose, his high cheekbones, his hard mouth.

"What are you doing?" he murmured.

"Kissing you better. Do you mind?"

He smiled under the brush of her lips, and his eyes opened, dark and soft as they met hers. "No. I don't mind."

She nibbled at his mouth, his chin, letting her lips drift down to the rough surface of his chest.

"Here," he said, guiding her lips to a hard, flat male nipple.

She smiled against his skin as he shivered, remembering how it had always excited him when she did that. Playing with fire, she thought dimly, knowing that she should stop, before she aroused him even more.

She sat up slowly, her eyes warm and loving as they smiled down into his. "I'm sorry," she said. "I've made it worse."

His chest rose on a shaky breath. "It couldn't get much worse." His body shifted and he winced. "I need something, honey."

"I'll get you some fresh water." She got up to fill a glass in the bathroom. She handed him his medicine and waited until he'd swallowed it before she put the glass on his bedside table. He was pale and drawn, and she wondered worriedly if the pain was a bad sign.

He opened his eyes, looking up at her. "Don't look so worried," he murmured. "I won't die."

"I hate to see you in pain," she said.

He smiled. "A likely story," he mused. "I told you what I needed, but you wouldn't do it."

"Your back isn't up to it."

"I guess not." He arched, grimacing, a hand going to his lower spine.

"I'm sorry," she said miserably. She brushed back her disheveled hair. "Can you eat something, or do you want to wait until the medicine takes effect?"

"Bacon and eggs," he murmured. "Butter me a biscuit to go with it, and sweeten and cream my coffee."

"That's a change," she said.

He laughed through the pain, his dark eyes sweeping over her. "Oh, I've changed," he agreed. "For the first time in my life, I've got my priorities straight." He caught her hand and pulled until she sat down beside him. He brought her palm to his lips. "You slept in my arms," he said huskily. "It's the first good night's sleep I've had since this happened. I woke once and saw you next to me. I wanted to wake you and make the sweetest kind of love to you in the dark."

She blushed a little and averted her eyes to his chin. "You can't manage that kind of exertion yet."

"My mind can." He rubbed her knuckles against his hard cheek, where a day's growth of beard rasped the soft skin. "How am I going to work in this condition?" he asked suddenly, his face going hard.

"Get on the telephone and give your board of directors

hell for letting me walk off with those proxies," she said, deliberately reminding him that she was trying to take his company.

He glared at her. "I'll get them back," he threatened.

"I'm counting on it." She smiled, tracing the stubble on his chin. "Oh, Cy, you're more of a man without the use of your legs than most men are with them, don't you know that? But it isn't going to happen. You're getting stronger every day. Exercise is helping."

"Are you going to stay until I heal?" he asked shrewdly.

"Yes." She said it without hesitation, without even thinking of the consequences.

"What about your own company? Your obligations?"

"Don is handling things. I'll keep up with the rest with the phone and the fax machine. Otherwise, I'm taking a few weeks off."

"You look as if you could use it," he said quietly. "Mother said that you haven't left me since I landed in the hospital."

She shrugged. "I didn't have anything else to do, and you needed watching. Your mother couldn't do it alone."

"I won't forgive her," he said doggedly.

"Yes, you will." She bent and kissed his stubborn mouth. "Now, lie there and heal. I'll get your breakfast."

He caught her arms, pulling her down so that he could reach her mouth. He kissed it hotly, with feverish need. "I want you," he said harshly.

"I want you, too. Now close your eyes and try to rest."

He let her go with an audible sigh. "I thought it might diminish a little over the years," he said, tracing her body with his eyes. "It gets worse."

"Addictions do, until you take the cure," she said lightly, trying not to react to the wounding the words caused. It was always physical with Cy. It had never been anything else.

"You aren't an addiction," he said shortly. "You're everything."

The way he said it brought a scarlet blush to her face. She wouldn't look at him. He was hurt and she was looking after him. It might be nothing more than misplaced gratitude. The past had taught her not to trust him. She couldn't relent now.

"I'll be back in a few minutes."

She left without another word, and Cy clenched his fist and hit the mattress in impotent rage. She wouldn't give him an inch. She was her own woman now, so self-possessed and confident that she made him nervous. Once, he could have reduced her to begging when he touched her. Now, she could walk away from him without even looking back. It made him less confident, less sure of her. She wanted him. But he wanted more than that. He wanted to be her world, as she'd long ago become his. The years without her had been hellish, anguished, lonely. Even under the circumstances, it was heaven to have her back. Her, and the child she'd given him. He groaned silently, hating the years he'd missed because of his mother. Why had she done that to him? His own son didn't know him, had another man's name, had called another man Father. Meredith would have spent her life as Kip Tennison if her husband hadn't died so unexpectedly. All that, because Myrna Harden hadn't thought Meredith was good enough for her son. How ironic that it was Meredith who'd given him the one chance he had of being able to walk again. Meredith, whom Myrna had discounted as of no importance. And now she could buy and sell the Hardens and most other people.

He could have cheerfully thrown his mother off the roof. But she seemed different since his accident. Less cold and haughty, less arrogant. Since the child had been in the house, she laughed. She was a changed woman.

As he considered that transformation, he considered the change in Meredith. She was everything he wanted. He couldn't let her get away again. He had to keep her here, whether or not his back healed, because he wasn't sure he could live without her.

But he might have nothing to offer her. Despite Smith's help with physiotherapy, he was barely walking. He cursed until his throat hurt. He wouldn't be an object of pity. He'd blow his damned brains out first. His heavy brows drew together. Of course, if he did that, he'd certainly never see Meredith or his son again. So much for easy ways out, he thought ruefully. Going down into the dark without the hope of eternity with her hurt him. He'd just have to walk again, he told himself. That was all there was to it.

MEREDITH WALKED DOWN the hall to the kitchen, where Blake and Mrs. Harden and Mr. Smith were all working to get breakfast together.

"Cook's day off," Mrs. Harden said with a smile. "Meredith, can you make biscuits?"

"Of course." She set to work while Mr. Smith fried bacon, Mrs. Harden scrambled eggs, and Blake placed napkins on the table.

"Isn't this fun, Mommy?" Blake asked excitedly. "This lady says I can play with her son's toy soldiers after breakfast."

"Cy used to have some metal ones," Myrna explained. "They're in a case. I thought, if you don't mind, he might have them."

"I don't mind," Meredith said. Impulsively she handed Blake a napkin and fork. "Would you like to take that to Cy?"

"To the man in bed?"

"Yes."

"Okay." He ran out of the room.

Myrna glanced at Meredith, her face worried.

"Trust me," Meredith told the older woman. "It's all right."

She sighed heavily. "He's said very little about Blake."

Meredith smiled. "He's curious about him. I want Blake to know his father, Myrna."

"You're going to tell him, then?" she asked, trying not to sound too anxious.

Meredith nodded, her eyes quiet. "He has the right to know the truth. I can't deny him his heritage."

Myrna bit her lip, and Meredith could see anguish in those dark eyes, in the lines of her face. Something tormented her.

Mr. Smith, ever sensitive to tension, finished the bacon and took it up. "I have to get gas. You and the boy be all right until I get back?" he asked.

"Yes. I promise," she said, smiling at him.

He chuckled, nodding toward Mrs. Harden as he left the two women alone.

"What is it?" Meredith asked. "Can you talk about it?"

Myrna laughed coldly. "You're very perceptive." She wrung her hands, finally sinking onto a chair. "How ironic that I should be able to talk about my problems to you, when I'm the cause of most of yours."

"Ancient history," Meredith said, sitting down in front of the other woman. "Come on. Talk."

Myrna hesitated. She lifted anguished eyes to Meredith's. "I have to tell you why I made you leave."

Meredith didn't speak, but she knew her face mirrored her surprise. Amazing that Myrna was actually willing to discuss something so personal with her. It was a milestone.

"Cy doesn't know, about my past. I've never told him the truth. I…I always seem to believe I've done the best thing for him, don't I, Meredith?" She leaned forward. "Part of Cy's problem is that he doesn't believe in fidelity. He thinks his father and I were deeply in love, but that his father was incapable of being faithful to me. I didn't care that Frank had affairs! My God, I couldn't bear for him to touch me, and he knew it. It was almost a relief when he died. He was unscrupulous, greedy and grasping, and a hopeless womanizer."

She grimaced as she continued her story. "I grew up in such terrible poverty. Even worse than yours, I'm afraid. My mother sold her body, when she was sober enough. My father...honestly, I don't even know who he was. I'm not sure she did," she confessed, her face gray from the strain of talking about it. "I deliberately got pregnant with Frank's baby so that he'd marry me. He was the best friend of the man I really loved, but my soldier was a full-blooded Crow, and he lived in poverty as bad as mine. He went off to war hating me for what I'd done, for betraying him with his friend. He didn't know, and I could never tell him, that I was terrified of being poor for the rest of my life. I married money and earned it. I never loved Frank Harden. Never!"

"You loved the man in the service, didn't you?" Meredith asked perceptively. "The one you said was killed in Vietnam."

Myrna nodded. "He was my world," she replied. "One of the reasons I fought Cy's involvement with you was because of your great-uncle." Her eyes closed. "I couldn't bear the memories. And there were people on the reservation who still remembered what I'd done to the man I loved, how I'd betrayed him for a rich lifestyle. I was afraid Cy might spend enough time on the reservation visiting you and your great-aunt and uncle and he might...hear of it."

Meredith felt cold chills rushing down her arms. She gaped at Myrna. "I see."

"If you'd married Cy, your great-uncle would have become part of our family. He...knew the man I loved, very well. I avoided you because I was afraid of you. I didn't want anyone vaguely connected with the Crow people around me. Not only because of the unbearable memories they brought back, but because I was terrified that someone might remember me, from the days when I used to haunt the reservation before I married Frank."

"I never dreamed…!" Meredith burst out.

"You can't tell Cy," Myrna said urgently. "He mustn't know."

"Why?"

"Because it's just one more thing he'll hate me for," the older woman replied. "I've lived with the shame and guilt all my life. I've already damaged his life. I can't bear having him know about his grandmother!"

"Oh, Myrna," Meredith said. "Don't you know that love forgives anything?" She leaned forward. "You don't stop loving people because of their shortcomings. You love them in spite of them. Love isn't conditional. How can you have lived so long and not have learned that?"

Her troubled eyes met Meredith's. "Do you really think Cy will ever forgive me? I've made so many terrible mistakes."

"You might try telling him why you did it," Meredith suggested. "Cy might surprise you. It might make a tremendous difference to him, to know the truth about your childhood, the real reason for your marriage."

Myrna stared at her for a long moment. "I…hadn't thought about that."

"Shouldn't you?" Impulsively Meredith stood up and bent to kiss the older woman's cheek. "You wicked woman, you," she murmured. "Why don't you finish those eggs while I get the biscuits out?"

Myrna actually blushed. She glanced at Meredith and smiled shyly. "I don't feel very wicked now. You have a way with words."

"My board of directors would agree with you. I hope Blake isn't bouncing on Cy's bed."

"Cy won't let him." She smoothed back her hair with a long sigh and went to dish up the eggs. "Confession is good for the soul, they say." She smiled at Meredith. "It must be, because I feel better than I have for years."

"We all have skeletons, you know," Meredith said. "It only proves that we're human. Your son isn't judgmental. In some ways he's a very nice man."

"And in others he isn't. Yes, I know."

"I only hope he'll work on those exercises," Meredith said solemnly. "He has to, if he wants to get back on his feet."

Myrna nodded. "He's so impatient."

While the women discussed Cy, he was watching his son meticulously arranging his silverware on a napkin by the bedside. He smiled gently at the scowl so like his own on that small face.

"There!" Blake said, satisfied at last. "My mommy is fixing biscuits. Do you like biscuits?"

"Very much," Cy replied softly.

Blake went close to the bed, looking up at the man with open curiosity. "You look like me," he said.

"Yes." Cy didn't enlarge on that. "Do you like horses?"

"Oh, yes, but we can't have a horse," he said. "We live in a city."

"Do you have pets?"

"Only Tiny." He sighed. "I wanted a dog, but my mommy said we'd have to wait until I'm older." He traced the pattern on the brown plaid sheets. "Your mommy says I can play with your toy soldiers. Is it all right with you?"

Cy had to struggle to keep a straight face. "Sure."

"I guess you don't want to play, too?"

"I might."

Blake's eyes lit up. "Really?"

"Really."

"I'll go and get them!"

"Wait a minute, sport." Cy chuckled. "Let's have breakfast first. I'm starving."

"All right," the boy muttered. "You sound just like my mommy."

"Want to have your breakfast in here with me?" Cy offered.

"Could I?!"

Cy's heart soared. His son enjoyed his company. Well, that was a milestone of a kind. "If you like," he said. "You'd better tell your mother."

"She likes you," Blake said. "She cried when they said you were in the hospital, and Mr. Smith fussed because she wouldn't even come home to sleep. Does my mommy love you?"

Cy felt something stir deep inside himself at the question, because he knew the answer as if it were embedded in his very soul. "Yes," he said softly. "Very, very much. Do you mind?"

"Well…I guess not," Blake replied. He looked at the tall man quietly. "Do you like me?"

Cy smiled. "Oh, yes."

"That's all right, then. I'll go and tell Mommy I can eat in here."

"Don't tell her what we talked about," Cy cautioned.

"Okay."

He lay back against the pillows, tingling with new sensations. Meredith loved him. He wasn't certain how he knew it, but the knowledge sang through him like music. He closed his eyes. No matter what happened, he had that.

Blake was back minutes later with Meredith on his heels. She was carrying a tray with two plates, milk and coffee on it, and she looked faintly amused.

"Blake says you don't mind if he has breakfast with you," she said.

"That's right." Cy levered himself off the bed and onto his chair, wincing a little as he began to realize that the damned exercises actually were helping.

"Does your back hurt, mister?" Blake asked.

"Yes, son," Cy said without thinking. "But it's not so bad."

"I'm sorry. Mommy, he says I can have breakfast with him."

"You've already told me that," Meredith said, putting the tray carefully on the bedside table. She was worried about Cy and unable to hide it. Was he telling the truth, that it was getting better?

He caught her worried gaze and sighed. "I'm all right," he muttered. "It's spasms more than real pain. It's healing."

So were his legs. She knew that without being told, although Mr. Smith had to help him into and out of the bathroom, which was another source of unrest in the household. Cy didn't like Mr. Smith, and the feeling was blatantly mutual.

Blake was busy talking to Cy about the toy soldiers. His dark eyes met Cy's. "We can play soldiers later," he reminded Cy.

"I promised, didn't I?" he mused, reaching out to ruffle the boy's dark hair. "I always keep my promises."

"So does my mommy," Blake told him. "She says you must always do what you say you will, so people will trust you."

Cy glanced at Meredith, nodding. "Trust is very important. Once you lose it, you have to work very hard to regain it."

Meredith didn't react. "Can I get you anything else?"

"Nope. I'm fine." He studied her with one dark eye narrowed. "I'll get out of this damned bed, one way or the other.

Then look to your laurels, Mrs. Tennison. I'm going after those proxies the minute I can walk without keeling over."

She laughed with pure delight. "That doesn't mean you're going to get them," she said, challenging him.

"Wait and see."

She arranged their plates on the table. "Dr. Bryner said that you have to come in once a week so that his physical therapist can make sure you and Mr. Smith are doing the exercises properly."

He grimaced. "I hate therapy!"

"You'll do it, though." She leaned closer. "Mr. Smith will make you suffer," she said with gentle malice.

"He already does," Cy said curtly. "Or has it escaped your notice that he works me like a damned horse every day?"

It hadn't, because they could hear him curse all over the house, not to mention the language Mr. Smith used when he finished the mutually irritating workout.

Meredith laughed out loud. "Well, at least you're used to each other, aren't you?"

Cy glared at her. She hurried out of the room before he had the chance to say what he was thinking. It was all too plain on his dark face anyway.

After he and Blake finished their breakfasts Blake fetched the toy soldiers. Cy sat there, brooding. He wanted to get out and drive his car, or go for a ride on his horse, and he couldn't. He knew he was moving around better than ever before, but he still felt impotent. He hated being helped around like a kid.

Blake's return to the bedroom, dozens of heavy, hand-painted metal soldiers in hand, took Cy's mind off his troubles. He explained the Napoleonic uniforms to Blake. It was like going back in time, to his own childhood. He remembered so many rainy days when he'd played alone in his room, with only the little metal men for companionship.

He looked at the boy and wondered how he would react to the knowledge that Henry Tennison wasn't his real father. There was only one way to find out, Cy thought, but he didn't have the heart to do it without Meredith's knowledge. She had the right to be in on any such decision.

He wondered if she really had planned to go back to Chicago without telling Blake. Obviously she couldn't run her business from Billings. Meredith had to be where the company was headquartered. She had obligations and duties that made her involvement with Tennison a full-time job.

It disturbed him to think that she might go. She'd left him once before. Of course, she hadn't been given a choice at the time. Now she had that option. Would she take it? Did she care enough to stay, if he asked her?

He didn't want to think about that. He couldn't ask her to give up her inheritance and her job. He scowled, letting the anguish of it wash over him. He'd have to let her go. And then what? The big, empty house would become a cold battleground as he tried to cope with his anger and hostility toward his mother. If it hadn't been for Myrna Harden, none of this would ever have happened. He and Meredith would have been married, and Blake would be his son in name as well as fact.

But he hadn't wanted marriage before. Amazing how he welcomed those ties now, how much he wanted Meredith and Blake with him always. But it was probably too late for them. He had so little to offer her, in comparison with what she already had.

Plus, there was Mr. Smith. The man lived in such intimacy with Meredith and Blake. Had Meredith slept with the other man? Did she love him? Blake certainly did. Every other word from his mouth was "Mr. Smith."

Cy had to admit that Smith took excellent care of the little boy and was obviously devoted to him. He brought to mind a fussy nanny, the way he made sure the child was properly dressed, the care with which he watched him. He was even teaching Blake martial arts. Amazing how much a part of Meredith's and Blake's lives he'd become.

That brought to mind the fact that Henry Tennison had employed him originally. His only real loyalty was to Henry and, because of him, to Meredith and her child. That could present a real problem if Cy ever managed to take a chance on asking Meredith to marry him. What would they do about Mr. Smith?

It didn't bear thinking about. He might not ever be in a position to propose to her. And right now he had other worries, foremost among them how to keep Meredith from walking right off with his company. Not that he thought she could do it, of course. That possibility he refused to accept.

CHAPTER EIGHTEEN

THE DAYS MEREDITH SPENT at the Hardens' passed so quickly that she had been at Cy's house for over two weeks before she realized it. For the first time since Henry's death, she'd had time to play with Blake, to take long walks outdoors, to slow down and look at her life.

Because of the amount of time she was spending in Billings, she'd enrolled Blake in the local Presbyterian kindergarten, where Mr. Smith took him each day. He seemed to make the change with very little adjustment, and he always came home laughing. That pleased Meredith, who was beginning to think of Billings as home all over again, without considering the implications or the consequences. Business, for the moment, seemed very far away.

She hadn't realized how much time she'd spent making money, closing contracts, making decisions, working. Blake was growing up, and as they spent time together, she began to see that her son's tastes and interests had changed subtly without her even knowing it. It was a sobering experience.

But if Meredith was becoming more relaxed through her introspection, having time on his hands was making Cy worse. He began to snap at everybody, especially Mr. Smith. The older man had been giving him physiotherapy mainly because the female physiotherapist Dr. Bryner had sent out had been reduced to tears after the first thirty minutes and ran for her car. Mr. Smith was adept and had the training to qualify him as a physiotherapist. Not that his qualifications impressed Cy, who raged every time the bodyguard came near him.

Meredith wasn't sure how to handle the situation. Dr. Bryner had told her that Cy's condition would improve rapidly if he followed instructions, but Cy wouldn't follow instructions. He was pushing himself too hard, impatient for results. It disturbed Meredith as much as it bothered his mother, but neither of them could find a way to slow him down.

Blake seemed to have the best shot at it. He spent most of the afternoon after school with his father, playing toy soldiers, coloring in his coloring books, or reading to Cy. It amused Meredith that Cy seemed to enjoy that most of all.

"He's bright, isn't he?" he asked her one night after Blake finished reading his nightly bedtime story to Cy and had gone with Mr. Smith to get ready for bed.

"Very bright," Meredith agreed. "He spells well, and he's got a feel for putting emotion into what he reads, as you've seen."

He studied her. "He likes school."

"Yes, I know. He's fitting in very well."

"Are you going to let him stay there, or uproot him again?" he asked with faint sarcasm. "Aren't you missing your job?"

She refused to let him bait her. "I like keeping busy. On the other hand, I'd grown away from Blake, and I don't like that. He's been changing under my very eyes, but I've been too preoccupied with business to notice. I'm ashamed of that."

"Business can blind you to life," he said quietly. "I know. It's sure as hell blinded me to most of the important things." He stared at his legs. He was sitting up, fully dressed. "I hate being confined like this," he said. "I ask when I can drive, when I can go back to work, and they keep telling me 'soon'. My God, it's been three weeks!"

"Dr. Bryner knows that. You've made remarkable progress. But you can't push too hard, Cy."

"If I don't, I may never get out of the house again," he said curtly. "I hate inactivity."

"You were badly bruised, and the surgery took a lot out of you. Everyone told you it was going to take time, but you want it all yesterday."

"Is that new? Patience was never my strong suit." He sighed. "The worst of it is that I'm so damned weak!"

She stood up, exasperated. "Cy…"

"Why don't you go home?" he asked, his eyes full of frustration and fury. "I don't need you."

"If I go, Blake goes with me," she said after a minute. "Who'll read you stories if he leaves?"

He didn't like thinking about that. His chest rose and fell heavily and he looked away. "I've gotten used to the boy."

"He's your biggest fan," she added with a faint smile. "It used to be 'Mr. Smith' every other word. Now it's you."

He shifted a little on the chair, his broad chest only partially covered by a dark blue silk shirt. "So I hear."

"You might try slowing down just a little," she suggested. "And not pushing yourself so hard. You're making progress. You can walk quite well now, except for those twinges, can't you?"

"Yes," he admitted. "But Smith smirks."

"That isn't a smirk," she returned. "Mr. Smith was badly wounded in one of the last guerrilla actions he participated in. They had to do a lot of plastic surgery. His cheek never healed properly."

He scowled. "Guerrilla action?"

"He was a professional mercenary, somewhere around the time he worked for the CIA," she reminded him.

"I see." He shifted against the chair's backrest. "I guess

he's been on the receiving end of physiotherapy at one time or another."

"Any number of times," she agreed.

His broad shoulders rose and fell. "I suppose it wouldn't hurt to slow down. Just a little."

She didn't dare smile, for danger of being accused of smirking herself. "It wouldn't hurt," she agreed.

The next morning, when Mr. Smith showed up for his regular session, Cy didn't glare or make acid remarks. He cooperated fully. For the first time.

Myrna Harden was almost exhausted with relief. "I never thought he'd agree to it," she said. "I thought he was going to try to get on a bicycle or take up skateboarding next!"

"We're not out of the woods yet," Meredith reminded her. "He's still muttering, and if he doesn't see some results pretty soon, he's going to get discouraged and step up the pace again."

Myrna looked at her levelly. "Any suggestions?"

"I've got one last card to play, if I have to," she replied. "He's been so depressed lately that he doesn't seem like himself."

"I know. I'm grasping at straws, I suppose, but I wish he could manage more than monosyllables when he talks to me," the older woman said wistfully. "He hasn't backed down an inch. I think sometimes that he hates me for what I've done."

"He'll get over it," Meredith said. "Give him time. He's had too many shocks in the past few weeks—most of them my fault." She studied her feet. "I came here for vengeance. That's not going to sit well with my board of directors when that comes out. And it will, if I know my brother-in-law," she added. "He wants me out of the corporation."

"Are you going to let him do that to you?" Myrna asked.

Meredith smiled. "No. I'm on to him. He doesn't know it

yet, but I'm one step behind him all the way. He isn't going to take the reins out of my hands until I give them up. I'm not sure I want to do that, just yet. My hold on Harden Properties may be the only thing that keeps Cy going right now. Every time I mention the takeover, he perks up."

"Yes, but if Cy doesn't start improving, I'm afraid even that may not be enough to keep him from backsliding."

Privately, Meredith agreed. Only his mother's obvious unrest stopped her from voicing the rest of her fears. Cy Harden wasn't the kind of man who would be able to take having a woman wrest his company out of his hands. She couldn't back away from her own responsibilities, but how was it going to affect her relationship with Cy if she had to use control of Harden Properties to thwart Don? She and McGee had already been burning up the telephone lines over the proxies, without Don's knowledge. She was getting a majority of the stock. But using it was going to be tricky.

THE EXERCISES were grueling. Cy was sweating as he completed the round of them and staring daggers at Mr. Smith.

"Go ahead, cuss," Smith said imperturbably. "I know it's uncomfortable, and I know you aren't seeing the results you want to just yet. I'd cuss, too, in your place."

Cy wiped his forehead and pushed back his sweaty hair. "My God, I don't know why I'm letting you put me through this," he said. "Take Meredith back to Chicago and let's forget the whole thing. She can go back to the life she had before."

"No, she can't," the older man told him bluntly. "You didn't see her the night they brought you in here, but I did. Taking her away from you now would be no less painful than cutting off one of her arms. Besides that, she wouldn't go. She's no quitter."

"Meaning that I am?" came the mocking challenge.

"I don't think you're a quitter," Smith disagreed. "You're just human."

Cy sank back onto the exercise table with a heavy sigh. He was so tired. Walking was easier by the day, but it took so much work for so little profit. Damn it, he thought furiously, why had this happened to him, now of all times?

Then he got up without conscious thought or much effort, moving easily for the first time. But Mr. Smith was watching, and he grinned.

"Do that again," he told Cy abruptly.

"What?"

"That," Mr. Smith said, and he actually smiled. "Look. You're walking without a limp, without even shuffling."

Cy held his breath. He walked around the room, amazed at his own fluidity. It didn't hurt. He didn't flinch. He chuckled softly, his dark eyes gleaming as they met Mr. Smith's.

"That's more like it!" he said.

He stood straight, bending at the knee and coming back up again; his back was a little less flexible than before, but the movement was comfortable now. He sighed his relief. All that work hadn't been for nothing after all!

"You'll do," Smith said with certainty. "Suppose we drift over to the hospital and see the therapist. We're overdue, and it would get you out of the house for a while."

"Hand me the telephone," Cy said, grinning.

"Here you go. If you don't mind, I think I'll pass along the news. There are two pretty hang-dog looking women downstairs."

Cy hesitated. But after a minute, he nodded, and Smith went out of the room.

Meredith made Smith repeat it twice before she really comprehended it, and Myrna cried like a baby. Cy was going to be all right, she was sure of it now. He might hate both of them, but he was definitely on the mend.

When the women got to the room, he was just hanging up the telephone.

"I'm going to see Bryner while I'm at the hospital," he told them. "He thinks I'm making a remarkable recovery," he added smugly.

Meredith didn't mention how much nagging it had taken, from all of them. She grinned. "Great! Now we can slug it out properly for control of your company."

He smiled through his fatigue. "I'll win," he said with cool certainty.

"No, you won't," she returned, feeling newborn, full of life. "Not without those proxies."

He smiled slowly. "We'll have plenty of time to discuss that little problem once I'm back at work."

"Discussion won't help," she said confidently.

"That depends on the kind of discussion we have," he murmured, and the look in his dark eyes made her heart beat faster.

"Out, while he showers," Mr. Smith said, holding the door open. "We don't want to keep the doctor waiting."

"Whose side are you on?" Meredith muttered as she walked past him.

"Yours. His. It's all the same," he chuckled.

Meredith didn't dare look at Cy, but she heard soft laughter behind her as the door closed.

They kept Cy for hours, running tests. He was literally cursing when they were through. But the result was worth the irritation, he supposed, because he and Mr. Smith learned that his back was healing beautifully and there was no nerve or muscle damage that wouldn't eventually repair itself. They were given some additional physiotherapy and exercises to do.

Cy became enthusiastic. No longer dogged by the fear of permanent disability, he worked on his therapy in a methodical way. He knew he had to be whole again before he could act on his plan to keep Meredith and his son with him. Saving the company was almost an afterthought now, because he knew exactly what he wanted. All he had to do was convince Meredith that she wanted it, too. He couldn't afford to let her confuse love with pity. He wanted to be back on his feet completely, so that he could gauge the exact extent of her feelings for him.

Cy no longer had any doubt about his own feelings. Meredith made the color come back into his drab world. He could look at her and feel his blood quicken, his heart lighten. He needed her, with a hunger that was more than just physical. The problem was how to undo all the damage he'd done in the past, how to convince her that he was no longer uncertain or unwilling about their relationship. To accomplish that, he was going to have to turn up the heat, and fast.

"YOU DO REALIZE that Dr. Bryner doesn't mean you're going to start skateboarding tomorrow?" Meredith asked hesitantly one morning as Cy was hard at work on exercises to strengthen his back muscles.

"I know it. If it takes time, it take times," he said.

"Excuse me, but are you the same man who was foaming at the mouth to double up on his exercises only four days ago?"

He chuckled softly, grimacing a little with movement, because he was sore and his muscles were beginning to wake up with a vengeance. "That was before I knew what I had to look forward to," he mused. His dark eyes slid up and down her body in an elegant black silk pantsuit. "Why don't you take off those sexy things and lie down with me?" He patted the thick exercise mat on the bedroom floor beside him.

"Not yet," she murmured. "And stop saying things like that. What if Blake or your mother walked in?"

"I don't give a damn what my mother thinks. And Blake is in school."

She went close to him and reached down to touch his hand. "Revenge is a cold thing," she said. "It's empty and unsatisfying, and it eats you up with guilt eventually. I could write volumes on that subject."

His fingers wrapped around hers and clasped them warmly. "Does that mean I can have my proxies back?" he asked with a slow grin.

"It does not!" she replied. "If you want them, get up and fight for them."

"At my earliest convenience." He moved his shoulders and grimaced.

"Need something for muscle spasms?"

He shook his head. "It's soreness more than that. The nerves are awake, and they want me to know they're still functioning."

"Is that it?" she asked, smiling.

His fingers slid in between hers with a sensual pressure. "Come here," he said huskily.

She sat down beside him and let him pull her down to him. His free hand speared into her soft blond hair, savoring its silkiness.

"I like it loose," he said quietly.

"I didn't have time to put it up this morning," she said, feeling faintly defensive.

"Don't, while you're here," he replied. "I like the way it feels in my hands."

"Cy..."

"Shhhh." His hand, which slid to the nape of her neck, brought her mouth down to his. Meredith's breath caught at the delicious hard warmth of his mouth, and she closed her eyes and gave in to it.

He kissed her gently, for a long time. He didn't increase the pressure or yield to the passion that usually fused them together seconds after they touched. His fingers brushed lazily against her throat, her cheeks, and the corner of her mouth while he savored the sweetness of her parted lips.

When he let her go, she seemed dazed. Her gray eyes were alive, burning, and her mouth was gently swollen.

"The next time we make love," he whispered, "it's going to be like nothing we've ever experienced. It's going to be just like that kiss, soft and slow and so tender that you're going to cry in my arms when I've had you."

She trembled. The words aroused her, just as the look in his dark eyes did. He'd never been tender with her. What they experienced together had always been explosive and urgent and almost too passionate. But this...this was something totally out of her experience.

She reached down and touched his mouth with just her fingertips. "I don't understand," she whispered, dazed.

"Don't you, little one?" He brought her palm to his mouth and kissed it with slow, lazy hunger.

He had her in his spell all over again. She looked at him and loved him. Even if she left Billings, the feeling wouldn't stop. She was going to spend the rest of her life loving him, and it would never be enough. All he had to offer was a blazing affair....

"No." She pulled away and stood up, looking and feeling threatened. "No! I'll be damned if I'll let you do this to me again!"

He scowled. She actually looked frightened. "Meredith," he said, "it's not what you think."

"Isn't it?" She laughed bitterly, pushing back her disheveled hair. "You want me. You can't get enough of me. I'm some sort of sexual zombie when I get around you, I don't even have enough pride to say no to you."

"You don't understand," he began, desperate to make her understand that he wasn't trying to entice her into bed with him for the sake of a little casual sex.

"Oh, yes, I do," she said shortly. "I have to help get lunch. I'll see you later."

"Meredith!"

But she wouldn't answer him. She went out of the room as if her shirt were on fire and didn't come back for the rest of the day, not even when he went to look for her. She locked herself in his study and wouldn't answer the door.

She did have work to do, she told herself. That was no lie. She had mail piled up, and that had to be dealt with even if she could pretend that she was on some indefinite vacation.

But she was preoccupied. Even Blake noticed. Yet it was Myrna who cornered her in the dining room the next morning while they were waiting for Mrs. Dougherty to finish fixing breakfast.

They were sharing a pot of coffee. Mr. Smith and Blake were having their breakfast with Cy.

"It's a man's world in there, I guess," Myrna said with a rueful sigh. "Not that I expect Cy actually to speak to me, but I didn't think he'd shut you out as well."

"He hasn't," Meredith said flatly. "I've shut myself out. I won't be used anymore."

Myrna's eyebrows arched. "What?"

"He wants me," she said, shrugging. "I'm helping him save himself from me."

"So that's why he's so explosive lately," Myrna said, and smiled. "Poor Cy."

"Poor me," Meredith corrected. "I'm not going to be your

son's plaything between takeovers and board meetings. I'm not a flighty waitress anymore."

"No, you aren't. You're a very capable young executive with independence and wealth on your side." She put down her coffee cup. "But it's a lonely life, Meredith. And an empty one."

"It beats chasing rainbows," she replied. "I've been living in a fool's paradise, enjoying being lazy, spending time with my son, watching Cy recover. I was so relieved that he wasn't going to die. But now he's on the way up again, and he doesn't need me. He did," she added quietly, "just for a little while."

"He still does," Myrna replied. "I may be banished, but I'm not blind. He doesn't look at you the way he used to. Something's different. Something's changed."

"It's just because he's been helpless."

"No." Myrna lifted her cup to her lips. "He looks at you," she mused reminiscently, "the way I used to look at Garson Hathaway."

Meredith raised her eyebrows to ask a silent question.

Myrna smiled and nodded. "The man I really loved. He was thirteen years older than I was, but the age difference never mattered. We fell in love, despite all the odds..." She grimaced. "About the time I got involved with Garson, my mother was going with a hardware merchant. He...told her that I was seeing an Indian, and she went wild. She actually locked me in my room." Her eyes had a sad, faraway look as she remembered. "Garson had asked Frank to come around and make sure I was all right. My mother and her sister had a fit over Frank. He was well-to-do even then, and they pushed me at him.

"I looked at my mother and saw what I could become, without money. I panicked. I started seeing Frank, and I never spoke or wrote to Garson again. When Frank seemed to be losing interest, I let him think he was seducing me. Garson went off to Vietnam hating me. He was killed two weeks later. I was pregnant by then. Frank married me. I never saw my mother again. I couldn't bear anyone to know who or what she was. I spent the rest of my married life devoting myself completely to my son and trying to be a society woman and all that it implied." She put her face in her hands. "Meredith, my whole life is a lie. I wanted respectability more than I wanted food in my stomach. Frank gave me wealth and power, but his behavior disgraced me. I thought that if Cy married well, I could live down the way Frank had humiliated me, that I could cement my place in society." She looked up. "But respectability isn't something you can borrow or buy. You have to earn it."

"Don't you think you have, in all these years?" Meredith asked. "I've learned a lot about you since I've been here. You sit on half a dozen charitable committees, you donate time to the hospital and the nursing home, you work with the literacy action program...you're a doer, not a figurehead. For heaven's sake, what does it matter who your parents were, or whether or not you were married when you got pregnant? You go to church, just as I do. Can't you believe that God understands how human nature can twist us into making wrong decisions for all the right reasons? He made us human. But you can't accept that you are, can you?"

"I think I'm learning to," the older woman said. She smiled at Meredith. "Because of you. You've made me look at myself. Truth is painful, but it's cleansing. I feel as if I've let go of my shackles."

"I'm glad of that. I was sorry about what I'd done, when you fainted at the board meeting," Meredith said. "If anything terrible had happened to you, I couldn't have lived with it. I was so bitter that I couldn't function normally. Maybe I was a little crazy."

"So was I. But we've come to an understanding, haven't we? And Cy is going to be all right."

"Yes. Now all we have to do is make *him* understand that people aren't perfect," Meredith said with a wry smile.

"I expect he'll come around," Myrna Harden said quietly. "He knows that I love him. But he blames me for the past, and I can't expect that he wouldn't, Meredith. I've cost him so much."

"That was a long time ago. Now you have a grandson who loves tea cakes and reading to his father."

Myrna smiled wistfully. "More than I deserve," she said. "But thank you, for the time I've had with Blake. You can't know how special it's been. Can he write to me when you go home again?"

"Of course." Meredith didn't want to think about going back to Chicago. She frowned as her position came back to haunt her. She had a company to run, people who depended on her. How much longer could she dodge her responsibilities now that Cy was going to be all right?

She worried the problem for the rest of the day. It didn't help that Cy didn't ask where she was again. She felt guilty about staying away from him, but she was too vulnerable when she got close to him. She hated being out of control.

Blake wasn't much help in that department.

"That man says you won't come and see him," he told her, his dark eyes accusing. "He's sick. Don't you care?"

She knelt in front of him. "I care very much. But he doesn't really need me. He enjoys your company much more."

"No, he doesn't. He and Mr. Smith argue all the time. Why does that man look like me?"

The question kept coming up. She didn't really know how

to handle it. But keeping quiet about it wasn't going to work. Blake was smart and curious. He wouldn't stop asking.

She toyed with a button on his shirt while she tried to decide what to tell him.

"Henry Tennison wasn't my real father, was he?" he asked suddenly.

She gasped. "Who told you that?"

"Mr. Smith. Well, I asked him. Mr. Smith never tells lies."

Mr. Smith was going to be put in an ice machine and turned into little balls one day, she thought furiously. But now wasn't the time to tackle that matter.

"That man in bed looks just like me," Blake repeated.

Meredith ground her teeth together. Intelligent children were trying.

"That man in bed," she said softly, lifting her eyes to meet his, "is your real father, my darling."

"That's why he looks like me?" he asked, accepting the information without any visible reaction.

"Yes."

He grinned. "I'm glad. Because I like him a lot. Can we live with him?"

Oh, boy, Meredith thought. Here it comes. She took a deep breath. "Blake—"

"Time for bed, my boy. Where are you?" Mr. Smith called.

Saved, she thought, and could have whooped with relief. She handed him over to Mr. Smith.

"What's the icy glare about?" he asked when Blake was perched on his shoulder.

"He already knew Henry was his stepfather."

Mr. Smith shrugged. "You never told me not to say so. I don't lie. Not ever."

She groaned. "I know that. But it's complicated everything. He wants to know why we don't live with his daddy."

Mr. Smith grinned at her. "Good question. Why don't you?"

And before she could think up a suitably acid reply, he bounded off toward the staircase with Blake.

CHAPTER NINETEEN

MEREDITH HAD PHONE CALLS to answer, so she stayed up much later than normal. When she'd finished, she sat behind the desk in the study and brooded for a long time. She'd let her life become so entangled with Cy's that she didn't really know how she was going to extricate it. And now Blake knew about his father. That was one big complication.

She started up to bed long after everyone else was asleep. Everyone except Cy. He called to her as she passed his room. His door was ajar, so she hadn't been able to sneak past.

"Still hiding from me?" he asked with a mocking smile.

"I'm not hiding."

"Pull the other one."

She went closer to the bed, tired and sad and a little pale from the late hours she'd been keeping. The slacks and gray knit blouse she was wearing were no more gray than her face.

"God, you look worn," he said, studying her. "Why don't you sleep?"

"I haven't been able to, since your wreck," she said. "It's like being on a merry-go-round, I guess."

"Want to sleep with me, little one?" he asked softly.

Her heart slammed against her rib cage. Just the thought of it brought color into her face, warmed her cold spirit. But she hesitated. He was doing it again—getting to her.

"No strings, Meredith," he added. "No pressure."

"But there doesn't have to be, does there?" she said. "All you ever had to do was touch me."

He reached out and caught her hand, pulling her onto the bed with him. "Now, listen," he said, and he didn't smile. "Hasn't it ever occurred to you that I'm just as helpless as you are? Just as vulnerable?"

Her eyes fell to his chest, where his dark silk pajama top was open over thick, curling hair and hard muscle. "No," she confessed. "I don't suppose I considered your side of it. I always knew you wanted me, even though you hated the wanting."

"Look at me."

She forced her eyes back up to his, fascinated by the expression in them. It was, as his mother had said, very new.

"There isn't going to be any more sex," he said quietly. "Not for a while. Besides the obvious fact that I can't, until my back heals properly, there's another consideration. I want a relationship with you. A real one, based on common interests and pleasure in each other's company. I want to get to know you and my son, Meredith."

Her eyes widened. "Honestly?" she asked, her voice unwillingly soft.

"Yes." He smoothed over her long fingers. "I've had a lot of time to think while I've been recovering. I suppose over the years I've become cynical about women, because of what I thought you'd done to me. Since I've learned the truth, the world has shifted several degrees." He searched her eyes. "Can you forgive me?"

Tears ran helplessly down her eyes, down her face. "Isn't that...the wrong way around?" she whispered. "I came back here with nothing in mind except revenge. I destroyed your relationship with your mother, I threatened your company, I denied you your own child...!"

He drew her to him and pressed her cheek to his chest. Under the thick hair that tickled her skin, she could hear the heavy beat of his heart, like a bass drum.

"Oh, sweetheart," he said, his arms contracting around her. His own eyes closed as he gave in to the anguish of the past six years. "I'd give anything to go back, to make it right for you. If I'd known about the baby, I'd never have let you go. Never!"

A broken sob tore from her throat. The emotion in his deep voice struck right at her heart.

"You didn't believe me," she said.

"I know." There was bitterness in the words. "I wouldn't allow myself to think it was anything more than desire. Then, when I discovered just how young you really were, the guilt ate me up." He smoothed her disheveled hair. "It didn't take two days for me to realize what I'd thrown away, to know that your age didn't make a damned bit of difference. But I couldn't find you."

The words were poignant—even more so because of the way he said them.

She drew her hand tenderly over his chest. "When I wrote you, and never heard anything else, I gave up. I was only just beginning to come back to life when Henry died. After that, business became everything. That, and revenge."

"No men?" he asked with quiet humor.

"No men," she replied. "Or don't you know that you're a hard act to follow? Even as much as Henry loved me, it was…always you."

His hands clenched in her hair. "Meredith," he whispered. His teeth ground together. "It was always you, too."

She managed a ragged laugh. "Really? How many women did it take you to find that out?"

His thumb pressed hard against her trembling mouth.

"Don't," he said quietly. "You can't know how ashamed I am of those women—and there were very few, despite what you think. I blame myself for those lost years. I could have trusted you, couldn't I? But I didn't know just how deeply you loved me. I was afraid to take a chance, because of your age."

"Maybe you were right," she said with a heavy sigh. "So much has happened since then."

"Yes. You grew up and became a tycoon. Or should that be a tycooness?" he mused.

She laughed softly. "Whatever." Her lips brushed his chest and she felt him stiffen. Her hand slid gently over a hard male nipple, her palm covering it. "Is it like this with other women?" she whispered.

"You know it isn't," he said huskily. His hand covered hers, brushing over it with his fingertips. "Meredith, I haven't…been with a woman for two years. Not until that day after we went to the battlefield. Sex wasn't even particularly satisfying anymore. I lost interest in it. Until you came back to me."

The way he put it made her heart leap. She lifted her head and looked down at him. "That's why…" she began.

He nodded. "Why I was so hungry for you. Not that I was ever anything else," he said. "I can remember so many times that I treated you like a Saturday night pickup, without tenderness or respect. That's ended, too." He lifted a rough hand to her face and brushed back a lock of her hair. "I meant what I told you before. The next time you and I make love, I'm going to be so exquisitely tender with you that you'll cry. It won't be quick, and it won't be rough."

She managed a shaky smile. "Careful, tiger. You'll make me think you care, talking like that."

He didn't return the smile. There was a dark, soft glow in his eyes. "Why shouldn't you think it? It's true. I do care. Very, very much."

It was like flying, she thought dizzily. He'd never said anything like that before. Of course, it could be the medication he was still taking, or misplaced desire, or…

He tugged at her hair and brought her mouth down over his. So softly, so tenderly, his lips teased and brushed and cherished hers. But long before he nuzzled her lips apart, she had yielded. He cupped her face in his big hands and built the kiss until tiny explosions rippled through her body.

He lay back, sighing gently. "We've never done it like that, have we?" he asked in the silence. "More and more, it's like two souls touching."

"Yes," she whispered.

He brought her palm to his mouth and kissed it. "You'd better go to bed," he said. "I don't want to spoil what we're building together."

"How could you do that?" she asked, dazed.

"I want you rather badly," he murmured, his eyes serious. "And this isn't the time."

"I want you, too," she said, smiling at him. "But I…want what you promised me. We've never been able to be tender with each other."

He traced her chin with gentle fingers. "You mean, I've never been able to be tender with you. But I think I can be, now. You see, your pleasure is more important to me than my own. Isn't that the beginning of love, little one?"

She bit back tears. It was love. But she'd never expected him to offer it to her. She'd never expected anything more than the helpless desire she kindled in him.

"Kiss me and go to bed," he said.

She bent, obeying him, her mouth trembling as it burrowed softly into his, feeling the warm, hard response with wonder. "I love you so," she said, her voice breaking on the words.

"I know." He pulled her head down and kissed her closed eyelids with incredible tenderness. "You won't get away this time," he said unsteadily. "If you go, I'll be one step behind you. To the ends of the earth, if it comes to it."

"Are you sure this isn't the pain medicine speaking?" she asked unsteadily.

He smiled up at her. "Wait until I get back on my feet, and I'll let you answer that question for yourself."

"All right." She sat up, sighing with pure pleasure. "Cy...I told Blake."

"Told him what?" he asked without really comprehending what she was saying.

"That you're his real father."

He stared at her blankly, and then he scowled. "Was that wise?" he asked. "You said that he thought of Tennison as his father."

"Mr. Smith told him long ago that Henry was his stepfather. I didn't know." She touched the button on his pajama jacket. "I thought he had the right to know the truth. Henry always said we'd have to tell him one day. It seemed the right time."

"What did he say?" he asked, and looked as if he were hanging on her answer.

She smiled. "That he was glad, because you looked like him."

He pressed her hand hard against him. "I do, don't I?" he said. "Same hair, same eyes."

"Same stubborn temper," she murmured dryly.

He chuckled. "Runs in the family. My mother has it, too." He sobered. "Damn my mother!"

"Your mother has suffered along with you," she said firmly. "She's not the ogre I used to think her. You might consider her own feelings. She hasn't had an easy life."

He scowled. "What do you know that I don't?"

"Do you know anything about her childhood, or the career soldier she was in love with?"

His eyebrows arched. "No."

"You really need to have a long talk with her," she replied. "For her sake and your own. You don't really know your mother at all, and it's a pity. She's much nicer than she appears."

"My father did that to her, you know," he said.

"Not entirely." She hated to blow Myrna's cover, but it was really becoming a habit. "She was desperately in love with another man. She gave him up and married your father because she was afraid of more poverty."

"She was poor?" he asked, shocked. "My mother?"

"Poor and unloved. You mustn't tell her that you know," she said gently. "She has to tell you. She said that she'd kept so many secrets from you, but this one would make you feel contempt for her." She smiled, her eyes loving. "Let me tell you about your mother, Cy. I think when you know it all, you may change your bad opinion of her."

So she told him, everything Myrna had said to her, about her childhood, about the man she'd loved—about her betrayal and his death and her grief. She talked, and Cy listened in stoic silence. When she was through he was pale, but there was something new in his eyes.

"I was never able to love my father," he said numbly. "I blamed him for Mother's unhappiness. I don't think I even cried when he was buried. I thought it odd at the time. There were periods when I thought I might even be adopted, but I knew he had to be my real father because I favored him so much, just as Blake favors me." He glanced at her. "My darkness is because of the French in my ancestry. But Blake's could be from your side of the family. Your Crow blood."

"Not really. Uncle Raven-Walking was my great-uncle, but not any real blood kin to me. Everybody assumed that I had Indian blood. Actually it's Dutch and Irish."

He smiled up at her. "Which gives Blake Dutch, Irish, English, and French blood. He's some mixture, our son."

"The best of us both," she said with feeling.

He nodded. His dark eyes searched hers. "Will you give me another child, when I'm able to help you conceive? Perhaps a daughter this time, with your blond hair and gray eyes."

Her heart raced. "I…I'd like that," she whispered. "But things are so complicated right now, Cy."

"Only until I'm back on my feet," he assured her. "Then I'll relieve you of those proxies and we'll get married."

She raised both eyebrows. "I haven't been asked."

"You won't be," he said. "We'll put it in the form of a bet. If I regain control of my company, you marry me. If you manage to oust me, you can name your own stakes."

She smiled. He made it sound like a challenge. "So I'm going to have to fight you and Don, too, hmm?"

"What do you mean, Don, too?"

"You didn't know that my esteemed brother-in-law is out to kick me out of Henry's company?" she murmured with an angry light in her eyes. "He'll have his work cut out, too. I hate being stabbed in the back by people who pretend to care about me. Especially so-called relatives."

"I knew Don was going to make a move," he said. "I didn't know that you did."

"Would you have told me?"

He linked her fingers with his. "Oh, I might have gotten around to it eventually. I was having some sweet fantasies about seeing you give up the world of business and come home to have my babies."

The anger faded and her face brightened. "And give up high finance and making money?"

That statement disturbed him, but he refused to let himself think about how wealthy she was. "You've got enough money, but only one child." He pursed his lips and his dark eyes sparkled with mischief. "Blake shouldn't be the only one."

"Well, you'll have to wait until your back heals first," she reminded him. "And I'm not going down without a fight. I won't give you back your proxies. You'll have to take them. So will Don," she added.

He chuckled. "I don't mind. A man needs a few challenges to keep him on his toes." He fingered a smooth strand of her long hair. "Want to sleep in my arms tonight?"

"More than anything in the world," she replied. "But it's too soon."

"All right. We'll take it slow and easy,' he said sensuously.

"That will be a change."

"Won't it, though?" His dark eyes slid down her body. "Do you know, of all the women I've been with—and in my younger days, there were a few—you're the only one who could accommodate me completely?"

She blushed and averted her eyes.

"Embarrassed?" he asked with a soft laugh. "Why? I always thought it meant something, that we were so compatible in bed. I didn't know the half of it. We made a beautiful little boy together."

She glanced at him shyly. "We did, didn't we?" she murmured.

"I'll talk to my mother," he said abruptly. "Don't mention anything you've told me to her, will you? I'll let her tell me."

She smiled down into his eyes. "You're a good man," she

said. "I always knew you had it in you. Of course," she added wickedly, "it took me to bring it out."

"Did it, now?" His hand fingered the sheet that covered his hips, and his eyes flashed merrily. "Want to see what else you bring out?"

"I can imagine. Get some rest."

"No chance of that, unless you want to slide in here with me."

"If I did, you wouldn't rest."

"Amen." He lay back with a long sigh. "You're still as beautiful as you were six years ago. Pretty as a picture. When we're married, you can fire Smith."

The sudden change of subject gave her mental whiplash. "What do you mean, fire Mr. Smith? Baloney!"

"I won't live with him," he told her. "And my son is going to have a father, not a burly substitute with scars."

"You'll have scars if you try to oust Mr. Smith," she said firmly.

"Is he your lover?" he demanded.

"You should be able to answer that all by yourself," she said in a quiet undertone. "Or don't you remember how hard it was, that day after we went to the battlefield?"

His jaw clenched. He remembered all right. He'd had to hurt her, and it had been too quick, too heated. "It won't be like that the next time," he promised her, his voice husky. "I'll never hurt you like that again."

"Oh, Cy, I know you didn't mean to." She moved closer to the bed. "It wasn't like that!"

"You were a particularly vicious fever in my blood," he murmured, watching her. "Two years of abstinence, memories of how it had been in the past, all of it just overwhelmed me. But I had no right to take you that way. I didn't even ask if you wanted it. I took."

"You knew I wanted it," she replied gently. "I didn't mind."

He turned his face away. "I did."

She bent and kissed him tenderly. "I love you," she whispered. "Anything you do to me is all right."

His jaw clenched. "Love doesn't include that kind of insensitivity. It means giving pleasure as well as taking it." He touched her face with exquisite tenderness. "I want to love you. Do you understand? I don't mean raw sex or feverish passion. I want to love you with my body."

She trembled. What he said, the way he looked, was so profound and new that her body burned with it. "Cy!" she whispered.

He returned that steady, hungry stare until he trembled. He chuckled angrily at his own helplessness as he managed to drag his eyes away. "Damn my back," he muttered. "Will you go away? Parts of me are in agony."

"I'm sorry about that. If you were in better shape, I could do something about it."

"You would, too, wouldn't you?"

She nodded, her eyes loving.

"Promise me you won't leave," he asked suddenly, his eyes dark and troubled.

She hesitated. "I'm going to have to go back to Chicago, at least for a while. I have obligations, responsibilities."

He sighed. "Then leave Blake with me."

That thought hadn't occurred to her. She wasn't sure how that would work out, although Blake loved his father and seemed happy enough with his grandmother. But as she looked at Cy, she wondered if it was another ploy, a way to keep Blake and get her away long enough to accomplish it. He said he cared for her, but did he, really?

"I can see the bricks going up in that wall you're trying to build," he said, watching her. "I'm going to steal Blake away and send you packing, isn't that the theme?"

She actually gasped, and then she blushed.

He nodded grimly. "I thought so. We've got a long way to go, haven't we, honey? You don't trust me any farther than you can throw me."

"I don't know you," she replied.

"That's true enough." He sighed gently. "Okay. I'll work on it. Maybe I can find a way to convince you that it isn't just Blake I want. I happen to want you, too. And not just for that delicious body that gives mine such agonizing pleasure."

"I'm used to working," she began.

"And making decisions and giving orders," he agreed. "Fine. Give some. Then come back, and I'll give you a few."

She glared at him. "I don't take orders."

He smiled slowly. "You will."

Her temper went over the top. She turned and walked stiffly to the door, cursing her own weakness for him.

"You're just frustrated, little woman," he said as he settled back onto the pillows and closed his eyes, smiling smugly. "As it happens, I can take care of that problem with relative ease, once I can use my back again."

"You conceited…!"

He opened his eyes and looked up and down her slender body with a possessiveness and sensuality that made her legs go weak. "I'm going to watch you, all through it," he said in a voice that rippled with meaning. "I'll exhaust you, but when it's over, you won't want to leave me. We'll never be apart again."

"You're not playing fair!"

"I'm not playing, honey," he replied, his expression somber.

She couldn't manage an answer to that. She was far too vulnerable right now, and the way he was looking at her made her aware of her own needs.

"Sleep well," she managed, opening the door.

"You, too. Good night, little one."

She paused, looking back at him. He smiled. After a minute she did, too. She closed the door and went upstairs.

The next morning Blake burst into the dining room where Myrna and a sleepy Meredith were having breakfast. Mrs. Dougherty had already taken a tray to Cy's room for him and Blake.

"Mommy," he exclaimed, leaning against her legs, "that man says I can stay with him while you go to Chicago! Can I really?"

"That man?' Meredith murmured softly with a glance at Myrna.

"My daddy!"

Myrna's hand trembled on her coffee cup. She put it down, her wide eyes going from Meredith to Blake.

"Yes, you can stay with Daddy," Meredith replied.

Blake glanced at Myrna and frowned. "You're my daddy's mama. Does that mean you're my grandmother?" he asked.

Myrna could barely get the word out. "Yes," she croaked.

Blake moved around the table and leaned against her legs, looking up at her with innocent fascination. "I never had a grandmother before. Do you like me?"

"Oh, yes," Myrna said huskily. She touched his dark hair. "I like you very much."

"I can read you stories, too, if you like," he told her. "My daddy likes it when I read to him."

"I'm sure he does." Myrna could hardly breathe. Blake grinned and ran out of the room again, leaving the two women alone.

"I told him last night," Meredith explained.

Myrna was dabbing at tears with her napkin. "Thank you," she said. "Under the circumstances, I hardly expected…"

"What circumstances?" Meredith asked easily. "You're

not the Witch of Endor, you know. In fact," she said, studying the older woman, "I wish I had you on my board of directors. You and I could give Don Tennison hell."

Myrna managed a watery laugh. "Aren't you going to give it to him anyway?"

"Indeed I am," she agreed, her eyes darkening with anger at her brother-in-law's treachery. She finished her breakfast and dabbed at her mouth. "I'm going to have Mr. Smith drive me out to the Big Horn Mountains. I have to have a little talk with your great-uncle about an offer he's probably gotten." She glanced at Myrna and smiled in a conspiratorial way. "Don't tell Cy, will you?"

Myrna grinned. "I should, you know."

"No. You shouldn't. I'm going to insure that your grandson has a company to inherit. You can't tell Cy that, either."

Myrna frowned. "What are you up to?"

"Wait and see," was the smug reply.

Down the hall, Cy was muttering as Mr. Smith helped him get up from the mat where he'd been exercising.

"Don't growl," Mr. Smith said imperturbably. "You'll upset the boy."

"He's my son," Cy reminded him. "Growling shouldn't upset him."

"Well, maybe not. Here, don't overdo. You're managing just fine, you'll be walking well in no time. Take it easy."

Cy glanced at Blake, who was lying on his belly on the carpet, reading a book with oblivious fascination. "He's quite a boy," he murmured.

"That he is. I hope you plan to make time for him, when you're back to normal. He needs a father."

"Does he? He has you," Cy said with venom.

Cy sat down heavily on his chair and stretched from the long strain. Mr. Smith put his hands on his hips and glared at him. "I'm not his father," he said shortly. "I'm his bodyguard. A few gentlemen from overseas had a go at him earlier this year. I was in the right place at the right time, and I foiled them. But he's heir to more money than even you've got, and that makes him a target. You can't watch him all the time. I can."

Cy was slowly revising his opinion of Mr. Smith. It disturbed him that he actually admired the man. He stared at his son with eyes that were concerned. "He's safe here, surely."

"Is he?" Mr. Smith gave a curt laugh. "Nobody that rich is safe anywhere."

Mr. Smith went off to take care of a couple of projects before he drove Meredith to see the old gentleman a few miles down the road. But he felt a little less concerned. Cy loved the boy, that was obvious. He had every reason to believe that Cy loved Meredith even more. Things were going to work out very well. He began to whistle as he went down the hall.

CHAPTER TWENTY

IT AMUSED MEREDITH that Lawrence Harden wasn't particularly surprised to see her. The old man actually grinned when he found her standing on his front porch.

"Well, well," he murmured. "I figured you'd be along. Want to know if I sold you out, I guess?"

She laughed. "I don't even need to ask. I'll go home."

"Not without coffee. Who's your friend outside?"

"My bodyguard," she said simply. And the way she was dressed, she looked rich enough to need one. If that wasn't an indication, the huge limousine certainly was.

"Bring him in. He can drink coffee with us."

Meredith laughed and called to Mr. Smith, who joined them with a minimum of fuss.

They drank coffee, and Mr. Harden told Meredith about his telephone call and the visit he'd had from one of Cy's directors—Bill, in fact, the director Meredith remembered as being so antagonistic toward Cy.

"He really wants that proxy." Lawrence chuckled. "Thinks he's got what it takes to oust Cy and take his place. But I said I'd think about it. I figured you'd be around."

"I'm not as dim as some people think I am," Meredith said dryly. "I appreciate what you're doing for me. Cy will appreciate it, too—although I imagine you won't care about that."

"He's not a bad boy, when he's away from Myrna."

Meredith frowned. "There are a lot of things you don't know about your great-niece," she said after a minute. "Someday it wouldn't hurt to get to know her. She isn't what she seems."

His eyebrows shot up. "I thought she was your worst enemy."

"So did I," she agreed. "But I don't feel that way anymore."

They talked for a few minutes, and then she and Mr. Smith left, having thanked Lawrence Harden for his support and promising to be in touch.

"He's a wiry old man," Mr. Smith said on the way home. "Good stuff."

"Yes. A real cattleman, in the best sense of the word." She leaned back and sighed. "I think I might like a ranch of my own."

"Buy one. You can afford it."

"Yes, but can I afford to live on it?" she asked. "My life gets more complex by the day. If I give up the company, I'll be letting Henry down. I can't do that. On the other hand, I'm not about to let Don take it away from me. Or Cy."

"Deal on your own terms," he suggested. "Get the upper hand and then bargain for what you want. You can do it."

She smiled, glancing at him. "You're devious, Mr. Smith."

"I'm shrewd, which is something else entirely," he countered. He stared straight ahead as they approached the city limits of Hardin, Montana. "Cy wants to marry you."

"I know."

He gave her a knowing glance. "You could do worse."

"So could he. I'm filthy rich."

"That isn't why he wants you. He's crazy about the boy. Even a blind man could see it."

She traced patterns on her skirt. "He wants me to leave

Blake with him when I have to go back to Chicago on business."

"Not a bad idea. I can stay with them."

Her eyebrows levered up. "You and Cy will kill each other."

"Oh, I don't think so," he said easily. "We're beginning to understand each other. Besides," he added, "he needs me to help get him back on his feet. He won't be much trouble."

Mr. Smith was soon to regret his words. Because as soon as Cy knew Meredith was talking about leaving, he gave the older man hell three times a day. The inversion therapy, which he did lying prone on a flat table that moved up and down like a seesaw, made him dizzy. The electrical stimulation therapy was unnecessary. He wanted to go back to work. He was furious because the doctor wouldn't let him drive. In between complaints, he cursed. He didn't exempt Meredith, his mother, or his son, either. He was in the worst possible temper, and it degenerated by the hour.

"You've got the entire household hiding under beds," Meredith said, exasperated with him. "You've got to stop snapping at everybody!"

"I'm not snapping." He glared at her. "I want to get back to work. I can't handle my office over the damned phone!"

"Why can't you?" she asked. "I'm handling mine that way."

"Smith won't do what I tell him to, and he won't let me go at my own pace."

"That's because your own pace will land you back in the hospital," she observed. "You're trying to do too much."

He let out an angry breath and turned off the treadmill. "God, this is slow," he groaned. "Like molasses. I feel as weak as a baby, Meredith."

That was probably most of the problem, she thought. He

hated being dependent on other people. He hated being helpless. Now that he knew he wasn't going to be paralyzed, he was getting irritable and impatient all over again.

She smiled and walked over to him. "Haven't you had enough for today, anyway? It's very early. Mr. Smith just left to take Blake to school."

He stared at her for a long minute, looking leaner than ever and especially tall in the dark blue silk pajamas and robe he was still wearing because of the earliness of the hour. His dark eyes slid down her body in her neat pink track suit, and he smiled gently.

"You're dressed for exercise," he murmured.

"I've been running. I do it every day, when I have time."

"Do you? I used to jog, but I ran out of free time."

She moved close, getting an arm under his and around his narrow waist. He smelled of cologne and soap, and the feel of that muscular power made her knees tremble.

"You've lost weight," she said as they walked back toward the bed. At least he could walk well now, even if he was a bit wobbly after a physical workout. He'd made tremendous progress since Mr. Smith had started the more strenuous exercises.

"I've been ill," he replied. His arm contracted around her shoulders. "You're thinner, too. Aren't you eating?"

"Oh, yes," she said. "Blake and I are being spoiled by your mother and Mrs. Dougherty."

He didn't reply. Things were still strained between him and Myrna. They spoke, and he didn't go out of his way to be hostile to her, but he was no friendlier.

"Blake reads me a story every night," he murmured dryly. "I look forward to his bedtime."

She smiled up at him. "He adores you. Can you tell?"

"It would be difficult to miss." He stopped beside the bed

and turned, taking his time, so that they were face to face. "Do you adore me, too?" he asked softly.

"With all my heart." She went up on tiptoe and put her mouth gently against his.

He nibbled at her lips with exquisite slowness, smiling as she followed the movement of his mouth and tried to stay it against her own.

"You like that, don't you?" he whispered. "So do I. I love the way your mouth opens when I touch it, the way you tremble when you feel my tongue going between your lips…."

She moaned, because as he said it, he did it. His hands went to her hips and pulled, gently, lifting her against the slow, raging arousal of his body.

"That feels good," he murmured. He pulled her closer. "Lift against me."

"I'll hurt you."

He smiled slowly. "No, you won't. Do it."

She obeyed him, careful not to throw him off balance. Her hunger for him had grown worse, not better. Abstinence was hard on both of them, but she began to feel its effect on her own nerves. A night in his arms would probably only make it worse, but she needed him as she never had before. Only the thought of the damage it might do gave her the strength to pull back from his firm hold.

"No," she whispered.

He gave a ragged sigh, his eyes dark with frustrated desire as they looked into hers. "Will we ever be able to love each other again?" he asked. "I feel like one long ache."

"So do I," she said. "But I won't help you hurt yourself. I care too much."

He drew her forehead to his chest and kissed her soft hair. "You could lie beside me," he whispered. "I could guide you with my hands, without exerting my back."

Her face burned with color. She closed her eyes, drinking in the feel and smell of him. "Just at the last, you wouldn't be able to…I mean, when you…" She faltered.

"When I started to convulse, you mean?" he whispered. He sighed heavily. "No. I wouldn't be able to control my body, would I?" He shivered a little, thinking of the pleasure he couldn't have. "Oh, God, it's so sweet, then! Like dying…"

"Yes." Her nails dug into his back and she clung to him, her breasts flattened against his hard chest.

His mouth found her eyes, her nose, her lips and pressed softly over them. While he was kissing her, his hands were searching under her sweatshirt. She wasn't wearing a bra under the bulky garment she had on, and he smiled as he discovered that with his warm, callused hands. He pushed it up, so that he could look at her breasts.

"You shouldn't," she said weakly, because she was enjoying it as much as he was.

"Yes, I should. Move back a little, so that I can see you."

She did, her breath catching as his eyes moved down to the soft mounds he was caressing so gently. His thumbs eased over the hard nipples and his eyes lifted to her face as she reacted to the sensual touch, her body jerking, her eyes dilating.

"Your breasts always were sensitive," he said softly, and without mockery. "I loved the feel of them in my mouth. I used to dream about the way you looked the first time I kissed you there, the shocked pleasure in your eyes, the feverish trembling of your body."

"You didn't know…it was my first time," she whispered.

"Not at first," he agreed. He held her eyes while he touched her. "Most women had a difficult time accepting my body. A few were actually afraid of me when I was aroused. But I learned that if I was slow, and very, very gentle, most of them could eventually accommodate me. That's why I didn't realize you were a virgin at first."

She colored as she looked at him. "I never knew, in the old days," she whispered. "You see, I'd never seen a man…like that, except you."

He bent, gently kissing her, while his hands made her body shake as if with a fever. "Go and lock the door," he whispered huskily. "No, don't argue," he added gently. "We're going to lie with each other for a few minutes, nothing more. I won't risk the progress I've made, but I need you very badly, little one."

She couldn't deny him. It was sweet, so sweet, to be intimate with him. She went to the door, closed and locked it with fingers that trembled.

She turned, leaning back against it. He dropped his robe and slipped off his pajama jacket. Holding her eyes, he reached for the snap that held his trousers on, popped it, and let them fall, stepping out of them slowly. He was fully aroused, and she looked at him with eyes that worshiped his blatant masculinity, the fit perfection of his bronzed, muscular body.

"There can't be another man, anywhere, as perfect as you are," she said huskily.

"Or another woman as perfect as you," he replied, his eyes on the swell of her breasts under the sweatshirt. "Undress, and let me watch."

Trembling hands moved to remove her track suit. She tugged off the sweatshirt and slid out of her sneakers before she slipped her track pants and brief lacy underwear down her long legs and stepped free of them. And all the while he watched her, his body throbbing, pulsating, with need.

"It's been so long, little one," he said, his voice unsteady as she came toward him.

"Yes." She went into his arms and pressed close, gasping at the contact with his heated flesh.

He drew her against him, bent his head over her. He shivered with anticipation. His lean hands slid down her back to her lower spine and slowly, tenderly, moved her in a sensuous rotation against the hot evidence of his desire.

He felt her shiver, too. "Here," he said huskily. "Lie with me."

He eased onto the bed, and she went down beside him. Then she lay facing him, her hands adoring on his hair-roughened chest, his broad shoulders, his muscular arms.

"Slide down a little," he whispered, smoothing over one perfect breast with his lips.

"Don't you mean up?" she asked dazedly, because the intimacy was making her body pulse with fever.

"No."

She slid down and only then realized what he had in mind. One steely hand caught her thigh and levered one of her long legs over his hip. In the same instant, his free hand slid to her lower spine. A second later he pulled her body close and she felt him go into her.

She gasped. "Cy, no, it's too soon…!"

"Shhhh. I'll take the risk." He brushed his mouth over her eyelids, closing them. His body ignited as his hands smoothed and caressed, easing her into a rhythm as slow as the tides, as relentless as time. "Feel me," he breathed against her lips. "Feel how completely I can fill you."

"Your…back!" she wept.

He smiled even through his raging desire. His mouth brushed over her flushed face, gentling her as the rhythm continued, soft and slow and worshiping.

"It isn't hurting me," he reassured her. And it wasn't. He kept his spine straight. The pain had diminished almost completely over the past few days and, except for infrequent muscle spasms, was rapidly becoming a memory. What he was doing to Meredith blotted out pain. All he felt was her soft warmth enveloping him, her body welcoming and submissive. He heard her soft cries as he built the steady rhythm, felt her hands clenching where they held him. He lifted his head, because he wanted to see her face. It was like a mask of unbearable pleasure, her eyes half-closed and blind with need, her teeth clenching with every movement he made.

"Cy," she whispered brokenly. Her eyes opened. When she spoke, each word jerked out of her in the same rhythm his body was enforcing on her. "I...love...you!"

"Yes." His hands tightened on her narrow hips. "Stay with me," he whispered. "Gently, sweetheart. So...gently. Take me. Take all of me, Meredith." Cy slowly deepened the tender movement with his hands as he pulled her closer each time.

"It will...hurt you," she managed, her last sane thought of his safety.

"If this is pain," he said through a building wave of sensation, "let me die of it, then!"

She gasped and tears began to shimmer in her eyes as the slow spiral to satisfaction began. She stiffened helplessly, oblivious to everything except what he was giving her. The tenderness was terrible, the ecstasy unbelievable. Nothing they'd ever shared was like this. She hadn't dreamed that two people could join so completely, so that bodies and minds and souls all seemed to merge in one colorful maelstrom of perfection.

"Let it go, my darling," he whispered as her face began to blur, sweat beading on his forehead, his muscles straining as his hands clenched and his powerful body began to jerk. "Let it go. It's all right, it's all right, Meredith, it's all right!"

She moaned in anguish and gave in to it. After that, reality blurred into regions of unexplored savage fulfillment. She heard him cry out, but she was beyond anything except pleasure as her own body began to convulse in mindless ecstasy.

Her nails were hurting him. She knew they were. She forced herself to release them from their stranglehold on his shoulders. She was trembling all over. She couldn't even breathe without gasping. Her body was totally without control.

"Cy?" Her eyes opened. Her head was lying beside his on the pillow, her hair damp with sweat, as was his. His body was shivering and his eyes were still closed, his thick lashes against pale cheeks. "Oh, Cy…are you all right?" she asked in anguish.

His eyes began to open, slowly. They were almost black, but it wasn't pain that dilated the pupils or caused that slow, tender smile that tugged at his swollen mouth. "Yes," he said, his voice drowsy with exhausted pleasure. "Are you?"

"I'm…fine," she said huskily.

His lean hand traced her face, lingering on her soft mouth, slightly bruised from his kisses. "Only fine?" he asked.

She began to color, her cheeks and then the rest of her. Shyly she averted her eyes to the hard pulse in his throat. "I can't find the words."

"Neither can I." He brushed his mouth against her eyes. "This is what love should be, Meredith," he said softly. "This incredible oneness. What we just did was more than a little casual sex. It was a total giving, and taking."

"I know. It…frightened me."

His hand tangled in her hair and brought her face to lie in the curve of his throat. "There's nothing to be afraid of. Not ever again. We belong to each other so completely now that there can't be anyone else for either of us. Not for the rest of our lives."

Her heart almost stopped beating. She burrowed closer, careful not to jar him any more than necessary. He was hinting at total commitment, but she was afraid to trust it. He'd been without a woman for a long time, and she'd satisfied him. If it was more than that, it would be everything she could ever want. But she was uncertain of him.

He felt her hesitation, but he only smiled. He could have her, now. It would take time, but she'd given herself completely, without reservations. She was his. He felt the joy of it all the way to his soul. He drew her even closer with a triumphant laugh.

"Is your back really all right?" she asked, trying not to react to his laughter because she was afraid that it was mockery.

"My back is fine. I didn't damage it. I told you we could make love, if we went about it the right way." He drew back, his soft eyes searching his. "It was what I promised you, too." He drew a finger under her eyelids and it came away wet. "You cried from the pleasure."

"Yes." She couldn't look away. Her body throbbed from the pleasure of such a tender encounter. She drew in an unsteady breath. "It was…never like that."

"I know." He looked down at her body, his own desire kindling again. He laughed with self-mockery. "My God. Even after that, it's still hungry."

She smiled shyly. "It always was."

"Not like this." He searched her eyes. "It isn't the same hunger. Before, it was for physical satisfaction alone."

"And now?" she asked, her voice hesitant.

He placed a hard thumb against her soft lips and caressed them. "Now," he said huskily, "it's for something that I don't think I can even express in words." He held her eyes. "I didn't pull away, at the last," he whispered. "I couldn't. I'm sorry. I meant what I said before—I didn't deliberately plan to make you pregnant without giving you a choice."

She hesitated. Her eyes lifted to his. "Cy…if a baby comes from this, I…I…"

His heart began to pound. "You wouldn't mind, would you?"

"No," she said breathlessly.

"Neither would I," he replied just as breathlessly. His eyes were fierce and unblinking. "Because I've never been able to give myself completely before, even to you. But this was two halves joining to make a whole. This was everything physical love should be."

She buried her face against his broad chest, her lips brushing through the thick, damp hair to his dark skin. "I thought it was only physical with you."

"If you still think it, after what we just shared, I'll jump off the damned roof."

She smiled against his skin. "You really do care, don't you?"

His heart leapt under her mouth. "I care. It took long enough for you to realize it."

"I'm not the only one. You never thought I was capable of it."

"Now I do. You proved it to me when you sat up with me, night after night. I stayed alive because of you. Maybe I always have."

She nuzzled closer. "I stayed alive because of you," she replied.

"Marry me."

She wanted to. More than anything. But there was still the matter of the proxies, of her takeover plans, of Don's treachery.

"It's the corporation, isn't it?" he asked, irritated when she didn't agree immediately. He hated thinking her job meant more than he did. Well, he had the advantage now. He laid a heavy hand on her belly and moved back so that he could smile down at her. "All right, do what you have to, but make it quick. I don't want you walking down the aisle to me in maternity clothes."

"It was just the once," she said, hesitating.

The smile grew wider. "How long did it take you to get pregnant with Blake? If I'm counting right, it was the first time we made love."

"I might be less fertile now," she muttered.

"You might not be." He smoothed back her hair, and the smile faded. "You've got some hard choices to make. You can't live in Chicago while you're pregnant with your second child. I want you with me. I want to watch you grow big. I want to sleep beside you, and feel the baby kick. I want all the things I didn't have when you were carrying Blake."

She sighed, because she wanted that, too. She smiled at him. "Give me a few weeks."

He nodded. He was too close to risk losing her now. She loved him. He could afford to give her enough rope. If she wanted a fight for control of the company, she could have it. It wasn't too soon to show her that he was always going to have the upper hand in business, if nowhere else.

She saw that grin and understood it. He thought she was going to be a pushover. But, then, he'd only seen her in action once. He had some lessons coming.

It disturbed her to think of beating him, because he had the usual masculine pride and ego. But he was enough of a man not to feel overly threatened by her and to accept defeat gracefully if he had to.

She couldn't give him the proxies, because Don was behind them. It was important to her to show her brother-in-law that she wasn't a figurehead, that she'd earned the position Henry had willed her. Her ego demanded it. Anger mingled with the need to come out on top. She'd trusted Don and he'd betrayed her. No way was he getting away with that!

After she regained control of her division, she could retire gracefully and give Cy those children he wanted. Surely Harden Properties was big enough to allow her a job if she wanted it. But in the meantime she could have the luxury of enough time to watch Blake grow to young manhood, to raise the child she might be carrying. Business was well and good, if it was all you had. But a child was a precious trust. He deserved enough of his mother's time to give him a good start in life. Not that he didn't need his father. She was impressed with the way Cy reacted to Blake, with the time he spent with him. It was going to be a good life, now that she was finally sure of his feelings, secure in them. But she wasn't going to hand him everything on a platter.

"I have to go," she whispered, reluctant to leave his arms.

"Do you?" he asked drowsily. "Why?"

"Because when Mr. Smith gets back from taking Blake to school, he might come along to check up on you, or your mother might decide to have a little chat with you."

He tilted his head with a rueful smile. "I suppose that's inevitable, isn't it?"

"You won't really mind, will you?" she asked gently, and he smiled. "Your mother isn't a bad woman. She had a lot of justification for her actions."

"Is this really you, singing my mother's praises?" he asked with dry humor.

"It really is. It's going to hurt her to have to tell you the truth, because she doesn't know I've already told you. You're doing the same thing to her that I tried to do to you. But I had reasons that you didn't know about. The same is true of Myrna."

"I suppose so." He sighed, cradling her close. "Reality keeps getting in the way of my dreams."

"Mine, too." She kissed his hard cheek and searched his

eyes, awed by the open warmth in them, the softness. She leaned close and kissed him with breathless tenderness.

He returned the soft pressure. "Dream of me tonight, when you go to sleep."

"I wish I could sleep with you," she said.

"Come to me when the rest of them have gone to bed," he whispered. "I'll love you again."

She swallowed hard. "I can't. Darling, I can't. I won't put you at risk again. If anything happened to you now, I couldn't bear it."

Her concern made him feel warm all over. He smiled wryly. "All right. I'll settle for stolen kisses and fantasy for a while."

"Once you're completely well, I'll make you glad you waited," she promised.

He whistled softly. "I don't know if I can handle all this excitement."

She grinned. "Oh, you'll manage, I think."

She got up and dressed in the track suit, with his quiet, hungry eyes on her. She tugged on her sneakers and took him his pajamas and robe. "Want me to help you into them?" she teased.

"Only if you want me to help you back out of those," he returned with a slow smile. "Get out of here."

"I get it. Now that you've had your wicked way with me, I'm persona non grata, is that it?" she murmured with mock anger.

His eyes slid down her body and back up. "Never that," he said dryly. "Feed me. A man gets hungry when he has to exert so much energy, and all I had was coffee for breakfast."

She laughed with pure delight. "Does he really? What do you want?"

"Dr. Bryner said lots of protein makes better muscles." His eyes teased hers. "Bring me a steak. I have to get stronger fast."

She flushed. "In that case, I'll see about a side of beef," she promised. "Now get some rest."

"Want me to call Dr. Bryner and ask him if making love qualifies as part of my therapy?"

"Better not," she mused, opening the door. "He might think you had evil intentions toward Mr. Smith."

"Damn you...!" He flung a pillow after her, laughing uproariously.

She met Mr. Smith coming down the hall and had to stifle a grin at the thought of Cy making eyes at the burly ex-merc—a ladies' man if ever there was one.

He raised both eyebrows. "Guerrilla warfare?"

"Only a pillow fight," she said with a straight face.

He grinned to himself as he went on to Cy's room. If they were able to laugh together, things were definitely on the mend.

CHAPTER TWENTY-ONE

CY HAD PROMISED that his back wasn't hurt, but the unfamiliar exercise had made it sore and brought back some of the pain. He could hide it from Meredith, but not from Mr. Smith.

"You've been overexerting," the older man accused.

"Maybe a little," Cy muttered without admitting anything.

"From now on, think before you try doubling up on those exercises, will you?" Mr. Smith said firmly. With a wry smile, Cy agreed that he would try to slow down again.

But when Mr. Smith happened to mention that Cy had suffered a minor setback, Meredith felt guilty. She avoided going in to see Cy, finding a legitimate excuse in business matters.

Cy noticed, and it made him irritable. So did a phone call he made to his office early the next morning, to Brad Jordan, his executive vice president.

"There are rumors that we're about to be taken over," Jordan reminded him. "Employees are going around in a panic, and someone's spreading tales that you aren't able to come back to work."

Cy was furious. "And who the hell's spreading these rumors?" he demanded.

"I don't know. I'm trying to find out. Proxies and stock are changing hands daily. I can't even keep up."

"It's your job to keep up," Cy reminded him. "I'll be back next week, doctor or no doctor. You tell my staff that. And heads are going to roll if I find out that anybody is trying to undermine my business," he added with cold authority.

Jordan laughed. "I'll do that little thing. Are you improving?"

"Daily. The pain's almost gone except for a few twinges, and I'd run if these damned doctors would stand back and let me."

"Kindly do what you're told," Jordan replied. "I don't relish having to have you carried in to the next board meeting in a body bag."

Cy grimaced. "Well, I can still use a telephone. I'll work on some of those proxies myself. Maybe I can provoke Lawrence into throwing in with me if I promise him a new bull."

"Bribery," came the dry reply.

"Anything, if it works," Cy said with graveyard humor. "I can't lose to Tennison International now. Keep me posted."

"That's my job. Get better."

"I'm doing my best."

Myrna went up to check on Cy minutes later and found him morose and depressed. "Something's wrong," she said.

Cy wouldn't answer her. He wasn't going to involve her in this fight. It was his baby. He lit a cigarette, the first he'd had since he'd been back home. "Get me an ashtray, please," he said curtly.

She found one and put it on the table by his chair, making no comment about the bad habit, even though she hated it. She sat down on the chair opposite him, her hands folded primly in her lap.

"I've been putting this off," she said at last, her eyes staring blankly toward the window. "I thought I was doing what was best for you, by hiding the truth. I seem to have done quite a lot of that over the years." She smiled apologetically. "Sometimes it's hard to remember that the tiny little boy you used to rock late at night is a grown man who no longer needs protection. It will be that way for you, one day, with Blake."

He was beginning to realize that. Discovering his own parenthood had made him less judgmental about his mother's actions. Even if he hadn't quite been able to put it into words. It was hard to talk to her, suddenly. He felt as if he didn't really know her at all.

"I'm getting a crash course in fatherhood," he admitted. He studied her closely, watching her face go pale at the scrutiny. "You had something to tell me, you said."

"It's about...Frank," she began.

He laughed shortly, pretending ignorance. "He had other sins on his conscience besides unfaithfulness?"

"No. But I have." And then she began her story. Her son listened raptly for the next half hour as Myrna repeated what she had told Meredith.

When his mother was finished, Cy drew in a sharp breath. "Why didn't you tell me this years ago?" he asked.

She shrugged. "I had to learn that respectability is something you earn, not borrow from someone else," she said. "It was a long, hard, painful lesson. I'm sorry. I've cost you more than I can ever repay."

"Did you love my father?" he asked.

Her eyes went sad. "No. I'm sorry. I never did. But I loved you. As much as Meredith loves you, although in a more motherly way," she added with rare humor.

He whistled softly through pursed lips. "That's a pretty powerful emotion."

She smiled, a little surprised. "You know how she feels about you?"

"I've always known. Lately it's been slightly more obvious. I don't think she slept five minutes during that week I was in hospital, or even after I first came home." His eyes darkened with other memories, too personal to repeat. "Yes. I know how much she loves me."

"You're very lucky, to be loved like that."

He studied her with new eyes, new respect. "I didn't know anything about your childhood. I don't remember your ever mentioning it."

"I was too ashamed. Silly, isn't it?" she asked. "Because I'm not my mother, or my husband. I'm me. Regardless of the bad things other people do, they only affect me if I allow them to. I'm not responsible for other people's sins. Only for my own. Lately that's more than enough."

He smiled slowly. "Oh, you're not so bad," he mused. "Blake loves you."

She flushed with pleasure. "I noticed. He reads to me at night, too, now."

He chuckled. "Did he read you 'The Three Bears'? It's got Red Riding Hood *and* the Teenage Mutant Ninja Turtles. They saved Red from the bears."

She laughed with delight. "Yes! And did he tell you the story of Sleeping Beauty? Now, it seems, the Prince was in an accident and hurt his back...."

He threw back his head and roared. "He's quite a boy, my son."

"Yes, he is." Her dark eyes searched his. "Are you and Meredith going to marry?"

"Of course," he replied easily. "I'm hoping to make it pretty soon. There may be a small complication."

She frowned. "The proxies, you mean?"

He smiled with wicked glee. "Of course," he agreed without adding that the one he meant was a second child. He wasn't about to admit that to his own mother, knowing how straitlaced she was. It might demean Meredith in her eyes, because she really knew nothing about passion, despite her first love. He could pity her for that. She'd never know the obsessive desire he and Meredith felt for each other, or the oneness they attained together.

"But I've got to keep Meredith from gobbling up my company, all the same," Cy added. "Not that I think she can do it. Meanwhile, I've got one hell of a takeover fight on my hands if I don't release those mineral leases." His eyes darkened. "I hate being backed against a wall. It isn't as if they even asked politely—they just started trying to absorb me because I refused. I didn't know who Meredith was when I said no." He stretched lazily. "Well, I'll sort it out without doing too much damage to Meredith's pride. But this is one fight she's going to lose."

Myrna didn't dare disagree. But she had a feeling that Cy was underestimating Meredith's capabilities right down the line. Having seen the younger woman in action, at the hospital when she was arranging for a neurosurgeon for Cy, she could imagine what Meredith was like in business. She was going to be formidable competition, but Cy didn't want to admit that.

"Anyway," she ventured, "if I were a gambler, I'd bet that she'll marry you regardless of what happens. She and Blake are stuck on you."

"I'm equally stuck on them." He shifted again with a hard sigh. "Where is she? I've been waiting for her to come in and check on me."

"So that's why you're still in here," Myrna said with a tiny smile. "Playing invalid?"

"Shame on you." He glowered at her. "You aren't supposed to read my mind."

"You're my son," she pointed out. "And shame on you for trying to play on her sympathies. Actually, she's been on the phone most of the morning. Mr. Smith mentioned something about her having to fly back to Chicago."

He grimaced. "I knew we'd come to that pretty soon. Tell her I have to talk to her, will you?"

"All right."

He caught her hand when she stood up, feeling its thinness with faint guilt, because he'd been difficult and he knew it. "I care about you," he said curtly. "Even when I'm giving you hell, that never changes."

She managed a wobbly smile. "Same here."

He let go of her hand, uneasy about displaying so much emotion. "And I'm not going to dwell on the past anymore. Maybe Meredith was right—maybe the truth is cleansing."

"She's a special woman," Myrna replied. "I'm sorry I didn't give her a chance six years ago."

"At least now I understand why. It wasn't snobbery at all, was it?"

She smiled and shook her head. "I can't really afford to look down my nose at people, considering how I grew up."

"You're quality," he said doggedly. "Regardless of your past."

"So are you." She cleared her throat and choked back tears. "I'll send Meredith in."

"Mother…."

She turned and saw the expression on his face. "Don't try to apologize," she said gently. "We all have a lot of guilt. We'll deal with it. You'll see."

She closed the door behind her. Cy had to fight a big lump in his throat. At last he understood everything. Why Myrna had chased Meredith away, why his mother was so alone and so sad most of the time. It explained all the mysteries he'd lived with all his life. He closed his eyes. Now all he had to do was come to grips with Meredith and the proxy fight. That shouldn't be too difficult, he told himself with dark humor. He'd done a lot of that in recent weeks.

Half an hour passed before Meredith walked into the room. She was pale and a little shy.

"Come here," he said softly, holding out his hand.

She paused beside him, obviously keeping herself under rigid control. Suddenly he knew why.

"Smith told you my back was worse, didn't he?" he asked. He chuckled. "It's only sore. No damage. Is that why you stayed away? Did you think I was going to end up back in hospital?"

"Yes." She burst into tears and sat down on the arm of the chair, going into his outstretched arms for comfort. "I'm so sorry. I couldn't face you. I thought…I thought…!"

"I'm tougher than you think," he said at her ear. "Don't cry, little one. I'm all right." He laughed softly and smoothed down her disheveled hair, enveloping her on his lap. "We only knotted a few muscles, that's all. I didn't strain my back."

"I felt so guilty," she said.

"No need. I'm not going to lose ground. I don't even hurt. Convinced?"

She lifted her head and looked at him. He wasn't in pain, she could see that even through her tears. She wiped at them, embarrassed. "I'm turning into a watering pot."

"You're just worn out," he corrected. "What's this about Chicago? I thought you were going to wait another week or two."

"Your mother told you, I guess?"

He nodded. "About that. And about my grandmother," he added with a smile.

"Thank God."

"It was hard for her, but she's a trouper. We understand each other a lot better now."

"I'm glad, Cy," she said.

"I wonder—" he touched her face with tender fingers "—if the baby we made yesterday will look as much like you as Blake looks like me?"

She flushed and a tremor ran through her. "You sound very sure of yourself."

"Yes." He searched her eyes. "Aren't you?"

She had been, and still was, almost certain of it. Somehow she sensed it, and Cy must have, too. It was as if they shared a mental bond these days, because of the intimacy between them. Not totally a physical intimacy, either. It went deep, almost soul deep.

"Yes." She bent and kissed him with aching tenderness. "I hope we have a daughter this time."

"So do I," he whispered back. "Do you have to go to Chicago?"

"Yes. I'm sorry. There are loose ends I need to wrap up, and I have to do it in person." She didn't mention his great-uncle, or the proxies, or the campaign she was going to mount to prevent Don's takeover of the domestic operation, or the fact that she might have to take over his company to save it. She couldn't tell him just yet.

"Okay," he said, nodding. "Does Blake stay?"

She hesitated. The thought of leaving the child disturbed her. "I'd rather take him with me," she said slowly, her eyes troubled.

"Meredith, he's safer here with me, and you know it," Cy said. "Not only that, you've just gotten him settled in kindergarten. Is it fair to disrupt him again?"

"Of course not," she said. "But I've left him behind far too often in recent years, don't you see? I'd almost lost him in the process. I can't desert him again, and this could take weeks…!"

"You can talk to him on the phone, just as you did before," he replied. "Besides that, little one, he's got me and his grandmother this time. He's in a settled environment." He smiled at her. "I won't let him forget you. I'll talk about you all the time."

She didn't like giving in, but she could see the logic of it. Besides, perhaps she could fly home for quick visits and she wouldn't miss too much of his young life. So much depended on her presence in Chicago now. So much! Her future, and Blake's.

"You're right," she said at last. "I can't take him out of school anymore and expect him to get to first grade next year. Mr. Smith will stay, too."

"You'll be alone," he said curtly. "I don't like that. Take Smith with you."

That was a concession of some magnitude, because she knew he was jealous of Mr. Smith. She smiled. "Thank you. But I'd rather he stayed with Blake. Wouldn't you, really?"

"I suppose so," he replied, remembering what the older man had said about the kidnapping attempt. "But I'm going to worry."

"I'll phone you every night," she promised. "I'll be all right. After all, Chicago has been home for six years. The company has a big security force. I'll borrow Holmes. Mr. Smith trained him. Will that satisfy you?"

"Not as well as you did, yesterday," he said with a warm smile, watching her blush. "But he'd better take care of you."

"I'll be back before you miss me. I promise."

"That wouldn't be possible," he said quietly. "I miss you already."

She bit back tears. It was so new, so beautiful, this communication between them. She thanked God for it, even while she worried about how it was going to work. She had a lot to do, and some heavy thinking. Minutes later she was packing.

Telling Blake was the worst of it. When he came home from kindergarten, only to learn that his mother was leaving again, he cried bitterly.

Meredith cradled him gently, trying to explain, but he was

furious. It took Cy to calm him down, promising special treats and a phone call from Meredith every night.

"Your mother can fly home on weekends," he added with a pointed stare at Meredith.

She agreed readily, even if she wasn't sure she could oblige. She knew from past experience that a good part of business was conducted socially, and back in Chicago she'd spend a lot of weekends working on those proxies she needed and undermining Don's treachery at her own office. In the end Blake was sulky and unconvinced, but at least he wasn't crying when she left for the airport. She kissed Cy good-bye gingerly, because everyone was watching, but her eyes told him how reluctant she was to leave. She got the same message back from his.

The trip to Chicago seemed to take a long time, even in the Tennison corporate jet. All the way there she pored over facts and figures that her own loyal staff had been digging out about Don's latest projects. Many of them touched on and even overlapped her domestic pursuits. She hadn't really noticed just how subtly Don was taking the reins out of her hands. And some of what she'd learned had her two steps short of homicide.

He'd been using her vendetta against Cy for his own ends, telling his key people—and some of hers—that she was acting out of petty emotional hysteria and not putting the interests of the company and its workers first. Well, he had her there. She'd allowed the thought of revenge to take her over, ever since she'd first learned that Cy Harden was blocking her mineral leases. She'd jeopardized the corporation from personal interests. No extenuating circumstances could smooth that fact over.

But she'd relented at the last moment, and that had to carry some weight. She'd already contacted McGee and two of the corporate directors who'd backed her when she'd first assumed Henry's role in domestic affairs. They were still on her side. But they wouldn't be enough. She had to keep Don from swaying enough Harden Properties shareholders to give him control. Then she had to undermine his plan to oust her. She had to have a vote of confidence from the directors. She smiled to herself. Well, they said business was shark eat shark. She sat back and began mentally to sharpen her teeth.

Don met her at the airport, looking puzzled and uncertain. "I didn't know you were coming until Harry McGee mentioned it at a marketing meeting this morning," he said in a faintly accusing tone.

"I thought I'd surprise you," she said sweetly, although her eyes were cold and calculating—something he didn't miss. "I did, didn't I?"

"Very much. Things are pretty much in flux right now…."

"No problem. I've been keeping up with the takeover while I was waiting for Cy to get well."

"Is he?" he asked shrewdly. "Will he walk again?"

"Most certainly," she said. "He'll be back at work soon." That wasn't quite true, but it wouldn't hurt to let Don think it. "Cy's no quitter."

"I told you that in the beginning," he reminded her.

"So you did." She turned on the back seat of the limousine and looked directly at him. "Neither am I. And very little gets past me these days, even when I'm distracted."

He looked uneasy. "I don't understand."

"Really?" She smiled even more, leaned back against the seat and closed her eyes with a sigh. "It doesn't matter."

Which had Don scowling long before they got to her home in Lincoln Park.

SHE SPENT a busy three weeks working to regain the ground she'd lost in her company during her absence. It was difficult, being away from Cy and Blake, but she phoned and talked to them every night. Cy had almost demanded that she fly home the next weekend, but there was a charity luncheon and a Sunday brunch, both of which she had to attend to drum up support. She tried to explain that, but he was livid because she wouldn't drop everything and rush back. Afterward he let her talk to an equally disappointed Blake. Except for Myrna's pleasure in hearing her voice, she felt like poison to the rest of her family. It depressed her terribly and made her even more remote from then on when she talked to Cy.

Cy was already back at work, in fact, for limited periods, but Meredith didn't know because he dared anyone to tell her.

Jordan had been shocked when he walked into Cy's big office overlooking downtown Billings and found the boss in residence, looking grim and determined.

"You aren't supposed to be here," Jordan remarked.

"Hell, no, I'm not," came the terse reply. "But if I stay at home another week, I can kiss control of my company goodbye. Millie, where are those stock averages?" he thundered.

His harassed little blond secretary came rushing in with a sheaf of paper, her face red, her hair disheveled. "Here you are, Mr. Harden. What next?"

"Get me Sam Harrison on the telephone, and then tell Terry Ogden I want to see him, pronto!"

"Yes, sir!" She rushed back out, closing the door with a snap.

"Poor Millie," Jordan mused under his breath.

"She'll survive," Cy told him. "She's used to me. Now, listen, what have you found out about Tennison International's progress?"

Jordan sat down on the chair across the desk and started quoting material he'd obtained. Cy was like a whirlwind, injuries and all. It was going to be rougher than ever until the takeover was settled, one way or the other. As Cy tossed out instructions to Jordan, and Millie, and the newly arrived Terry Ogden, Jordan could almost feel pity for Don and Kip Tennison. It was going to be like beating a tree branch against a stone wall.

Back in Chicago, Meredith was smiling to herself as she looked at Harden Properties stock on the exchange via the news channel's money report.

Cy didn't want her to know that he was already gobbling up proxies, with the help of his own support people. But she knew it. She'd watched the transactions not only on television, but by computer, and it didn't take a lot of guesswork to discover the difference between the proxies Don was acquiring and the ones Cy was obtaining. But Meredith still had enough to outvote both of them. Don obviously thought his people were loyal, because he didn't seem to realize that proxies he was sure he'd snapped up were dribbling right through his fingers. What Meredith was getting were verbal promises, so that she didn't have to play her hand too soon. She had one big surprise to spring on both the men in her life when the next vote came up at the Harden Properties board meeting. But meanwhile, an emergency meeting of the Tennison board had been called. Meredith knew instinctively that it was Don's idea, and she was positive her position was going to be challenged.

The irony of it was that she had no real desire anymore to continue as head of the domestic organization. She'd put in her time, and she was tired. She still owned a hefty chunk of stock, which would pay her a handsome dividend for life, and she had property and investments as well. Henry had left her very well fixed, without causing Don to suffer, either. Don had money of his own. But he wanted power. And Meredith might want to relinquish some of hers, but no way on earth was she going to let her sneaky brother-in-law take it away from her.

She went the cocktail party round, back in harness again, wearing designer clothes and sharing sophisticated conversation while she worked subtly to undermine Don's hold on her corporation. She managed to get to every one of her directors socially, and she used her charm and business acumen to the hilt to undo the damage her brother-in-law had done. It was more work than play, but she noticed an even more arctic cooling in Cy's attitude when she told him she was going to parties in Chicago. It was worse because she couldn't tell him what she was doing. She wouldn't put it past him to back Don. She knew he wanted her to give up the company, and she remembered how ruthless he could be. This was one fight she couldn't afford to lose.

Blake was no more enthusiastic about her absence than Cy, and some nights he hung up without even saying, "I love you, Mommy." All he talked about was his father. That should have pleased her, but it only made her more afraid. Business was no substitute for her child. Why had it taken her so long to realize it? She only hoped that the damage her neglect had done wasn't being corrected too late. She couldn't bear it if Blake turned against her. It was just as bitter that Cy seemed to be less pleased than ever to hear her voice, and his earlier affection was so lacking as to be blatant. Perhaps all along it had only been his weakness and vulnerability that had caused him to be so tender with her. Now he was getting better, and maybe he'd cured himself of his obsession for her. It might have never been anything more than desire after all.

She missed Cy and Blake terribly. But she grew more tired by the day, and her phone calls dwindled to one every few days because she came back to the house too tired even to talk. The distance between herself and the others in Billings grew daily, and she was powerless to leave Chicago until the board meeting.

She missed the gossip at the restaurant where she'd worked, and especially the sound of Blake's little voice as he read fairy tales to his father. She missed being with him, and with Cy. She felt desperately alone, more so when she remembered the closeness she and Cy had shared in intimacy and the way he'd seemed to care so deeply for her. Even that was gone now.

She missed Myrna and Mr. Smith and Mrs. Dougherty's delicious cooking. So easily, she'd stepped into a new life in Billings. Now the old one seemed somehow artificial, without substance. And here she was, tied to it again.

The worst thing about her enforced absence was the nausea that dogged her as she moved into her fourth week away from Cy and Blake. But she had a very good idea of what it meant, and she only smiled as she refused drinks and canapés. A light blazed in her gray eyes, and her face had a radiance that made her beautiful. This might be the best peace offering she could make to Cy. When he knew, it might bring him back to her. She wouldn't even let herself consider the fear she was going to feel if it didn't.

"THE EMERGENCY BOARD MEETING is tomorrow," Don reminded her a week later as Holmes—a thin man with a nervous demeanor—waited to escort her back to the house after a dinner party where she'd obtained the last vote she needed to retain her seat of office.

"I haven't forgotten, Don," she said, and smiled at him.

That smile was beginning to make him nervous. Henry had smiled like that just before he gobbled up a new company or sent someone's head to the block.

"Meredith… I really do respect the work you've done these past few years," he said hesitantly. "Henry would be proud of the load of responsibility that you've shouldered, the profits you've made for his company."

"I know he would," she said. "It's been fun."

Interesting phrasing, he thought. His eyes narrowed. She sounded as if she knew what was going to happen to her, and he felt the familiar twinge of guilt. He wanted his brother's company back, but he didn't like the way he was being forced to deal with Meredith.

"This Harden Properties takeover…" he began.

"We can talk about it tomorrow, Don," she said. "I'm really tired."

"I've noticed. You've hardly made it past nine o'clock any night this week," he said with reluctant concern.

She raised her eyebrows, and her hand rested absently on her stomach. "Yes, I know. Too much lost sleep, I guess," she said evasively. "Good night, Don."

He nodded, watching Holmes escort her down to the limousine. He didn't quite understand what was going on these days. She was in love with Harden, and he with her, if gossip meant anything. Blake was still with the Hardens in Billings. So was Smith. And the last time the untiring Kip Tennison had been totally without energy was when she was pregnant with Blake. He was doing some quick adding, and interesting answers were coming up. Well, tomorrow it would all be over. Kip would be out and he'd be in. Then maybe she'd go back to Billings for good, and he could go on with his own life.

Cy, meanwhile, had promises of the proxies he needed to undercut Tennison International's stranglehold on his company. He also had a vote of confidence from his directors—with one abstaining. The abstaining vote caught him off guard, because Bill had made it. He knew the man disliked him, but this was a company under siege, and it disturbed him that one of his directors wouldn't stand behind him. It gave him food for thought and made him uneasy. Regardless, he felt confident enough to proceed with his own plans now. He had no inkling of what was going on in Chicago, although there were rumors that a board meeting was scheduled and one of the corporate leaders was under fire. He smiled to himself. Meredith was about to be ousted. Good. Now he could get her back where she belonged and away from the business life of which he was bitterly jealous. He'd had enough of her poorly excused absences. From now on she could let him be the businessman in the family.

MEREDITH WENT TO BED EARLY that night and slept late, almost too late. The next morning she dressed hurriedly in a neat oyster cream silk suit with a pale blue blouse and tan accessories, put her hair into a neat twist at her nape and headed downstairs. She could barely keep down two sips of coffee, and she didn't dare try for breakfast. She had to keep her wits about her this morning. Everything depended on it.

The limousine deposited her at the Tennison International building. It was like history repeating itself. Just so had she arrived for the Harden board meeting, and she'd surprised the directors there. She had a real surprise ready for Don. She hoped he wasn't going to be too disappointed when his sword didn't take off her head.

The directors were already in their seats when she walked into the boardroom. She smiled down the length of the table and seated herself. Don looked unusually nervous. Meredith, however, didn't have any such misgivings. She had everything she needed in her attaché case, having waited until the last minute to call in those votes and proxies that Don and Cy were certain they had committed. She was ready for anything Don sprang on her.

After the meeting was called to order, and the minutes were read, Don got to his feet to address the directors. He glanced at Meredith briefly before he began to speak.

He outlined his interpretation of her approach to the Harden Properties takeover—touching on her vendetta, on her endangering Tennison International by having offered an exorbitant buyout figure per share, and showing the other places in Arizona where mining leases for molybdenum could have been obtained without a corporate takeover bid or by risking Tennison's profits on a company with a CEO as financially successful as Cy Harden. He didn't mention the transportation costs for such alternative ventures, Meredith noted. Then he called for a no-confidence vote against Kip Tennison.

Meredith was allowed a rebuttal. She stood up.

"First, let me emphasize that everything Don Tennison has told you is gospel," she said, shocking Don and the directors whom she hadn't approached about her position—there were only two. "I did risk the company by underestimating Cy Harden's financial situation and by offering an exorbitant buyout figure. However," she added slyly, "I now have controlling interest in Harden Properties and I can tell you flatly that we will refuse a buyout. We will, however, negotiate on the mineral leases."

Don looked stunned. "But I have the proxies," he said slowly. "I was promised enough votes to oust Harden and buy out the company, at a considerably lower price than we originally offered."

"Sorry to say your friend Bill sold you out," she said, her tone steady and firm. "When it came down to it, he wasn't willing to go against me without a majority of the stockholders behind him." She held up a fistful of proxies. "I regained the proxies you thought you had," she told Don, amused at his wide-eyed shock. "Including those Lawrence Harden seemed willing to give you. And despite the fact that you had Cy helping you, I undermined your hold on the company. I'm certain," she added cuttingly, "that Cy didn't realize you planned to turn his own strategy back on him. But then, he doesn't know you as well as I do."

Don leaned back in his chair. "I'll be damned," he managed huskily.

"Now," she continued, laying down the proxies. "On to the no-confidence vote. This was my husband's company. He started it, he ran it, he built it into what it was. I never asked him for control of the domestic branch of operations. Henry gave it to me, trained me to run it, sent me to school to teach me what I had to know to keep it going. We've shown a ten percent profit every year I've had control of it, and I've managed not only to diversify our holdings, but to increase them. Our public image is improving daily, our clientele is growing. We are beating out the competition on almost every front, from the computer hardware and software production divisions to the mining operations to the steel mills. My brother-in-law, Don, has told you that I allowed a vendetta to stand in the way of what was best for Henry's corporation. That is true," she said quietly. "I'm human. I had grievances that I should have taken through the civil courts. But emotions can blind you. Mine blinded me. I never meant to risk Henry's corporation, but I suppose I came very close to it. For that, I'm sorry."

She looked down the faces of the directors, lingering until she'd focused on every one. "You have to decide whether or not you want me to continue as vice president of domestic production. If you think I deserve a second chance, fine. If you don't, fine. But I want you to know that double-dealing and under-the-table politics cut no ice with me," she added with a cold glare at her brother-in-law, who looked ready to climb under the table. "If I'd gone after you, Don, you'd have seen me coming. As it was, I turned the tables on you by dealing in your own coin. I'm sorry about that, too. Henry never stabbed anybody in the back, even for corporate gain."

Don flushed. He averted his eyes to the table.

"Now, go ahead and vote," Meredith invited, sitting down. "You have a choice between two low-down, dirty-dealing worms. All you get to decide is the sex of the one you want to head your domestic division."

There was muffled laughter. The vote was taken and passed down to the corporate attorney. He counted them and shook his head.

He stood up. "Two votes against. The rest for. Looks like the worm is going to be a lady."

Meredith laughed delightedly. "Thank you, gentlemen. You'll never know how much that meant to me."

One of the directors was called to the telephone. His absence dragged on and Meredith was glad that they still had a quorum when she reached for the envelope in her purse. Time was too precious to waste.

Don sighed heavily and leaned forward. "I'm sorry," he told Meredith, meeting her eyes and then avoiding them. "You're right. It was dirty pool, all the way. Henry would be ashamed of me."

"Of both of us, actually," she agreed. "Before we adjourn, I have one more small bit of business to conduct."

Eyebrows lifted when she pushed a sealed envelope to the center of the highly polished boardroom table, its whiteness stark against the dark wood, like a skeleton.

"What's that?" Don asked.

"My resignation from the corporation," she said, grinning at their astonishment. "I am stepping down as vice president in charge of domestic operations."

"But we just gave you a vote of confidence," a director exclaimed.

"I know. And I appreciate it," she added. "But my priorities have shifted recently. I'm planning to move to Billings to accept a merger of another sort. I expect to be happy, and very busy, in the coming years. I will retain my seat on the board at Tennison, Henry's will and my own holdings in the company assured me that. But the next time someone comes out to Harden Properties with a takeover bid, you should know that I'll be on the opposing team."

Don chuckled. "God help us."

"He'll need to," she assured him. She held out her hand, and Don shook it. "I'm sorry," she repeated. "But I had to leave on my terms. You'll do well. Just delegate a little more. Business has become your life lately. You need to take time out to look at the world around you."

He shrugged. "Business is really all I need. Thank you," he said solemnly.

"My pleasure."

"There is one small fringe benefit," he added after they'd adjourned.

"What's that?" she asked.

He smiled slowly. "Mr. Smith and his lizard will get to live with you in Billings. I can get a new dog."

The meeting ended shortly afterward. Meredith smiled all the way to her car, passing the director who was still on the telephone and nodding politely. She didn't notice his sudden flush or his nervousness.

"She just walked past," he was telling the party on the other end of the line. "It took me long enough to get through to you."

"I'm on my way to a meeting, and I won't be accessible for the rest of the night. Just as well you caught me," Cy Harden said. "I'm pressed for time. What is it?"

"She's got you by the seat of your pants."

"What?"

"Kip Tennison," the director said shortly. "She produced

enough proxies to gain control of your company and used them to force the board to give her a vote of confidence. She's obviously decided that the best way to get the mineral leases is to own them."

Cy didn't stop cursing for a full minute. He was shocked, hurt, enraged, by her defection. She'd taken over his company while she was under his roof. Had it all been toward that end? Had she slept with him to keep him off balance? Damn her! She'd done nothing but plot against him ever since she'd come to Billings, and now she'd stabbed him in the back!

"Can't you stop her?" the director asked.

"I don't have hurricane training," Cy muttered. "But she'll need armor when she gets back here."

"She's headed for the airport now."

"Thanks. She'll have a reception she'll never forget when she walks back into my house. I owe you one," he said, and hung up.

By late that night, a tired, blessedly oblivious Meredith was taking one of her last flights in the Tennison International jet back to Billings, having phoned ahead to have Mr. Smith meet her at the airport. She'd never felt quite so happy in all her life. Now all she had to do was face Cy and confess what she'd done. By winning control of the company for herself, she might have cost herself that personal merger she'd wanted. But she hoped and prayed that she was mistaken—that Cy was big enough to take defeat in his stride and not let his pride separate them.

CHAPTER TWENTY-TWO

MR. SMITH SEEMED solemn as he drove up beside the Tennison jet. Meredith noticed that he didn't have Blake with him.

"Is anything wrong at the house?" she asked just before she stepped into the car.

He took in her teal green cotton pantsuit with its gold shell and multipatterned belt. "Just the usual. You look tired."

"I am," she said, her smile wan. "Dog-tired. It's been a long five weeks. How is Blake? And Cy?"

"Blake is reading a bedtime story to all the adults in the house," he told her.

"And…Cy?"

"I can think of several adjectives," he said ominously. "Care to hear a few on the way to the house?"

She grimaced. "That bad, huh?"

"The better he gets, the worse he gets," Mr. Smith replied. He glanced her way. "I think having you back home may improve him a little."

She leaned her head back against the seat wearily. "I'd reserve judgment until he finds out what I've done," she replied. "I swore Don and the board to secrecy, so that I'd have time to tell Cy myself before he had to hear it through the grapevine."

"By that, I gather you foiled Don's plans."

"Indeed I did," she agreed, without adding that she'd handed in her resignation at the same time. That bit of news would have to wait until she saw how Cy reacted. "But in order to foil them, I had to gain control of Harden Properties."

He pursed his lips and whistled softly. "Someone's not going to like that."

"Tell me about it." She looked out the darkened window at the passing silhouette of the landscape. "That hole I'm digging for myself gets deeper and deeper. I think I should have stayed in Chicago to begin with, and not come out here trying to play God."

"Well, we live and learn." He pulled out into the sparse night traffic. "Harden bought Blake a dog." He gave her a brief look. "A *big* dog."

"Great. Maybe when we get back to Chicago, we can sit it on the patio and have a room built around it," she suggested cynically. Because it might come to that. Cy might be angry enough to send them packing back to Chicago, *big* dog and all.

"You don't understand," he said. "Iguanas hate dogs."

"Oh." She had to bite back a smile at his tone. "In that case, maybe we can build Tiny a room of her own. How about that? With a fountain and lots of ficus trees for her to climb."

He looked as if he'd just found heaven. "Honest?"

"Honest and truly. Don't worry. We'll cope."

"Where?" he asked bluntly. "Here or in Chicago?"

She had to grit her teeth, because she had no idea. That was going to depend on Cy, when he found out what was going on. She was really concerned about it, especially in light of her probable condition.

Her mind gave out halfway home. She closed her eyes and just listened to the radio until they got to the Harden house.

The place was ablaze with light. Meredith noticed the front curtains pull open as the car stopped in front of the porch. She dreaded what she was going to have to do, but she felt she had no choice. The fact that she was pregnant—almost certainly pregnant—was going to complicate everything. If Cy threw her out again, having lost his company to her, it would be like history repeating itself. And what about Blake? Would there be some horrible custody battle…?

"Mommy!"

So much for wondering if her son was still mad at her, she thought, standing in the front hall. Meredith laughed as she held out her arms and hugged Blake warmly. She didn't try to pick him up, as she usually did. If she was pregnant, it wouldn't do to strain herself. "Oh, Blake, it's so good to be home," she said, tears stinging her eyes as she held him close. He smelled of soap, and he was so little that he wrung her heart. She loved him with every thread of her being. "I missed you so much, little man! You'll never know how much."

"I missed you, too," Blake told her. "Mr. Smith doesn't like my dog," he said accusingly. "My daddy bought him for me, and he's black and white, and his name's Harry."

"Mr. Smith is going to get a whole room for Tiny, and then he'll like Harry," she promised.

"Is my daddy going to build the room?"

She hesitated. Her eyes went to the open kitchen door, where Myrna stood, smiling broadly. "We'll talk about it later, darling."

She walked inside, leaving Mr. Smith to deal with luggage and child. Pausing at the kitchen entrance, she asked Myrna, "How are you?"

"Doing very well. And you?" It was the old formal way of greeting that she remembered from long ago, until Myrna smiled gently and softened the icy hauteur she'd assumed automatically. "You look so tired. Come in, and I'll have Mrs. Dougherty make us a pot of coffee. Have you eaten?"

"I had a sandwich before I left Chicago," she said. "I really am bushed."

"Too much work and too little rest." The older woman nodded. "Cy does the same thing."

"How is he?" she asked, because her conversations with Cy on the phone had grown briefer each time she spoke to him, as if distance were affecting his attitude toward her. Their conversations had been, she had to admit, abrupt and less than satisfying. He'd changed the subject every time she'd asked about his condition or tried to discuss the takeover bid.

"Why, he's back at work full-time," Myrna said, surprised.

Meredith wobbled. "Full-time! But his back…"

"It's healing fine. He can't do a lot of lifting, of course, but most of his work is done mentally or sitting at a desk. He's just had to give up working with his horses for a while, that's all." She frowned. "Surely he told you?"

It didn't bode well for the future, Meredith thought. Secrets again. She grimaced, ignoring the question. "Is he home?"

Myrna shook her head. "He was, but he had a late meeting."

"He's driving, too?" Meredith asked miserably. Time had blurred since she'd been away.

"Yes." Myrna set about getting them some coffee while Meredith and Mr. Smith took a reluctant Blake up to bed, where his puppy was sleeping peacefully in a custom-made indoor dog house in the corner. No allergy problems, Myrna had promised, because air filters and central heating took care of that problem. Blake understood that when the puppy was just a little older, he was going to have his own enclosure outside. This was temporary, because the pet was new.

After tucking Blake in for the night, Meredith returned to the living room.

"How did it go?" Myrna asked with some concern.

"I gave my brother-in-law a very hard kick in the head," Meredith replied with faint satisfaction. "He'll think twice before he tries to double-deal with me a second time."

"And your job?"

Meredith hesitated. "I...haven't decided about that just yet," she lied. She didn't want Cy to know that she'd resigned from her high-pressured position. Now that she'd done it, she wondered with cold apprehension if she'd made a terrible mistake. Cy had been badly hurt, and everything he'd said and done could have sprung from his vulnerability. Now that he was back on his feet again, he might very well find that his feelings weren't as involved as he'd thought. And did he know that she already held controlling interest in his company?

"I've had so much on my mind lately," Myrna was saying, "trying to keep Cy from overdoing it. He threw himself back into the job with a vengeance when he found out that Don Tennison was trying to grab up those remaining proxies." She smiled gently. "He knew that Don was moving on you, you know. Don offered him the proxies if Cy would side with him to help him oust you from the corporation."

Meredith felt cold all over. "And Cy agreed?"

"I don't know," Myrna replied. "He was furious when he left here tonight. I don't know why. The company means a great deal to him, but I don't know if it means so much that he'd go behind your back to help your brother-in-law plot against you. I hope not, Meredith," she added quietly.

But Meredith wasn't so certain. Cy had changed since she'd been away, and she knew how much he resented her work. She grimaced as she sipped her coffee. It was worse than she'd expected, it seemed.

They hadn't been in the living room long before the front door opened and closed with a rough slam. Heavy footsteps thudded toward the living room, and Cy stood there, dressed in a dark navy blue suit, his cream Stetson curled in one hand, his dark eyes cold and accusing.

"You've got my damned proxies, haven't you?" he demanded.

Meredith didn't flinch. So he knew. He probably had spies right in her own office, and that would explain his vicious anger. But he had to know that she'd resigned, too, so she wasn't worried. She lifted her head and looked at him levelly. "That's right," she said.

"Including my great-uncle's."

"You shouldn't have trusted Don so much," she mused. "He and one of your directors have been stabbing you in the back for weeks."

"Which director?" he shot at her.

"Your friend Bill. Didn't you know?" she baited him, furious with the way he'd confronted her. He hadn't even bothered to say hello. Well, she'd expected trouble. Here it was.

"No, I didn't know," he said coldly. "And you couldn't tell me, could you? No aiding and abetting the enemy, is that how it goes?" He tossed his hat onto a chair and sat down on the sofa beside his mother. He looked worn, but he was sitting straight and apparently without too much discomfort.

"You might at least welcome Meredith home," Myrna told her son.

"Why bother?" he asked, his eyes stabbing at her. "She won't be here much longer. Isn't that right, Meredith? Now that you've got what you want, you're going back to Chicago to run your husband's company. But it may not be that simple. I'm not going to lie down and let you run my damned company!"

Incredibly, he didn't know about her resignation. All at once she remembered the guilty-looking Tennison director on the telephone and put two and two together. That director wouldn't have known about her resignation until after he'd telephoned Cy, and Cy obviously hadn't talked to him since.

"Yes, I have control of Harden Properties," she began, ready to explain why.

But he didn't give her a chance.

"See how long you can keep it," he said, feeling as if he'd been kicked. Ms. Businesswoman, he thought coldly. He'd thought she was ready to step down from her pressured job and give him children. "Do you really think I'm going to stand by and watch you dismember my company?"

"I know better," she replied. "But I have controlling interest."

He laughed without humor. "Not for long, honey. While you're in Chicago, I'll be right back regaining control." He stared at her. "When are you leaving?"

Her heart felt like lead in her chest. Was that what he wanted? He didn't look as if he really cared one way or the other. His eyes were arctic, like his deep, cutting voice.

"Or have you decided to stay here and try to run Harden Properties?" he added, even the set of his dark head challenging. He smiled mockingly. "If that's the case, you'd better move back into your great-aunt's house, because I don't tolerate subversives under my own roof."

"Cy..."

"My son stays here, of course," he added flatly. "You aren't taking him away with you."

Her eyes popped. She got slowly to her feet, furious. She was tired and worn and shocked. Now she was angry, also. He was making altogether too many assumptions for a damned arrogant man who couldn't be bothered even to listen to her. "Like bloody hell, I'm not," she raged. "He's my child! Until a few weeks ago, you didn't even know he existed!"

"I do now," he said, crossing one long leg over the other with a faint grimace. "Having him in Chicago isn't convenient. I want him here, so that I have access to him. I won't have a long-distance relationship with my only child."

That was a laugh, because Blake wasn't going to be his only child for long. But she wouldn't tell him that. Not now.

"You aren't giving me orders," Meredith said shortly. "And if you aren't careful, I'll throw you right out the front door of Harden Properties!"

"Try it," he invited, his eyes flashing.

"No," Myrna said finally, standing to get between them. "No, I won't have this. You stop it right now," she told her son. "Meredith's just home after weeks in Chicago, and before she can even rest from the flight, you're jumping down her throat about business."

"She deserves it," he said. "My God, don't you realize what she's done? It's your livelihood, too."

"Is your company really more important to you than Meredith and Blake?" Myrna asked.

"You're damned right it is," he said out of uncontrolled fury. She'd betrayed him, and he hated her at that moment. All he knew was that she'd gained control of his company while pretending to care about him, while he was helpless. He couldn't forgive it, not even if she'd done it out of revenge for the past. "You can't equate a life's work with a few hours of pleasure in bed," he added with pure venom.

Meredith went white in the face. She lowered her eyes to her lap and didn't say another word. She was tired and nauseated, without even the will to fight back. She'd had to fight so much, to get where she was, to stay where she was. Now she was pregnant and helpless and he was putting a knife into her heart, the cold brute. The irony of it was that she'd done it for him, to save his company from Don's control. Don would have fired Harden Properties' entire board of directors and replaced them with yes-men who'd have ousted Cy without a second thought. She knew that, even if he didn't. She hadn't wanted to take over the company for herself. She'd been thinking of Blake, who would someday inherit it. But Cy didn't know that. As usual, he always thought the worst, no matter what she did.

"Cy, how could you?" Myrna said miserably.

He uncrossed his legs and got to his feet, his face as hard as ever while he glared down at Meredith, hating the look of defeat about her. He'd loved her, and she'd sold him out. She'd beaten him at his own game. He couldn't bear what she'd done to him.

"I won't throw you out tonight," he said quietly. "But tomorrow, I want you and your lizard-loving bodyguard out of here."

"My lizard-loving bodyguard and I will be delighted to vacate the premises, with my son," Meredith replied in a voice like warmed-ever death.

He stood there vibrating with anger, but she wouldn't look at him. Seconds later he left the room, still bristling.

Apparently he'd moved back upstairs, because Meredith heard his heavy footsteps going up the carpeted staircase. A door slammed far away.

"I'm taking Blake with me," she told Myrna as she got unsteadily to her feet. "If Cy doesn't like that, he can lump it."

Myrna grimaced with compassion. "I don't know what's gotten into him," she said apologetically. "I'm so sorry, Meredith."

"It's not your fault," Meredith replied. "It's just the old pattern, you see. If anything's wrong, I did it." She shrugged. "Why do I always expect it to be different?" She let out a long breath. "But you'd better tell him to keep an eye on his friend Bill. He and Don were hand in glove on the takeover. I prevented Don from assuming control, but Cy's only safe as long as I have those proxies. When I give them up, he's on his own. Don won't back down, and he's perfectly capable of replacing Cy's entire board of directors just to have a free hand on those mineral leases. With the increase in strategic metals right now, Don won't hesitate, believe me. And I'm no longer in a position to fight him."

"You're giving up the proxies? But why?" Myrna exclaimed.

"I have no choice," Meredith said without explaining that once her resignation was voted on next month by the board of directors and she was officially released from corporate obligations for Tennison, she would no longer have control over the proxies. In point of fact, she would have little left except her wealth and her pride and Blake. She'd gambled and lost. Now she wondered why she'd even bothered. She should have gone elsewhere for those mineral rights. Why hadn't she?

"Go and lie down," Myrna pleaded. "You look really bad, Meredith. Perhaps you should see a doctor."

"I will, later in the week. Right now I just want to sleep," she said, her voice slurring from weariness. "Good night."

"Yes. Sleep well."

That was probable, even if her heart was broken. She could barely keep her eyes open long enough to get to the guest room and change into her long lemon cotton gown. Just one minute after her head touched the pillow, she fell into a deep sleep.

MEREDITH GOT UP and dressed quickly the next morning. She packed, too. If Cy wanted her out, she wasn't about to argue with him. She had pride, too.

Blake was dressed already, but when she told him they were leaving, he started to cry.

"Damn you, Cy," Meredith muttered. If only he were still here instead of already at his office, she'd probably crack a chair over his arrogant head!

She calmed Blake as best she could and had Mr. Smith get everything together while she dealt with him. Myrna was also sad, but Meredith promised her son she would make sure he had plenty of time with his grandmother—and his father, too.

She hated having to send Blake to school in this state of mind. She went in with him and explained to his teacher that his home life was upset, without mentioning why. The woman was very understanding and promised that she'd call Meredith if he didn't settle down.

Then she and Mr. Smith drove back to Great-Aunt Mary's house and settled in.

A week went by, during which Cy didn't call and didn't make any attempt to contact her. Meredith heard through Myrna that he was ignoring the situation, although he did seem to find plenty of excuses not to be at home. Myrna thought it was because he missed her and Blake. Meredith wasn't sure about that. She was too depressed and miserable to think very much about it. The nausea seemed to get worse every day, although she didn't mention that to Myrna. Like Cy, she preferred to ignore the whole situation. The only contact she had with him now was through his mother, who phoned and came to visit Blake. The little boy, too, was missing Cy. Even his friend Mr. Smith didn't seem to be an adequate substitute for his beloved daddy.

The first flakes of snow were falling that next Saturday. Mr. Smith was in the kitchen making sandwiches for lunch. Blake was out in the fenced backyard, bundled up while he threw sticks for Harry. Meredith had no appetite at all anymore. Well, except for Cy's heart on a platter, she thought icily. She could probably force herself to eat that!

While she rested, she made telephone calls, reassuring herself that Don wasn't helping himself to her proxies before she could throw them back in Cy's face. She planned to make them a going-away present, because she'd convinced herself that he wasn't going to budge. She might as well go home; there was nothing left for her here. It had better be soon, too, she thought miserably, because they could get snowed in if they weren't careful.

"Everything okay?" Mr. Smith asked hesitantly. She was stretched out on the couch in a royal purple track suit, which was loose and warm, her long hair disheveled, her face almost as pale as the snow outside.

"I'm just tired," she replied defensively.

"You need a doctor," he said firmly. "You look awful."

"No, I don't," she snapped.

"I'll make an appointment for you," he said, and went off to do it. None of her angry protests made a bit of difference. He did it anyway, setting up an appointment for her at Dr. Bryner's for the next morning. "And you'll go," he told her. "If I have to carry you over my shoulder."

She bristled, sitting up to glare at him. "If you dare, I'll lay a coffee table over your head! I'm sick to death of men. I hate you all! I wouldn't be in this condition except for Cy."

"You're the one who wanted to keep Don from ousting you…."

"That isn't the condition I meant," she raged. "*This* is the condition Cy's responsible for!" she added furiously, laying a deliberate hand on her stomach.

Mr. Smith's eyebrows arched, and he began to grin from ear to ear. "Another baby?" he asked, his voice indescribably tender. "Maybe a little girl this time, Kip?" he added softly.

She burst into tears. That tenderness was so familiar. She remembered it vividly from when she was carrying Blake.

Henry and Mr. Smith had always been tender with her. She cried even more, remembering how tender Cy had been with her the night before she had to go back to Chicago. That tenderness was what she'd wanted when she'd returned last week. She'd planned to tell him everything, especially about the baby, and she'd dreamed of having him hold her and be the way Mr. Smith was being about her pregnancy. But it had all gone wrong.

"Oh, damn him," she sobbed.

Smith picked her up off the sofa and smiled, sitting down with a watery Meredith in his lap, rocking her gently in his arms. "Now, now," he crooned. "It's all right."

"I hate him!" she raged, hitting Mr. Smith's broad chest with her fist.

"Yes, I know."

There was a knock on the back door, but Mr. Smith didn't answer it. The door was unlocked, and he had a good idea who it was.

"Somebody's at the door," she sniffed.

"I guess so."

As he spoke, a door opened and closed. Cy came into the living room, looking as worn and unhappy as Meredith did, but when he saw her in Mr. Smith's lap, his dark eyes exploded.

"Put her down," he told the older man in a tone that sizzled.

"Don't you do it," Meredith said, her arms linking around Mr. Smith's neck as she glared at Cy from a red-nosed, red-eyed face. "You go to hell, Cyrus Harden!"

He stiffened a little, but he didn't back down. With that snow-speckled cream Stetson slanted arrogantly over one dark eye, he looked as threatening as an old-time gunfighter. "What are you crying about?" he demanded. "Guilty conscience again?"

"I don't have anything to be guilty about," she shot back.

"Stealing my damned company out from under me doesn't bother you?" he asked with a mocking smile.

"If you don't like it, go steal it back," she challenged.

"Thanks. That's just what I had in mind." He lifted his chin, glaring at Smith. "You're the new love interest, I gather?"

Mr. Smith grinned. "Lucky me."

Cy actually vibrated. "Put her down and step outside," he said, his voice ominously low.

"Glad to oblige, but not until the snow stops," Mr. Smith said pleasantly. "We wouldn't want you to slip and fall on your back."

Cy started toward him with barely leashed rage.

"Don't you touch him," Meredith dared, clinging closely. "He cares about me. He doesn't yell at me or doubt everything I tell him or flaunt his women in front of me. He doesn't use me to get to my child, either!"

He stopped dead. "I never did that," he said.

"Didn't you?" Her red eyes filled with helpless tears. "You seduced me, so that you could keep me at the house, so you'd have access to Blake." The tears began to roll down her pale cheeks. "But when you found out I had control of Harden Properties, you stopped caring about either one of us. You said so last week. Maybe you never cared at all, anyway. Because the only thing you want is your damned company." She buried her face in Mr. Smith's shirt, sobbing brokenly. "Well, go run it! I don't want it! I never did!"

Cy didn't know what to say. He'd never felt quite so helpless. She really believed that he'd only used her to get to Blake, that he didn't care about her. Well, she was probably justified in thinking so. He'd been hostile since she came home, he'd thrown her out of his house, he'd accused her of selling him out without bothering to ask her side of it; he'd even told her that all he wanted from her was sex and that his company was worth more to him than she and his son were.

He almost groaned out loud at his own stupidity. The absence from her had driven him mad. When she didn't come back, he was afraid that he couldn't offer her enough to keep her with him, and he'd panicked. He hadn't meant the things he'd said. He didn't even mind that much about the proxies, because he knew he could get them back if he worked at it. It was the thought that Meredith had beaten her own brother-in-law at the game, that she'd proved she was capable of fending off sharks and holding her position. His pride was hurting.

He hesitated. "Meredith," he began, "maybe we could go for a drive. Talk this out."

"You go and talk to yourself, Cy," she replied, sniffing as she sat up, taking the handkerchief Mr. Smith handed her. "I'm through talking to you. Tomorrow I'm taking my son and my friend back to Chicago. If you want to get a lawyer and drag us all through the courts trying to get Blake, go ahead. But you'd better have a good lawyer and plenty of time and money. Because you'll have to find us first!"

His face contorted as he realized just how upset she was, how far he'd pushed her. She might run, and he'd never find her. It would really be the past all over again.

"It's not like that," he said softly. "Meredith…"

Her lower lip trembled as she dabbed at tears and glared at him. "Go away."

He threw up his hands. "Will you at least listen to me?"

"No!" she said arrogantly.

His lips compressed. "Look here—"

"Daddy!"

Blake came running out of the backyard, through the house, and threw himself into Cy's arms, hugging him warmly. Cy's eyes closed as he savored that enveloping love. He put the child back down, smiling at him even through his turmoil. Blake was so much like himself.

"Daddy, did you come to see me? Harry's in the backyard, and he can chase a stick! Want to watch?"

"In a minute, son," he said, diverted.

"Your daddy has to leave, Blake," Meredith said. "He's very busy."

"Why are you sitting on Mr. Smith, Mommy?" Blake asked with wide-eyed curiosity.

"Because he's more comfortable than the floor," she told him absently.

Cy's lips tugged into a reluctant smile. He'd been ready to kill Smith, but it was getting through to him at last that Meredith's emotions were wildly out of kilter. That was his fault—maybe more his fault than he'd thought at first.

He listened to Blake's monologue about his puppy unconsciously while his eyes went slowly to Meredith's stomach and lingered there with quiet, steady curiosity.

Meredith was wiping her eyes and missed the look. Mr. Smith didn't.

When Cy glanced at the older man Mr. Smith winked. Not another muscle of his face moved, only that one eye. And Cy's breath expelled in a harsh rush and his cheekbones turned ruddy with shock and delight.

Mr. Smith gave Cy a short, sharp jerk of his head, cautioning the younger man not to give himself away. He knew Meredith. If Cy showed that he was aware of her condition, she'd cut and run. He didn't want that. She loved Harden. If that look was any indication, Harden was dying for her. It was a stupid misunderstanding, but he wasn't going to let them suffer another miserable six years because of this one.

He wasn't quite sure what to do, but he had to think of

something before Meredith made a truly disastrous decision out of hurt pride. She wasn't in any condition to think rationally, so he was going to do it for her.

CHAPTER TWENTY-THREE

CY DIDN'T KNOW HOW TO COPE. Even though he'd hoped there might be another child, the reality of it was overwhelming. Smith was silently warning him not to push Meredith. She was obviously out of control emotionally, and what he'd said to her the night she came back had made it all worse.

They'd been so close during his recovery. Then he'd let his own doubts and insecurities warp his feelings for her. He'd pushed her out of his house and almost out of his life, because it had never occurred to him that he could lose that proxy fight. Even though his board of directors would side with Meredith and refuse the Tennison takeover bid, Meredith still held all the aces. She had controlling interest in his company, despite his plotting and scheming. She owned him. His pride had taken a hard blow with that knowledge, and it had gone straight to his head. He hadn't been thinking at all when he'd ordered her out of the house. He certainly hadn't dreamed that she was pregnant. He'd hurt her so much that he could hardly expect her to give in easily. Pregnant, and he'd turned her out. Again. He hadn't given her a chance. Again. Would he never learn from his own mistakes?

"God, I'm a first-class heel," he said aloud. He let out a long sigh, watching the shock widen Meredith's red eyes. "Oh, you heard me all right," he said bitterly. "I never learn, do I? If anything goes wrong, it's always your fault, not mine.

I lost the proxies to you, and my pride couldn't stand that, so I threw up everything we'd been building on and sent you packing. Even that wasn't enough. I told you the company meant more to me than you and Blake, and I threatened to take you to court to get custody of him. Oh, I'm a prince, Meredith." He laughed without humor, his hands rammed angrily in his pockets. "If I were you, I'd have Smith throw me through the damned window."

Meredith didn't know how to handle such a head-on assault. She was expecting accusations, anger, even outrage. She certainly hadn't anticipated humor. She wiped her eye again and stared at him, birdlike, without speaking.

"Better wait until you're properly healed," Mr. Smith suggested. "We wouldn't want to undo Dr. Danbury's hard work. Besides, we'd have to replace the window." He eyed the tall man. "You'd make a hell of a hole in it."

"Good point," Cy agreed. "You can have a rain check."

Blake had long since disappeared out the back door to play with his puppy, shaking his young head over the strange argument the adults were having.

Mr. Smith glanced toward the back door with a rueful smile. "I'd better go out and make sure young Blake isn't making a snowman out of his puppy. He needs a thicker coat on, too."

"You can't leave me here with *him,*" Meredith wailed, nodding toward a grim Cy.

"Now, Kip," Mr. Smith said gently, rising to deposit her on the couch. "You can't run away forever."

"You and Henry always built walls to make sure of that," she grumbled.

"We knew you." He turned and looked at Cy. "She's already packing to leave here. If you want to do anything about it, you'd better make haste."

"Traitor!" Meredith accused Mr. Smith.

He just tugged a lock of her disheveled hair and grinned at her on his way out.

The back door slammed, and they were alone. Meredith felt vulnerable with Cy, nervous and unusually shy. She couldn't quite meet his eyes, and he didn't say a word.

He pulled a cigarette out of his pocket and lit it absently, fingering the lighter she'd given him so long ago and smiling at it. "You know, I've carried this thing around with me ever since you left Billings," he said. "You gave it to me, do you remember?"

She nodded, dabbing at her eyes. "I didn't have much money, but it was the best one I could afford. Silver-plated," she murmured. "I thought you'd probably give it to one of your men or throw it away after I left. It was a shock to see you still using it when I came back."

He didn't smile. His eyes searched her wan face. "It was all I had of you," he said huskily. "Every time I touched it, it was like touching you, triggering the memories all over again."

"I thought that was the last thing you'd want."

"Did you?" He eased closer and sat down on the armchair across from the sofa, leaning forward so that he could see her better over the coffee table that separated them. "I said a lot of stupid things last week. I came this morning to apologize for them. I should have come sooner, but my pride has been pretty well dismembered, and I wasn't even sure I could get in the door here after the way I treated you. All the same, I'd like for you and Smith and Blake to come back home."

Her lower lip trembled. "That isn't home."

"Yes, it is, little one," he said in a tone so tender that tears spilled from her heavy eyelids again. "Home isn't a place. It's the people who live in it." He shifted on the chair and smiled ruefully. "I miss the green lizard. Place is empty without him. No claw marks on the curtains, no scales on the carpet, no fresh vegetables put out in the kitchen for him. My heart is breaking."

"Mr. Smith might loan Tiny to you," she said, not giving an inch. "Or you could buy an iguana of your own."

"I might have a relapse if you aren't around," he went on, watching her warily as her attention perked up. "I overdo."

"Your mother was worried about that," she said involuntarily.

"She's right. I've been pushing too hard." He pursed his firm lips and smiled, his dark eyes sliding over her possessively. "If you'd come home, I could slow down again. Blake could read me bedtime stories. Smith and I could fight over you."

"Mr. Smith is my friend," she said in a hostile tone. "He's a better one than you've ever been, too."

"I don't doubt that," he agreed without protest. "He looks after you with the ferocity of a rooster. Nothing will ever happen to you or Blake with Mr. Smith around. I've changed my mind about him. He'll have to stay with us. He can head up my internal security for the company in his spare time. Give him a challenge, shaping those boys up."

"Mr. Smith goes with me," she said, "and I'm going back to Chicago."

"You'll be alone," he replied, his dark eyes quiet and searching. "So will I. Even Blake and Smith won't make up for that."

"I've been alone a long time, Cy," she said in a weary tone. She leaned back against the sofa and slumped, her eyes still meeting his. "I'm used to it now. The corporation is all I need."

"No. I don't think so."

"You did when you threw me out," she accused.

He took a long draw from the cigarette and blew out a cloud of smoke. "I was an idiot," he said carelessly. "Men get that way when they feel threatened, didn't you know?"

"If I hadn't laid claim to those proxies, Don would have taken you over without a qualm," she said suddenly. "He'd have fired your board of directors and put his own people in. You'd have been out on the street. He's Henry's brother. Henry taught him how to cut throats, and he's good at it. I don't have the killer instinct, but Don does."

His eyebrows arched. "I thought you were getting control of my company to show Don he couldn't have yours."

"I was saving your precious business for your son," she said flatly. "I assume you do intend to retire one day."

He sat watching her, almost without breathing. So that was it. She'd been protecting his interests. And he'd thought… He groaned inwardly at his own misassumptions.

God, she was lovely. Long, tangled blond hair, soft gray eyes, radiant complexion. Meredith… He sighed and his lips curved as he looked at her. It was like feeding his heart just to do that.

"Somebody had to save you from Don," she was saying.

"What?" he asked when she stopped speaking.

"Cy, are you listening to me?"

He nodded absently. "Your face has more color than it did last week. You look a little better." He scowled. "But you're still much too pale. Are you eating?"

She nodded. "In between cursing you."

He smiled, the forgotten cigarette firing up curls of smoke. "If you'll come home with me, I'll make love to you again," he said in a deep, coaxing tone. "We won't have to stop at one time, either, now that my back's mostly healed."

She glared at him. "A few hours of pleasure in between

the most important thing in your life?" she asked with biting sarcasm.

"Ouch!" he murmured.

"That's all I've ever meant to you," she said icily. "Somebody to roll in the hay."

"We never did it in the hay," he mused. "There's a possibility."

"I'm not sleeping with you!" she raged.

He shrugged. "You'll get cold. The house is pretty drafty in winter, even with central heating."

"I'm not living with you, either," she informed him.

"Remember the night before you went back to Chicago?" he asked in a tone that made her toes curl.

She flushed and sat up straight. "You stop that."

"I can't forget," he murmured. "It was the most erotic thing we've ever done together, so slow and soft. Even the rhythm was bluesy."

"I won't sit here and listen to you," she said angrily.

"Sit on my lap and listen to me, then," he invited. His face hardened. "You sat on Smith's."

"I was upset," she muttered. "He made me an appointment with Dr. Bryner that I didn't want."

"Good for him. You don't look well."

"Thanks so much," she said viciously. "I love you, too."

"You do, don't you?" he said, his eyes steady and soft. "You told me so time and time again, and I don't suppose I listened well enough or I wouldn't have hurt you the way I did. I'm not sure of you," he added with a crooked smile. "It plays hell with my temper."

She blinked. "Sure of me?" she asked hesitantly.

He put out the cigarette with a long sigh. It was tell the truth time, he thought bleakly. "Meredith, you're worth millions," he said, staring at her. "You've been head of a corporate structure that makes mine look like Tinkertoys by comparison. You're used to making decisions, giving orders, taking command." He leaned back in the chair and crossed his legs. "I could have offered you marriage when you were a waitress in my restaurant and it would have felt comfortable. But to offer it to Henry Tennison's widow is a different proposition. What can I give you that you don't already have?" he asked with a faint smile. "How can I ask you to give up an empire to come out to Montana and just be my wife and Blake's mother?"

She felt, and looked, shocked. "But you did offer me marriage," she reminded him.

"Even when I said it, I knew I was dreaming." His jaw tautened as he looked at her. "I want you like hell. That's no lie. When I see you with Blake, I get goose bumps, thinking what it would be like to have you in my house all the time, to watch Blake grow up with you at my side. But it's just a daydream. It isn't even realistic. As you said when you went back to fight it out with Don, you've got obligations and responsibilities that you can't shirk. You're used to being a corporate executive. After that, sitting at home with a child wouldn't begin to satisfy you." He stared down at his hands, oblivious of her blank stare. He didn't want to say these things, but they were being dragged out of him. It was always what *he* wanted that took precedence, it was *his* comfort he thought about. For the first time he was looking at things from her vantage point. That was when he knew he couldn't force her back into his life. It was much too late for that. Now he had to give her freedom. If he did, she might come back to him one day.

"Cy?" she prompted, because he was so quiet. This wasn't what she wanted. Didn't he *know?*

"If you want to go back to Chicago, I won't say anything. I'd like to see Blake occasionally. If you'll let me have him for a weekend now and then, or maybe for a few days in the summer..."

Her heart felt as if he'd put a knife in it. He couldn't have known how it hurt to see him so humble, totally without self-interest. Her throat felt thick and full of pins.

He stood up abruptly. His face giving away nothing, but the pain in his eyes was so intense that he couldn't even disguise it. Her lips trembled with the depth of emotion she felt. He was going to do it. Actually going to walk out and let her go, because it was what he thought would make her happy. He wasn't going to try to change her mind or ask her to stay with him, because he didn't think he had anything to offer her.

"What are you saying?" she whispered.

"That I finally understand what you've been trying to tell me all along. That you're not the teenaged girl I used to know." He drew in a slow breath. "Until today, I didn't realize how totally selfish I've been. But it's not too late to correct that mistake. Take Blake and Smith and go back to Chicago, if that's what will make you happy." He managed a faint smile, his eyes loving her. "God knows you'd be better off without me, little one. I knew that six years ago, even if you didn't." He didn't dare think about the child she was carrying or he'd go out of his mind. He had to put her needs first, for a change. Besides, she might not want the child. He was pretty sure she couldn't still want him, after what he'd done to her. She'd made that clear. "Good-bye, little one," he said softly, his eyes adoring her one last time. It was going to tear the heart out of him, but he had to give her time.

He turned toward the door, and a sob tore out of her throat as she saw the past repeating itself. Her priorities sorted themselves in a fraction of a second.

"No!" she almost screamed after him. "No! If I lose you again, I don't want to live!" she choked.

He whirled on his heel, his face livid with emotion, his eyes blazing with it. "What did you say?"

She held out her arms, trembling, her tear-wet face telling him all her secrets as she threw her pride to the wind. "I said I love you," she whispered. "I don't care what you have to offer. I just want to live with you! Oh, please. Don't go—" Her voice broke.

He reached her in two long strides, sinking to his knees in front of her, his hard arms folding around her as she clung to him. Her face pressed into his neck. She was trembling as he pressed her close to his chest.

She moved then, turning her head so that she could search for his mouth. She found it, moaning when his warm lips returned the hungry pressure and then became suddenly insistent, devouring.

He groaned and forced himself to lift his head. Her face was flushed, radiant, her eyes almost worshiping. He touched her cheek with fingers that were faintly unsteady before he eased up beside her on the sofa and turned her so that she was lying across his legs, her cheek against his broad, hard chest, feeling his pounding heart. He stroked her long hair.

"We'll work it out somehow," he said. "You can leave Blake with me when you have to go on business trips. Smith can travel with you, look after you…"

"You don't understand." She drew back a little, her fingers tracing his lean face. "I quit."

"You quit what?"

"My job," she said, and smiled through her tears at the expression on his face. "I told my board of directors that Don would do a much better job of it than I had, and I tendered my resignation." She reached up and brushed her lips against his chin. "I told them I had a merger of another kind in mind."

His body tensed. "You didn't tell me."

"You didn't give me a chance," she reminded him. "You barreled in with your guns blazing the minute I got back from Chicago. I couldn't make you listen."

"I had a phone call—"

"From one of our directors," she interrupted. "Yes, I know, but he left that meeting early." She leaned forward and kissed him, loving his instant response. "I was going to tell you the night I came home, but you jumped the gun."

"I can't quite take it in," he said. "You gave it all up, for me?" He couldn't comprehend the enormity of it. He felt absolutely humble. "But the corporation was everything to you!"

She shook her head slowly, her gray eyes fearless and proud. "You are that," she whispered. "You, and our son."

His arms contracted hungrily and his face buried itself in her hair. He shuddered from the force of the emotions her confession kindled.

"And there's…something else, Cy," she added after a minute, her voice worried.

"Yes." His hand slid down to her belly and pressed there with aching tenderness. "Oh, yes, there's something else," he breathed.

She trembled against him. "You know?"

"I know." His mouth searched along her cheek until it found her soft lips. He parted them with slow mastery and kissed her almost reverently. He lifted his head, his dark eyes smiling into hers. "I won't miss a second of it this time. I'll watch you grow big and I'll take care of you. Smith and I," he added.

Her heart overflowed. She touched his lips with the tips of her fingers, tracing around them. "Oh, I love you so," she said. "I didn't know how I was going to stay alive if you let me go a second time."

"I'd have come to my senses," he said. "In fact, I already had. But my mother threatened me with one of Mrs. Dougherty's iron skillets when I hesitated about coming over here. She was furious because I sent you away. Imagine that," he murmured dryly.

She gave him an indulgent smile. "Your mother and I have grown close," she reminded him. "Between us, we'll take care of you, too."

"I missed you." He searched her eyes. "Every day, every night. The longer you stayed away, the worse it got, until I started finding reasons that didn't exist."

"Fighting it again," she said knowingly. Her eyes grew wistful. "You don't trust it, do you? You're afraid to love, because it's such a risk."

"I'm afraid of losing you," he said. "I thought you were too young to love when you were eighteen. Then I was afraid you were too full of bitterness and revenge when you came back to me. When I discovered who you really were, I was certain that you couldn't settle for the only life I could offer you. I've fought you for years, Meredith," he mused. "Because I knew if I ever gave in to it, there was every chance that I wouldn't be able to keep you."

"I thought it was because you hated the effect I had on you," she recalled.

He shrugged. "That, too. You made me into a lusting boy, without a shred of control." He searched her soft eyes. "But even then, the world began with you," he told her. "You were every color of the rainbow. When you left, the light went out of my life."

Her eyes were troubled as they searched his. "Do you care enough to stay with me?" she asked hesitantly. "Because it can't just be for Blake or the new baby, or because you want me…."

He caught her hand and brought it roughly to his lips, his eyes closing as he kissed it. "You want words I've never given anyone," he said gruffly. "Words I've never said in my life."

"No." Her voice was sad, resigned. "I...only want to know that you want a real commitment. I'll settle for that. I don't have any pride left." She laughed. "I'll settle for crumbs, Cy, if they're all I can have."

"No..." His eyes were glittering as they met hers, dark and full of secrets. "No, you don't understand. I've never...*said* the words."

Her heart stopped beating. She stopped breathing. Because if she'd been blind, she would have known everything he felt. It lay naked in his face, in his breathing, in the way he touched her, in the flush of his cheekbones, even in the scent that clung to his dark skin. Perhaps it had been there all along, and she'd been too confused to recognize it. He was telling her that he hadn't spoken the words, not that he hadn't felt them. And she knew suddenly, and without a single whisper, that he loved her. Not just loved. He looked at her, and she was the world and everything in it to him. He was telling her so as clearly as if he'd shouted it.

"Oh...my," she whispered.

"Yes," he replied quietly. "Oh, yes, you know, don't you? You knew it before you left my arms, that last time we loved. Because it had never been like that. We shared something so precious that I choke up just trying to talk about it." He shaped her face with a tender, loving hand. "We made the baby then, didn't we?" he asked.

"Yes." She shivered with the force of the emotion that washed over her. "How do you know, about the baby, when I'm not even sure myself?"

"I looked at your stomach and Smith winked," he said, smiling. "I got cold all the way to my feet thinking about what would happen if I couldn't talk you out of leaving me. Imagine that, Ms. Corporate Magnate. I can eat ten-penny nails, but the thought of living without you terrifies me."

"I can identify with that," she whispered. She curled her hand around his strong neck and pulled. "Kiss me," she breathed.

"What if I can't stop?" he asked.

"You can. You have to marry me very quickly," she said, her eyes holding his. "So that our baby has a name. The right name."

He brushed his mouth over hers. "I'll marry you tomorrow if we can arrange it."

"Blake is your son, too," she said, searching his dark eyes. "We have to do something about his name…."

"We'll talk about all that later," he said. He gazed at her hungrily. "Do you know how beautiful you are? I look at you and my heart aches."

She smiled, snuggling closer. "I feel the same way when I look at you." Her arms encircled his neck and she sighed. "I'm so tired lately. I don't sleep well."

"You'll sleep with me from now on. I'll rock you in my arms until you drift away."

"That sounds nice."

He kissed her eyes closed. "I'd kill for you," he whispered at her forehead. "I'd die for you. You are my life."

Tears burst from her eyes and she clung to him, her heart so full that it hurt to breathe. "I thought you couldn't say the words," she managed on a watery laugh.

His nose nuzzled against her cheek. "The next time I make love to you," he whispered. "I'll say them."

Her arms contracted. "You say it without words, when you love me, Cy," she said, smiling against his skin. She moved slowly, sensuously, so that his body hardened at the contact. "You want me, don't you?"

He chuckled. "Did you figure that out all by yourself?"

"Oh, I'm very observant," she whispered, and her hand slid down and stroked him.

He jumped, his breath catching at the unexpected action, his face cording with shocked pleasure. "My…God, don't do that!" he gasped, jerking her hand away.

"You prude," she accused, sitting up on his lap.

"Prude…the devil!" he got out, trying to get his breath. "You still don't know a lot about men, do you?"

"I know that when men get like you are, they're very susceptible to suggestion," she whispered wickedly. "Want to hear a suggestion?"

"There are two people in the backyard," he said through his teeth. "One of them would snicker, and the other one would have one hell of a story for show-and-tell at kindergarten."

That was true, she thought. "In that case, you'll have to take me home with you, won't you?" she asked.

"Will you go?"

She nodded. "All of us will. If you're sure it's what you want," she added slowly.

He frowned. "You're the one I'm worried about. Meredith, you're giving up so much…."

"I haven't given up my seat on Don's board of directors," she said, "or my inheritance, or my holdings. I still have them. But when the children are bigger, if you have something open at Harden Properties, I might be tempted back to work."

"You'll have to keep your hand in," he advised. "So that you don't get rusty."

She laughed. "And those proxies?"

"If we get married," he murmured, nibbling at her lower lip, "what's yours is mine, Mrs. Harden. It's all in the family."

She opened her mouth to accommodate the slow, soft stroking of his lips. "So it is," she whispered. She moved against him sinuously and he groaned, staying her with lean, rough hands on her hips. "Guess what you've got that I want?" she murmured dryly.

"Meredith!" he groaned.

"Being pregnant seems to affect my hormones," she whispered, "because all I've thought about for days is being naked with you."

"For God's sake, stop!" he gasped.

"If we go and pack, we can be home in thirty minutes," she breathed. "And tonight, I can come to you, or you can come to me, and we can make the softest, sweetest love to each other."

"Yes..." His eyes met hers, blazing with need. "Oh, God, yes!"

"It will be like the first time," she said huskily as she held his gaze. "Because there are no more secrets."

His hand rested on her flat stomach, idly caressing as he kissed her with wonder. "I'll make it all up to you, Meredith. I swear it."

She kissed him back. "We both have some making up to do, my darling," she whispered, smiling against his mouth. "I'm looking forward to it."

He managed a husky laugh of his own before he gave in to the temptation of her mouth and arms. The heated interlude was barely begun, though, when Blake and Mr. Smith came bursting in through the back door. And then explanations took precedence. Not that Mr. Smith needed any. The radiance in those faces told him everything.

With an ear-to-ear smile, he and Blake went to pack.

CHAPTER TWENTY-FOUR

MEREDITH AND CY were married a week later in a small, intimate ceremony in the local Presbyterian church, with Myrna, Mr. Smith, and Blake for witnesses. Afterward Blake and Mr. Smith returned to the house with Myrna while Cy and Meredith boarded a plane for Canada, where they were to spend a brief weekend honeymoon at Lake Louise in Alberta.

"I wish we could stay longer than this," Cy told her regretfully as they stared from their balcony at the towering Canadian Rockies looming over the valley where their hotel was located.

"So do I," Meredith agreed. "But we've both got our little chores to attend to." She smiled up at him, her eyes full of joy. Last week Dr. Bryner had run tests, and since they'd proved inconclusive, he'd had her come in again the day before the wedding. Just as they were getting ready to go to the church for the ceremony, the doctor had called them with some not unexpected but wonderful news. Meredith was, indeed, pregnant.

"It isn't too soon, is it?" he asked, concerned for the first time that he'd forced her into a decision she had the right to make for herself.

"Don't be absurd." She slid her arms around his neck, feeling the immediate response of his body to her nearness. They'd been very circumspect before the ceremony, preferring to wait for further intimacy until they were legally married. This was the first time he'd even touched her since the night she'd agreed to marry him.

"You might not have been as willing to give up your responsibilities if I hadn't take the choice away from you," he said quietly.

"Oh, Cy." She sighed, smiling against his mouth as hers teased it. "Do you honestly think any job would stand a chance when I could have you?"

His teeth ground together and his eyes closed as she kissed him. He didn't deserve this, he thought as he half lifted her against him. He didn't deserve such devotion, such headlong love.

"I've hurt you so badly," he breathed.

She nibbled at his lower lip. "Kiss me better," she whispered, deliberately brushing her thighs against his in a sensuous sweep. "Love me."

His eyes blazed down into hers, dark with feeling. "With my body, I thee worship," he whispered.

"Cy!" She closed her eyes and moved against him, her body throbbing with kindling desire as she felt him go rigid with arousal. "Yes," she whispered, shivering. "Yes, now you can…."

He laughed through his own urgency. "You aren't suppose to notice that," he bit off against her feverish lips.

"Who could miss it?" She teased at his mouth. "I'd have to be numb."

"Meredith…" he lifted her, despite her protests, and carried her back into their bedroom, his mouth covering hers hungrily.

They undressed each other with hands that barely fumbled even in their haste, so intent on getting closer that reality began to blur around them until they were in a sensual world of their own.

He spread her out across the green-and-gold coverlet, his

eyes adoring the soft evidence of her condition: the swollen fullness of her pretty breasts, the growing darkness of her taut nipples, the faint swell of her belly.

"Did you look like this when you were carrying Blake?" he asked, tracing her stomach with reverent fingers.

"Yes," she whispered, smiling sadly. "I'm sorry you missed it. But this time you'll be with me all the way."

He nodded, but there was a deep regret in his eyes as he sprawled beside her, his hair-roughened torso poised just above her while he gazed at her nudity.

She reached up and touched his cheek. "Cy, don't look back. It's in the past, where it should be. You have no reason to resent Henry now."

"At least he cared about you, took care of you," he said reluctantly. "I'm grateful for that."

She drew his hand to her breast and held it there. "I love you," she said softly. "We have the rest of our lives, and a beautiful son. And another child on the way." She touched her stomach and smiled. "You can walk again. The bitterness and hatred are all gone. So many blessings, Cy," she said, searching his eyes. "So much to be thankful for."

"All right," he replied. "I'll stop dwelling on the past." He bent toward her parted lips. "Touch me," he whispered as he took them.

She followed the thick arrowing of hair down his chest to his flat stomach and lightly drew patterns in it, feeling his powerful body tense and arch.

"No," he groaned. "Not…like that, sweetheart."

Her eyes opened and looked into his as he took her hand and taught her what to do, watching her the whole time with the muscles in his face cording like drawn rope.

"I never taught you, did I?" he asked.

"No one ever did," she emphasized, loving the feel of all

that tense masculinity under her fingers. "We never had time for foreplay, in the old days."

"We've got time now," he whispered, bending to her breasts. "I'm going to be good to you, little one. No rough loving. Tonight it's going to be the way it was the night we made the baby, all velvet and blues."

"Your back..."

He smiled against a hard nipple, feeling her arch as he drew on it with his warm mouth. "Remind me to read you a passage from the book I bought on backache," he whispered. "It mentions the beneficial massage of lazy, rhythmic lovemaking."

"Really?" she whispered.

"Really." He moved slowly until she was beneath him, his forearms catching most of his weight as he brushed his body against hers. "See how exercise pays off?" he whispered, watching her shiver with the incredibly sensual caress.

"Oh...yes!" she gasped. "But wouldn't it be better...for you...on your side?"

"Maybe. But I want you under me this time." He held her eyes while his powerful leg parted hers so that his hips could settle between them. "Help me, little one," he whispered, feeling her body move to accept the fierce arousal of his. "Join us."

She trembled all over from the sheer sensuousness of his husky deep voice, the slow teasing of his body. She arranged her hips to accommodate him and started to close her eyes when she felt him begin the exquisite process of filling her.

"No," he said huskily. "Open your eyes."

She blushed as her eyes met his. "Watch me while we make love," he said, his voice as slow and tender as the movements of his hips as he teased and probed and withdrew. He bent, brushing his mouth over the parted curve of hers. "Yes, like that. We've never watched each other this way before."

"There was never…enough time," she said, gasping as he deepened the slow movement.

"Never like this," he agreed. His breath caught. His jaw tautened as he looked down into her eyes. "I want to drag my mouth over your breasts," he said unsteadily, "but I can't do that…and watch your face. I want to see your eyes when…you lose control."

She shivered with pleasure. He was possessing her now, almost totally. She had to stop herself from tensing, because he was more potent tonight than he'd been in a long time. Her nails bit into his powerful arms as he hung just above her lips.

"Relax, now," he whispered, sensing the contraction of her muscles. "Just relax. You can take all of me. Slowly, my darling. So slowly." He brushed his mouth with tender reverence over hers and lifted it so that he could see the torment building in her wide eyes. "Like the blues, deep, slow rhythm that climbs up from the depths and shoots like lightning to shatter against the night. Yes," he breathed as she began to move to the rhythm of him, tiny sobs tearing from her throat as her body gave in to him completely.

He gasped, too, at the shock as she eased the way for him and he felt the complete union of their bodies all the way up his spine.

"All…the way," he bit off, his hips moving now with short, sharp stabs that were slow and smooth even as they aroused. His fists clenched by her head on the pillow and his face began to contort. "Oh, God, baby, all…the…way…now!"

She couldn't answer him. The terrible, sweet rhythm had her in its coils, too, and she answered him with her body, measuring it to his as the rhythm deepened to unimaginable oneness. She felt him as she never had, felt the agonizing completeness as they reached with painful slowness to grasp a thread of pure electricity and then gave themselves to the staggering jolt of fulfillment.

In the back of her mind, she heard his hoarse groan at her ear, felt him convulse helplessly over her. She went with him, into the maelstrom, into the heat, laughing brokenly as she fell into a hot, black oblivion where ecstasy was the only occupant.

She couldn't breathe. A heartbeat was shaking her body, and she was drenched in sweat. She opened her eyes, feeling thick hair against her tender breasts, powerful legs brushing abrasively against her own as he moved with a slow, predatory laugh.

She managed a weary smile for him, her hands possessive as they touched his hard face, his damp, unruly hair.

"I love you," he whispered, and it was in his eyes, in his face.

He'd told her that he'd never said the words before. Tears stung her eyes. "I'd have known already," she whispered back. "But it sounds like sweet heaven."

"Yes. Say it to me."

"I love you," she obliged lazily. She reached up and nibbled his mouth with her teeth, smiling at his instant response. "Do it again."

"Optimist," he chided.

But she knew better. She smiled wickedly and moved her hips, very gently. His response was instant and intense, and she laughed. "One man out of twenty," she reminded him, gasping as he reacted slowly to the teasing words and movements.

"Is capable of multiple orgasms," he finished for her, his eyes sparkling as he bent again to her mouth. "I can. Can you?"

"Oh, yes," she sighed with pure delight. She smiled under the warm crush of his mouth. "All night."

"When you've had enough, whisper uncle," he said into her open mouth, and she laughed.

It was almost dawn when she whispered it, and by that time he was exhausted, too. They slept in a tangle of bare arms and legs and didn't wake until well after dark.

She could barely move when her eyes finally opened, and her first thought was of his back. How could she have forgotten?

She sat up jerkily, her eyes horrified.

He opened his lazily and then wide, arching a thick dark eyebrow at the look on her face. "Did you think you'd killed me?" he asked politely.

"Your back!"

"My back is fine. How is our baby?" he whispered, sliding his hand over her warm belly. "We didn't hurt him, did we?"

"He, or she, is just fine, thank you," she said with a loving smile. She slid onto his body with a tired sigh, drinking in the ecstasy of being loved, being close to him. "I love you."

"That goes double for me." He kissed her hair and folded her closer. "Try to get away now."

"I wouldn't dare, you might let me go."

"Never again. Not unless I go with you." He eased her over onto her back and looked down at her tenderly.

She traced the thick hair on his chest. "But what we did last night was like dying."

"Every time we love will be like that, from now on," he said quietly, searching her eyes. "Because for the first time, we aren't keeping secrets, flying false colors. We love with everything in us, no holding back."

"Yes." She smoothed her hands over his chest. "I'm glad I came back to Billings, Cy," she said. "Even if it was originally for all the wrong reasons."

"So am I. Although, if I'd known where to find you, I'd have been looking long before this. I've looked for years,

Meredith. I don't think I've ever stopped. And here you turned up, all by yourself."

She nodded. "Out of revenge."

"You had that." He touched her belly. "But it backfired, didn't it?"

"Oh, I wouldn't say that," she murmured dryly.

"No? Then what would you say?"

"That he or she is the product of an extremely satisfying merger between two industrial giants."

He burst out laughing. "Well, he or she is marketable and shows a steady profit," Cy said outrageously, gathering her smiling face in his hands to kiss it soundly.

A LITTLE OVER seven months later, Russell Lawrence Harden was born, despite a completely pink layette that his mother had painstakingly assembled.

"I told you to have the amniocentesis," Cy murmured smugly when he was holding his son in his arms. "My father came from a line of boys, didn't Mother tell you? Not a girl in the bunch. And it's the father," he added with unforgivable superiority, "who determines sex."

"Wait until I get home and well, and I'll show you who determines sex," Meredith said with a challenging twinkle in her weary gray eyes.

He stood over her lovingly, his son cradled against the hospital gown they'd made him put on to hold the infant. "That would be a first," he mused. "I almost had to get a fly swatter to keep you out of my bed this last month."

She made a face. "Can I help it if you're so sexy, you make my knees go weak just by walking into a room? I get turned on just listening to you talk on the telephone."

His eyes twinkled. "Useful knowledge, that. I'll have two new phones put in."

"You do that," she said with a demure smile.

Myrna Harden came in, gowned like Cy, her wrinkled face beaming as she was allowed to hold her second grandchild.

"How's Blake?" Meredith asked her, because Blake and Mr. Smith were still at the house.

"Missing you, and very anxious to meet his new brother," Myrna replied, crooning to the tiny infant. "Isn't he beautiful?"

"Handsome," Cy said with a glare.

"He's a baby, he can be beautiful if he wants to be," Meredith fussed.

He threw up his hands. "Oh, for heaven's sake…!"

Meredith laughed. "Grumpy…."

"I'm entitled to be grumpy. You were in the recovery room for hours, and this is the first day you've had any color at all in your face. I've been worried."

"I'm going to be fine," she reassured him. "And you were with me every minute, until they took me into the delivery room," she said, smiling at him. She grimaced a little, because she'd had to have another C-section. They'd anticipated it, though, and she'd checked into the hospital on the date Dr. Jacobson, the obstetrician, had named. "You must be tired."

"You're the one entitled to be that," he said, clasping her hand as he bent to kiss her forehead. "You can come home in four days."

"That will be lovely."

"And Blake can read *you* bedtime stories," Myrna offered.

Meredith laughed. Her eyes held her husband's for one long, lovely instant, and then she dragged them away to watch first her son's tiny face and then the radiant elderly one bending over it. Three of the dearest people in her world, she thought, two of them finally displayed in their true colors, long having discarded the masks that hid their pain and guilt and doubt.

"Colors," she said absently.

"What?" Cy asked.

She just shook her head, smiling. "Nothing. Just thinking out loud."

She closed her eyes as the fatigue began to catch up with her, compounded by drowsiness from the pain medication. But when sleep finally arrived, like the sun after the storm, she dreamed of rainbows.